T

BASICS

OF

FUNDAMENTALS

Book Three of
The SON

A Novel

By

Doug Dahlgren

RH
Publishing

ISBN : 0983376735
EAN : 978-0-9833767-3-6

Printed in the United States of America

Ridge House Publishing

Decatur, Georgia

Cover Concept and Design by :   Linda Stephens Dahlgren
Memory Magic
memorymagic@mindspring.com

Dedication

I dedicate this work, with total thanks and utmost appreciation, to three people who have been supporters beyond belief.

They are contemporaries.
All from the same class at the high school I called home.

My seniors by a decade, they come from a time in which "Class" was earned...not simply claimed.
When loyalty and patriotism were more clearly defined.

Independant of each other, and in uniquely seperate ways, each has been a force and an inspiration to me in this new effort of story telling.

From the Albany (Georgia) High School Class of 1955

Charles H. (Chuck) McCorvey Sr.

Beverly Smith Herrington

Janice Faye (Mitzi) Cook

Acknowledgements ...

My proof reading crew: Don Brooks of Pea Ridge, Ruth Donald in Snellville, Ga. Mr. Elliott Brack of Gwinnett County, Dot York of Stone Mountain, Scott Young of Decatur, Ga. and of course my wife, Donna.

They suffered through my grammar and spelling, so you might enjoy

Thanks to each of them !

The

Basics
of
Fundamentals

Book Three
of

The SON

Prologue

Lester Bean had noticed the signs for the past several weeks. Trash strewn along a nearly straight line to a low spot in his fence. That morning the trash was heavier and the bottom two strands of his wire had been cut. Air moving towards him was thick and bitter.

"Easy..." he commanded as his quarter horse reacted to the smell. Pulling on the reins, he turned her head away, but there was no escaping it. The rider leaned forward and reached down to stroke the underside of her neck.

"Steady, Sheba...whoa now," the rancher spoke softly this time.

The location was twenty miles in most directions from anything else. Lester Bean's ranch swept down near the Rio Grande and a shallow ford in that river across from Coahuila, Mexico. He kept a three-strand fence along that line simply to keep his wandering cattle in place, or at least he tried to.

"Damned Coyotes," Bean exclaimed under his breath as he climbed down from the saddle. Sheba continued to pull her head back in attempts to avoid the odor. He tied her to a post to be sure she would stay put and wrapped his bandana around her nose.

The "coyotes" he referred to were the two-legged kind, the ones who smuggled human cargo into the country. He could see the skeletal remains, of what was to have been the federal border fence, several yards below his. The rusting steel standards, pieces of mesh and concertina wire hanging limply from them, still brought anger to him. Lester was not a man who wasted time on anger or hate. But the trash left just beyond his property, on his side of where the border fence should have stood, stirred emotion in him.

This should not be happening, he told himself again. But lately, it had been worse.

Finding a large stick to pry with, he scattered one pile of debris to see what it was. The noise now spooked his normally steady horse.

"Easy, girl." He stretched his empty hand toward the horse, "steady, now." Empty cans of fish, lots of them, and wrappers from saltines had caused the odd sound. Rags, that had been makeshift shoes, were also among what he could make out in the pile. Their smell, along with the fish cans, created the pungent aroma.

He walked south toward the highway, which was nearly a mile away. US 90 ran along a stretch of south Texas east and south from Bean's land. Tire tracks lay in the sand. They had been partially rubbed away with a section of brush.

Somebody brought in supplies, Lester thought as he grabbed his phone. *This is big… and organized.*

Service this far out was minimal at best and he was beyond range. Lester walked at a brisk pace back to his fence line. He slid under the gap in the wire. Protecting his hat carefully, he untied Sheba and then reached forward to retrieve his bandana.

As Lester grasped the saddle horn he thought he heard it. He would later tell his wife he had, but he wasn't really sure. Sharp pain can blur the mind.

The round pierced his right side from the rear and went through his right arm just above the elbow. The bullet then bounced off the heavy leather of the cantle binder on his saddle, leaving blood and a scuffmark. Leaning forward toward Sheba's nose had saved his life.

"Git!" he screamed and Sheba lunged forward. Lester's adrenaline provided the strength for him to pull himself up and onto the saddle. Slipping and sliding on the slick leather surface, he held on with his good arm until his feet found the stirrups and balance was restored.

Lester heard more shots, three or four at least. Those were what he was sure of. That sound, the atomic powered bees whizzing past his head, was undeniable. He'd heard them before in Afghanistan.

Instinctively, his horse jogged right, then left as though she was dogging a calf. Sheba continued her dodge until they were several hundred yards away and out of range. Lester held on for dear life with his left hand and tried to ignore the pain. When the ride finally straightened, he lay across the saddle and Sheba's neck, his wounded right arm flailing like a rag.

It was twenty minutes later when they rode up to his ranch house.

Lester's wife, Abby, called 911 in a near state of panic. The service answered on the fifth ring.

"Pecos County Sheriff, is this an emergency?"

"Yes," Abby was crying. "My husband has been shot."

"Where are you, ma am?"

""Near the Big Canyon... northeast of Dryden." Abby was regaining her composure. Lester needed her now and she knew that.

Doug Dahlgren

4

1

" One man with courage is a majority."

Thomas Jefferson

Sweat formed on his brow and dripped into his eyes. It was early June and the harsh heat made his mind reminiscent of spring. What little rain there was only drove the humidity higher. The windows of the Mercury fogged up, actually running down in streaks. The heavy air was difficult to breathe. Yet he chose to be there.

He'd have parked under a tree had he found one, but West Laciede Street was bare of vegetation. Old, brick two-story commercial buildings lined the street. Many of those were now unoccupied. Traffic for mid-afternoon was light, very light.

The economy takes a long time to recover in some places, he thought quietly. The rough, prolonged recession had reached into this town like so many others. There had been nowhere to hide. Now what the media called a "steady, slow recovery" felt more like a continuation. The very word, "recovery," brought grimaces to the faces of those who lived in the hard hit small towns. Only crime appeared to be unaffected.

This stakeout was old school, sitting, waiting and watching. He had employed a couple of new wrinkles, but the idea was the same. It required patience above all. He found he still had those main assets, his persistence and tenacity. The rules Silas demanded were again in force as he carefully kept his vigil. There was no contact or distraction from the outside world, not even Ben or Marsha.

Stubblefield should never have gotten that far, he chastised himself again. Allowing distractions had been his fault. *Should have thought that case through and not moved on like I did.* Jon had checked out Congressman Stubblefield and did not find enough to remove him.

The truth was there, he complained. *I just didn't see it. I got sidetracked.*

Stubblefield later killed several more members of his family...and then himself. But Jon had been concerned about his own friends and didn't see what was coming.

That won't happen again, he promised himself. *It can't.*

His concentration on this case was meticulous and stoic. The rules demanded it, and he was determined to get back to those rules.

Once again it was necessary to start the engine to run the defogger and the wipers. The light and scattered raindrops served up little more than a blurred view. The local police drove by, slower this time. It was eighty-six degrees outside, ninety-three in the car. Malden, MO, was being less than hospitable this afternoon, but he resisted the temptation to run the air conditioning.

Through the streaked windshield he watched for activity from the building. It stood just down the road, perhaps a half a block from where he had parked. He had information that a man used that building for his crimes, but that was yet unproven. The new wrinkles he had put to use were a microphone and a small camera, both near the large garage type doors on the building's street side. So far, neither had picked up anything worthwhile. The building wasn't empty; there just wasn't any movement inside.

The smallness of the town had no bearing on the seriousness of the charge alluded to by one of Jon's unnamed associates. In the past year, nine high school students had died from bad drugs all within a two hundred mile perimeter of the small, southeast Missouri town. Most were found to have gotten into a bad batch of methamphetamine.

Speed, or "crank," as it is known on the street was regaining popularity with its lower cost made available through the moving meth labs. The cooking process was extremely dangerous, even in the steady confines of a building. But the elaborate set-up needed was too easy to locate and bust. The mobile labs made location much harder for law enforcement to nail down and therefore cheaper and more profitable. That is, until one of those mobile labs blew up.

The chemicals used in the process were not only volatile during the cooking, but could react to movement without warning. There had been two recent cases of vans exploding in that general area of the state. The mobile lab concept was confirmed.

That small fact brought Jon to Missouri. Mobile labs have to be built and stocked somewhere. This takes money, lots of it. Jon's informant had linked the building he was now watching to that process. Jon sought his proof.

The money required to fund a drug operation often accompanies power. The building in question was owned by a group of investors. The major stockholder in this group was Congressman Fred Everett of Missouri.

State Police and even more so, the local law enforcement officials were cautious and timid about investigating this man. Everett had power. The congressman's clout carried far and wide. The case won Silas' interest and here he was.

Regardless of what was found this trip, the mission was not "removal," Silas demanded solid confirmation before removals would occur. This visit to Malden was for verification and solid proof.

~

Texas Ranger Neal Garcia was investigating a backpack found near the junction of Howard Draw and the Pecos River. One of the rancher's dogs had reacted violently to the backpack though it was empty.

The reason for concern was well justified. This particular dog had retired from the Odessa Police Department last fall where he had served as a bomb sniffing K9 for five years. When this dog got excited, it was worth paying attention to.

Garcia's test kit proved negative for the normal explosives with the exception of traces of TNT laced with barium nitrate.

"You got some traces of Baratol there, Neal," the lab tech told him by phone.

"What is that?" the Ranger asked.

"You don't want to know, brother. They used to use that stuff to set off A-Bombs."

Garcia looked at the backpack and was about to tell the technician he would bring it in for further tests, when his radio beeped.

"Hang on a second, I've got another call," he told the lab. "Rangers, Garcia here."

The sheriff's operator advised Garcia of the situation and he acknowledged he was on the way. Rangers didn't ride horses these days unless it was necessary. Garcia had a reconditioned Hummer geared for cross-country travel.

"I'm in Val Verde County, about twenty-five miles away from there," he told the dispatcher. "Tell 'em I'm on my way."

He threw the backpack into the rear of the vehicle and headed west. As he reached the Big Canyon River a helicopter roared overhead. Garcia eased across the shallow, yet quick running river and still kept an eye on the copter. It led him to the ranch house.

~

The next few days were frustrating to Garcia, the Pecos County Sheriff and law enforcement from several surrounding counties and townships near the border.

The DEA and Border Patrol would not get involved. Officially, there was not enough evidence in either situation for them to expend resources.

The Sheriff had argued he found more signs of large groups coming through, staging near the US highway and then continuing on north. Federal officials were not swayed. The government's stance was firm if not clear. Undocumented immigration was currently very sensitive and they couldn't show it in an unfavorable light.

News coverage of Lester Bean's ordeal was limited to one local radio station, and that report went out one time.

"How can this not be a story?" Lester's wife complained, "They shot him." But things worse than his being shot were going untold. The new law allowed the media to pick stories based on presumed effect. If that effect was considered negative toward certain issues, the story was killed.

"They won't talk about anything controversial or that shows the government in a bad light," the Sheriff explained to her. "They call it National Sensitivity."

The new law was the Information Equality Act. Within the months that followed its enactment, all radio stations that had offered an open "talk" format and one cable television station were silenced and removed from the air.

"I never watched that station, but things are sure different since they're gone," Mrs. Bean had noticed. "Now you don't know what to believe." She wasn't alone.

The public was not being told about incidents like this one, so the federal authorities could simply ignore it. Locals could complain and they would be asked to file reports that would be "looked into." From time to time, networks would offer specials on the importance of "positive programming."

"Workers, needed to keep the economy going, were for everyone's good," the reports proclaimed. "Be they legal or otherwise."

Lack of trust in the news wasn't a new concept. This expansion of that mistrust had little impact on the nation as a whole. Most people paid little attention to the news anymore. Even before the new law. These restrictions had quickly become a way a life and people adapted the best they could. But in the southern region of Texas, fear had become injury too many times. If the feds wouldn't help, the people would handle it themselves.

The local ranchers were getting organized on their own. Plans were made on a local level to gather more conclusive evidence the Feds couldn't ignore. A task force of five county sheriffs, twenty-one deputies and four local ranchers set up along the area Lester Bean had found. Ranger Garcia went with them.

The high overcast sky made the conditions nearly pitch black that night. It was after 2 A.M. when they first heard and then could see the eerie images. People, one after the other, stayed low and kept moving. Coming north through the dark.

Every fourth man carried a pack on his back and they all followed a leader, using only a tiny flashlight to find his trail.

When the quiet line of smugglers reached the fence, the lead sheriff stood holding his Colt .45 and an oversized flashlight. The task force was armed with standard issue rifles and side arms. The ranchers had hunting rifles. As they all took aim, the sheriff shined his flood beam toward the approaching line and hollered, in both English and Spanish.

"Stop... throw up your hands."

Members of his task force rose to their feet exposing themselves just as the chaos began. Large lights mounted on unseen pick-up trucks flooded the area with harsh light from the south. Loud, heavy caliber weapons sounded from just beyond the brightness, catching the stunned posse like deer in headlights.

The sheriff fell before he could get off a shot. Others of the task force opened fire in return, but they were out-manned and out-gunned. The battle lasted no more than five minutes and the thirty local members of the task force lay dead or wounded. Ranger Garcia was hit in the leg and shoulder as he spun trying to draw his weapon. He landed face down with sand flying up from impacting bullets just in front of his face. Rolling over a clump of pincushion cactus to get into a gully, he lay there perfectly still for nearly an hour.

No one approached the downed men. Garcia could hear the line of smugglers continue on through the fence line and then to the northeast. As that noise dissipated it was overtaken by the sound of the trucks cranking and leaving the area. They went back south from where they had come. The Ranger attempted to get to his feet, but became lightheaded and consciousness left him. He was found the next morning with the others, still alive, but just barely.

2

It was 10:45 AM that morning when the phone rang on the desk of Brownwood Sheriff Horace Wilbury. It was a private line used mainly by his friends and family. The sheriff sat his coffee cup down and leaned forward. Answering the phone in his normal manner.

"Sheriff's office, this is Wilbury."

Brownwood, Texas was the home of the late Senator Warren Bilstock. The senator had died the year before in an accident along his property's fence line. Or so it seemed.

A reporter from back east, Daniel Seay, came to Brownwood a few weeks after the death searching for details of what had happened. He brought with him a theory and hoped to find proof or at least a trace of evidence. Daniel Seay believed the senator was a victim of a serial killer. Officially, that case was never resolved. It was simply allowed to fade away as an accident.

"Uncle Horace," the female voice whimpered through her tears.

"Susie?" Wilbury recognized her instantly, his only sister's only child. "What is it child?"

"Neal's been hurt. He's shot, Uncle Horace. They shot him."

"What...what happened, girl?" The sheriff was now on his feet, and the tone of his voice brought a deputy into the office to see what was wrong.

Susie Garcia explained what had happened to her husband with all the details she knew. This included the lack of interest by the government.

Wilbury listened, tried to console her the best he could and assured her that he was on the case. As he put the phone down, he noticed his deputy standing there, looking concerned.

"Damn this mess. Damn this fool government anyway," the sheriff muttered. He looked to his deputy as he tried to think of where to start, what to do.

Wilbury's thoughts oddly enough included the reporter from Pittsburgh and his stories about a man who was beyond the law, a man who did what was required to be done. Horace Wilbury had resented Daniel Seay's involvement in the investigation of the senator's death. The old country sheriff had found the visiting reporter's questions intrusive and chose not to be as helpful as he could have been about the incident.

He told the reporter there were no pictures of the scene where Bilstock was found dead, and he failed to mention to him that Murray and Slick were family of the senator. The situation was their local affair in his mind and no business of outsiders. Yet he remembered Daniel Seay and he remembered reading follow-up stories written by him. The sheriff had made it a point to keep the reporter's contact information.

His deputy stared without speaking while the sheriff looked down at his desktop as though the answer to his problem was there. A red streak of color ran down the sheriff's neck, and one large fist rose above his head and slammed hard on the desk.

Then he glared at the deputy and more ordered than asked, "Do we have the number for that reporter fellow who was here last year, the one looking into Bilstock?"

The deputy had to think a minute. "I think so... I've got it somewhere in the file."

The sheriff leaned back and looked at the chair Daniel Seay had occupied those many months ago. "Get him on the line for me...quick."

~

A patrol car approached slowly from the rear along West Laciede Street. Jon slumped low in the seat and toward the driver's door as the Malden Police unit cruised past him once again. Checking his watch, he figured that was about it for this afternoon. The officer had driven by three times in the last four hours. The frequency of those drive-bys was increasing and Jon knew the Missouri cop was becoming concerned about his presence. Not only did he need to leave for the time being, but the Mercury was probably done for this mission. A rental, or better yet a cheap used van, was now called for.

Easing away from the curb Jon headed south and out of town. Through the sleepy town of Clarkton and on to the larger Kennett, MO. Kennett's main street had neon lights sprinkled in among the painted signs for businesses. There was even a used car lot a few blocks down from the motel he chose.

This will do, he told himself as he pulled into the motel.

The rain had stopped, but the humidity level seemed to rise. It was uncomfortable outside and Jon, registering as Stanley Wilson of Oglethorpe, Georgia, asked for a room with a good air-conditioner.

"Room 123 has its own unit, but its way toward the back," the clerk informed him.

"That's fine, I like being away from the road," Jon told her as he checked his watch. It was 5:00 P.M.

"Say, do you know how late that car lot down the street stays open?"

Looking at the clock on the wall behind her, the young woman smiled,

"Dan usually goes home for dinner about this time. Willy should be there."

Then she gave him an odd look and added, "You need a car? That's a real nice Mercury you got out there."

Jon realized he probably should not have asked such a question, but what was done was done.

"I need a part for an old truck back home," he said with a straight face. "I look everywhere I go. Thought I'd check in and see what they have."

The clerk smiled back and nodded.

If there's anything folks from a small town understand, it's looking for auto parts, he assured himself in silence.

Parking behind the main building at the motel, Jon went into the room and turned the air on "high." When satisfied with the output, he locked up and headed on foot toward the car lot. He checked his wallet for the ID he wanted to use, if he found a vehicle that would work.

~

The phone call was immediately transferred to a receptionist. Daniel Seay did not care much for mechanical answering machines. If he was tied up when a call came, he preferred the caller get to speak with a person not just a machine.

The soft female voice answered, "Mr. Seay's office. May I help you, please?"

"I have a call for Mr. Seay from Sheriff Horace Wilbury. Can you connect us?"

"Mr. Seay is on another call. Can I have a number where he can reach the Sheriff?"

"Sure," the caller responded and offered a number.

The receptionist repeated the number and then asked. "Can I say what this is about?"

"They know each other, ma-am. That's all I know."

Daniel was indeed on a call with a friend, police captain Phil Stone of Shreveport, Louisiana.

"So, he still won't work with us on this, huh?" the officer asked.

The reporter glanced down at the envelope in his hand. It was now dog-eared from being filed and retrieved. That envelope was the reason for this discussion and many others in the last four months.

"Phil, that's not what he's saying." Daniel couldn't think of another way to explain his other friend's position on the matter of the Sponsors. "He needs something solid to verify, that's always the way he works."

The envelope had appeared on Daniel's desk within a week of the mysterious death of a Hollywood big shot. The postmark on the large, yellow mailer and the location of the death were both Malibu, California. Neither the lists inside nor the letter that came with them were signed.

Captain Stone had not contacted Daniel in several weeks. They tried a couple of time before to get Jon interested in the group Stone organized to fight crimes. Those the law couldn't reach. A large drug bust forty miles south of Shreveport got Stone's adrenaline pumping and he thought about the Sponsors. So he called Daniel yet again.

"That list you got matches the one he found in Texas. Why ain't that enough?" the veteran cop challenged in frustration.

One of the lists did indeed match another that Jon had found in the Texas biker gang's hideout. One even included the name of a sitting Supreme Court Justice. The information seemed to tied everything together in Phil's eyes, but they were only lists. There was no confirmation and to Jon, that simply wasn't enough.

"We've been through all this, Phil." Daniel was getting frustrated again. "It's not my decision. Jon has been different since all that. He's quieter and much more reserved. Ben says that's the way he was before."

There was definite meaning to Daniel's use of "before." It meant before Ben even knew who Jon really was. Back when the Congressional Killer, or as the media named him "The Son," was little more than a hunch to the outside world. Barely over a year ago, but "before" was, in some ways a long past, former lifetime.

"Can't Ben talk to him? I mean, damn, Daniel... people could be killed any time on account of these creeps. We can't even investigate them, you know that."

"They'll mess up soon enough and give us what we need," Daniel said with hope coming through very clearly in his words. "Then Jon can and I know will act on it."

And so he had. Just a few weeks before the arrival of this strange envelope, Jon had tackled threats and incidents too numerous to name at virtually the same time. To top it all off, the Argus drug business was closed down, this time for good.

So much had been going on then that everyone welcomed the peace that followed. Many, mainly the closest of the group, had gotten back together for Ben's graduation right after everything settled down. He and his wife Lori, Lt. Marsha Hurst from Charlotte, plus George Vincent, the local Dalton DA and Doris, Ben's mother had stayed in touch, but contact with Jon since then had been sparse.

The mysterious envelope had lain on Daniel's desk for several days before he opened it. Though the lists were not signed he knew it had to have come from the man police in Malibu found dead on his beach house deck. The main one listed names of many people in government and other prominent figures. The other list named the victims the first group intended to harm. A hand-written note claimed the information to be damning evidence. But there was no proof, just the lists.

It was several weeks after that when the police in Florida put the case of the attempted assassination at Disney World together with the Sponsors. The only captured gang member to have contact with anyone within the Sponsors, possessed a phone number that traced back to California. Nothing could be proven and that case, like everything else, quieted down after that. There had been no further attempts on any of the listed victims in the last three months.

"How about your group, Daniel?" Phil Stone asked.

"Same as you guys, we're keeping our eyes and ears open."

Daniel led a group of newspaper people across the country that also understood the value of a man not restrained by the complexities of the law. Laws that powerful people could hide behind, people like the Sponsors.

Daniel's vision of a rebirth of the Sons of Liberty had taken two forms. One filled by members of law enforcement, led by Stone and Lt. Marsha Hurst in Charlotte, North Carolina. The other, some half dozen of Daniel's trusted media friends. Neither group had Jon's personal involvement, though each had tried.

"Show me something I can verify," Jon made clear to both groups. It was his most basic requirement.

Daniel remembered a discussion he had with Ben in which the young man explained his mentor's attitude toward what he does.

"Virtue to Jon is fundamental," Ben had tried to explain. "That's the foundation of his ideals and it is basic to anything honorable in his eyes."

Daniel went on, quoting more of what Ben had shared in his defense of Jon's position. "He has rules he once abandoned for a time."

Daniel told Phil how he would never forget the sincerity in Ben's voice. How he had paused to compose himself after the comment about the rules.

"Phil, it might as well have been coming from Jon himself," Daniel shared with him. "Ben understands what and why Jon is doing this. I don't think speaking with Jon directly would change any of it."

Daniel went back to quoting Ben's words from their conversation.

"But now Jon has returned to his basic foundation," he had expressed. "The reasons and the rules Silas first set up and worked under."

Daniel himself paused a moment. "Phil, the way Ben put it, Jon feels he let someone down by ignoring his rules. He didn't say who, but he feels strongly about it."

"So," Phil asked. "He's going solo again, huh?"

Daniel thought back to how Ben had stated it. He tried to say it the same way.

"He's going back to his rules. He's returning to the basics of those fundamentals."

Phil stayed quiet. He didn't argue or add anything. He too knew the man, and though it sounded strange, he understood what it meant.

At that point, they were interrupted. A messenger knocked and came into Daniel's office. Hand delivering a note sent by the receptionist about the call from Texas. The name on the note shouted at Daniel from the paper, Horace Wilbury.

"Phil, I need to go," he told his friend in Shreveport. "I've got a call I need to return."

"Alright Daniel... Matt says 'Hi' and to come see us."

19

"I'd love to. My best to Matt as well," and the reporter then hung up.

Horace Wilbury, Daniel thought, his hand still resting on the phone. *What could he need with me?* The answer to that came to him as he dialed the number. *Probably like everyone else, access to Jon.*

3

Dialing the west Texas phone number, Daniel's mind was a bit conflicted. His instinct was to call right back and yet, this was the man who went out of his way to lie to him about the pictures of Senator Bilstock's death scene. A deputy answered and put him through before he had settled his internal discussion.

"Horace Wilbury," the heavy voice answered.

"Sheriff, this is Daniel Seay. I'm returning your call, sir."

"Mr. Seay, thank you for calling back."

Then oddly, the line became very quiet. Daniel could hear the sheriff breathing so he waited. After what seemed like too long, Daniel tried an icebreaker. "Call me Daniel, please."

"I'm sorry, son. I wanted to talk to you, but I can't figure out how to ask what I want to ask."

Daniel gave him a few seconds and then replied, "just ask away, Sheriff."

The sound of a deep breath preceded the next words, "That fella you were writing about, the one they call The Son. Did you ever prove he was for real?"

"To my satisfaction, yes," Daniel told him. "Others may not agree."

"I've got a situation down here. Stuff like it has been talked about for years now. But this is close to my home," Wilbury lamented. The large man paused and Daniel could again hear the labored breathing. "First time in my life, I don't know what to do."

Daniel sat back in his chair and considered his next statement. This didn't sound like the huge, self-confident country sheriff he had met last year. What could be going on? He went with that thought, "what's going on, Sheriff?"

Horace Wilbury explained the details about the ambush and the shootout, the dead, the wounded and the aftermath. He explained almost every detail.

Daniel had been hearing of killings near the border, but Wilbury's town was much further inland. "When did this happen?"

"Three days ago."

"Sir," Daniel opened his laptop and tried to find the story. "How does this affect you so closely?"

"My niece's husband is a Texas Ranger. He got shot up pretty bad in the deal."

"Oh...I'm so sorry. Is he going to be alright?" Daniel was beginning to understand though he could not find any mention of the incident on line.

"She ain't sure." The sheriff gathered himself at that point. The worst part to tell was over, but there was more. "Look," he started with a stronger voice. "It's whats happened since then that has me pissed off and confused."

"You've talked with Homeland Security?" Daniel asked.

"Them... the DEA, ICE and the damned FBI. Won't nobody do nothing."

"You said people were killed?"

"Yeah...eighteen dead and thirteen in bad shape. All they want us to do is bury the dead and move on."

Daniel knew some of the border conflicts were being ignored because of "sensitivity" and political correctness. But this many lives lost should be different.

"They told you they won't do anything?" he asked the lawman.

"Not in so many words...but I've done this work a long time, son. I know when I'm being put off and intentionally stalled. The law can do that kind of thing and you're helpless to deal with it. Damned bureaucrats."

"So...how can I help?" the reporter wondered while trying another search engine on his computer.

"Look... everybody knows what Bilstock was up to...maybe not then, but now for sure. That guy that took him out did all of us a favor."

Though he stayed quiet, that comment brought Daniel to attention.

"Bilstock had the law on his side," Wilbury continued, "protecting him. That Son fella, didn't wait for the law. He did what was right and what was needed."

"O...k?" Daniel knew, but still asked.

"We need his help...we need that attitude applied here again. This stuff can't keep happening like this."

Now it was Daniel who didn't know what to say. The sheriff waited nearly a minute and then went on, "Can you get in touch with him or not?"

"I'll do what I can...no guarantees."

He grabbed a piece of paper and made a note, "Is this a number you would want him to call on?"

"Sure, if they're listening and come shut me down it won't matter anyway."

"You think you are being monitored?"

"Hell, son...I don't know what to think."

Daniel caught himself shaking his head. He took a deep breath and offered, "My best to your niece and her husband."

"Thank you, son. I appreciate your help."

The line went dead and Daniel sat there with the phone still in his hand. *What have I committed Jon to now?* he thought. *How do I get him to respond?*

He pushed the button on the phone's cradle down and got a tone, then he hit 232 for the National desk. A young reporter answered and Daniel asked about the story he couldn't find.

"When did this happen?" was asked.

"This week...within the past several days," Daniel told him.

After the sound of ruffled papers and a shout across the room, the young reporter came back on the line. "Mr. Seay...there's nothing about that anywhere."

"You sure?" Daniel challenged.

"I even asked Fred." Fred Newcomb was the Chief Editor for the National section. He would know about it if anyone did.

"Thanks, Jimmy." Daniel hung up and dialed his boss, Editor Bill White. "Bill, I just got word of what should be a huge national headline. There's nothing on the wire about it, not one thing. Can you help?"

"What's the story?"

Daniel gave his boss a brief synopsis of the tale to which White responded, "Damn, Seay. I don't have time for jokes like that."

The boss leaned back over his desk. With the phone line still open he continued his work. "Something like that should be on everything," he muttered loud enough for Daniel to hear.

Daniel just stood silently, phone in hand until White finally spoke again, "You sure about your source?"

The thought about Wilbury lying to him once before raced through Daniel's mind, "Yeah...I'm sure," he blurted out. *Wilbury wouldn't make this up.*

"Let me make a call, you come on down to my office while I do that."

Daniel knocked and pushed the door open at the same time. Bill White was still on the phone. The look on his face was puzzled.

"Thanks, Tom. I appreciate it. My love to Jenny... Yeah...bye now."

The stern expression on the boss's face foiled any surprise.

"That was Tom Adams at the AP in Washington." He noticeably blinked and leaned deep into his chair. "There is no story."

"What?" Daniel couldn't believe this was all made up. "That can't be..."

"There should be...but there isn't," White continued over him.

Daniel Seay hushed, his anger now replaced by worry. He sat in a chair and simply waited for his friend and mentor to explain.

"The NSA has a spike on the story, national security," the editor said calmly.

"What?" That was the second time that word was all he could form to ask.

"It's more than mules bringing in drugs or people, Daniel. Something big is up and nobody's talking."

"So it is real?" Daniel stood and started to turn then looked back at his boss. "I need to go to Texas."

"Not yet," White stared him down. "Soon... but not yet. Didn't you tell me that young man in Georgia has a network of informants, nationwide?"

"Ben?" Daniel knew instantly what his boss was thinking. "Yeah...of course." He turned away again and took several steps this time. "Good catch, boss. I'll reach out and see what he can find."

4

The car lot in Kennett, MO. was a dirt space just off the paved road. Pits of untold depth were filled with rainwater. They gave the grade a more level appearance than it deserved. Jon looked toward the corner of the lot and could see a young man sitting at a computer terminal in the office building.

Must be "Willy," he thought as he went right past the concrete block structure and stepped around a couple of puddles to get to where the cars were parked.

The selection at Dan Bull's Good Used Cars wasn't deep by any imagination, but out of the corner of his eye, he noticed a beat-up van sitting near the back of the lot. The young salesperson had bounded from the building and approached him almost instantly.

"Evening, sir. Looking for a car are you?"

"Tell me about that van back there." Jon pointed at his interest and then looked toward the young man.

"We ain't cleaned that one up yet," the salesman offered as an excuse and tried to move his customer's attention back to the front area. Jon remained interested in the van.

The quick thinking salesman tried to change the subject. "You walking, tonight? I didn't see you drive up."

Staring a hole through the other man, Jon restated his interest. "Tell me about the van... please."

"Yes, sir... let's go take a look at it."

The vehicle was painted proclaiming "Wally's Wi-Fi and Computer Service" on its sides and the phone number appeared to be local. It looked to be about five years old.

"Is Wally still in business?" Jon inquired.

"Oh, yeah..." the salesman assured him. "He's from up the road a bit, in Holcomb. We got the van at an auction after Wally traded it in for a new one."

"Does it run at all?"

"Hell, yeah!" The salesman was feeling a sale coming and ran to get the keys. "Hang on a second."

Jon pulled the driver's door open and an unpleasant smell quickly attacked him. It was enough to cause him to step back. He exhaled and rubbed his nose while checking the tires, "fairly new," he mumbled out loud as he noticed the salesman returning with keys, and three cans of "Car Fresh" spray.

"They get kinda gamey sometimes." He tossed the keys at Jon and began spraying the interior with two cans at once. "That'll clear her right up."

"Did Wally bathe...ever?"

"Ha- ha!" The spraying stopped for a second and the salesman turned. "You wouldn't think so...huh? Actually, they tell me something spilled in here and he didn't get it cleaned right."

With the smell knocked down for the moment, Jon climbed in and fired the engine. A quick spin around the dirt lot left Jon nodding and smiling.

"How much...as is?"

"Well, Dan was gonna ask $3500.00 after we cleaned it up and painted it. I think he'd be happy with $2500.00... as is."

"Two thousand and you throw in more cans of that spray," Jon countered.

After trying to look disappointed for a minute the salesman stuck his hand out, "that's a deal, my friend."

The paper work took about thirty minutes. The cash transaction moved the process along and as the transfer papers said, a

Keith Webber of Ozark, Arkansas soon drove away with his new...used van.

~

Ben Shaw heard the cell phone and rolled it over on the table to check the caller ID. It showed Daniel Seay and his number. That usually meant one thing.

"Hey Daniel, he's not here."

"Ben...Don't sell yourself short. I wanted to talk to you."

Ben sat down his copy of <u>Washington at Valley Forge</u> and leaned back against the chair in surprise.

"Me? Okay... I'm sorry. What can I do for you?"

"Has there been any chatter from your contacts about a gun fight inside the Texas border?"

"There's been several near the border in the last couple years."

"No...no..." Daniel's tone asked for focus. "This was a big deal. Bunch of guys killed and just in the last few days."

Ben went through his papers, the reports were organized by sector and one SW informant said he had something big, but didn't say what.

"Daniel, let me check this one thing out and call you right back."

"You've got something then?"

"Not sure, sir. Let me check it out."

Ben sent the unknown informant an e-mail asking him to meet in a special electronic chat room, ASAP. Logging in himself, he then waited. The wait was less than ten minutes.

"Is this Silas?" the screen suddenly asked.

"Negative, I won't lie to you. This is his assistant."

The screen stayed blank for a minute. Ben went further adding, "I need help with info about a big gun battle your way."

"Hush-hush...no news about it at all. Not even here."

"It happened?"

"More than twenty dead from this side. Many more hurt. All hush-hush. Scary."

"When was this?" Ben typed.

"The seventh. Early morning of the seventh."

That was three days ago. Daniel had said it was this week. Ben asked for more info.

"Texas Ranger involved. Named Garcia. He's hurt bad, but alive."

"You mean like the Lone Ranger?"

"Yeah...they do exist."

"Where is he now?"

"Don't know...source too afraid to say."

"Okay...thanks." Daniel typed and then added. "We'll be in touch."

The person on the other side logged out and was gone. Ben's mind whirled until he thought of Franklin Webster, a former science teacher who now lived down in Atlanta. Dr. Webster left teaching to take a job at the Fernbank Science Center.

The electronic Rolodex came up with a number and Ben dialed before he realized how late it was. The phone rang in Atlanta.

"Hello?"

"Dr. Webster. This is Ben Shaw."

~

Jon drove the van several blocks to a self-service car wash. The place didn't appear like it was operational. He tried the sprayers and they did work.

With the rear van doors opened, the source of the odor seemed to be a spot on the floor carpet. Jon cut the spot and a large section around it out and tossed that carpet in a dumpster besides the building. Then it was back to his motel room to put the informal uniform on.

He parked about a block away and walked to his room. It was almost still too hot for the jacket that held the arm enhancer, but he couldn't chance going without it. The thin Glock pistol was checked and slid into his pant leg pouch.

The monitors for the camera and sound were transferred into the van along with two pillows from the room. He took a sniff of the interior and noticed the smell was less than before.

Good, he thought and half smiled. *That smell could have made for a rough evening.*

Jon checked once again through the supplies he had loaded and headed out.

The drive back into Malden was quiet. Without the rain, the ground showed no signs that it had ever been wet. No steam, no anything. The twenty-five miles to Malden went by quickly and his thoughts turned to something to eat.

A burger, fries and a bit of hard listening, was the thought of the moment. Then back to monitor the building after it turns dark.

Passing a side street as he got back on West Laclede Jon noticed a small flat building with a big sign. The main letters were worn, but it read Ennis or maybe Ernie's Country Kitchen. Several trucks and cars were parked in front and another guy was walking from an empty lot, about half a block away, where he had parked.

Jon pulled the van into the lot and tried to park behind the other truck. He sprayed another can of "New Car Smell" into the van before closing it up.

Drawing attention the minute he stepped inside the diner was not avoidable. The others customers paused their conversations to take a look. He was new, obviously new.

The menu was written on the back wall in chalk. Didn't look like it changed much. "Two Veggies and a Meat" was across the top, "Drinks and Bread Extra" in slightly smaller print just below.

Jon found a table and sat down. The young waitress threw a rag over her shoulder and asked if he knew what he wanted.

"How about a ground steak and some fries?" he smiled.

"Comes with two veggies...you want some beans?" Her eyes never really focused on him as she spoke.

"Double order the fries, please," Jon asked. The girl nodded and headed toward the back. Glancing around, he was met with questioning eyes from every corner. He dipped his head and tried to say "Hi" to one table with no response coming back. There was a newspaper rack in the corner so he got up, paid fifty cents for a thirty-five cent paper and returned to his table.

The crowd slowly began to act as though he had either disappeared or become one of them. Conversations started up again, though softly at first. With the newspaper held in front of him, Jon tried to concentrate on voices as their volume rose. One group caught his attention and he overheard a question.

"What time is Jerry opening up tonight?"

Zeroing in he heard another voice answer, "Don't know, maybe nine or so...and don't use his name in public, fool."

"Yeah, sorry."

Ruffling the paper, Jon rocked back and leaned toward the voices.

"I've got a bunch of stuff to drop off, is all," the first voice said in frustration. "I don't want to get caught hauling it around."

"What do you have?" the other voice asked him.

Jon needed to strain to hear the softer, near whisper that followed.

"Sudafed, fifty capsules I traded for at the hospital, for some weed. And some HCA." That was sometimes short for Hydrochloric Acid. "Had to go to four paint stores to get enough to bring. Told 'em I was cleaning bricks from getting tagged."

"That shit is supposed to be mixed, you dumb ass. That's sulfuric and salt."

"It's all the same in the end man. Besides, the HCA was cheaper time I got it together."

"I still think you're leaving out a step." His friend shook his head and looked away, toward Jon's table.

"Naw...hell, I checked it on the internet, man. It's cool."

Without looking their way, Silas could see in the reflection on the front glass window that one of the men would look towards him every few minutes. He remained cool and showed no sign of interest or even having heard.   His dinner came and the plate was piled high with French fries. The young woman leaned in and put the plate down. Folding the newspaper, he looked toward the waitress and beyond her to get an image of the man with the first voice. The green tee shirt he was wearing had a hole near the right shoulder and his shoes were heavy black boots.

The waitress cocked her head and asked if he needed anything else.

"You got any ketchup?" Jon smiled.

5

Daniel Seay tried to work on another story while waiting to hear from Ben. Finally, he closed the notebook and gave up on that. His mind kept wondering if he had done the right thing. Sheriff Wilbury sounded sincere and Daniel believed him...but the man had lied to him before.

Opening his cell phone, Daniel scrolled down through his phone numbers to M. Bilstock. After a slight hesitation about bothering yet someone else with this, he hit "call" and rocked back in his chair. The phone rang three times.

"Well, Daniel Seay," a voice announced loudly. "How the hell are ya?"

"Hello, Murray. Hope I'm not interrupting anything."

"Wouldn't have answered if you were...what's up?"

"I had a call from Horace Wilbury today."

"Sheriff Wilbury?" Murray sounded confused. "How did he know how to reach you...and what the heck for?"

"I had left my card with him back last year. I met with him right before I came out to your place."

"Okay." Murray was still interested.

"Would he make up some weird story and lie about it?" Daniel came right out with it.

Murray was quiet for a few seconds, and then responded. "That's kind of a tough question. He might lie to protect somebody or if he thinks something ain't any of your business. But the old crow is pretty much as honest as you get."

"Does he have a niece that you know of?" Daniel asked.

"Susie... oh, yeah. We dated way back in high school. Nothing serious. I heard she married a ranger a few years ago... Why?"

"Well, that ranger got hurt in some big shoot out earlier this week. The strange thing is there is no report of it...anywhere."

"How big a shoot out is 'big' to you?" Murray halfway challenged.

"I'm hearing twenty dead on our side and a bunch wounded."

"Christ!" Murray started flipping through newspapers and Daniel could hear it.

"It's not in the paper, Murray. That's the problem. Would Wilbury lie about this?"

"Damn...I'd hate to put my reputation on it, but...no. I don't think so."

"Ok. Well I'm checking it out, but if this is true and it's being kept quiet, you don't want the wrong people to know you know about it."

"Yeah... really." Murray paused. "How bad is the ranger hurt?"

"That I'm not sure of. Wilbury didn't say...or where he is."

"This is your cell number, right?"

"That's it and if I go anywhere I'll have it with me."

"Alright, if I hear anything I'll call. Oh...by the way...how's Capt. America doing?"

"Ha!" That barb caught Daniel by surprise. "Only the Shadow knows," he fired back.

"Good one!" Murray laughed back. "Not bad for a Yankee."

"Actually, I haven't talked to him for awhile. I've spoken to Ben about news reports. Haven't heard back yet."

"Ok, later my friend."

"Thanks, Murray." Daniel hung up and stood immediately. He paced around his office like an expectant father. *What's going on?* He kept thinking. *This is too big to keep quiet. Something is wrong, bad wrong.*

~

Ben Shaw was searching through his bountiful records for any other activity on that part of the Mexican border when the call from Dr. Webster came back.

"Ben, Frank Webster here," he said in very formal tones.

"Yes Sir, doctor. Anything on the films?"

"I...ugh." The learned man was caught without words. "I've never heard of this happening. I have a friend who operates the satellite cameras for those coordinates of the southwest, 29 degrees, 80854 north by 101 degrees, 55873 west. They copy whatever gets recorded because it's all motion activated." The scientist paused for a few moments. "The tapes for the evening of the sixth through the next morning were erased."

"Erased?" Ben wanted to be sure what he was hearing. "Recordings were made... and then erased?"

"That's all it can be." Dr. Webster was clearly upset by what he had discovered.

"Who could make that happen, doctor?"

"My friend doesn't know and I certainly don't have any idea. It has to somebody way up."

"Thank you anyway, sir," Ben started.

"I'm not finished...there's more," Webster interjected. "My friend checked for several days prior to that night and found what appears to be a rancher getting shot as he was running from something. His action made the cameras follow him, we didn't get the shooter."

"When was this?"

"The evening of the fourth." The doctor again stopped for a minute. "Ben, there's no police record of that incident either, none that we could find. They just forgot it was filmed I guess, because the tape was still there."

"I hadn't heard about that shooting yet...but I'll bet they are connected."

"Be careful, my young friend," the doctor advised. "I don't like any of this."

"Thanks, Doc. I'll do that."

~

Jon Crane had again assumed his Silas mantle. This ulterior identity required he wear the defensive armour Jon brought for survallence missions. Tonight that included his Kevlar jacket with its hydraulic powered right arm. Lightweight, yet very highly resistant to ballistic impact, the clothing drew no unwanted attention by its appearance.

Riding in a secret side pocket of his pants, which were also constructed from the protective Kevlar KM2 material, was the special Glock pistol. This weapon's thinner profile made it hard to detect as he carried it within reach.

Silas left the diner in Malden, Mo. around 8:40PM local time. He drove the van away from the area of interest and circled back.

The building he was watching appeared to be dark from the front windows. But Jon noticed some light coming through a crack in the sidewall.

There are lights on inside, he said to himself as he parked across the street. After powering the arm and checking the Glock, he got out on the passenger side of the van and ducked low behind three other cars parked along the same side of the road. He crossed and moved slowly up to the building. All was quiet.

Standing at the front glass, Jon could see the false wall that stood about four feet inside the windows. It was covered in flat black paper and gave the appearance of an empty building. Now he just needed to find out what was going on behind that fake wall.

"Straighten up real slow," the voice said firmly. Within a few more seconds, Jon could feel the barrel of a gun pressed into his back.

"Easy, now," he tried. "I'm just here with a delivery."

"Is that so?" The voice was on top of him now.

Jon thought it sounded familiar. He tried to calm the situation.

"Yeah man, I've got some batteries to sell... lithium."

"Knock off the bull and tell me where you got Wally's van?"

That didn't sound good to Silas. Not only was he caught; he had bought the absolute wrong vehicle. Suddenly that smell in the carpet made more sense to him. *Think, man. Say something.*

"I bought it. I knew Wally was part of the team," he offered sincerely.

"Dude, you're just full of crap, aren't you. Get inside." The man pushed him with the barrel of the gun and they walked in the direction of a small side door.

Jon slid his left hand to his belt and pushed the buttons.

"Alright, man. Don't get excited."

The door opened into a small, still completely dark area. *They had thought this through,* he told himself. Once in the small space, the gunman pulled the outside door closed and opened another sliding door. There was the light.

The interior was a large open garage space with four bays on the back wall. Two men were working on one truck and another loaded boxes into a car.

"Look what I found snooping around outside," the gunman announced.

"Hell, that's the dude from the diner," one answered as he picked up a large wrench and came their way. The others stayed where they were and looked on.

The odds were not comfortable to Silas. He didn't know what those others would do or what kind of weapons they may have, but he had to move and fast. Bending rapidly at the waist, Jon reached through his legs and grabbed the gunman by one of his ankles just above the heavy black boot. The gun fired and the round grazed off Jon's coat and on to the ceiling. His powered arm pulled that man's leg with the force of fifteen men. The gunman's head impacted the floor with a loud crack. The other approaching threat raised his wrench and began to run in Jon's direction.

Jon blocked the blow from the wrench with his Kevlar protected left forearm and reached under with his right hand to the man's throat. Shock and fear filled his eyes and the wrench-wielding attacker was unconscious in seconds. Jon laid him on the floor and quickly looked to the others.

Stunned by what they had witnessed, they slid slowly forward a couple of steps and raised their hands. One pleaded, "No trouble, man. We just work on the trucks."

"Who do you work for?" Jon demanded.

"Jerry Blake," the one offered right away.

"Do you know a Fred Everett?" Jon asked.

"Who?"

"Everett...Fred Everett."

"No sir," the first said and then the other, younger man interrupted him.

"I don't know about any Everett. I heard Jerry mention a Fred to someone on the phone once."

38

At that, the first man turned with a sharp glare at the other. "You've killed us both, you moron."

Jon stepped in and stared down the first man. "Why is that? Did you lie to me?"

The man bowed up and swore he didn't know any Everett. "This Fred fella is a bad guy, lots of pull somehow. That's all I know." His lip trembled as he spoke.

"Why are you that afraid of this guy?"

"Look." The man rolled his head like his neck hurt. "People disappear, ya know? They just go missing if this Fred ain't happy... with something they done."

"Where do I find Jerry Blake?" Jon demanded.

"I don't know. He finds us."

"You got a cell phone?" Jon came back.

"Yeah."

"Does he call you on it."

"Aw... man, don't go there, please. He'll have me killed for sure." The fear in the voice was building again.

"Tell me where he is and I'll give you time to get gone."

"Who the hell are you, anyway. A cop?"

"Don't worry about who I am. Just tell me what I need to know."

Jon got the cell number from which the mechanics were contacted. Then he went back to the two men on the floor. The one with the gun lay perfectly still. Blood oozed from his head onto the floor, soaking his green tee shirt. The one with the holes in it.

Rifling through the downed men's' pockets, he came up with several hundred dollars. Jon handed it to the other two.

"If you have families, go get them and leave this state... Tonight," he ordered. "Go far away till this is over."

"Over?" one asked as they went out the door.

"You'll hear about it. When it happens, you'll know. Now go."

They climbed on motorcycles that were behind the building and fled north. Jon walked across the street and looked the van over carefully before getting in. Retrieving four lipstick cameras and two audio microphones, Jon set them at various angles in the lighted space of the building. Through his remote monitor he would be able to see who, if anyone, came back to the building.

Driving directly back to the motel, Jon transferred his belongings into the Mercury and checked out. He left the area driving west at first, should anyone be watching. He would change course after two hours and head for home. Driving all night wasn't new to him. He would find a motel around mid-morning and get some sleep.

After driving about eight hours, at around 6:00AM on the east coast, he used one of his drop phones to call the number he had gotten from the men in Malden. It rang nine times.

"Hello..." a groggy voice answered.

"I need to speak to Everett," Jon told him.

The line got very quiet, but he could hear someone struggling to sit up. Then the voice barked. "Who is this?"

"Everett...I need to speak with Everett," Jon repeated.

The line went dead.

That would likely be one of the last calls that particular number would take, he thought with a small smile.

His point had been made. The bushes should be rattled enough to draw out his quarry. Congressman Everett would soon be aware that someone was on to him. How he reacted would be monitored. Jon already figured he had enough to go on. Still, Silas wanted to be sure.

It's a rule, he reminded himself.

6

Retired Naval Commander Mack Torrance was on the phone to a former Seal teammate. Mack was currently a sales manager for an auto parts company in New Mexico. He was calling his old friend from Austin, Texas.

"Tim, hey...this is Mack."

Tim was Special Agent Timothy Spiegel of the New Orleans office of NCIS, the Naval Criminal Investigative Service. Mack and Tim had worked together as part of Seal Team Bravo-six. To both men, that now seemed like another lifetime ago.

Spiegel's NCIS job fit him like a glove. He liked the atmosphere of New Orleans, having come there after the flood. Tim had met Capt. Phil Stone and Matt Turlock in Shreveport last year. Phil Stone stayed in touch from time to time. About as often as he heard from Mack.

"Commander, how the hell are you, Sir?" Spiegel shot back at his old friend, clearly glad to hear from him.

"I'll get right to it, Tim." Torrance was uncharacteristically abrupt. "I'm in the middle of a weird experience and wondered if you could ease my mind a bit."

Conversations that start with statements like that one are never good. But Agent Spiegel would not turn away a fellow Seal.

"What's going on, Mack?"

"Sharon and I are in Texas. Austin, right this minute. We came over here to take her Dad to a doctor's appointment. He still lives over in Junction and doesn't drive much anymore."

Tim got out a pad and pencil, said nothing. He listened intently to his friend.

Mack continued, "Just below Johnson City we noticed some buzzards. A bunch of them... circling low over a carcass."

"Ok," Tim said enough to let Mack know he was still there.

"Something wasn't right about the carcass...too much time seeing dead Marines on the battlefield, I suppose. Anyway, something about it made me stop and go check."

"Human?" the agent asked.

"Yeah, very much so. He was laying on his face with an empty backpack strapped to him. The bag had a hole and a tear in it...looked to me like it had been shot with a high caliber weapon. Whatever had been in there was gone."

"Could you tell how the guy died?"

"Oh, yeah...shot in the back of the head. And it was a fairly fresh wound, the blood pool was still kinda liquid, you know. And the body wasn't in rigor yet."

"Robbery, then?" Spiegel guessed and grimaced. He wished immediately he could have taken that back and just listened. A stupid guess like that showed little respect for his friend's concern. *Mack wouldn't call me over a robbery*, he chided himself.

If his old friend was insulted, he didn't let on.

"That's part of the weird stuff...I don't know about that, Tim. The body had dried blood, I mean old, dried blood under his nose and the corner of lips looked cracked and dried out. There was dried vomit on his chin, near the mouth and on the ground. This guy was really sick before he was shot."

Agent Spiegel knew what Mack was describing and sat up a bit straighter as he listened. This time he did stay quiet.

"That's when Sharon's dad got out of the car to see what was going on." Mack went on, "as he got close, his Dosimeter went nuts."

"His what?"

"He's a cancer survivor," Torrance said bluntly. "It took a bunch of Chemo and Radiation Therapy to get it under control so now his tolerance to radiation is really low. He carries a personal Dosimeter to register radiation exposure. The thing goes up to 300 mR on the scale...it pegged and actually beeped. He'd never heard it do that before."

"You're telling me the body was radioactive?"

"Hear me out, Tim," Mack pleaded. "I got Sharon's dad away from there, about a hundred yards up the road and then called 911." The old Seal was rolling now. "The local cop interviewed me at length and then within an hour there were Homeland Security people crawling all over it."

Mack took a minute to organize what else he wanted to tell. "Tim, they never said a word to me...nothing. The agents never asked the first question. Just sent us on our way."

"That's not normal protocol for any agency," Tim wrote as he spoke.

"Didn't seem right, but that's not all. As they loaded the guy up on the gurney... I got a better look at his face. I had assumed he was Mexican. But when they rolled him by, I could tell that wasn't the case. The guy was Arab, Tim. Either Syrian or maybe Iranian."

"Do the authorities know you saw that?"

"I don't think so, no."

"I'm looking at our wire reports. Something like that should be broadcast all over pretty quick." Spiegel said.

"That's another thing, Tim. This happened two days ago. We've been in Austin since later that day. I've checked the news each day...nothing. No mention at all."

The agent was quiet for several minutes. He finally spoke in authoritative tones. "Mack, did anybody ask where your father-in-law was from?"

"No. Nothing was ever mentioned about that."

"Get him and go to his house. Take a different route to get there. Just go, and if anyone approaches you, call me right away."

"What do you think is going on, Tim?"

"I don't know. That's what bothers me Mack. I don't know. I'll get back to you when I do."

~

Ben called Daniel to fill him in on the growing mystery, the incident that had no record. Daniel had briefly talked with Phillip Stone again, letting him know about the situation. Stone told Daniel that was how the government worked these days. Some things just weren't reported on, so they didn't happen.

"There's times when public safety can justify that type of action, but it's used way too often for other reasons. We just don't know what this deal is all about...and we may never know," Stone told the reporter. "You guys are the ones who can stop it if you would."

"What did you say to that?" Ben asked Daniel.

"Didn't get a chance to say anything," the reporter confided. "Phil had another call come in, so I let him get away with it, for then."

Ben was perplexed at best.

"Everything I do simply verifies there is no record of this mess, yet several people know it happened," he lamented.

"Have you talked to Jon at all?"

"No...he's on a mission. I'm not even supposed to say that much. He's really serious about getting back to his rules and the one man show."

"Can't you call him in an emergency?"

"Not this time. He'll call me or he'll just show up here...one or the other."

"Probably not much he could do right now, anyway," Daniel sighed.

"I'll keep looking and asking around from here," Ben said.

"Ok, talk to you later."

~

Another news story went out national, but was not picked up too far from its local origin at first.

The dateline was Austin, Texas:

"Major Downtown Hotel closed this week due to Gas Leaks caused by Eroding Infrastructure."

The problem was explained as collapsing water pipes, some as large as six feet in diameter had disturbed gas lines directly under the hotel. Guests were evacuated and the hotel was closed till further notice.

This cover story would hold for about a day.

~

Something about the innocuous Austin story, a mere paragraph on the AP wire, caught Daniel Seay's eye. He had a sixth sense for bullshit and this didn't quite add up in his mind. He checked his on-line phone directory and found the name of a reporter he had dealt with before, Jim Langston of the Austin Statesman.

The call had to be transferred twice, but he finally reached the younger reporter.

"Jim...Daniel Seay in Pittsburgh. How are you?"

"Well, well, Mr. Seay. How's the hunt going? Or did you find your serial killer?"

"I'm glad you at least remember who I am. Even if it is a joke." Daniel tried to sound disappointed and let down.

"No joke intended, sorry if you took it that way. Sure, I remember you."

"Jim, I'm interested in your gas leak situation. Anything new on that?"

The voice became a whisper and lost a great deal of its former confidence. Daniel could hear Langston walking. The Texas reporter moved to another room, and then closed the door.

"Daniel, I can't really talk about that," he asserted. "It's a weird deal."

"Can you tell what's weird about it?"

"I've been down to the site, twice. You can't smell gas at all. The city puts an agent in their gas so it will smell bad. There's nothing, no smell at all."

Langston was now talking fast. "The place is roped off. The whole square block around the hotel, and yellow caution tape is everywhere."

"Can you tell who's in charge of the scene?"

"Nobody's talking, and I mean nobody. There's guys in full-blown HAZMAT suits going in and out." Langston could be heard moving again and added, "I've seen several of them with Geiger counters."

"Geiger counters?" Daniel thought as he spoke. "Doesn't your paper have some of those?"

"Not now, we don't." The young man's tone was of disgust. "They're all gone. This whole thing is hush-hush and my boss looks scared to death. We've been warned not to talk, to anybody. National Security they say."

Daniel could hear another muffled voice and then Langston went on.

"Rumor is the area of quarantine is going to be expanded, sometime soon. When that happens, the lid might come off this thing. Maybe we'll learn something."

"How are the citizens reacting down there?"

"Curious... but they seem to buy the water pipe story so far. We've had sink holes for the last number of years so, they're buying the cause as neglect."

"Alright, Jim." Daniel found himself whispering. "Thanks and be safe. This is my cell phone so if you hear or see anything..."

"Yeah...will do. I'd better go."

"Take care." Daniel said as he heard the line click.

National Security? he thought. *Could this be coincidental to the other story*? He doubted it. He doubted it very much. What could he do except wait? *Others have taken great risk in talking to me. I have to respect that for now.*

~

Phil Stone's call was from a fairly new friend and standoffish member of his law enforcement group, a Special Agent of the Naval Criminal Investigative Service.

Tim Spiegel had served as a Navy Seal for eleven years. At the age of thirty-five he retired from the service and was asked to apply to NCIS. The idea intrigued him.

After six months at Glynco, Georgia's Federal Law Enforcement Training Center, Spiegel was assigned to the Washington, DC office as a probationary agent. His training time was shortened due to his Seal experience.

He worked on a four-man team under a legendary Special Agent by the name of Lamar Jerome Grimes. Grimes had investigated the USS Orman incident in Yemen and arrested several of the men responsible for the attack, single-handed. He had other noteworthy accomplishments, but that was the biggie.

Grimes was tough, fair and honest as the day is long.

He could have been a Seal Team Commander, Spiegel thought when he discovered his supervisor had been a Marine Sniper before joining the agency. His close friends still called him Gunny.

Working in Washington also exposed Spiegel to the Director of the Agency who saw a leader quickly forming in the new probie. Within two years he promoted Spiegel to Special Agent in charge of the New Orleans office. It was through his duties there he came to meet the homicide Captain in Shreveport.

They met following a large, drug related bust at a Shreveport hotel where a Naval Commander was a guest. Special Agent Spiegel was called up to look into and clear the Commander of any involvement. The significance of that event brought players from several law enforcement agencies together for a couple of days. Stories were swapped, friendships were formed and though Capt. Stone had later tried to recruit Spiegel into his secret team, the Special Agent declined. Though he did promise not to interfere.

Now he was making contact about another situation.

"Hello Tim, what going on in New Orleans?" Phil asked as he answered the call.

Without a hello or a howdy, the agent went directly into secret mode, "Phil, this is something I need you to call me back about, Ok?"

"Call you back?" Stone was intrigued by the idea. "Sure."

"Here's a number," came back and Spiegel gave Stone an odd twelve-digit phone number for him to call. "It's a secure satellite phone you're calling and it will be encrypted. Call me right back."

Before Phil could ask anything else the phone clicked and the NCIS agent was gone.

Phil went into a private office and got on one of the departments secure lines. He checked out the glass door and no one was paying any attention to him. He pulled the blinds down and dialed the strange numbers. Rather than a ring...the phone buzzed.

When Tim Spiegel answered, it did sound different...and delayed.

"Thanks, Phil," the voice with echoes and hollow sounds answered. "I have something I shouldn't share that I need to tell you about."

Tim explained the call he had received from his old Seal buddy and that he had called another friend in Washington, a member of the National Security Agency, and gotten more disturbing information.

"The big thing is that Washington got a call several days ago from somewhere in Iran. Al Qaeda claimed to have a bomb in Austin, Texas that they would set off if prisoners were not released from Gitmo."

"What? What kind a bomb?"

"Thermonuclear."

"Bull-shit."

"Naw...I'm afraid it ain't. This is straight from Homeland Security."

"When the hell is the deadline?" Phil asked him.

"That's the big deal, Phil... It was yesterday."

Capt. Stone was quiet as that soaked in. Then he announced, "Well... they were bluffing, right?"

"I wish," the garbled voice continued. "A radiation signature was located and traced to a room at the Hilton in downtown Austin."

"We found the bomb?" Stone interrupted.

"They found where it had been. It must not have worked. It leaked something bad and the room has been cordoned off. They may have to destroy the whole hotel if it can't be scrubbed."

"So what now?"

"The experts say a container of U-238 must have been damaged and was leaking pretty bad. Bad enough it degraded some other components. That's what the guy my buddy found by the roadside must have been carrying. It killed him...or got him killed when he got sick."

"Where are we now?"

"The NSA says they should find the leaking container any minute. But... the threat is still on. Al Qaeda will just bring in some more parts, we think through Mexico."

The police captain's mind was spinning. *Al Qaeda, nuclear bombs and Mexico, this is nuts.* "What on earth can I do from here?"

The hollow, echoing voice did not hesitate. "We need someone who can get inside... and quick. Someone who doesn't worry about political correctness or even the law if need be. We need that guy you were telling me about."

Phil didn't have to ask who that was. He was the reason for the group, known only to most of them as Silas. Phil knew him as Jon Crane, but he had never mentioned that name to Spiegel.

"Yeah...I'll try to get word to him, Tim. But damn, where would he start on such a mess? He's good... I know that. But this is crazy."

"I have some names of their contacts and sympathizers, Spiegel offered. "It's all we have and we need to move fast. Time is critical... A new deadline could be set anytime."

7

The Mercury parked on the backside of the Southaire Motel near Dickson, Tenn. He had checked in shortly after 6:00AM as a traveling salesman from Little Rock.

Jon was tired and though he was only three hours or so from home, the morning rush hour through Nashville would add another hour and a half he'd rather not drive. Once in his room, Jon set up the laptop he had programmed to contact Missouri.

The cameras and microphones would not reach this far on their own, but wireless Internet was a wonderful thing. The monitoring units were connected to an I-Pad Jon had carefully wrapped in plastic and left in the dumpster at the motel in Kennett, Mo. One button push on the laptop and the I-Pad came to life and relayed the feeds from the building in Malden.

The man with the gun still lay where he had been.

That head bouncing off the concrete didn't sound good, Jon told himself. *Looks like it really wasn't.*

There was no sign of the other man, the wrench wielder.

So much for the live feed, he thought and hit a rewind key. The I-Pad began to play a recorded visual of the hours that had passed. In high speed, time lapse, of course.

At the five-hour mark, about three hours ago, there was slight activity inside the building. Two unidentified men came in... looked around for a few minutes and then a third man came in. Jon got a good look at this one; his face rang a bell with him.

Opening the file he had collected on the congressman and his associates, Jon thumbed through to the pictures and quickly found what he sought. That third man was Abe Sinclair, an aide to Congressman Everett.

According to the file, Sinclair was the main strong arm for Everett. He got things done and handled the dirty business of punishment, when needed.

Sinclair made a call while standing there. The audio wasn't clear, but Jon could figure who he had called. Within thirty minutes, live time, another man stepped into the interior of the chemical building facility and warehouse. It was Charles Fern, one of Everett's partners in the real estate holding group listed as owners of the building.

That was enough for Jon. This guy, and his friends were dirty. He had his proof, now he needed to go home, plan how to remove Everett and deal with any others necessary to close down their meth business.

Jon stopped the recording and the feed went back to live action. The scene was quite different now. Flames rose through heavy smoke from the floor and within a few seconds the picture went dead. The building had been torched. Soon, nothing other than the concrete block and slab would be left.

"They don't play nice," Jon smiled and said out loud. He thought about calling Ben to check in, but decided against it.

He's fine, I'm sure, he told himself. *We both need to get used to my working alone and being out of pocket more anyway.* Besides, he was exhausted. It was time to sleep a few hours.

~

After a couple hours of sleep that just overtook him, Ben continued with his search. The follow up calls began to put the pieces together, though not completely. There was enough to tell something major was happening. A bomb threat, it appeared, that the government was either unwilling or afraid to share with the public.

The three main contacts set up a secure conference call to compare notes and figure out what to do. Contacting Jon was the main consensus. But that would have to wait for him to call in or simply come home.

Ben suddenly realized a bad exclusion had happened.

"Has anyone talked to Marsha?" he asked sheepishly.

The others were quiet until Daniel finally muttered, "Damn, I just thought...no I didn't think. This all has come together so fast there wasn't anything to call her about till just a few minutes ago."

"Let me see if I can get her on the line and jump her into this call," Ben told them. He was off line a couple of minutes and then came back.

"Marsha, you're on the line with me, Daniel Seay and Capt. Phillip Stone of the Shreveport Police."

Marsha cleared her throat audibly and then asked straight out, "Something's happened to Jon?"

"No...no, no," Daniel jumped in. "Didn't mean to scare you. Fact is...we haven't heard from him and wondered if you had."

"No... he usually calls when I'm getting up or getting off duty. This day schedule I'm on keeps me pretty busy most of the time. What's going on, guys?"

Daniel tried to explain the situation as the others listened. He included all the details he knew. No one offered any corrections, so he assumed he had done a good job.

"It's time we made Jon aware of this. It seems too big to ignore," he declared.

"So, Ben...you obviously can't reach him, right?" she asked.

"He's gone native. I know he must have talked to you about it," the youngest one responded. "I don't really know where he went. All I know is... he's on a mission."

"Truth is..."Marsha started. "I was just going to try to call you, Ben. I have something weird I wanted Jon to know about. A message just got to me from a contact in DC."

Marsha could be heard going into a different room and closing a door. "May be connected to all this other, then again... it may not."

"Right now, we don't know what to think about any of it," said the frustrated reporter. "I'd like to believe we're all making too much of everything. What have you got?"

"A contingent of Israelis, two men and a woman, came into Reagan Airport late last night with no fanfare. They were escorted right out, no customs or anything."

"Diplomats, most likely," Daniel offered. "An advance team, I'm guessing. Must be some big meeting coming up."

"My contact didn't think so," Marsha continued, her tone now a bit more worried than before. "They didn't go into DC, but went straight to Langley. They haven't come out since."

Phil Stone was the first to speak up. "Langley...that's CIA. Makes sense to me."

"What? How does that make sense?" Daniel demanded.

"If something is over your head, you call somebody who has more experience with it, right?" The homicide captain was feeling a connection, a big one.

"They've called in the Mossad." Ben interjected flatly.

"Bingo!" Phil concurred. "This is too new for our guys. They've called in the big guns, the ones with experience in threats from Al Qaeda."

~

The Headquarters of the CIA was not a place domestic issues were to be discussed. Those were left to the offices of the FBI and other agencies. The CIA was forbidden to operate within the country. But this was special.

Seven men and a woman sat around a large, egg shaped table in the Secured Conference Center for the CIA in Langley, Virginia. Huge maps and an eight-foot wide video screen covered the walls while hundreds of unseen LED lamps lit the room with an erie glow.

The Section Director of Homeland Security, Darin Doyle, considered himself to be leader of the group. Their host for the event, CIA Director Wilson Farley, sat on the far side of the table, quietly moving his eyes from one guest to the next, never saying a word.

"Mr. Harel," Doyle said while looking toward the eldest member of the Israeli group, "I certainly know you by reputation."

Indeed he should. Yinon Harel was one of Israel's most decorated war heroes. He led the incursion into Iran a couple of years earlier. His team had neutralized the main nuclear facility producing weapons grade material the Iranians had. They were in and out before the world knew Israel had taken action. When the site was attempted to be restarted a week later, it blew. The blast was not nuclear, but materials released into the air were both lethal and embarrassing to the Iranian government.

The Mossad leader did not look at Doyle. Rather he tilted his head in the slightest of recognition gestures.

"I don't believe I know your team members," Doyle added.

Yinon Harel looked up and across the table toward Jason Shuck of the FBI. He paused there for a moment before glancing at the speaker with the oversized ego.

"I don't think it's necessary that you do, Mr. Director," he countered in a course tone. "Besides," Harel lifted his arms and continued, "Where is Jerry?"

"Jerry?" Doyle asked as he looked to Shuck who had straightened his sitting position abruptly.

"Jerry..." The FBI Operations Officer now stood. "He means Jerry Grimes. Jerome Grimes of NCIS," Shuck explained.

Doyle frowned sternly and uttered one word. "No."

"I believe Yinon has worked with Mr. Grimes in the past, Mr. Director," the FBI agent offered. "He has trust in him."

The Israelis remained quiet.

"Look, Yinon," Doyle smirked while attempting to sound official and in-charge. "We're trying to keep this situation as quiet as we can. We really don't think we need to involve the NCIS." His tone was condescending. "This is not a Navy matter."

Farley of the CIA smiled a huge, wry smile. But said nothing.

"Mr. Director," The Israeli leader stared straight at Doyle this time. "It does not matter to me what unit Jerry works for in your organization. I would like him on this team."

"And I told you that isn't necessary." Doyle now tried a forceful tone and folded his hands in front of himself on the tabletop. A gesture showing that was his final word on the subject.

This time Farley put his elbows on the table and his head in his hands.

"Very well," Yinon Harel said calmly as he stood and motioned to his team members to follow. "Good luck to you, then."

He again nodded to the Homeland Security chief.

Darin Doyle's complexion went gray and he looked desperately to Jason Shuck for support. Shuck stood up and raised his hands, palms out in front of him.

"Whoa...whoa now! We can work this out," he blurted. "I'm sure we can get Jerry here if you'd like, Yinon," Shuck assured him.

"Shuck!" Doyle shouted and offered a look that was lethal.

Shuck stood and walked at a quick pace to Doyle's end of the table. He grabbed the Homeland Director by the arm and half carried him out of the room.

"Turn loose of me, sir," the director commanded, shaking himself free. "Do you know who you are manhandling?"

"Oh...Yes, sir." Shuck released the grip and leaned into the Director's face. "I sure do."

"What is your problem, Shuck? I'll have your damned job."

"You just might," the FBI Section Chief glared. "If they walk, so do I." He gave the other man a second to let that settle in, then ripped into him again. "We need them and what they know, you... political fool."

Shuck stepped back. His volume lowered but his intensity did not. "You let them go and I'm not only leaving...I'm calling the Washington Post on my way out."

The politician knew a good bluff when he saw one. This wasn't one. The Post was one of the larger publications still fighting the news blockade.

"Ok...call the NCIS Director and see if Grimes can help on this."

Shuck nodded his head once at the Homeland Security leader and replied as he turned to go. "Now...that's leadership." He stepped back into the room and directed his next comments to his CIA host. "Wilson, can you get Director Scott on the line for us?"

The head of the Central Intelligence Agency smiled again and spoke his first words of the evening. "I believe I can Jason. Be back in minute."

8

Daniel Seay remembered he needed to get back to Sheriff Wilbury with some form of explanation about what they had discovered. His call did not get the Sheriff in his office, but a deputy transferred the call to his mobile unit.

"Yeah, Wilbury here," he answered.

"Sheriff," Daniel started. "This thing is bigger than we ever thought."

He then offered his best, condensed version of what he felt he could tell the man.

"It's being kept quiet for National Security reasons, Sheriff. They don't want a panic over it."

"Panic? Over some bomb threat?" Wilbury scoffed.

"Pretty big bomb though," Daniel reminded him.

"Well, I'm more concerned about my friends and my niece's husband. I'm on the way down to that area now."

"Do you think that's wise, Sheriff?"

"Wise?" Wilbury shot back. "Wise isn't the deal right now, son. We got bad folks bringing shit into my country, right out in the open and there ain't nobody I see doing squat about it."

"Please, listen to me..." Daniel tried.

"Son... three counties along that stretch have dead sheriffs because of this. They need some law."

Daniel thought fast. He needed to come up with something. "Sheriff Wilbury, do you remember Murray Bilstock?"

"Murray? Sure. I know Murray... what of him?"

"I know where he is and how to reach him. Let me see if he can't organize some help for you."

"Murray's not law."

"You want law...or do you want help?" Daniel pleaded.

The line was quiet for a minute. Then Wilbury spoke again, sounding more in agreement.

"I'm gonna look around a bit and then head back to Brownwood. If you get Murray, have him call me," Wilbury declared. "But be quick about it."

"Thanks, Sheriff. I'll do that."

~

The panel truck bounced hard as it pulled off from Interstate 35 North.

"Careful you fool," the passenger shouted in Arabic. "You'll blow us to Allah's doorstep."

"It didn't work, remember?" the driver answered. "The detonator was ruined."

The exit lane was long and well paved. The flat landscape was almost like home to the men in the truck. A building on the right appeared to be abandoned even from a distance. As they drove past the former truck stop and restaurant, the passenger twisted his body to look the entire building over. Sitting back in his seat he smiled.

"There is much emptiness now in this country. The Jihad is having its affects. Allahu Akbar." He coughed as he spoke and could taste blood. He said nothing of it. "This is why Mithras recruited us...to correct this mess."

"Think what you like, my friend. Our cause has little to do with that."

Their three days in Texas had shown them many signs of a failing economy and lost promise.

"They did this to themselves," the driver declared emphatically.

The neatly paved and well groomed expressway and exit roads were a contrast to the closed businesses that littered those concrete ribbons. The government had spent money it didn't have on things it didn't need. The world had watched and scoffed at their actions for years.

At the end of the side road all the signs pointed west, to the left. Texas Highway 195 the main sign said. With little choice, the driver turned and headed that direction. The road soon narrowed and brought memories of another Texas road they had traveled a few days earlier.

"I still say it was a mistake to leave Ashur lying there," the rider noted, still continuing his argumentative tone. "They will identify him."

"Demyan, he was contaminated," the driver shouted this time. "They would have found him ten feet under ground." His hands trembled as his thoughts added up their predicament. "They know what we tried to do. Think man! That hotel is hot from the leak." The driver's emotions boiled over. He slammed the brakes till the truck stopped and looked at his companion. "We...we are hot from it."

"We are dead, you mean," Demyan muttered in a defeated, weakened voice.

The driver blinked his eyes and filled his lungs with a breath that he held rather than speaking. He pushed the gas pedal down and drove toward the town of Florence, Texas. When he finally exhaled he said firmly and defiantly. "It is Allah's will."

The back compartment of the vehicle held the salvaged parts of the bomb that didn't work. They had made contact with their controller who told them to go north and wait for further word.

There were five of them when they started. Ashur, a Syrian national had carried the uranium canister in his backpack. It had been hit in the gunfire near the border. When it became obvious just how sick he was, they ended his suffering. Trying to reseal the contents of the broken container only damaged the detonator as well.

Vafa, the Iranian chemist who had waited for them in the Austin hotel, knew right away there was a problem. He had tried to set the bomb off at the appointed hour using what he thought was a manual trigger. That exercise only hastened his own death and spread the radiation through the hotel.

Following their instructions, they took Vafa's body to a lake near the town of Marshall and weighted it down. Now Demyan, the driver Mohsen and Hamid, who rode in the back with the bomb parts, headed north to find a place to wait.

"It must be hot in the back," Demyan said. "Hamid is awfully quiet."

They had drawn lots to see who would ride with the parts to prevent any further damage. Hamid lost the contest.

Unknown to the passengers in the truck's cab, Hamid now lay in a pool of his own vomit with blood running from his nose and eyes. It was not from the heat. But from the invisible poison raking through his body, killing cells by the millions. Within minutes he would be dead.

His co-conspirators had only hours left themselves.

~

Daniel first thought he had the wrong number. He even contacted Ben again to verify it.

"Oh well, must have dialed wrong in all the excitement," he told the younger man.

"Didn't you just talk to him?" Ben asked.

"I must have dialed wrong, sorry to bother you."

The second try worked much better. Murray Bilstock answered on the third ring.

"Murray...Daniel Seay from Pittsburgh. How's the new house coming along?"

"Hey... Daniel. We're getting to be two Chatty Cathys ain't we?" With no immediate response to that joke, he moved on. "The house is doing just fine. We're painting...or should I say arguing over colors, right now."

"Been there..." Daniel cracked back. "I thought I had your number wrong at first. I dialed a few minutes ago and didn't get you."

"Oh, yeah..." Murray explained. "I was over at the barn where I keep Lucy. I had it lined with lead to keep certain things out. Ya know what I mean? Got a new hanger, too. It's basically for show and a place to do maintenance."

Daniel tried to move the conversation forward.

"Murray, you remember I asked you about Sheriff Wilbury a day or so ago?"

"It was yesterday, Daniel. Are you losing your grip, boy?"

"Lots going on, man. I may well be losing it."

Murray could tell the situation wasn't funny and he dropped the humorous tone. "What's going on with all that? You sound worried."

"It's a big mess, Murray. National Security, bombs and dead people."

Murray did not respond to that, though the word "bombs" got his attention. He listened and waited for his friend to continue.

"Wilbury has taken it upon himself to go police the entire border where the first incident took place. I don't know what to do...you got any ideas?"

"Well... you're not gonna stop him or change his thinking, I'll tell you that," the cowboy concluded. "So, the Feds are still doing nothing about this?"

"It's all bottled up. Nothing is being said...or done."

The cowboy spoke up. "I may best get down there and see how much trouble he could be getting into." Before Daniel could speak, he added. "Heard from Jon yet?"

"No. Like I know what he could do about it anyway. This is nasty business."

"One bite at a time, Daniel. That's how you eat a mouse or an elephant. Look, I'll head out in the morning. I can be down there in a couple hours flying time. Should you hear from Jon...tell him I'll have this number with me."

"Murray...do you have a Geiger counter?"

"What?" The question was sharp and pointed.

"A Geiger counter...that warns about radiation..."

"I know what a Geiger counter is, Daniel," he interrupted bluntly. "You really think it's at that level?"

"I afraid I know it is. That's not public information just yet. Please keep it to yourself."

"They brought an A-Bomb into Texas?"

Man..." Daniel hesitated. "A hotel in Austin is quarantined because of radiation."

"You know this? How?"

"One plus one...from the information I've gathered."

"Like I said...I'm on my way down there."

"Murray, I thank you. And be careful."

"Yup...that's how we do it. Talk to you later, Daniel."

~

The eight-foot video screen lit up as Wilson Farley reentered the room and hit a button on the remote he held. The image was of a dark room with many screens and a large logo over the door that read MTAC. As the focus sharpened there were two men standing in view, one in the foreground, the other in the shadows.

"Director Scott, glad you could join us," the host offered.

"Wilson, nice to see you again. I notice you have company tonight."

The CIA Director motioned towards Harel and his team. "I believe Jerome is familiar with Mr. Harel here, at least."

Jerome Grimes stepped forward, "Yinon, my friend. How has life treated you?"

"Quite well, Jerry. You're looking fit."

Grimes laughed. He looked toward his director briefly and then back at his old friend from the Mossad. "What brings you here?"

The question was not totally sincere. Grimes had contacts in other agencies and was quite aware of the situation. His question was directed at those who thought they were controlling the information and keeping his agency out of the loop.

"It seems your country has a problem..." Harel began and went on to bring Grimes and Wilfred Scott up to speed.

Scott spoke up, pretending to be addressing his counterpart at the CIA. "Damn, Wilson. You guys still keeping all the good stuff secret these days?"

The CIA Chief looked down to cover his smile as he thought of what to say. "Old habits die hard, Wilfred. What can I tell you?"

A glance at Doyle made the Homeland Security Director aware it was his turn to talk. "The decision was made up the chain. NSA and above wanted it kept quiet. Far as I know POTUS was in on the decision."

"Ah...over our heads, huh?" the NCIS Director addressed his Homeland Security counterpart and made sure his comment was taken as sarcastically as he meant it.

Both rooms became quiet as the two high-level department heads stared each other down through the flat screens.

The head of the Mossad broke the standoff. "Gentlemen, if we're through pissing on each others shoes, can we get on with it?"

Special Agent Grimes began adding the details he had just heard to what he already knew about the case. Speaking to Harel directly, he asked. "Yinon, we need to stall them. Has there been a new deadline set yet?"

The Mossad leader looked to Farley who shook his head, "No."

"Good." Grimes was clearly taking control of the discussion. "That cover about the gas leak is good. Just expand on it... clear the city."

Doyle piped in, "Clear the city?" he scoffed. "Are you out of your mind? We don't want a panic situation."

"Then don't create one," Grimes countered calmly. "Do it professionally. Tell the folks they've discovered possible sink holes forming and the erosion could break more gas pipes and collapse buildings." He gave them a second to absorb his idea. "It's extreme, but it'll work."

"That's good." Harel was nodding in obvious agreement.

"How does that accomplish anything?" Doyle was attempting to regain control of the meeting, but only exposed his ignorance further.

With his face taking on a disappointed expression, Grimes explained, "We make the bad guys pick a new city. It slows them down." Then his eyes went straight to Doyle as he asked, "Get it?"

Doyle stiffened his back at the insult. "Scott...are you going to stand there and let your man continue this insubordination? This is my meeting and we'll do this my way."

"They wouldn't want to threaten an empty city," Farley said softly with a hand over his mouth.

The Homeland Security official turned red, and he wasn't blushing.

"I understand the concept, damn it. I just don't know that I agree with the tactic."

Yinon Harel waved again to his Mossad team. He stepped to his right and picked up his jacket.

"Nice to see you again, Jerry," he said calmly.

Through the large screen Jerome Grimes answered, "Same here, my friend."

"Wait just a minute..." Doyle commanded. He looked around the room and could feel the lack of support. His only hope was to acquiesce and he knew it. He rubbed his forehead hard and looked at Farley.

"Do it," the Homeland Security official declared.

Harel looked at the screen and addressed the men at MTAC. "We need to set up out there...near the border." He walked to a map and circled the area with his open hand. "To find out where they bring this stuff in and where they will go next."

"Can we be sure they will pick another city in Texas?" Farley asked.

"Yeah...they're all set up to hit Austin so they'll try for somewhere within a couple hundred miles of there." Grimes had already thought it through.

"Dallas?" Doyle questioned.

"Nope...too big."

"I guess Waco, Odessa or San Angelo," Harel said while looking at the map.

"Agreed," Grimes confirmed. "We'll meet there in the morning. Your people and mine."

"Who are your people?" Doyle demanded.

Grimes looked at his director. "I'll need Barker from L.A., Spiegel from New Orleans and Wilson..." He paused and looked at screen. "If you're available, Sir. We could use you."

The CIA section chief smiled. "I retired from field work several years ago," he said. "I'm a bit out of shape, and shouldn't work in the country anyway... but I wouldn't miss this."

"We need what and who you know." Grimes grinned. "None of us are as kick-ass as we used to be. But even that won't fix this mess. We need to think our way through it."

"I'll need to get approval on all this," Doyle tried to inject.

"Yeah...you do that...Sir," Grimes said. He then looked at his Mossad friend. "We all travel separate. Meet at terminal B, the San Angelo airport, 7:00 A.M. Okay... fine?"

Harel nodded, Wilson Farley grinned and Darin Doyle looked disappointed, like he'd been passed over. Farley picked up his remote and pointed at the screen.

"Okay and fine," he said as he hit the button and the big screen's picture went black.

9

Murray's Bell 407 copter cruised southwest at thirteen thousand feet. The tail numbers identified the craft as NMB407T, but Murray preferred to call her "Lucy." The name was displayed on her sides, below the rear windows.

Lucy's current altitude was considerably lower than her maximum ceiling of twenty thousand feet. But Murray wanted to stay out of harms way. He chose to fly at night for the same reason, less traffic around him.

After splitting the difference between Dallas and Waco, he leaned Lucy due south until he could see Lake Whitney. It was about there that the two G5's roared overhead, some ten minutes apart. The silhouettes and running lights were distinctive. Murray was personally familiar with the G5 and recognized them immediately. Both jets were heading west and only a few thousand feet above him, quite low for that type of aircraft.

"Naw, it couldn't be," Murray heard himself say as the first passed. More to himself he finished the thought, *not yet, couldn't be him. Not enough time for him to react.*

His new friend, Jonathan Crane often used a G5 for transport. *Besides, I'd have heard from him if he were coming this way.*

He rolled Lucy back to starboard until they were in a western track. Forty minutes later he could see the lights of Brownwood Regional Airport. It felt strange to be "home."

Deputy Irv Stallings stood waiting for him. Leaning against the hood of his car, Wilbury's number one deputy grabbed his hat as the prop wash swirled around him.

Irv's eyes squinted against the dust and the glare of the sun just peaking over the horizon. When the door of the copter opened, he walked around toward the rear of the machine to greet its pilot.

"Murray, how the hell ya' been, man?" the deputy started.

"Hey, Irv. Thanks for coming out."

"Wilbury called, he's on his way back," the deputy said as he grabbed Murray's bag and led him toward the car. "Driving right this minute, matter of fact."

"Irv," Murray was always one to cut to the chase. "What do you think is going on?"

"Smuggling," he answered stone cold factually. Then he stopped and looked at his old acquaintance. "Just what... bothers me...about it all..." He started and stopped. "You don't kill sheriffs and Texas rangers over a couple bags of dope."

"Did Garcia die?"

"No...sorry, I forgot you knew Susie. But he damn near did."

The ride to the sheriff's office was quick. Irv got Murray some coffee and went straight to the two-way radio.

"Mobile one...this is Brownwood dispatch to Wilbury...come in, over."

"Wilbury...go ahead," the radio answered.

On hearing that Murray Bilstock was there, the sheriff instructed Deputy Stallings to take him into the sheriff's private office. "Show him the file on my desk," he added.

The file contained Wilbury's mostly hand written notes and accounts of what had happened. News reports were almost non-existent. But what had been reported was also in the file.

Pretty thorough for a old country sheriff, Murray told himself. He was impressed.

~

The Gulfstream jets that Murray had noticed landed in San Angelo about fifteen minutes apart. The agent, from Los Angeles, Terrace Barker having arrived first, waited for the planes at the gate. A commercial flight from New Orleans would land an hour later with the remaining member of Jerome Grimes' task force.

The Mossad leader and Grimes had flown with Farley in an FBI plane, borrowed from that agency's rapid response unit. Harel's other team members had left DC after gathering supplies to add to what they had already brought with them. Their CIA contracted plane was heavy with equipment and weapons.

The three leaders had time to discuss what they knew on the flight, a discussion that didn't take long. Much of the time was spent in thought and contemplation of how to uncover the facts they desperately needed to know. Their mutual conclusion was groundwork, old school detective legwork. Something they were all good at.

Terrace Barker had been with the NCIA for three years. A Los Angeles police officer for two years prior, following his tour in Afghanistan with the Tenth Mountain Division, Barker was a welcome addition to the team on the west coast.

Barker waited until Tim Spiegel's plane came in from New Orleans to share what he had learned from a contact in the Texas Rangers.

"A panel truck has been found off a highway just south of Florence, Texas. Three dead inside, two in the cab and one in the back, all radiation poisoning."

"How can they be sure of that?" Grimes asked.

"The source of the radiation was in the truck," Barker smiled. "We found what's left of the bomb."

~

Horace Wilbury had noticed the SUV before they both went through Brady, Texas. The headlights got behind him at Menard and had stayed about a quarter mile back ever since. US Highway 377 between Brady and Winchell was more than twenty miles of nothing. At the half waypoint, the Suburban closed the distance to less than 100 yards and then held that gap. Early sunlight was now illuminating the object in his mirror and Sheriff Wilbury had seen enough.

"Mobile One to Brownwood dispatch, come in," he radioed. Then laying the microphone down next to him, Wilbury unhooked his seat belt so he could get his service revolver out of the holster. He checked the huge weapon and placed it in his lap.

"Brownwood dispatch to Sheriff Wilbury, go ahead, Sir," the radio crackled.

"Brownwood, I'm 10 miles north of Brady on 377 and I've grown a tail. A black SUV is closing on me and I do not know its intentions, over."

"Roger that, Sheriff," Irv waved for Murray to come over as he responded to his boss. "Are you sure he's following you? Over."

"I'm getting ready to take the Placid turnoff and will get back on 377 at Mercury," Wilbury stated calmly. "If that shakes them off me, I'll report... over."

"Roger, Sheriff." The deputy rubbed his chin as they waited. Two, then three minutes passed until the radio squealed and the sheriff's voice came over it again.

"Brownwood, they're still on me. Turnoff didn't shake 'em. I'm gonna try to out run them."

Murray grabbed the microphone. "Sheriff, this is Bilstock. I'm on my way in Lucy. Haul ass, old man."

The drive back to the airport took less than five minutes. Lucy was in the air shortly after that. Irv Stallings slid a four round magazine into his Browning 308 rifle as they roared south over Browning. Murray then followed the highway toward Mercury, Texas. He never took Lucy above three hundred feet as she screamed ahead at 130 mph.

As they approached the town of Winchell, Murray could see the speeding vehicles coming their way. The sheriff's cruiser tracked back and forth across the road with a black Chevy Suburban right on his bumper.

Murray looked over at Irv who nodded and pulled back a side window. Lucy dove low and buzzed the vehicles, making her presence known. A larger gap between the SUV and Wilbury's car developed as Murray swung out wide left and then dived down low, coming from out of the sun. Roaring toward the side of the larger ground vehicle, Irv leaned back, sticking the barrel of his weapon through the window and took aim.

Considering the closing speed on a moving object, it was a great shot, hitting the right front quarter panel of the Suburban just above the wheel well.

Lucy arched upward and to the left as she turned for another pass. Murray could see the Suburban slow down, and a blacked out window rolled down. As they slid back into the path of the SUV, automatic gunfire erupted from the opened window. One round hit Lucy's windshield and cracked the outer shell.

The cowboy pulled back on the stick and again nearly rolled his machine. The engine coughed and nearly stalled through the direction-changing maneuver.

Murray caught a brief glimpse of the highway and could see the sheriff's car pulling further ahead of the SUV. The sun caused him to lose sight of both ground vehicles for a second, but then he leveled off and bore down once again on the offending Suburban.

Irv tried to take aim and they both could see the barrel of a weapon emerge from the window of the SUV. Murray started to pull back when suddenly the Suburban veered hard right and went off the road.

It bottomed into the Texas dust and bounced high one time prior to rolling over. The huge vehicle flipped several times before Irv hollered out. His attention had moved.

"Would you look at that?" he yelled while pointing below.

Sheriff Horace Wilbury stood in the middle of the highway, no more than fifty yards from where the SUV left the road. He had braked his cruiser hard and slid it sideways across the road. From there he had stepped out and was still holding his .357 revolver in both hands.

At that point the attention of the men in the helicopter was again distracted. On its fifth roll, the SUV exploded in a fireball. The energy released stopped the rolling, and what was left ended up on its left side, still in flames. By the time they looked back at Sheriff Wilbury, he was in his car heading towards the wreck.

Murray sat Lucy down on the dirt, upwind of the fire, and he and Irv ran to see what they could do. The heat kept them back, and it was obvious the men inside were already dead. What was also obvious was the missing right front tire on the Suburban.

Wilbury had fired two shots. One ripped through the windshield on the driver's side, and the other had destroyed the front tire and nicked the rim. When that metal wheel hit the pavement, it pulled the vehicle out of control.

Murray turned to see the old lawman now standing just outside his cruiser, microphone in hand calling for assistance. Despite the circumstances, Murray smiled and tipped his hat toward the sheriff who did not respond.

It would take authorities some time to identify the men from the SUV, if at all. But Irv made a discovery that didn't make sense to him. The item had been thrown from the rolling Suburban and lay in the dust. The deputy picked it up and walked toward Murray.

"Check this out." He handed the cowboy a small black book with writing he couldn't understand. "What do think this is?"

Though he couldn't read the text either, Murray recognized and knew what the book was.

"It's a Koran, Irv." His face showed the confusion that mixed with his concern. He looked hard at the burning hulk of the vehicle in front of them. "What the hell is going on here?"

10

The offices of Congressman Fred Everett sat on the second floor of an old retail building. The corner of North Main and West Pine had once been the center of commerce in Poplar Bluff. As with most semi-urban cities, business had long since moved to the suburbs. The space was adequate, accessible and still secluded. Everett enjoyed being in the town he had grown up in.

Constituents would likely never see the renovations the congressman had done to the room he now called his home office. The opulence there far exceeded his Washington assigned space, where he preferred to have his official pictures taken.

The coffered ceilings, expensive paintings and oversized leather furniture accented the heavy oak paneling and bookshelves in the Poplar Bluff office. The meetings held there were not for the public's scrutiny. The one this morning was no exception.

A new freeway between Kennett and Poplar Bluff was being discussed. Federal money, lots of it, would be needed and that was Everett's domain. The course of the new road would cut through a section of Arkansas, and a representative of their interests was in attendance. Arkansas wanted a share of Missouri's funds to help with their costs.

Everett faked a protest while fully in favor of the plan. That road would help distribution of goods from Malden into Arkansas, and expand the business.

A knock at the door disrupted the meeting, and an aide stuck his head into the room.

"Mr. Everett, I need a word, sir."

"Can't it wait a minute?" the annoyed congressman challenged forcefully.

"There's a situation with resource," the aide insisted, "that needs your attention...now."

Everett excused himself and left the room with his aid. The word "resource" was an operative word.

"What's going on?" Everett demanded.

"Malden has been compromised."

"Malden? How the hell did that...?"

"Some guy found it. He was snooping around and the guys jumped him."

"So...get rid of him. What's the problem?"

"He killed Stan and nearly choked Billy to death."

"What of the mechanics? Weren't they there?" Everett asked, his face losing color.

"Gone...don't know where yet. Both of 'em, families and all."

"They're gone?" Everett was confused. "How do you know they didn't do it?"

"Cause Billy woke up when Jerry got there. Billy saw the guy, saw him good."

"Who was he? A druggie?"

"May have been," the aid told him. "Billy said he was stronger than a guy that size should be. Could have been on something."

The congressman turned away and stared at the wall. "We have to move the operation," he relented. "Destroy everything there."

"It's already been done, Sir," the aid said solemnly. "There's one more thing, Sir. Jerry got a strange call on his cell not long after this happened."

"Have him ditch that phone and start planning to regroup," Everett ordered.

"Where... do we regroup?"

"Good question..." Everett said. "Let me get rid of these guys and we'll talk about it." He pulled the door open and thought of something else. "Find out who that SOB is, you understand me?"

"We're working on it, sir."

"Working on it ain't enough," Everett glared. "Do it."

Returning to his meeting the congressman was brief and abrupt.

"Gentleman, I can't see any worth in more asphalt poured over farm land down there," he stated.

"What?" The Arkansas representative stood angrily and protested the sudden change. "We had a deal, Fred. What the hell is with you?"

"Look..."Everett raised his hand. "I've thought about it. Please, let's just leave this alone, for now." He walked to the office door and opened it, motioning for his guests to leave. "Perhaps a better location may come up."

As the men quietly left the room, each met Everett's glassy stare and knew not to challenge the man. Not now anyway.

~

Jon's alarm went off at 8:45 A.M. He rolled over with some reluctance, to turn it off. The TV remote lay next to the clock and Jon punched the on button. He normally had little time for television, but the noise would make a good back up for the alarm.

Rolling on his back to stretch, the "News Alert" bong got his attention, and he struggled to focus on the picture.

"Major city to be evacuated, infrastructure faults main cause." The pretty blond read from her prompter. The story was unusual enough to keep Jon's attention and he sat up to hear more.

"Lack of normal maintenance on water and sewer lines puts area in danger of sink holes and damage to more gas pipes." The story went on.

More gas pipes? Jon was not aware, like most of the country, that there had been a problem under the big hotel in Austin. His sixth sense threw red flags all over this entire story. But he went on with his shower and got dressed.

Jon loaded the Mercury and was checked out by 9:30AM. He considered calling Ben to see what he knew about the strange story on the news, but didn't.

I'll be home in a couple of hours, he thought. *Then I'll have to figure out how to deal with Congressman Everett.*

Interstate 40 was only three miles away and it would take him into Nashville. From there it was on to Interstate 24 South for a couple of hours. Time to think about what he had learned in Missouri.

~

Professor Steven Walden had been in his office early. His first class at the Boulder College of Philosophy wasn't until 2:00 P.M. But he had messages to deal with. These messages had to be handled through channels, secure channels.

The failure in Austin was described as a "capital wash-out," one which would be rescheduled and soon. Walden's reaction to the news was odd. He smiled and folded the piece of paper twice and then stuck it in his pocket.

The professor's job, in the plot, was to recruit zealots who would sacrifice everything for the cause. His ranks were loyal, though becoming thin.

The professor openly taught his radical ideas under the guise of a class structure. He espoused the teachings of Saul Alinsky and other progressives about the evils of capitalism and other virtues of this country.

"One's concern with the ethics of means and ends varies inversely with one's personal interest in the issue." He would often quote Alinsky about his proposed tactics.

His lectures were quite popular among students who tried to understand how wealth could be so vastly fickle. The correlation of work and wealth didn't make sense to them. They wanted everyone to share equally in the goods earned by the nation and the professor helped push their beliefs away from individual effort to mass ownership.

Some were more impressionable than the majority.

Walden had been born in the late sixties to Hollywood Society parents in Redondo Beach, California.

"Most Likely to be a Terrorist," one student had written in his high school yearbook. The joke wasn't funny to Walden who had few friends in his formative years.

Though their names were not household words, his parents were well known and regarded in the movie industry. Their only son grew up in a home filled with Oscars and Emmys. His father was a master lighting technician of great demand, and his mother had been a publicist with a major studio for many years. The Hollywood community was mostly tight knit, in relationships as well as politics. But the younger Walden found himself talked about, more than with. He was extreme even for the Hollywood Left.

Steven studied journalism in college and even wrote for a local paper. He was never taken seriously, his ideas being far to the left of most in his peer group. That drove him into politics. He unsuccessfully ran for office twice and then settled on working for other candidates. None of whom ever won.

His disillusionment led him to teaching. There he found likeminded fellows who proffered him along. When Journalism groups soon tired of his preachy lectures, he found a home teaching Philosophy.

The cause de jour for the moment was the continuing struggle in Iran, it having been de-clawed by Israel a few years ago. Walden spent much of his time espousing his hatred for Israel and of course its defender, the Imperialist United States.

He had been accused of connections with Al Qaeda before, but nothing was ever proven. His positions put him in a minority. That label carried weight in a society that valued feelings of guilt over substance.

It was early in the investigation, but even those who had dealings with Walden before did not connect him with the situation in Austin, though they should have.

Walden had arranged for the shipment of the final pieces of the bomb into Texas. The assembler was sent by Syria and came in through Canada, but Walden had trained the others. He helped them with customs and conduct for travel within the US, conduct that would not draw undue attention.

The "capital wash-out" message was followed by requests for more couriers. He had responded he would need some time.

"Several candidates near potential, convictions not yet tested." He wrote. His messages were signed, "M"...Mithras.

Mithras would be notified of a new message through a date code on a social networking site. The account holders name was Sharon Able. Sharon did not exist, but from time to time, one of her forty-three "friends" would have a birthday. The notification of that birthday would be a date of shipment of a message. Walden had four "students" charged with monitoring for birthday notices, all on different days.

Two days after one was received, Mithras or Walden, would pick up his mail from a commercial post office box listed to Paris Publishing.

The reverse method was similar. He directed his messages to his contact in Massachusetts. The address would never be to the same name, though he knew his contact as "Bogart." Mithras' messages would often be post cards, appearing to be from a family member on vacation or a notice of a sweepstakes entry. Words written and out in the open, meaning little to anyone except the intended viewer.

This one was more sensitive. It would travel appearing to be a bill from a consulting company. The variances were too many to track.

~

Wilson and Grimes, with Harel and Nava Golan of the Mossad team, flew by helicopter to Florence, Texas. Nava was the nuclear physicist on the team as well as a trained killer. Her father was the Prime Minister's bodyguard for ten years and she had learned much from him. The science was a natural gift. She learned quickly and could develop theories to use in field situations.

The bodies had been sealed in special contamination containers as were the parts found in the truck. Nava took sediment readings from the ground and the vehicle. She quickly agreed with the NSA official there that the truck should be sealed where it sat.

"Can't we just burn it?" someone asked.

"Oh, my God...no!" The guy from NSA shook and waved empathically. "The uranium would spread even more as it burned."

"We have a containment vessel." Wilson offered. The FBI had borrowed an idea from Russia, one that they kept quiet. "It's a trailer with walls filled with sand, boric acid and lead." The others looked at him in puzzlement. "They used bags at Chernobyl to seal the reactor. It worked so they developed these frames that can make a container."

Nava nodded with a slight smile and the NSA official looked disappointed.

"The weight needed to contain this much debris would be staggering," Nava told him. "Don't you have containment foam?"

"That will work for this?" Wilson seemed surprised.

"In a hurry up situation, and this certainly is," the NSA guy answered. "It will take four containers of spray foam for this job. I have it on the way."

"How does foam stop the radiation?" Wilson was fascinated.

Nava again spoke up. "We developed a formula with your government that uses a high-density, closed cell foam that is impregnated with boric acid and lead fiberglass."

"How much does it take?" Grimes joined in.

"About sixteen inches thick will seal 1000Gy of gamma with a residue level of 40 roentgens," she told them.

Wilson and Grimes looked at each in complete loss of what they had just been told.

The NSA officer smiled, "It'll turn instant death into a dental x-ray."

"Oh!" Grimes laughed and instinctively stepped back from the truck even further than he was. "What level is that thing putting out now?"

"We measured the radiation at 28Gy of gamma within five feet exposure," Nava read from her pad.

"That's bad, huh?" Wilson surmised.

"It was worse in that cab," she answered and looked to the ambulance with the bodies.

11

Dalton, Georgia was busy with traffic at 11:00AM. People were too busy to notice the Mercury that pulled into the old warehouse building and disappeared.

Jon grabbed a bag and some leftover equipment boxes and threw them into the Jaguar. Stepping back to look at the car, he shook his head a bit. It was still hard for him to be so pretentious, even though the wealth was real. The car played into the new image he had agreed to. Daniel and Ben convinced him that the traveling salesman cover wouldn't float anymore around town. Jonathan Crane was now a wealthy philanthropist. The head of Crane Investments, Inc. could live in his huge mountain home and not hide his money, just what he did with some of it.

The warehouse doors opened and the Jaguar glided out onto the roadway.

This is sweet. He admitted to himself as the engine purred. The pure power of the car consumed your thinking if you didn't watch yourself. The urge to "just let her run" was always there.

I bet I could make that light, he thought at the sight of amber. But he didn't try. In a small town full of carpet millionaires and their gaudy carriages, this car stood out. Folks would stare and many waved as he drove by. Running red lights would not go unnoticed. In an odd way, *it was a good place for Silas to hide.*

The thought raised his eyebrows and made him smile. *Besides...Marsha liked it.*

The red light had changed, and he turned right pointing the car toward home.

~

Daniel Seay was already packing his briefcase for a road trip. It was still dark in Pittsburgh when he left home, but he knew his approval would come this time. News of the bodies found near Austin would be enough for Bill White and Daniel had anticipated his response.

"You're in kind of early." The boss pushed the door open and noted with a smirk.

"Yeah, what took you so long?" Daniel threw back at him and smiled. "The sun's almost up already."

"There's a story down there that needs to be covered." White had come to Daniel's office to discuss it. "Be mindful of the security lid on most of this stuff."

"Looks like the lid may be loosening," the reporter grinned at his boss.

"Don't take lightly the irrational acts of government, son." Bill White tended to offer advice with a heavy hammer. His comment stopped Daniel in his tracks and the reporter looked back at his boss and nodded.

"I understand."

"So, what route you going to take? You can't fly into Austin."

"Murray Bilstock has gone to Brownwood to help the sheriff." Daniel told White. "I'll go there and try to find him."

"Brownwood? That's a long way from the find, isn't it?"

"Yeah, but I can fly there on a regional out of DFW... and Murray has a helicopter."

"If that makes sense to you..." White responded and headed for the door. He turned back from the hallway, "Just be careful."

The Basics of Fundamentals

"Thanks, boss," came out automatically as he checked his watch. His flight left at 9:25 A.M. He had an hour to get there.

As he climbed into the cab that was waiting downstairs, Daniel pushed redial on his phone. He had already tried to call Murray, twice, with no answer. *Come on, Murray. Answer the phone...*he thought as he pulled his briefcase off his desk and moved toward the door. *Where are you, man?*

~

Murray Bilstock and Irv Stallings had walked up to the highway and stood with Sheriff Wilbury. The three men watched the burning SUV and said very little as they waited for help to arrive. Death was serious business, even if the victims had been trying to do harm to you. Each man knew they were lucky that fireball wasn't them.

Murray felt of his pockets and looked back at Lucy.

"I left my phone in the copter," he told the others. "Be right back."

~

Flight 6532 pushed back and awaited clearance to depart. Daniel Seay's phone was turned off and in his pocket. He watched the news report on the mini screen TV in front of him.

"Breaking News" the picture said. "Two incidents in Texas concern authorities..." Then the screen went blank as the attendants began the departure instructions. The plane moved forward and the pilot announced, "We are next in line for take-off."

Some five minutes later, at about 24,000 feet, the TV screen returned and the news was now going over baseball scores from last night.

Daniel shook his head and leaned back. *Timing is everything,* he thought quietly.

~

Murray's phone had fallen behind the pilot's seat during the excitement. He pulled it out and saw the flashing light, four missed calls. All were from Daniel Seay.

No Daniel, I haven't heard from Jon, he thought as he pushed the dial button on his phone. *I've got a good bit on my own plate right now.*

The recorded message explained that Daniel's number was not available.

"At the tone..." it continued, "please leave a message.... Beep."

"Daniel, it's Murray. I have not...repeat...not heard from him. It's kind of busy down here, I'll talk to you later, Ok?" and he pushed "end" so hard he thought he might have broken the phone.

The fire to his right was easing off and he could hear sirens coming from the north. Sheriff Wilbury was still on the radio, cool as a cucumber. Murray laughed to himself.

How old is this guy? Sixty-nine...seventy? He closed Lucy's door and walked back toward the police cruiser. *Still the tough, official lawman.*

~

The highway in front of the mansion was quiet. Even in rush hour periods the Dalton traffic stayed several blocks over. That was one of the main reasons this site was selected for the house. The old, abandoned gas station down the road was icing on the cake.

Normally Jon would park the Jaguar in the main garage up top, but he decided to use the old gas station entrance this morning. A busy road would make this problematic, but planning can be a beautiful thing. This road lost most of its users years ago when the expressway came in.

As he passed the house, Jon hit a button on the dash of the Jaguar. A panel flipped up and came to life. Monitor cameras from the gas station sent images back to the screen. Jon could see there were no witnesses around so he hit a second button. Unseen steel doors behind the holographic picture of a stonewall opened wide. That stonewall was the back of the gas station's service bay.

He couldn't help the self-satisfied grin that came over him. *Some things just work out better than others,* he thought and turned into the station at over twenty miles per hour. The Jaguar went through what appeared to be solid rock and disappeared.

Once in the tunnel, he had paid a fortune to construct, sensors closed the steel doors behind him and the Jaguar headed toward the house. The tunnel's lights came on ahead of the car and at the halfway point; another sensor opened the doors to the third level garage of his home.

He checked the monitor again. It now showed a view of just inside the garage. There was nothing parked in the way of his entrance, so he slowed to about ten miles an hour and slid inside. The steel doors behind him closed and the tunnel became dark.

The slot for the Jaguar was third on the right, just past his beloved Jeep and the pick-up truck. He noticed the "activity light" on the elevator come on as he parked and climbed out of his car.

An alarm had sounded upstairs and in the other sub-level areas that woke Ben from his sleep. He had been up most of the night and fell asleep with his head next to the keyboard on a work desk in his shop.

"You look like crap," Jon laughed as Ben stepped off the elevator.

"Man...am I glad to see you."

"Now what?" Jon was dismissive and walked to the rear of the Jaguar. He pushed the trunk release on his key and looked back to Ben. "More 'Sponsors' stuff they want me to look into?"

"Jon...have you heard anything on the news?" Ben stood with slumped shoulders and waited.

~

The FBI agent in charge of the scene at Florence, Texas had reviewed the pictures of the bomb parts. He called into his office that was now in Waco, having been relocated from Austin.

"I need full search warrants for two businesses in Austin," he told the agent who answered. "Yes, Brody. I understand the situation, but we need to get into these businesses and find out what we can." He listened for the man to get paper and a pen.

"Ok...go," the man on the phone said.

"Burnside and Griffin Safety Equipment, and Burrell Luggage and Gifts."

The man in Waco asked for addresses.

"I don't have any more that that, right now. Figure it out. Some of the stuff used for this bomb was bought in those two places. Now step on it."

~

Setting the bag from the car trunk on the floor, Jon turned his head to look at Ben before he straightened up. The look on his changed dramatically as he spoke.

"I heard about a city being evacuated...there's more to it. Isn't there?"

"A bunch," Ben started. He then told the entire tale, as he knew it. Jon listened while walking to a pair of chairs and motioned for

Ben to sit as he talked. Ben told him about Murray going to Brownwood and finished by telling Jon about the latest news of the bodies being found in the truck outside Austin.

With so much to absorb, Jon spoke to the obvious, "You've been up all night about this?" he asked.

"No...not really." Ben then reconsidered and amended his answer, "Well, most of it... I guess. I was going through some older correspondence from our network, looking for anything, any clue."

Jon's look hardened as Ben stopped short. He leaned forward in his chair.

"I can tell you've found something...what is it?"

"I don't know for sure...maybe nothing to do with it, but it bugs me."

"Ok, let's hear it."

"I found where a contact had picked up on some discussion from a college campus in Massachusetts. This has been going on for weeks. The group or individual up there goes by the handle, 'Bogart.' They were getting messages to a 'Mithras' out in Colorado. Some electronic and some other ways."

"Mithras?" Jon leaned back and rubbed his chin. "What's does that mean?"

"Mithras was a Persian warrior god of some sort." Ben had looked it up.

"Yeah? Persia...that's Iran now isn't it?"

"Yep, Iran... The name isn't as bad as what they seem to be talking about." Ben's tone went a pitch higher. "This is where it gets weird. It's parts... for some big event."

"Ok..."

"A big event that went fine... 'as planned.'" Ben then paused, he cradled his chin with his hand for a second considering what he was about to say next. "Now they're planning new shipments for another event... and they need new helpers."

"Who is your source for this stuff?" Jon asked as he stood.

"It's a college student up there. He claims this group or person is recruiting terrorists and he's going along with them to see what he can learn."

"Why doesn't he tell the authorities?"

"He did...they didn't believe him." Ben knew it seemed weak. "All he has is what he's heard. Nothing solid."

Jon walked back to the car and picked up his bag. He walked back to the chairs and tossed the bag down.

"How do you know all of this? You said some of the correspondence was sent other than by computer."

"It was," Ben assured him. "But they used two computers in the college library to type the messages out."

Jon thought he understood where Ben was going with this, but he stayed quiet and waited for the explanation.

"That's why I've been up most of the night, Jon." He started. "I identified the IP addresses of the computers being used and hacked my way into them. They used a simple Word Processing program to type out the other messages. The originals were not saved on the PC, but I got into the college's server and found archive copies of everything. " He opened a folder he had brought down with him. It was full of printouts. "I've got it all right here, except who 'Bogart' is."

Jon reached for the papers and then pulled his hand back.

"You need to give those to the Feds, Ben," he said sternly. "This is too big for us."

"What I did wasn't legal, Jon...They can't use this stuff if they wanted to."

Here we go again, ran through Jon's mind as he picked his bag up once more. Throwing it over his shoulder, he headed for the elevator. "Ben...I know you think there's something to this. You wouldn't bother me if you didn't believe it...I know that. Tell me, what makes this stuff real?"

Ben took a deep breath, realizing what Jon had just said. He stepped forward and walked to the elevator door as well.

"The timeline fits," he said. "All the information this guy has sent out matches with dates of stuff we know of...officially. And also... with some I'm not supposed to know about."

They were both quiet as the elevator doors opened. Jon put his hand on the casing of the doors and looked at the floor.

"You've got notes for me?" he asked. "Stuff I can understand, that is."

"Notes, maps, everything I could gather."

"Good." And they both stepped into the elevator. As they moved to the living-quarters level of the mansion, Jon looked at Ben and smiled. "You might just be a national hero with this. I knew that evacuation story was bull. Somebody is trying to extort something out of this country or worse."

They walked into the kitchen and Ben asked him, "So...which way are you going? North or West?"

"Sounds to me like all the activity is out West," he answered. "I'll check that out and then we'll close down whatever operation is going on in Massachusetts." Jon looked at Ben for approval. The younger man nodded in agreement.

Jon suddenly looked as though a light had flashed in his head.

"This contact in Massachusetts," he started through a wry smile. "Can you research his system and see where those messages to him came from?'

"Jon...I'm proud of you, man," Ben exclaimed.

Jon's expression fell. "You've already done that, haven't you?"

"Seriously...that's great thinking Jon. You're coming along with this technology."

"You've already done it," Jon repeated, his look back to serious.

"Didn't get very far, though," Ben said. "They were all text messages that were bounced round through several G4 networks and a couple of secure satellites."

"And that means...?"

"Bogart may not even be in Massachusetts. He could be anywhere."

"Alright, we'll deal with him later. I hope you warned our friend to be very careful."

"Oh, yeah," Ben asserted. "As this thing unwrapped he got scared. He realizes it's serious."

12

"Judge, there's a call for you on your private line." The clerk had been instructed to interrupt no matter what, so he did.

"Thank you, Charles," District Court Judge Nevin Byers of the Western Texas Federal Court answered. He excused himself from the meeting he was in and abruptly went into his chambers. The attorneys left in the conference room looked at each other with concern.

"That was weird," one finally stated with no response from the other.

The clerk entered the room and offered the men coffee.

"Or would you rather reschedule, gentlemen. Judge Byers may be a little while."

The attorneys again glanced at each other, but asked no questions. They did ask for some coffee.

The Judge, in his private chambers, opened a drawer on his desk and retrieved a cell phone. He held it in his hand and waited.

When it did ring, he nearly jumped and then sat down in his large leather chair. The caller ID said the number calling was 111-111-1111. He flipped it open and stammered out,

"Yes...this is Byers."

A mechanical voice began its orders. "This is from Mithras...do you understand?"

"How is Suzy?" the judge demanded.

"Do you understand?" the voice repeated.

"Is my Granddaughter alright?" Judge Byers unconsciously stood as he challenged the caller.

The line was quiet for nearly a minute. Then the voice came back.

"Much better than if this call is terminated, as it is now."

Judge Byers shivered and sat back down. "Please...don't hurt her."

"One last time. This is from Mithras. Do you understand?"

"Yes," a weak, meek voiced Judge replied.

"There will be requests for search warrants for two businesses this morning. Delay both."

"I get lots of requests," the Judge pleaded. "How do I know, which ones?"

"Then you'd best delay them all," The voice instructed.

The Judge tried to respond, but heard a tone come on. The voice had hung up.

A knock on the door shook him from the stupor left by the call. His clerk opened the door and stuck his head inside.

"Is everything alright, Your Honor?"

"Yes... Yes, Charles. Thank you."

Charles was a long-time and very trusted aid to the judge. He knew what the calls were about. The ones that came first to his desk with five minutes warning of a special call for the judge.

The granddaughter had not been kidnapped, nor did she or anyone else know she was in potential danger. Photographs of her daily routines, dozens of pictures, had been sent to the judge with a warning that they could reach her at any time, her and anyone else around her.

Charles knew about the calls, and he worked to keep them private.

~

Foaming operations went smoothly. The panel truck was now covered and looked more like a dirty snowball than anything else.

Readings from the edge of the foam now registered twenty Roentgens of radiation, far below the hazard the truck had once been.

This took a while and Nava Golan spent the time talking up the FBI agents who were the first responders. After getting to know them a bit, she finally asked the questions she wanted answers to.

"You took pictures of the bodies and the parts from in the truck, right?"

"Yeah..." Said one agent glibly. "Not much to see really."

"Could I have a look?" Nava gave it her best curious schoolgirl smile.

"They're classified." The agent reacted. Then he looked back at her and sheepishly grinned, "but heck, so are you, right?"

The bodies looked as she expected. The amount of radiation they had been exposed to take a toll on the human body. The pictures of the bomb parts caused her expression to change. She looked at each one several times.

"Was this all there was...the parts I mean?" she asked.

"That's everything. We pulled the boxes apart and laid everything out to inventory it all." The agent did a double take and then asked her. "Why...?"

Nava quickly cast a smile to dissuade him. "Just wondering," she replied.

The truth was she saw parts that did not make a complete unit. Even with allowances for the detonator to be missing, the parts lacked a container strong enough for the nuclear compression stage of an explosion to occur. The cylinder in the pictures was merely a lead lined fire extinguisher. It may have held down radiation some, but was not remotely heavy enough for a nuclear bomb.

Nava excused herself from the FBI agent and walked to her boss, Yinon Harel.

"Sorry to interrupt you," she looked at the Mossad leader and Jerome Grimes. "I need to tell you something."

~

Jon got upstairs to his room. He threw his bag with the info on the Missouri case on the bed, and then just stared at it.

If I don't act on this quick, they'll move everything. I'll have to start over and that won't be easy. His mind tried to sort out all the possible ways he could be in more than one place at a time. *Removing Everett won't be enough. I have to do it before he sets up shop elsewhere.*

Ben stepped into the doorway.

"Did I tell you Murray is down there already?"

"Yeah..." Jon looked up for an instant. He obviously wasn't listening and Ben could tell.

"You know, Mom used to do that when she had too many cases in her head."

"Do what?" Jon was annoyed by the inane reference. He continued going through his files and then realized Ben had not answered him. He put his hands down on the bed and braced himself for a minute. Then standing, Jon smiled at Ben and nodded.

"I do know what you mean," he said. Jon turned away, walked to a large wing-backed chair Marsha had insisted he buy and sat in it, for the first time. With his elbow perched on the overstuffed arm, he rubbed his forehead and then cupped his chin with his right hand. Looking up at his loyal friend still standing in the doorway, he had made up his mind.

"Ben...you have been handling this for a day of two already. Murray is on it. Daniel is on it... for whatever good that'll do," He halfway chuckled. "I'm going to finish what I've started in Missouri.

But, I'll need a large bag to take with me. With everything I might need, should I get involved with this other deal before I get back here."

"What all do you want in it?" Ben asked him.

"Buddy...you know what's going on better than I," Jon reminded him. "If there's radiation I'll need a suit, strong as you can come up with and other gear to warn me about all that stuff."

Ben was making notes and spoke without looking up. "I agree. But that could take a few days."

Jon paused and then added, "Make that two suits. Ship them up to me if you need to...or better yet, ship them out to Murray and I'll get mine from him when I get there."

"I can get some Geiger counters locally, I'm sure." Ben said under his breath.

"Got any books on nuclear bombs?" Jon grinned. "Never messed with anything like that. My chemicals were all pharmaceuticals."

"I know you're kidding," Ben got more than serious. "But how do we stop people with a bomb like that?"

"We take 'em out of the gene pool," Jon stated firmly. Then he stood and moved back toward his notes and the bag on the bed. "By the way...I'll have a list of things I'll need for Missouri by tonight. Soon as I decide what they'll be."

Jon then reached into the bag and pulled out a videocassette. After giving it an approving glance he tossed it to Ben.

"There's a face that shows up, real close and just before the film goes black," he told him. "See if our facial recognition stuff can ID him, will ya?"

Ben smiled and nodded in agreement. Slipping the cassette into his pocket he turned to go back downstairs. Ben thought he could hear a ringing noise and as he got further down the stairs he could tell it was his phone. He had left it on the kitchen table.

~

The assembled investigative group near Florence, Texas prepared to leave for Waco. Foaming was complete and everything loaded for transport. The senior FBI agent in charge received a disturbing message from his office as he checked the convoy.

"No warrants for those businesses," the man on the phone said.

"What?" The agent in charge couldn't believe what he heard. "It's standard procedure. What's the problem?"

"Two things...the quarantine of the city and the fact that the owners can't be there. We'll just have to wait."

"That's crazy. We've got people trying to assemble nuclear bombs to blow up our cities and we can't get a warrant? Who was the Judge?"

"Nevin Byers."

"Can we go around him?"

"Not till the quarantine is lifted...we tried already."

"Okay...we're ready to leave here. Should be in Waco in about ninety minutes."

13

Daniel's flight from Pittsburgh landed at DFW airport ten minutes late. He got to the concourse area and immediately called Lori to let her know he was there.

"Anything new?" he asked her.

"There's been a shooting incident south of Brownwood, Texas. Nothing said if it ties in with this or not. Isn't that where you're headed, Daniel...Brownwood?"

"That all depends now," he answered. "I haven't talked to Murray yet. Maybe he'll know something about it."

"Daniel..." Lori started.

"I know..." he cut her off quickly. "I know... I will be careful."

As he hung up, Daniel realized he had been walking with the crowd and was now at the baggage terminal. He thought about calling Murray, but decided to get his bag and grab a cab where it would be quieter.

Nava had explained her concerns and her boss took them very seriously. Harel looked at his old friend from the NCIS. The inspection, foaming and loading all went without a hitch, but Nava's report on the components of the bomb concerned him.

"We could be in severe danger," he told Grimes.

The senior NCIS agent had not seen Harel this worked up in years. "You think there's more than meets the eye here?"

"Definitely." Harel walked away from the earshot of anyone else and Grimes followed. When he felt comfortable he turned. "Call your man and find out what's going on around us."

"Around us?" Grimes was puzzled. "We're about ready to leave."

"On the ground...in the air." He pointed up with his index finger. "Get them on the global satellite feeds... and fast."

Jerome Grimes called Spiegel and told him to patch into MTAC's system. "Get these coordinates from my phone's signal and check a two hundred mile perimeter, all directions."

Spiegel immediately flipped open a laptop and logged in. The face of a pretty female in a lab coat appeared on his screen. "Emily...locate the bosses GPS coordinates from his phone and check SkyBird for all activity within two hundred miles of his location."

The lab tech went into motion and spoke as she worked, "What's wrong, Tim?"

"I don't know...I'm hoping you'll say nothing."

~

"I'm staying till the investigation is over," Sheriff Horace Wilbury scolded his deputy and the old acquaintance. They wanted him to go on to Brownwood after the chase and "take it easy" for a while. He would have none of it.

A pair of Texas Rangers and a deputy from Santa Anna were on the scene quickly. They were concerned with Wilbury and could do little else while the burning vehicle raged.

The FBI took more than an hour to arrive. They flew in by copter from Waco and by then the fire was out. All anyone could see of the victims was the still smoking skeletons in a hulk of twisted steel.

Murray Bilstock had wandered down to the wreck before the Feds arrived. Though the heat was still oppressive, he managed to find a metal plate near where the windshield had been. The plate had a VIN number on it and Murray copied it down. The VIN is a Vehicle

Identification Number. That number is the key to all records about the vehicle, including the owner. He was still walking around the burned out SUV as the agents landed and swarmed around him.

"Don't touch anything," they yelled. "Get back from there."

"Yeah," Murray scoffed. "Don't touch scalding metal...there's an idea. That's a good start, boys. Real sharp."

One of the agents demanded to see ID and Murray pointed to Sheriff Wilbury. "I'm with him."

"I still need your ID, Sir," the agent insisted. He then pointed to Lucy. "Whose helicopter is that?"

"That's a Bell 407 and she's mine," the indignant cowboy informed him.

Sheriff Wilbury, flanked by the Rangers, was now walking toward the wreck and shouted out. "He's with me, gentlemen. The young man may well have saved my life from..." He pointed to the remains in the smoldering pile, "whoever they were."

The uniform apparently wasn't enough for the FBI, so Wilbury pulled his ID card and his badge for them to check. He began to tell the tale of his ride home from the southern border area.

"This...car followed me for over twenty miles. Then suddenly pulled close in a very threatening manner." As Wilbury spoke, the agents listened but said nothing. "At one point they were right on my bumper."

"Were shots fired at you, Sir?" one Fed asked.

"Not at that point, no..." Wilbury started to explain.

"So..." the agent interrupted him. "What was threatening about it? Maybe they just wanted to pass you."

Murray and Deputy Stallings started to step in, but Wilbury held his hand up. Looking straight at the two FBI agents, the old lawman didn't flinch.

"Young man," Wilbury addressed the one who had challenged his recall of the events so far. "I haven't been in law enforcement for all these years to stand here and take crap from you." He stepped closer to the agent and continued. "Get your field super out here...and now."

The lead Ranger stared the agent down and nodded in agreement.

"Sheriff," the young Fed tried. "I apologize. I'm just trying to find out what happened."

"I'm trying to tell you what happened, son. If you want to listen, then listen. If you want to cross examine me...you can forget it." He turned and began to walk back up to his car.

"Sir, we will listen," the agent hollered out.

Wilbury then finished the tale, right down to where he shot the tire out and watched the big Chevy go off the road.

The agents and one Ranger were making notes. The FBI agent then looked up.

"Why would these guys be after you, Sir?" he asked.

"That's your job young man," Wilbury told him. "They attacked an officer of the law. That's a federal crime. I expect you to find out what's going on...here and down at the border."

The two Federal agents looked at each other. The one spoke again, "Sheriff. If this is connected to the border deal, in any way, we can't help you."

"The border deal?" Wilbury bowed up and got into the face of the agent. "That's what you call three dead sheriffs and a bunch of other citizens killed and wounded? Including a dad-burned Texas Ranger."

"We're restricted by National Security concerns, Sir."

Wilbury pulled his huge hat off and slapped his leg with it. "U.S. citizens getting killed on U.S. property and you hide behind

National Security?" he screamed. "What's wrong with this blamed country anymore?"

"It's all classified, Sir. Personally, I agree with you, but that's all I can say about what you refer to."

Stalling grabbed Wilbury by the shoulders trying to calm him down.

Murray felt in his pocket, he had the paper with the VIN number buried deep inside.

Ben can trace this for me, he thought as he smiled at the agents.

14

The United States Supreme Court convenes from October through April of each year. The five off months are spent giving speeches and reviewing potential cases for the next session.

Clarence Wofford had been on the court for twelve years. He was not immune from the divisive struggles that preceded most cases lately. Politics always seemed to bring a five to four decision in the last, too many, years. Wofford never spoke of it publicly, but not all of his fellow justices followed the same rules.

The Court had become more polarized and now featured justices who complained about the "fairness" of some decisions. They used terms that only incited the public rather than settling down disputes. The tension last year was thick, and in Wofford's opinion, it was unbecoming of the Court. It was time for him to speak up.

Several weeks earlier, Wofford picked up his tackle box and a pad. He headed to his dock while his guard detail went to their boats to get ready. Soon, he was sitting in his beloved bass-boat near the middle of Rocky Fork Lake. With a line in the water and his mind formulating a speech, Wofford paid little attention to the shore or the water around him. His mind was completely occupied by his thoughts.

The Justice's farm sat on the south side of the lake near Marshall, Ohio. He would usually go out about two hundred yards, just off the wetlands at the far west end of the lake. Large-mouth bass and crappie loved the submerged island that lay slightly further out where the depth would become only eight feet or less.

Justice Wofford had long insisted the bodyguards stay back so he could fish. So he negotiated the distance he would venture away from them. As the years went by, that distance grew wider.

The anchor rope he used was twenty-two feet long and normally would scrape the bottom. Drifting ever closer to the hidden landmass, the depth lessened rapidly.

When the bass-boat tilted harshly to the port side, the startled guards fired their outboards and rushed to the scene. Justice Wofford was instantly nowhere in sight. Two guards dove into the fifteen feet of brownish water, but Wofford was not found.

Trained drivers later found the body tangled in a submerged log's branches some ten feet down. The justice was 74 years old.

The process of naming a replacement began the next day. The bitter process of selection and confirmation would take months. The President was of the basic persuasion of Justice Wofford, so the appointment would not have any effect on the decisions of the court.

~

Sheriff Wilbury allowed Deputy Stallings to drive his cruiser back to Brownwood so he could ride with Murray. The sheriff needed to get back quickly. So he could plan his next step.

"Let us handle this," the Feds had warned him. But in Wilbury's mind they weren't doing enough of anything.

Murray and Daniel finally connected while Lucy was airborne. Daniel asked for an update and Murray was his typical self.

"Update? Are you kiddin' me? This thing makes no sense at all," Murray told him.

Daniel asked if Murray could come get him in Fort Worth, "or should I rent a car?"

Daniel could hear a conversation between Wilbury and Murray, then, Murray came back on the line.

"Daniel, we'll be up there in a couple of hours. The sheriff wants to fly by, or close as we can get to Austin just to take a look."

Lucy touched down in Brownwood for fuel, and Wilbury went into town to make a few calls.

When they got back into the air, Murray asked him, "How do you want to go, which way?"

"Slide down to Goldthwaite and follow Hwy. 183. We'll see how close we can get."

Somewhere south of Lampasas, Texas, at 6,000 feet, a small craft glided under them moving northeast at what Murray estimated to be 150 knots.

"What the hell was that?" Wilbury exclaimed.

"That, Sir...ain't supposed to be up here," Murray told him.

~

Special Agent Tim Spiegel of the NCIS was frantically trying to reach his mentor, Jerome Grimes. When the call finally got through, he practically yelled into the phone.

"Skipper, where are you in that convoy? I'm looking at two trucks and three units."

"We're in the trailing car, Tim. What's going on?"

"You're about to be under attack. Get off the road," Spiegel tried to sound more rational.

Grimes nudged Harel and looked around. "Attack?" he repeated. "From where, from who?"

"The satellite shows a drone closing on you fast. It's at 4500 feet and due southwest of your current location."

"A drone? You're kid...." and then transmission went out.

Spiegel could see the explosion in the satellite image being relayed to him. First, in the middle of the convoy, then another blast to the front, which directly hit the truck, carrying the parts.

"Skipper!" Spiegel hollered. "Jerry, come in." There was no answer.

The final blast hit into an area already smoldering.

The satellite also picked up a private helicopter that at first rushed toward the attack site but then pulled back and landed upwind from the smoke. Dialing into air to ground radio traffic, Spiegel found a transmission in progress.

"Waco control, this is NMB407T. Emergency traffic please!" The caller requested.

"What is your emergency, NMB407T?" the tower responded.

"I've just witnessed an attack on a motorized convoy, Interstate 35 north near Temple, over," the voice stated. "It was a military drone...one of ours."

The tower did not respond right away. The delay was unusual and nerve-racking. When they did answer, that too was highly out of the ordinary.

"NMB407T, clear all air traffic. Repeat clear the airwaves. Your transmission is not authorized at this time."

Spiegel looked at the men with him. Amzi Reiss, one of the Mossad team reached out and grabbed the microphone Spiegel was holding. He covered it with his hand and calmly warned the others.

"Don't let them know we heard that," Reiss said.

Spiegel's face looked as though he'd seen a ghost, but he knew very well the Israeli was correct. They could still hear the copter pilot complaining and another voice talking over him. Looking straight at Reiss he said, "I've got to do this." He keyed his microphone. "NMB407T, this is not Waco, repeat...this is not Waco... but hear me clearly...get the hell out of there... now."

He saw a slight nod of agreement from the Mossad officer and then after a pause, heard the radio answer.

"Roger that...'not' Waco, whoever you are. Freaking Roger that!" came the reply.

The men of the NCIS and two Mossad agents watched the satellite image of the chopper leaving and heading north. They had not yet had time to consider grieving for their lost friends.

Tim Spiegel looked at his Los Angeles counterpart, Terrace Barker, and asked, "Terry, can you get hold of your contact at FAA and find out who that copter jockey is before they do."

"Yeah, what was that call sign again? NMB407T?"

"That's him," Spiegel noted. "The boy is in real danger from what I see."

~

Wilbury was still cursing audibly as Murray flew and dialed his cell phone at the same time. When the voice answered he was relieved.

"Hey, cowboy," Jon jested. "What's going on with you?"

"Jon, I need your input on a situation I got happening here."

Jon could tell this was not a time for jokes. "You're in trouble?"

"It sure looks that way, partner. Big trouble. Bigger than you'd believe."

"Look, Ben has told me what he knows from his end and I know you went out there. What did you find?"

"Well, do you know what a unmanned drone is?" Murray asked.

"Sure, I do. I was a Army Ranger, remember?"

"Well...I just watched one blow up a line of cars on a US Interstate highway. I don't know what going on, Jon. It's some kind of war that nobody is talking about."

"Where are you now?"

"I'm heading to DFW airport to get Daniel and then back to Brownwood, I guess."

"I don't think you should go to Brownwood, Murray." Jon's gut reaction came out in words. "If they're on to you, that's one place where they'll go."

"Where then?"

"Did you insulate that hanger building like we talked about?"

"Sure did. It's the only hanger with a...."

"Let's not talk about it over the phone. Go there. I'll see you there tonight. Call Phil when you get to Dallas and let him know what going on. Maybe he knows some people who can help."

"That's what I needed...a cool head to think for me. I'm a bit wound up right now." Murray was trying to thank his friend.

"See you tonight, cowboy. Hang tough."

"Yeah, man. You and Silas travel safe, ya hear?"

"I hear ya," Jon said. He hung up the phone and yelled for Ben.

"I'm gonna need some stuff... quick. And call the G5 pilot for me please. I need to leave in an hour."

15

Congressman Fred Everett had heard the rumors of the gun battles in Texas, but he had issues of his own. Someone was on to his operation and they knew too much about it. Up to and including his right hand man, Jerry Blake.

His private cell phone rang from an odd number. *Must be Jerry's new phone*, he told himself.

"Yeah..." He answered cryptically.

"It's me." Jerry Blake's voice was quite familiar to Everett. "Anything new?"

"You're asking me? That's your job," Everett snapped.

"I'm working on that...but I need to know where you want to go, boss."

"I have been thinking, not about that directly, but about what's happening."

Blake had no idea what his boss was talking about. "Ok...what's that?"

"There hasn't been much more in the news about that 'Son' guy since the Columbian cartel went under."

Blake held back a laugh, but did say something he wished he could take back right away, "Come-on boss, you're combining paranoia with ego just a bit, aren't you?"

"I'm not paranoid, I'm pragmatic and I plan ahead. What if this guy is after me now?"

Blake's voice sounded different as he attempted to calm his leader's fear. "Man, we're no cartel, certainly not Argus. We're just a small time operation. You've been sure to keep us that way so we wouldn't attract too much attention."

"I'm telling you to look into it. You've got a description of the man from Billy, right?"

"Yes Sir," Blake answered.

"Get an artist that can draw from his description. I want a picture of this guy."

"I'll get right on it."

~

Another secretive, high-level meeting was taking place, face to face, in luxury suite of a hotel in the Buckhead area of Atlanta, Georgia.

"The drone hit was sloppy."

"It will still work in our favor. Stay cool. We control the information we want out about it. We're fine."

"We better be," the female warned. She was slight of build to start with, and her age made her appear smaller. Yet she was forceful in demeanor and attitude.

"Did your Judge Byers do his job?" she asked while fiddling with a triple strand of diamonds that hung around her neck.

"Yeah, just fine. They won't be able to get into those businesses for a couple of weeks."

"Where did the owners go when they evacuated?"

The man pulled a piece of paper from an inside coat pocket. "Griffin is dead, has been for years, Burnside went to Shreveport to stay with a daughter. The Burrell Company is a chain. The manager went to Dallas and is staying with a sister."

"We're done with all of them...including the judge," the woman instructed him.

"Done?" the man's face squinted in concern.

"Don't wimp on me now, Cyrus." The woman stood from her overstuffed chair. "We're close on this."

"Well, yeah...but with bodies piling up it's going to be hard to keep a lid on everything. Especially a sitting federal judge."

"You worry too much," she laughed. "Think about it...Byers is an old man. They die everyday. The manager for Burrell is in a city we control. And Burnside... well...Shreveport has a paper that still leans the other way. They'll report it, but it will all be coincidental."

"You thought all that through...just now?" Cyrus asked wide-eyed.

"What?" she flared at him. "I'm just doing my job."

~

Jonathan Crane was shifting gears. His hard-nosed approach against getting involved with others was out the window. Trying to concentrate on what was going on and what he would need was a transition from his planning for Missouri. He reached back for Silas and actually became more at ease.

Good, he thought. *Silas sees this as important.*

He turned on the TV in his room while he packed. A game show was winding down and a Special Report broke in. It told of a cartel hit squad in a gun battle deep into US territory. "The quiet town of Florence, Texas... only ten miles from Interstate 35, but north of the state's capital city of Austin..." the report started.

The mention of I-35 caught Jon attention. *Murray said he had been near I-35*, he thought as he sat down to listen closer.

"Several people were killed, mostly Mexican citizens," the report continued. "Highly unusual, but not unexpected in the escalation of drug cartel activity along the southern border."

Murray wouldn't mistake a ground battle for a drone attack. Jon called for Ben on the intercom system.

"Hey, don't you have a contact with a satellite monitoring system?"

"Yeah...I was talking to him just yesterday...maybe that was two days ago."

"Whatever...get him to pull up any tapes for earlier today, I-35 north of Austin, Texas. See if anything shows up."

"I'll see what I can do."

The news media is getting worse, Jon thought. *Used to be they just leaned away from the truth. This is an outright cover-up.*

The "Information Equality Act" had come to life as an attachment to the repeal of large sections of the Health Care bill. The desire to reverse the hated legislation caused the congress to overlook the reach of the new law they were enacting.

Its ultimate effects were to remove "talk radio" from the airwaves and cut into the programming of the one National TV News network that went against most other media outlets. The biggest name in talk radio had taken his program offshore, to a ship he had purchased for just such an occurrence. His broadcast came from beyond the seven-mile limit for over a year. Then, as reports say, a fake missile hit the ship. It bounced off the hull and floated for several hours before sinking. A message sent to the ship the next day simply said, "The next one will be real."

The broadcast of that evening pled desperately for listeners to spread the word of what had happened. There was some talk and a few stories in newspapers not controlled by the main media, but even that soon died down.

Several lawsuits had been filed in twenty states. The rulings were fourteen to six against the law. Pressure was still on, and three appeals were to be heard by the Supreme Court this fall.

Though too few cared, information currently being broadcast was unreliable by any standard.

"Everything Ben has uncovered could be a sham," Jon said out loud, but to no one. *Where do I start? How do I find out what's real?*

~

Daniel sat in the waiting area of gate B6 in Terminal B at the Dallas-Ft. Worth Airport. The news on the TV was reporting a shootout north of Austin involving Mexican drug gangs. A brief notice of a similar incident below Brownwood earlier that day followed the Austin reports.

"Gang violence was on the rise due to the strict nature of our immigration laws," the talking head stated with what appeared to be a smile on his face.

Daniel pulled his cell phone and looked up Matt Turlock's number in Shreveport.

"Matt...Daniel Seay, how are you sir?"

"Daniel, Good to hear from you. I was just talking with Capt. Phil Stone, you remember Phil, don't you?"

"Of course. Hope he's okay."

"Funny thing is...he just had a call from Murray Bilstock."

"You're kidding." Daniel was taken back. "Murray's supposed to be on his way to pick me up."

"He is, from what he told Phil." Matt paused a second. "Are you where you can talk?"

Daniel looked behind him. The waiting area was almost empty except for him. "Yeah, I guess," he whispered.

"Murray was all upset. He's been witness to two incidents today, neither was being reported as he saw them."

"Witness?" Daniel pressed.

"Saw 'em both happen. Played a role in one." Matt went on, "Somebody tried to kill a sheriff out there that he knows..."

"Wilbury, Horace Wilbury."

"Yeah...that's the name he used." Matt was a little surprised by Daniel knowing that. "Where are you anyway?"

"I'm in Dallas, at the...."

"Don't say anything more," Matt cut him off. "I don't know what's going on, but I know Murray enough to believe him. Something way out of line is happening right now. You don't want to give away where you are...understand?"

Daniel took a deep breath and muttered, "I'm afraid I do. Say, Matt, is there anyone over here I can trust, media type?"

"In Dallas? I don't know, man. They pull the company train, if you know what I mean. Everything. It's as bad there as New York or LA."

"Let me ask you this...the reports, national reports I'm seeing about drug gang stuff. Stuff that happened today, any of it true?"

"All bull-squeeze, my friend. Every bit of it."

"Damn...okay. I'll wait for Murray and see what he thinks we should do."

"Be careful, Daniel."

"You, too."

~

The chambers of Judge Nevin Byers were empty. The Judge was away at a meeting. Dear friends would ask him at that meeting about his knowledge of Austin and the evacuation and quarantine there. The judge would only say the situation was critical and that fears of total collapse on streets through the city had brought on the action.

Charles, his longtime assistant and law clerk was alone in the offices. He stood at a worktable in his area, flipping papers and going over the agenda for the next day's caseload.

The muted sound of phone rang at his desk. It was a cell phone he kept in a drawer. The caller ID number startled him, but he answered anyway.

"Is this Charles?" the caller's voice asked.

"It is."

"This message is from Mithras. The judge has outlasted his usefulness."

"No...that can't be," Charles immediately pleaded in earnest. He had feared that message for months.

"Again...this is from Mithras. It is not for discussion."

Charles looked toward his friend's chambers. He felt like he couldn't breathe, but he managed to respond to the voice. "I understand. I'll take care of it."

"We expect to hear the news before tomorrow."

"Yeah," Charles answered and then heard nothing.

~

The Terminal Concourses at DFW resembled horseshoes. The doors from the landing area, which surrounded the outer arch of the terminal, were secured and guarded at all times.

Daniel had just finished a call to Earl Johnstone at the Burlington Hawkeye and noticed a warning light over one door flash, and then the door opened.

The large, burly man was dressed in a uniform and wore a very large ten-gallon hat. He thanked the guard at the door and glanced around the waiting room. His eyes locked in on the only person sitting there and Daniel realized who he was at that same moment.

"Sheriff Wilbury? What are you doing here?" Daniel rose and walked towards him.

"Got on a tilt-a-whirl ride I can't seem to get off, son," Wilbury answered. "How are you?"

"Good, I guess. I take it you're with Murray."

"Yep. Look," he said as he looked around almost nervously. "We need to go, Murray is on a short leash with the parking for that thing he drives."

The guard shook Wilbury's hand and reopened the door for them. Daniel could see the Bell 407, blades still rotating while getting refueled. Murray was up on a rolling ladder looking at his front windshield.

"Murray Bilstock..."Daniel hollered so as to be heard. "Good to finally see you again." Murray looked down at him as he rubbed the crack and pushed on it slightly. "Daniel...hey man. Are you ready for all this?" he said as he climbed down and extended his hand.

"I don't know," Daniel winced. "How deep am I getting?"

Murray waved his fingers across his neck, "I'm in up to here." and then glanced at Wilbury. "How 'bout you, Sheriff?"

Wilbury turned his head and spit.

"Where to now?" Daniel asked.

"My place," he answered. "Jon is coming in tonight. We'll figure out what's next from there." He looked at the briefcase and small bag Daniel carried. "Is that all you got with you?"

Raising both arms and nodding, Daniel silently said, "yes."

"Okay...let's get out of here," Murray proclaimed. He grabbed Daniel's stuff and threw it in the back section of the vehicle. "Daniel Seay...meet Lucy," he said.

Daniel looked puzzled for a second. Then he remembered hearing the stories, and who Lucy was. "Hello there, Lucy. May I come aboard?"

Murray winked and climbed in. Sheriff Wilbury took the right side front seat leaving Daniel the bench on the second row. He climbed in and fumbled with his seat belt as the helicopter slid backwards and then leaned him left and up.

Daniel found he had placed both hands on the seat beside himself for balance. His first ride in a copter was starting out strong.

Murray stayed low till he cleared the airport's air space and then climbed several thousand feet at a thirty-degree front tilt. Lucy's course changed to northwest and the three men were on their way to Caddo Mills.

16

The home on the northeast side of Atlanta was nearing the 100-year-old mark. Tender, well-timed maintenance and renovations had kept the building sound and sturdy. English Tudor by design, the three-story home stood atop the steep incline through tall, skinny pines and a few young growth hardwood trees. A narrow driveway wound its way to the side portico that acted as the main entrance. The front door may not have opened in years.

Some of the renovations were cosmetic and most of that was interior. But many were necessities like roofs and asphalt for the driveways. A much-needed rewiring project, a few years ago, had included the addition of electronic infrastructure that many office buildings would envy. Cat-5 and Cat-7 wiring linked the owners to the outside world and beyond. The small satellite dishes on the separate garage/apartment located behind the main house could bring in entertainment, communications and more if necessary.

A prestigious golf course and country club lay directly across the winding road on which this home stood. The view of this immaculately groomed landscape from the home's perch added to the total value. Still, some considered its age and the steep climb to be drawbacks. Beauty lies in the eye of the beholder. While there were those who thought of the house as a spooky old mansion, others viewed it as a symbol of the city's rise to prominence in the early prior century.

One family had raised three generations in this house until economic circumstances, a few years ago, forced the heirs to sell. Some in the ranks of the local gentry claimed it had sold for three million.

Such discussions of money were unseemly in southern society, so the story never rose above rumor status.

The new owner kept to herself, though she was known to be an important lawyer from the northeast. Massachusetts was the best guess going around.

Proper invitations to local parties were sent, but never answered. Attempts to visit were brushed off by the household staff. The owner remained an enigma and was soon accepted and all but forgotten. As time passed, the neighbors began to treat the property as unoccupied.

~

Spiegel, Barker and Reiss left San Angelo within minutes of viewing the attack via satellite. Their only delay was calling in for the directors of Homeland Security and NCIS. Neither were available, and that message didn't take the team long to add together with what they had witnessed.

Flashing his badge, Spiegel commandeered a police MD 600N helicopter and pilot to fly them to the site south of Florence, Texas.

Scorch marks were all that remained of the violence that had happened. The cleaning crew, whoever they were, had been quick and thorough. As they spread out to search the area, Barker yelled out.

"Get over here, now." He was running to the edge of the roadway and knelt down in a dip off the pavement.

She had heard their voices and tried to talk. All he heard was a muffled moan, but that was enough to find her. It was Nava. She was alive and just barely conscious.

"Golan...Golan, wake up," Reiss urged her while gently shaking her shoulders.

"Go easy with her, man," Spiegel warned. "We don't know what her injuries are yet."

The Mossad officer moved his hands and began to check her for broken bones. He turned her body in a slow, even motion to look for wounds that may be hidden.

"She's scraped up and her arm is broken, but the bump on her head concerns me the most," Reiss said as he looked up to the others.

"Can we carry her in that bird?" Spiegel asked the pilot.

"Sure," he responded, his eyes obviously flickering as he thought how to make it happen. "We can take the rear seats out and lay her on the floor back there."

"Let's do it," Barker agreed and pushed the pilot toward his machine.

Reiss stood and looked around, prompting Spiegel to ask for what.

"We need a board to carry her on, at least four feet long to support her head and body."

Spiegel nodded and the two looked for anything that would work for the task.

The pilot grabbed his microphone and started to call in to base. Barker ran over and stopped him.

"Don't do that, man."

"I need to let the hospital know we're coming," the pilot pleaded.

"No...not yet. We don't know what's going on or who we can trust."

"I don't understand."

"Look around you, man. There should be twelve to fifteen bodies and parts of several vehicles all over the place...from just two and half hours ago."

The pilot's stunned face became ashen as he thought about what Barker had said.

"Then where do we take her? She needs help," he asked calmly.

Barker walked over to Spiegel and told him his concern.

"Don't you know someone around these parts?" he asked Spiegel.

"Shreveport. I know a police captain in Shreveport," he said as he grabbed his cell. He rolled through his phone book and then hit "call."

"You've got Stone...go," Phil offered his standard answer.

"Captain Stone? This is Tim Spiegel from New Orleans."

"NCIS!" Phil blurted out. "What's up?"

Tim gave Stone the brief version of his morning and asked if he knew a safe harbor with medical care they could count on.

"So, this has got you into it too, huh?" Phil asked.

"Are you already involved?" the agent asked in response.

"My friend Silas is on the way here now. We're going to Texas tonight."

"I've got a Mossad agent with a bad concussion that needs to be looked at."

"Mossad? My God...never mind that...let me think a minute." Phil grabbed a Rolodex and thumbed, "where are you?"

"Near Florence," Spiegel answered. Phil wasn't familiar with Florence, and as the pilot offered, "below Killeen," he clicked in the news of the day.

"That drug shootout! You guys were there?"

"It wasn't a drug shootout and yes...we're here now. It's been cleaned up, oddly enough. But we found a survivor, a witness."

Phil had found a trusted location. "Can you get to Tyler?" he asked.

Tim looked at the pilot who nodded his head.

"Yeah...we can get there."

"Alright," Phil gathered himself. "The East Texas Medical Center...just about the center of town."

"Do they have a helipad?" Tim asked abruptly.

Phil thought a second, "Yeah...yeah they do. I'll call the PD there to watch out for you. They're ok. They see things as they are."

"Got it...thanks Phil." Then Tim added. "What are you and this Silas going to do?"

"Don't know yet," the police captain answered with a phony laugh. "He'll figure that out as we go."

Spiegel couldn't think of anything else to say, though his mind was reeling with the activity this day had brought.

"Take care, Sir," he offered to Stone and they hung up.

Reiss pulled down a road sign and bent it in half. With Barkers help, they had it folded flat enough to use to carry Nava. Reiss knelt next to his moaning team member. Gently, he pulled Nava to him as Barker slid the sign under her. With her head and torso secured, the men lifted her and walked to the aircraft.

"Yinon..." She began to stir and mumble.

"Yes, Nava...we know," Reiss whispered to her.

"Yinon...and Grimes." Her eyes opened wide and she stared at her friend. "They are alive."

"What? Where are they?" Barker leaned in to ask.

"The men took them...they are alive," she repeated.

~

Cyrus Grant had just gotten home. His condo was large for the area, two stories and a large covered porch off the back that faced the ocean.

His bag still sat in the living room, and he rested on the porch with a double scotch. The thought came to him, *just let it ring*, but he got up and walked to the bag. Digging the phone from a pocket on its side, he flipped it open.

"Yeah," Grant barked in a stern, short northern accent. "What?"

His reaction to what he heard made him glad he was alone. Explanations of his expression to his wife and staff would have been difficult to pull off. He leaned hard on a side table and winced as the voice continued.

"Do you understand?" it asked.

"I do," Grant stated solemnly. "There's no turning back, you know?"

The call ended without an answer to his question. Cyrus Grant folded his cell phone and looked at himself in a mirror over the piano.

"Here we go," he said out loud.

Congressman Fred Everett had a message to call Jerry, ASAP. He stepped into his private offices on the second floor and picked up a cell phone. It rang once.

"Hello?" Blake answered.

"You've got something for me?" Everett summoned from his aid.

"Yeah, but I don't know...I don't know what to make of it."

"Tell me, man," Everett nearly yelled.

"Billy did a good job working with the artist guy you set up. The picture from his memory is a guy, mid-thirties...nothing special about him."

"Did you run it through the computer?"

"That's the thing. It came up a positive hit, some guy in Georgia. A big shot millionaire and that's about all there is about him."

"A millionaire?" Everett couldn't believe what he was hearing. "You got his name, don't you?"

"Jonathan Crane...that's with a 'ane', no 'i'," Blake explained to him.

"Never heard of him...find out if this guy was around these parts this week. Find out anything you can about him. I don't want to waste time on this if he was in Europe or something. You got me?"

"Yes, Sir," Blake responded and heard the phone click. Walking to his car, Blake frowned.

Crap...he thought to himself. *I thought he'd be pleased with that.*

17

Lucy touched down in Caddo Mills on her fairly new, round concrete pad. As Sheriff Wilbury climbed out, he looked at the house some fifty yards away and grinned.

"That looks like your Dad's house," he said to Murray.

Daniel had only been to Brownwood once, but he too remembered.

"It sure does, Murray," the reporter smiled.

"Supposed to," the cowboy agreed. "Will even more when we're done."

The house wasn't quite finished. It could have been. But extra time had been taken for a project Jon had insisted on. The barn for Lucy sat fifty yards away, opposite the house. It was two stories high and as they walked in the wide double doors, they could see the shiny lining on the interior walls.

"Lead," Murray explained before they could ask. "Something to do with radio signals. Blocking them, I believe that's what Ben said."

Come this way Murray pointed. The next building was a hanger. Sitting to the side of the barn, away from the house, it was one story and made of much thinner material.

Aluminum, Daniel guessed.

The sixty by eighty foot building had cabinets on three sides with what appeared to be toolboxes and benches between them. Murray walked right past them all, leading the others to the far left corner.

He opened the door of yet another cabinet and placed his right hand on a glass plate that was framed and mounted just inside. The plate lit up and a streak of light ran down his hand. Wilbury and Daniel said nothing. They simply glanced at each other in wonder.

"This is where it gets neat," Murray smiled at them.

The back wall of the cabinet slid open and exposed a staircase to the right. Lights came on and Murray stepped into the cabinet.

"Come on," He coaxed the others. "It doesn't stay open that long."

Daniel and the sheriff quickly followed and Murray lead them down a set of stairs that went down about twenty feet.

"We're under my corral...cool, huh?" Murray smiled.

Another glass panel at another door required Murray's left hand. Again, the panel flashed and the door opened, this time leading to a hallway of about six to eight feet.

One last door opened with the simple turn of the doorknob, and they were standing at the entrance of a large space. The lights came on across the room, and they could see it was furnished and fully stocked.

"Jon wanted me to have a 'safe room' he called it. It's a bit much, but he had the contractor already started on it when I got home." He walked in as the others stood and stared. "Once they dug the hole, the forms went in fast. Then all they had to do was fill it in and build the corral above."

He went to the refrigerator and retrieved three beers. "Pretty neat, huh?"

"How did you get the stuff down here?" Daniel asked. "All this furniture and stuff."

Murray walked to a far wall and pushed a button. The wall opened to a shaft that began level, but didn't stay that way. A Hummer vehicle sat waiting for use.

Just ahead of the Hummer, the shaft angled up thirty degrees and went out of sight.

"There's a set of steel doors at the surface. They have explosive bolts holding back springs I can set off from inside the Hummer."

Murray had forgotten the situation for the moment. He had not yet shown this to anyone, except Slick.

"I brought everything down through here." He turned back to his friends. "It was a snap."

Wilbury smiled a forced smile and sat on a sofa with his beer. But quickly jumped up again.

"I need to check with Stallings," he all but shouted, "should have called him a couple hours ago, really," and he pulled his phone from a pocket. His deputy had driven the sheriff's patrol cruiser back to Brownwood for him.

"That one won't work down here, sheriff," Murray told him. "Over here. Any of these are wired to antennas up top."

Wilbury gave him a funny look. But picked one up and dialed the number for his office.

"Yeah, this is Wilbury..." He barked into the phone. "Get Stallings for me."

The sheriff waited as he listened. His facial expression changed dramatically.

"He ain't there?" He listened a bit more. "No, he's not with me. He was driving my car back to town. You haven't heard from him at all?"

Murray walked over to the sheriff. He realized something was wrong.

"Get out there and look for him," Wilbury ordered over the phone. "I'll be home quick as I can."

The sheriff put the phone down and stared at Murray.

"They got Irv. Nobody's heard a word from him."

"They'll find him..." Murray assured him. "Or we'll go back and find him ourselves."

"I don't know who these boys are we're playing with," the sheriff was turning red in the face. "But I don't care for this game."

~

The phone rang at the Dalton mansion. Not one of the cell phones, the listed phone, the number from the phone book. Ben had to think to remember where it was.

"Hello," he answered, finding an extension in the kitchen.

"Is Jonathan Crane there?" the voice asked.

"No...I'm afraid he's not in at the moment," Ben responded casually. "Can I take a message for him?"

"Is he expected in soon?"

"Anytime now..." Ben chirped. "Be glad to have him call you."

The line disconnected. Ben looked at the caller ID info. "Private Caller" was all it registered. Hanging up the phone and went to his system on the kitchen counter. He keyed in the house phone number and "control *" twice.

A number from Missouri showed on the screen. Ben made a note of it and the time of the call.

~

Steven Walden ended a class early. He had two recruits to interview and little time to make up his mind about them. Walking to a private lounge used only by professors, he called for them to meet him.

Walden sat near a window inside the lounge and watched. Within twenty minutes, a young man walked up to a large tree with a seat wrapped around its trunk. He looked around nervously and sat.

Walden walked out of the lounge and straight to the tree.

"Lamar Jakes?" he asked as he approached.

The young man rose and extended his hand, "Yes, Sir. Dr. Walden. I'm Jakes."

"It's Professor..." Walden corrected him. "I'm not a PhD. Please... sit"

The men talked. Small talk at first, and then Walden suddenly pressed him about his feelings for the government.

"Oppressive, capitalistic aggressors," Jakes answered with venom in his words.

"You are not Muslim, are you?"

"No. Sir. Not yet. But I am studying."

"What would you give for Allah?" the professor asked bluntly.

Jakes stared at Walden without blinking. "I would give my very being."

Walden stood and took two steps away from the seat around the tree. Jakes did not move or speak. The professor stuck a hand in his pocket and turned back to the young man. Pulling a small note, he handed it to Jakes with simple instructions.

"Meet two others at this address tonight. The leader will be apparent to you and he will know what you are to do for Allah."

Jakes nodded and looked up at Walden who offered a warning as his last words to him.

"Speak of me to anyone and you will die." The young man did not flinch or speak. "You understand?" Walden smiled as he asked.

Jakes nodded. He sat still and watched as the professor left the area.

A similar meeting with the same basic results occurred forty minutes later outside the campus library. Walden had his orders and now he had his team.

Stage two, he thought. *Soon chaos will reign over this land.*

~

Lt. Marsha Hurst had a note on her desk to call a local number. It was one of her CIs. Confidential Informants were a normal part of police business. This one in particular was off the grid, as they say. This informant was special.

"Yes," Marsha responded when he answered. "This is Hurst."

"The Jews have disappeared from Virginia. No news on where."

"What.... When? Do you know when they left?" she asked.

"Contact says right after they got there. There's more though."

"Ok." Marsha grabbed a pencil.

"I'm hearing that things are about to change." He was now breathing faster and somewhat labored. "The lid was on for a reason... and now they want to alter everyone's thinking."

"Make sense, will you?" Marsha let a bit of frustration show in her tone.

"The cover-up of the bomb story... it's over," he told her.

"Just like that? They're changing the story just like that?"

"Mind games, Lieutenant. Not on yours...the people's. Those trusting souls who believe in their leaders."

"They're playing with the people's minds? What the hell for?"

"This is big, Lieutenant. I don't have it all. We put this together from different sources. But it all adds up to this."

"Who's in charge of this thing?"

"Bogart," the informant said. "I'm gonna have to lose this phone."

"Bogart?" Marsha repeated. "Where do I find this Bogart?"

"All we know for sure is that he is not as it would appear."

"You're doing it again."

"Bogart is not who you will first think he is."

"Is that all?" Marsha asked him. "When does this start?"

"I have to go..." He took a deep breath and whispered, "I'll need another phone...this one has to go. They'll find me."

"Okay...Okay, I can get you another phone." Then she listened for a few seconds more, but he was gone.

18

Murray was still trying to calm Wilbury down and convince him he couldn't leave just now. The sheriff was being adamant about it though he had little choice in the matter.

One of Murray's underground phones rang and broke up the discussion.

"That'll be Jon," he announced and grabbed the unit ringing.

"We're here," Jon told him.

"We?" Murray was confused.

"Phil and Matt came with me. Phil had a police pilot fly us in. He's gone already."

"You want to come down here or should we come up?"

"It's fine up here for now," Jon told him. "Let's meet in the house."

By the time Murray, Daniel and Wilbury stepped from the cabinet Jon was getting off the phone with Marsha. She had shared her latest information, as cryptic as it was.

Jon told her to be careful and then turned away while the others shook hands and exchanged hugs and introductions. He cupped the phone with his hand and whispered, "I love you, too."

Turning back to the others, he was greeted by Murray, grinning widely and holding an item in each hand.

"What have you got?" Jon asked.

"This...is the VIN from the SUV that tried to kill Wilbury." Murray held out the piece of paper he'd kept in his pocket. "This," he held the small book towards Jon, "is a copy of the Koran that Stallings found near the wreck."

"Who is Stallings?" Jon quizzed him while looking at both items.

"Sorry...that's Wilbury's deputy. Who is now missing, by the way." He noticed Jon's brow wrinkling in confusion so he went on. "You think Ben could run this VIN number for us?"

Yeah," Jon took the paper. "But how about we all sit a minute... and get on the same page here."

"Sure, that's a given. We can't act till we know what we need to know." His mind spinning, Murray continued. "You want to go back to the dugout?"

"Is your system up for the house?"

"Oh, yeah. Works fine." Murray's head bobbed as he headed into the house. "I just need to turn it on."

The dining room was "finished," so to speak, and held a large table with ten chairs. Murray walked across the room to a doorframe and grasped the trim just over head-height. As he squeezed the wood, a screen emerged from the sideboard cabinet sitting along one wall. The cabinet had been made to blend with the old table, but it was new and quite special.

The screen lit up and displayed a radar blip monitor, registering forty miles out at 360 degrees and 40,000 feet in altitude. Any intruder would be picked up from the surface to the sky.

The men sat around the table to talk, two lawmen, two newsmen, a cowboy and Silas.

~

Lamar Jakes followed his instructions and walked down a dark alley to the rear of a small hardware store. Two other men were waiting there, neither speaking to the other as they waited.

As Jakes approached, one of the others became more animated.

134

"Give me your cell phones and wallets," he said waving his arms in front of him. "We're going to be away for a while...if we come back at all." He looked hard at the others for a negative reaction. "If and when... you'll get 'em back."

Jakes and the other man showed no change in attitude as they removed their phones from pockets and handed them over.

Pointing to a van barely visible in the dark, the obvious leader spoke again.

"Get in the back and stay down. The trip will take several hours. There are bag lunches and a cooler with drinks. No talking, understand?"

Jakes nodded and glimpsed over at the other man. He looked to be older. His clothes were very dirty yet he didn't smell bad.

Not yet anyway, Jakes told himself.

They walked to the van in silence. Jakes looked at him a couple of times, but the man showed no interest in talking.

The trip started slow, and Jakes had the feeling they were going south. He couldn't see, the back of the van had no windows and the rear glass was blacked out. Still, the young man felt he had a compass built-in somehow and the sensation was he was going south. After a half-hour they turned abruptly. It was a ramp, one that circled around nearly 360 degrees. When they straightened out, Jakes knew they weren't going straight at all.

Elevations in this part of the country are extreme. You can "feel" how high you are. Had they gone north, the elevation would have dropped slightly, but enough to tell. South, and the sensation would be increased height. East would cause the feeling of rapid descent, while west would feel like you were going straight up.

After two hours of riding, Jakes concluded they weren't really going anywhere, except in circles around Denver.

19

The police copter from San Angelo touched down in Tyler, Texas with the survivors of the investigative team from Washington, DC. A local officer ran up to the machine with the emergency crew of the medical center.

"You Spiegel?" the cop asked of Terry Barker who simply grinned.

"That's me," Tim responded from the other side of the copter. "These are my partners, Terry Barker, Amzi Reiss and Nava Golan. Agent Golan is hurt pretty bad."

The officer glanced toward the Israeli lying on the gurney and nodded. Medical personnel were working feverishly with her so he turned back to the others.

"Capt. Phil Stone sends his regards," the local officer tipped his hat and offered his own wry grin. "Other than that, you weren't here." He stepped back a little. "Let me know if there's anything you need... while you're 'not' here, that is."

"Thanks, officer," Barker reached for and shook his hand.

Barker then leaned into Spiegel and asked him a question. Spiegel nodded and tapped the pilot on the shoulder thanking him for sticking with them. "You'd best get back to San Angelo."

The copter pilot acknowledged that was probably true and as Tim and Barker pulled the doors closed, he powered up and then lifted away.

"I need to call Phil and find out where he and this Silas guy were going."

Barker stared at him and responded. "You got a plan after all this?"

"Well...we're going to get our people back..." Tim said in full bravado. The statement was sincere yet it gave him pause. The realities of the situation washed over his momentary swagger. "Don't ask me how just yet, but that's number one," he added.

Barker's nod was subtle, but in full agreement.

"Number two...good as we are...we're gonna need some help." Tim grabbed his buddy's shoulder and cocked his own head sideways. "And I don't know who all we can trust."

"Your friend Phil seems to think a lot of this Silas fella."

"Yeah," Spiegel muttered under his breath as they watched the chopper disappear into the sunset. "That he does."

~

The oversized mahogany table and chairs were compliments of Murray's sister, Charlene. They were to be hers from their Mom's estate. She just wanted to see the set in a house like they had been in before.

The sideboard of course, was new. Other than that, furniture was sparse in the house. Murray didn't have a Marsha, like Jon did. He was working on it, as he would tell you with a smile. But his Air Force pilot friend was still in the early stages of their relationship. He and she were both, old school in that regard.

Daniel smiled to himself as the others entered the huge dining room. The table had been covered in boxes and packing materials when he last saw it. It looked completely different now. But the small round table, sitting just outside the room in a corner, he remembered more clearly. It was the one that had held the two-way radio Charlene had used to call Murray from the old Brownwood house.

Seems like a long time ago, he thought while seeking out a place to sit.

Horace Wilbury assumed the head of the table position. It never struck him that he was a guest, but no one objected. His age allowed for unspoken respect, which he didn't acknowledge if he even noticed it. They also asked the sheriff to start the process with his story. He was interrupted first by Matt Turlock.

Matt became indignant at the tale of the ambush that killed the sheriffs and so many others.

"Whoever did that needs to be locked up and forgotten about," Turlock suggested.

Wilbury took his oversized hat off and sat it on the table in front of him. "Where I come from, we just bury 'em when we catch 'em. And for less than that, I might add."

Several chuckles followed the sheriff's comment. It was cute to some, but not all.

Phil Stone bounced a fist off the table, his face red. "Look guys, let's put the jokes and kidding around away." His eyes searched the room for a dissenter. "This mess is bad business. Those were lawmen that were killed. There has to be folks in really high places approving what's happening." He looked around again then leaned back in his chair. "And that's scary...as hell."

Things got quiet for a minute. Though Wilbury's story was just the beginning, they all knew what was happening was extremely serious. More to the point, they didn't understand exactly what it was or why it was happening. Phil's reaction to the exaggerated remark by a small town sheriff refocused all of them.

And then Jon's phone rang. It was Ben calling from the mansion in Dalton. Jon put him on speaker and tossed the phone on the table.

"Ben, you're here with the whole crew...I'll introduce everyone later. For now, speak freely," Jon assured him.

"Ok...That VIN number you asked me to check out," Ben started. "It's from a 1964 Pontiac GTO. Last owner, a guy in Staten Island, New York."

"How could that be?" Murray asked.

"Recycling VINs," Stone spoke up and pointed out. "We've got a bunch of that in Louisiana."

"I don't get it," Daniel admitted his naiveté.

"Chop shops are too much trouble these days. Sometimes they just replace the Vin numbers with old numbers they steal off the system." Phil looked around the table and everyone was listening. "They have to have access to the old records to do it, our boys seem to be highly connected already."

"What does that accomplish?" Matt Turlock threw in and others nodded in agreement.

"When you've had time to reregister the number on a stolen vehicle and pull the old record, you're golden. This SUV had to have been a new one." Then he corrected himself, "Newly stolen at any rate. Guess they didn't expect to lose the chase with our sheriff."

He looked down at Wilbury for an expression. He got nothing. The sheriff instead leaned onto the table and folded his arms in front of himself. Looking up at the group, he spoke.

"So...I don't suppose they would go to all this much trouble for just one car, do you?" His tone was past sarcastic.

"Nope," Phil agreed and nearly became animated. "There's no telling how many unregistered vehicles are out there. Or what they plan to do with them."

There was no answer to that statement. The group again went quiet as the possibilities piled up in their minds.

"Ben," Jon realized the young man on the phone couldn't tell what was going on through the silence. "Stay on the line, will ya? You're a part of this."

"Sure," he answered. "Should I say what the pictures of that Koran book turned up?"

"Well, we haven't really gotten that far yet," Jon tried, but got cut off.

"Koran?" Phil asked impatiently. "What Koran?"

"Murray found this small copy near the crash site of that same SUV." Jon tossed it on the table.

"Actually, it was Deputy Stallings who found it," Murray corrected him.

Ben took over the conversation so they could move forward. "It's a pocket copy they sell in gift stores. The inscription reads, 'to Joel, from Mithras.' And it's in English."

"So, we've got local, homegrown talent trying to convert," Phil smirked. "What's new?"

"Joel sounds like a Jewish name, doesn't it?" Wilbury asked.

"Doesn't have to be...but that would be weird, huh?" Phil leaned back to ponder that thought.

The recounting of the individual experiences picked up again. Murray went next, followed by Phil Stone. As Phil recounted his call from the NCIS agent, he referred to him as "Spiegel." Jon did a small double take. That could be a common name in parts of the country, so he let it go. Then the police captain talked about this special agent being part of the team that got shot-up along the expressway, Murray leaned forward and asked for details.

"He could be our 'not Waco' voice. The guy that talked to us before we cut out from there."

"Yeah," Phil agreed. "Tim said something about a copter setting down. They saw it on the satellite feed."

"Tim?" Jon stared a hole into Phil Stone. "This Tim... is Tim... Spiegel?"

"Yeah..." Stone confirmed. "He's NCIS out of New Orleans. Matt and I met him early last year. You know... after that big raid we had in Shreveport, you remember."

Jon unconsciously laid his head on one hand and rubbed his forehead like it ached.

"What's the deal?" Phil asked him. "You know Tim?"

"Possibly...most likely it's another guy with that name." Spiegel isn't that common and Jon knew it, but they needed to continue. "Let's move on, okay?"

"Jon," Ben spoke up suddenly.

"Go ahead."

"I need to tell you something in private, okay?"

"If it's about this mess let's save the time and tell everybody now," Jon advised him.

"Well, I'm not sure if it is...I'll have to let you decide that."

Jon glanced around him apologetically and picked up the cell phone. Stepping away from the table, he punched off the speaker and said, "Ok...what is this all about that couldn't wait."

"Sorry, man. But you had a call from a non-published number that I traced back to Missouri."

That did surprise Jon. "No kidding?" he asked.

"The guy wanted to speak with you directly. Asked for you by name."

Jon tried to think of how he could have left anything tied to him and Ben finally spoke again, "Coincidence, huh?" he tried.

"I wish...." Jon had no idea what was going on, but was glad to know it had happened. "Thanks, Ben. Good call to interrupt us. I'm putting you back on speaker now."

"Ok."

As Jon returned to the table Matt Turlock's phone rang. Looking embarrassed while checking it, he rose and stepped into a corner of the room.

"I need to get this," he apologized.

20

The van carrying Lamar Jakes and his mute accomplice came to a stop sometime before sundown. Jakes could hear the driver get out. Then there was nothing for several minutes. That concerned him.

He tried the rear door but it was locked. He tried yelling, nothing came of it. Looking back at the other man with him, Jakes suddenly got a chill up his back.

"What's with you, dude?" he asked the conscious, yet uncaring fellow captive. The man said nothing.

Jakes crawled over to him and shook him by the shoulders. That's when he knew something was wrong. The silent, sullen face with the open eyes was a death mask. The man fell over on his side and revealed the remains of one of the sandwiches that had been in the bags. The lunch bags provided for them.

Whatever it was had been quick. The man had little more than two bites and made no sound of distress when the poison kicked in.

Now, the radical student looking to make a name for himself, realized he had been duped. His willingness to give his all was apparently being abused for some show. In a panic, Jakes began kicking the rear doors with both legs while on his back. After several tries the doors flew open.

Jumping from the van and running, Jakes took little mind of where he was. But that soon became clear to him. The city skyline looked familiar to him. He stopped running for a minute and turned to look back. The van was parked in a service bay just outside of Coors Field in downtown Denver.

In the twilight that obscured him from view, he could hear the sound of approaching trucks. Jakes moved quickly to his left and dove behind a row of shrubbery. An explosion from where the van was parked lit up the sky and rocked his eardrums.

"Damn," he heard himself nearly shout. Turning around to see, he threw a hand over his own mouth to keep from yelling out again. The van was now a fireball and pieces were still landing in the lot as the trucks pulled closer. The men climbing from those trucks were dressed as cops.

"What the...." Jakes muttered softer this time. *They were here before the truck blew up. Those aren't cops.* He shook all over as he lay beneath the bushes. The air temperature had to be seventy-eight degrees yet he shook like he was freezing.

Five of the men walked toward the burning van's remains and opened fire with automatic weapons. They sprayed the area with gunfire for several minutes. Then incomprehensively, two of the men exchanged their weapons with others from inside one of the trucks. They walked closer to the fire while their accomplices moved out of the way. Then turning back, they shot at their own empty vehicles. Peppering the windshields and truck bodies, but careful not to hurt the wheels or hit the engines.

Jakes lay perfectly still through the fear that racked his body. He stayed put for more than two hours, until the "investigation" and clean up was well under way. At one point he noticed men in odd looking suits with hoods going through the remains of the vans.

Pushing himself back along the line of bushes, he finally found a low spot where the ground was terraced. Quietly, he rolled down the embankment and ran for his life.

Now what do I do? He asked himself as he ran. *Where do I go?*

~

Fred Everett had been doing math in his head. The face of the man his employee had described as a Georgia millionaire didn't add up at first. But when he remembered reading about the vigilante rumored to be killing members of congress, the numbers came together. Their total scared him.

Looking through old files he had come up dry. So frantically, he got on the Internet and searched through archives of the local paper.

"When was that Washington thing?" he asked himself out loud finding no names listed. The problem he was having, was that Jon was never mentioned, by name, in any of the stories. Not even in the hospital incident in Charlotte. His picture graced national headlines for two days, but there was no name. Daniel had made sure of that.

The overpowering strength Billy had told of was considered, but then discarded by Everett. This millionaire wasn't likely to be a drug addict looking to score in Missouri. That didn't make sense so he threw it out of his equation.

The more Everett searched and thought, the more he became convinced he had figured it out...*even without any proof.* When Jerry Blake called with the news that Jonathan Crane was not in when he called the house, the congressional drug dealer issued an order.

"Find him," he said in serious tones. "Find him and get rid of him."

Blake was stunned. "Boss...come on. A guy like that has bodyguards and stuff. It won't be that easy. He's got money...he's got juice."

"Just do it." Everett was adamant. "It's him. I know it is."

~

Matt Turlock returned to the table in Caddo Mills, Texas. His expression was not confusion. It was clear anger. He still held his open phone in his hand, but before he spoke Daniel's cell also rang.

Matt sat down in sullen silence and watched Daniel as he reacted to his call.

"Ok guys," Phil broke up the quiet. "Enough of the drama, what's the deal?"

Matt continued to look at Daniel who finally returned the stare and spoke, "My niece has sent a birthday list. There's an e-book on the list."

"Sirens Dance by W. Neilsen?" Matt asked.

"The same," Daniel responded without looking up. "Have you looked already?"

Phil jumped in this time. "Ok damn it...that is enough guys! What the hell is this?"

Matt leaned into his stiff backed dining chair and began his explanation. "The Information Equity Act took a huge toll on news when it went into effect." He glanced again at his fellow newsman who simply nodded and sunk into his chair. "National stories get approved through either New York or Los Angeles these days. Without that, the story doesn't float. Anyone who tries to report without their approval is black-balled."

"Nobody listens to the news anymore anyway," Murray threw in.

"Yeah...maybe not," Matt answered him. "But this situation is tough for us who still believe in the truth, however it looks. There are law suits working their way through the system to rescind the law." He looked at Murray and challenged him, "You didn't know that did you?"

Murray sheepishly acknowledged he did not.

"It's being kept quiet as they can, like some of our stories here. If they don't report it, it didn't happen." Matt's face was red, "That's how they see it."

"People won't stand for that," Murray looked around quizzically, "Would they?"

"There have been law suits filed by over forty states. The case gets stronger with each win at that level. It could get to the U.S. Supreme Court next year and if it does it'll get declared unconstitutional." Matt breathed a deep breath and went on, "Wofford's death was a scare, except that we have a President who will nominate a like minded person for his replacement."

"I did hear about that," Phil said. "So that won't change anything really?"

"It shouldn't, but who really knows?" Daniel added.

"But for right now, we do have a network for spreading word that needs to be told." Matt nodded to Daniel who motioned for him to continue. "Do you have your e-book reader application on your phone?" Matt asked Daniel.

"Yeah, but I haven't ..."

"Let me save you the time." Matt stood and began walking around the room, showing the others his phone and the program he had on it. "This book isn't a book at all. It's a code for news we need to share."

Jon looked and then leaned back. "Can I get that for Ben?" he asked.

"I'll copy mine for him," Daniel said.

"This sample of the book suggested by the e-mail," he held his phone now for Murray to see. "Contains the story the national media doesn't want to get wide spread coverage."

"So, what's going on now?" Sheriff Wilbury wondered.

"The stories you guys know about, the ones that were all buried, are now being let out with a slight variation in the details. Plus, there are many more reports of attacks, all over the country. Al Qaeda, and other Muslim groups are being blamed."

"So they're reporting the attack at the border?" the sheriff jumped.

"Not quite the way you tell it, but similar. The big thing right now is reports of incidents in Las Vegas, Denver and Phoenix."

No one asked. They all waited for the rest of the story.

~

In her law offices overlooking Peachtree Street, she sat and waited for the updates. They knew she expected to be kept informed. At twelve minutes past eight o'clock her special phone rang.

"You may proceed," she answered.

"Stage two underway. No issues. Reactions as expected."

The voice was clearly that of Cyrus Grant though he did not identify himself by name. His reporting himself explained the lateness of the call. Cyrus had collected the info from his surrogates and compiled it for her. She liked that.

"Very well," she responded and hung up.

Cyrus Grant closed his phone as his assistant entered his office in Washington, D.C.

"You know to knock before you come in here..." he chastised him. "Now what is it?"

"Sir, the representative from California is here. He says he has an appointment."

"Oh...that's right. Send him in, please."

"Sir, I didn't have this appointment on the schedule. Is that my error?"

"Don't worry about it, it's my fault. I probably didn't mention it. Now let him in."

"Yes, Mr. Speaker," the assistant said.

21

Ben Shaw had another phone ringing. He excused himself from the meeting in Caddo Mills and answered the other line. It was Dr. Franklin Webster in Atlanta.

"Ben..." The doctor started. He seemed a bit excited.

"Yes, Sir," Ben replied. "Nice to hear from you again so soon."

"Well, you may not think so when I tell you what I'm calling about."

Ben said nothing. He listened intently.

"I started running other programs with the satellite imagery after we talked. Different locations along the border within three of four days of that incident."

"I take it you found something." Ben was now anxious about what he might hear.

"Bunches of something," Webster said. "Looked like an invasion with nobody stopping it."

The doctor could be heard grabbing some notes from which to be sure of the locations.

"Ok...you had me check the area around Langtry and Dryden." He went on, "When I looked south of there at El Indio, there were many men that came across one night after the shooting at Dryden. Then north...to Ruidosa the next night, even more came across with heavy vehicles. Must have been twenty to twenty-five trucks or big cars."

"How far did you track them?" Ben asked.

"The cameras only showed them going east toward Highway 67. They headed north from that point."

"The others? The ones to the south, where did they go?"

"They seemed to be on foot. They all walked out of camera range going northeast. Ben...I've never seen anything like this, what is going on?"

"Dr. Webster, there's a group working on that question right now. You're information is a big help and I'll see to it they get it."

"That's great and all, but I get a sick feeling when I watch those images coming in like that. Especially with all the vehicles." Franklin Webster took a pause and then added, "The news media should be all over this, you know? Where are they?"

"There's a real good question," the young man confirmed. "Where are they?"

~

Lamar Jakes was alone and afraid. The would-be terrorist, turned should-be dead patsy had walked several blocks from Coors Field. Darkness had settled in. The street lamps gave everything an eerie glow. Jakes wanted to get out of the light. He wanted to hide. He needed a place to stay.

The university wasn't that far, but he could not go back there, he was supposed to be dead. No money, no phone and few ideas, he turned right and continued to walk in the shadows. A looming overpass for Interstate 25 came into sight and he approached it cautiously. There didn't seem to be any squatters there already, so he climbed high on the steeply angled abutment. There, just below the concrete beams for the bridge itself, Jakes found a flat ledge area. Summers in Denver could still get below sixty degrees at night. He lay down and curled up into a ball to wait for morning.

~

Matt Turlock's explanation of his "book" message was interrupted by a loud beeping noise. Everyone in the room looked to the radar screen.

"That's them," Murray explained. "Coming in from southeast." He stood and walked closer to the screen. "They are thirty-five miles out...should be here in about fifteen minutes."

Phil Stone got up, as did Matt. They had met Spiegel before and wanted to be a greeting party outside. Daniel and Sheriff Wilbury decided to go with them and followed them out the door side by side.

Murray was still watching his radar screen. He turned to look at Jon who was still seated at the table. "You coming?" Murray asked him.

"Yeah, in a minute. I'm waiting for Ben to call back so I can tell him what's going on."

"Ok," the cowboy waved as he joined the others just off the porch.

Jon picked up his cell phone from the table and walked to a window in the front foyer. He stood listening for Ben and wondering just who might step off the approaching helicopter.

The small house sat behind a Shell Gas station on the main street of Rocksprings, Texas. The dirt front yard held an elderly White Oak from which an American flag flew, all the time.

This house had five rooms in all. Two were bedrooms. The current tenants were not using those rooms as they were intended. Three men were tied and gagged in the front most bedroom. One other lone prisoner was held in the same condition across the hall. In the room with three, one was badly hurt.

Wilson Farley lay on the opposite side of the room from Grimes and Harel. His breathing sounded shallow and labored to Grimes. *But he is breathing*, Grimes told himself.

They were all tied, hands behind their backs and at the ankles and knees. Resting on their sides facing away from each other, Grimes and Harel could at first see Wilson, but not each other.

"Are you there?" the NCIS agent whispered.

"Good," the Mossad leader responded. "I wondered if you were awake."

"Hell, I've been awake. What can you see? Anybody in here with us?"

"No."

"Ok, good," Grimes grunted as he stretched his legs out and rolled over. "I have a beacon I can set off. I'll need your help, though."

Harel stiffened his legs and rolled toward his friend. "Your boot?"

"Hell of a memory, Yinon."

"I'm still alive, aren't I?"

Grimes rolled back as he had been and bent his knees as much as possible. Harel spotted where the boots would be and slid himself down a foot. Then rolling back to his original position he could feel the boots with his bound hands.

"The left one," Grimes muttered.

With their posture, Harel had to think a minute about which that would be, then grabbed the heel of the boot and twisted it until it clicked softly.

"That's it," Grimes told him. "Now turn it back."

Looking back over their shoulders, the men smiled at what they had accomplished. But that was short lived.

Within five minutes a cell phone rang in another room of the house. A dark haired man in a black suit burst into the room with them.

"Where is the signal?" he demanded.

Grimes and Harel tried to appear confused, but the man pulled a handgun and cocked it.

"My boot!" Grimes shouted. "It's in my boot."

The man pulled off both of Grimes boots and left the room. They could hear water being poured into a tub and then the boots throw in.

"It'll still work for ten minutes under water," Grimes told his friend. "But there is one more major problem...."

"How did they know about the signal?" Yinon finished the statement.

Nodding, Grimes told him, "Only my unit and Homeland Security has that frequency information...we've got a leak inside somewhere."

~

Jon was still waiting at the window when Ben came back on the phone. Ben told him about the call and Jon wasn't surprised.

"We've got people missing from the two incidents we know about. Can your professor look closer at those locations after the main trouble?"

"I can ask him." Ben sounded confident.

"Good," Jon sighed slightly and Ben knew why.

"So much for the old basics, huh?"

"Not necessarily," Jon countered. "I'm going let this group do as much as they can. They really are amazing and if my guess is right...about to get better."

The sound of the approaching aircraft could be heard over the phone.

"Capt. Stone's friends?" Ben asked.

"Yeah...let me let you go for now. See what more your professor can do for us, anything at all. A direction if not a location, okay?"

"Will do." And Ben hung up.

Jon watched the whirlybird that was marked Tyler Police on the sides land and two men climbed out. As they stepped away from the blades, Jon got a good look at the face of an old friend. One he had not seen since Afghanistan.

22

The call came while she prepared her dinner. Lt. Hurst's shift had been over for some time yet the phone call was from the precinct.

"Lt. Hurst?" the young voice asked.

"Yes, what is it?"

"There's an important call for you with a message that you should call back immediately."

"Immediately? Who's it from?"

"They left the name Sharon and a number in DC," the caller informed her.

The name Sharon meant nothing, but the DC reference could be one of her contacts. They never used names when calling in. Informants were known by the credibility of what they offered, not who they were.

"Give me the number again," Marsha asked as she grabbed a pencil. "Thanks."

She started to return the call right then and there, but something Jon had told her snapped in her brain. Turning down the stovetop burners, Marsha went into her bedroom and searched through a bottom drawer. There were three "burn phones" still there from a group Jon had given her to use. They were not traceable.

Slipping a battery into place on one, she walked back toward her kitchen and dialed the number in DC.

A shaking female voice answered, "hello?"

"This is Lt. Hurst of the Charlotte PD. Did you call for me this evening?"

"Yes... yes, I did."

"Are you Sharon?"

"Yes...Sharon Yates. My brother said you were the only one who could get help."

"From what?"

"He's been 'detained' as they put it." The female voice tried to gather herself, "I call it arrested without charges. They said he was just being 'detained'."

"Who took him?" Marsha asked. "The police?"

"Homeland Security officers. There were no police involved."

Marsha tried to think and understand what this could be about. Nothing except terrorism came to mind.

"Did they say why they took him?" she asked the frightened girl.

"Josh told me he had sent you some info about people coming into the country. He didn't offer any details.

The Mossad team that came in, Marsha realized they were being monitored beyond their knowledge. The government knew someone had reported them being here.

"Your brother's name is Josh?"

"Yes. Josh Yates. He's nineteen."

"Try to stay calm. I will see what I can find out, okay?"

"Thank you...I don't know what else to do," the voice stumbled.

Marsha pushed the "end call" button and started to dial Jon right then. A voice in her head screamed at her, *don't use a 'burn phone' twice.*

She pulled the battery from the one in her hand and went back to the bedroom to get another. The female on the other end had also closed her phone. She looked up at a man standing near her.

"Did she buy it?" he asked.

"I think so."

~

Jon stepped out onto the front porch as the men came around the machine. Spiegel and Phil Stone looked up to see him at the same time.

"Tim..."Stone started with his introduction.

"Why...well, what the hell?" the NCIS agent blurted out and stopped in his tracks. "What are you doing here?"

Jon smiled and moved closer. "I could ask you the same, old friend."

Their handshake became a quick, sincere hug as Phil and the others waited for an explanation.

"I'm working," Spiegel said in jest. "I usually am... when I run into you."

"Touché," Jon grinned. "I'm just trying to learn a few things from these guys."

Murray's face went from one confused look to another at that comment, but he didn't question it. "Well...now that we're all reacquainted. Let's get inside and back to work, huh?"

"Don't forget Terry." Spiegel reached back for his partner.

Barker nodded at the others in the primitive way warriors acknowledge each other.

Agent Spiegel grabbed Phil Stone's arm as they walked to the house. He pulled the man close to him and said something near Phil's ear. Stone looked back, a bit surprised at first. Then he went to Matt Turlock to share what Spiegel had told him.

"Remember the story of the lone Army Ranger they rescued in Afghanistan?" Phil whispered and pointed to Jon.

"You're not serious?" Matt stopped perfectly still.

"Yep, our boy is one and the same."

Murray grabbed another chair from the den as they moved back to the dining room. The table was now more than full and the talk got even grimmer as the NCIS and Mossad agents added their stories.

"Do you suppose they are holding Stallings and your people together?" Sheriff Wilbury threw out.

There were nods all around and Murray finally spoke, "If we're dealing with the same group for both cases, yeah."

"I believe that will be true," Phil Stone added.

An odd sounding beep went off and Spiegel reached into his side pants pocket. Turning the unit he read the text message that was on it.

"Signal beacon received. Rocksprings, Texas. Short duration, discovery suspected." He quoted from the transceiver and pushed the keyboard to reply. *Roger, will respond with local resources.*

When asked what he had told them, Murray then wondered, "What's a local resource?"

"You, for one thing," Spiegel smiled and added, "You and that bird out there, I'm hoping."

Murray nodded his head in agreement and Spiegel then asked, "What kind of weapons do you have here?"

". 50- caliber and down," Murray told him.

"You got a fifty? Great! We might need it."

"How are we gonna do this?" Jon asked that time.

"We?" Spiegel smiled. "You coming with, Kemo..." and then he stopped himself.

Jon sternly looked at him with a start. "Remember where you are, Master Chief," he teased the newcomer. "Lone Ranger jokes won't fly around here."

The NCIS agent tried to appear sheepish, "We'll just have to figure it out when we see what we are up against. I've got good coordinates as to where the signal came from. We need to get there before they move them."

Murray was at his map. "It's about 280 miles as the crow flies. It'll take a good two hours once we're airborne." He spelled out for them.

Murray and Jon went to the armory in the house's basement level to retrieve the weapons. Sheriff Wilbury threatened to shoot anyone who tried to leave him behind, so the four-man party was set.

Phil opted to stay with the newspapermen so he wouldn't be caught out of his jurisdiction. Murray led them back into the underground "safe room" to wait and monitor the progress. Agent Barker offered to stay, as security should things get rough.

Lucy lifted off with Murray and Tim Spiegel up front. Sheriff Wilbury sat behind the pilot. Jon was sitting next to Wilbury and he motioned to Murray as they leveled off at around 3500 feet. He had his bag sitting on the floor between his feet. The suits were in there. Murray took a look and his head bobbed like a doll as he leaned into the throttle. Lucy lurched and roared through the night toward the southwest.

~

Marsha Hurst walked toward her cabinet that held the other "burn phones." The intent was to get a clean one. She was anxious to contact Jon about the call she had completed. Her mind was swimming with concern for the "detained informant" yet small red flags began to go off within those thoughts.

With the drawer pulled open, she suddenly stopped and stepped back. Sitting down on the edge of her bed Marsha replayed the thought she had just processed. *Even if all that was true, how could the contact have known who she was?* Then a final thud added to the revelation. *Much less find her precinct phone number to call her?*

The phone she had used to return the "call" was still in her right hand. Turning it over, she pulled the cover and found the card and its serial number. It wasn't Jon she needed to call right now. It was Ben.

Grabbing her regular cell, she hit Ben's auto-dial number. He answered on the third ring.

"Hey, Marsha. What's up?"

"The call is over, but can you give me any idea where the last call came from?"

"Did they call you?" he asked.

"No...I dialed from a burn unit."

"Give me the SIM number and I'll see if it comes up." Ben didn't sound too positive.

Marsha read off the number and sat back to wait. Ben called up a program and searched for records of that SIM's activity. After a couple minutes, he came back on line with her.

"I can't give you a exact location, but it was in the city."

"Washington, huh?" Marsha asked.

"Washington?" Ben seemed surprised by that. "Heck no...it was much more local. The number you called was a cell phone being used in Atlanta."

The information stunned Marsha. "It wasn't going to Washington from there? I mean...I thought I was talking to someone in the D.C. area."

"Nope." Ben was firm about what he had found. "You called into Atlanta. Somewhere right downtown." He was still working to zero in on it. "That's the best I can do. The last tower was in Mid-town, just north of the Varsity Drive-In."

Rubbing her forehead, Marsha thanked Ben and hung up. *She had been discovered,* her mind shouted. *They knew who she was.*

23

Murray sat his Bell 407 down on the northeast side of the town. Rocksprings was not large and helicopter traffic was likely not a normal occurrence.

They did find the house they were looking for. The coordinates would be in the dark this time of the evening, but the gas station right in front of the house lit the area and they could see it from the air.

"We're about a mile away," Murray told the team. He looked to his left and saw a livery with a dozen horses standing at the fence. They were staring at the men and their machine in wonder.

"I say we commandeer the horses we need," Sheriff Wilbury declared. He looked at the others who were simply smiling and added, "I can do that. I'm a sheriff in Texas."

"Ok," Murray waved his hand in agreement. "We'll ride hard south around town and come in from the other side, slower." He paused and then added, "Everybody does ride, right?"

The others nodded and Spiegel headed off toward the barn while Jon stood with a blank stare.

"You do ride, don't you?" Murray asked directly.

"I have..." Jon replied. He inferred that his limited skills would not match the others. "It's just not my second language, okay?"

Murray didn't know what to say. Then a question came to mind. "How you gonna get to the house, then?"

"Don't worry about me," Jon assured him. "I'll be there and I'll set up a diversion." He stepped back toward Lucy to get his bag.

Tim Spiegel had missed the discussion. He was returning from the barn with several large blankets.

"We can use these as ponchos, hide our weapons and gear," He announced.

When the obvious quiet got to him, Spiegel added. "Okay, what's up?"

"Jon doesn't ride," Murray mumbled.

"I can ride," Jon corrected him with his back turned to them. "Just not like you guys will need to...now get on with it." He turned towards them. "I'll see you at the house in fifteen minutes."

Tim and Wilbury stood on their toes as the sound of vehicles came close from the north. It was three black vans moving in convoy on the road heading into town.

The team all knew where the vans were going.

"Make it ten minutes," Spiegel suggested.

The three riders mounted, bareback and covered themselves with the blankets. They headed south from the corral and disappeared into the night at a full gallop.

Jon quickly changed into his black suit and pushed the other under Murray's pilot seat. Walking toward the corral, he stooped to pick up the fourth blanket and picked out the darkest brown horse left in the livery. Without a bridle, he grasped the horse under its jaw and gently led him from the corral. The suit startled the horse a bit at first. But Jon's confident, easy moves quickly calmed the creature down. He swung his right leg up and over, tied the blanket around his neck like a cape and with a soft kick they lunged toward the town.

Jon hated lying to his friends, but it was necessary. He needed some alone time with the men in those vans. This was the only way he could do that.

~

Ben was working on another system, trying to identify the caller that Marsha had spoken to when the machine across the room beeped. It was the computer he had locked on the number Marsha had called. It was being used again.

He rolled his wheeled office chair across the floor and hit "enter" on that system. The monitor showed both the number being called and the location, an office in the Peachtree Center, the old Georgia Gas Light building right on Peachtree Street in Atlanta. He couldn't tell, which of the twenty-five floors that office was on, but he could trace the number called.

That phone was listed to a Marshall Forrest, aide de-camp to wealthy businesswoman and attorney, Sheri Shanahan, whose offices were located on the twenty-second floor.

Ben leaned back in the rolling chair. He knew this name. Shanahan had connections in Washington. *She's been on the news.* Ben thought nearly out loud. *One of those talking head guests on the cable shows.*

Suddenly Forrest, the phone's owner, was insignificant. Shanahan was the big fish. Ben needed to check into her activities a bit deeper and report to Marsha and Jon. Maybe even a road trip to the "Big A."

~

Congressman Fred Everett was still in his office. It wasn't the country's business that kept him up. It was his drug business. He had been shut down and forced to move the center of operations. That not being bad enough, there was a mysterious man out there who seemed to know it was Everett's business.

This man had to be eliminated and fast, replayed in his mind.

Everett had issued orders that this be handled and in his mind, yesterday was too late.

A phone rang in the outer office and an aid soon stuck his head in the door.

"It's Jerry Blake," the man said.

"Are you there?" Everett demanded as he raised the phone.

"In the morning," Blake answered. "We've driven all afternoon. We're going to eat something here...we're in Chattanooga, and get some sleep. We should be in Dalton by 6:00AM."

Everett wanted to complain yet reason told him to accept what he heard.

"Alright," he breathed out with a hesitant resolve. "Get it done."

"Will do," Blake assured his boss.

~

The lights of the gas station in Rocksprings, Texas seemed to radiate for blocks. Jon could clearly see the house and the three vans parked along the front side. An American flag flew from a stick on the large oak tree near the driveway. That struck Jon as odd, but he didn't waste time thinking about it. The others would be here any minute.

He pulled the horse up by its mane and jumped down. Then turning the steed back toward where they had come from, he slapped the horse's hindquarters. The animal jumped forward without a sound and was gone.

With the old blanket still wrapped around him, Jon walked across the street to the front of the gas station. He watched his step carefully on the road that had once been paved. Cracks showed at least two or three layers of black tar, but it was now more dirt than asphalt.

A diversion was needed to assist his approaching friends, and there was little time. Spotting an old wreck parked at the far rear of the gas station gave him an idea.

That will have to do, he told himself.

He walked past the front of the building and noticed the only attendant was asleep at the counter, his head resting on his arms. Jon eased into the building and gave the man a slight tap on the back of his head, assuring he would sleep a while longer. Then, looking over the counter, he found the switch for the gas pumps and turned them on.

The wrecked car had only three wheels and two of those were flat, but Jon was able to pull it with ease. The added strength to his legs, back and arm provided by the suit made the task simple.

He filled the vehicle's tank and doused the interior thoroughly, then moved the wreck one more time. Making sure it was far enough from the pumps for what was to come. He could hear the three horses approach and stop about a block south of the house.

Checking his watch, Jon planned his timing.

Two minutes should let them get into position, he thought while checking his route to the house. A small, four-foot high concrete wall separated the house from the business. From there, the distance to the exterior of the house was only a few feet.

Jon glanced at his watch again. Nearly a minute and a half had passed. He reached for a match, waited a few more seconds and then lit it.

Tossing the match into the wreck, he quickly moved over the short wall and to the house. From his spot near a window, Jon looked back to the gas soaked car. It burned evenly at first. The small orange glow expanded and Jon leaned toward the window, straining to hear inside the house.

When the burning vehicle exploded into a loud, fierce fireball, the noise did as it was intended. Men began rushing from the house and the vans to see what had happened. Jon could only assume his friends would react to the opportunity as he began his own attack.

A head appeared through the window near him and Jon grabbed the man under his chin. A quick pull with the powered arm and he was launched from the window. The limp body landed unconscious in the yard, just short of the concrete wall.

Another man ran around the side with an AK-47 in his hands. Jon stepped from the shadows and delivered a single, short, devastating punch.

Breaking glass, shouting and some gunfire now came from inside the house. In that chaos, others who had come outside stopped and turned back to the house. Jon knew his team was now inside so he moved quickly, overtaking those going back in.

He ran up behind one of the armed men and kicked him in the small of his back. The heavy framed body flew into the building headfirst and did not move further. Four others turned to attack Jon who was still moving forward. Shots from point blank range bounced off his suit. The right arm swung, catching one man just below his chin. Another attacker grabbed Jon's left arm and paused for a second. Baffled by the material of the suit, he looked up to see Jon's fist flying straight at him.

The two shooters had thrown their guns down and fled. One toward the gas station, the other jumped into the passenger seat of the second van.

"Go...go!" He could be heard screaming.

Two of the vans cranked and began to back out onto the road. The first one straightened out and fled north through town. Running to the second van, Jon pulled the side door open and was met with gunfire from within. Those rounds also bounced off his suit, one striking the front seat passenger in the head. Jon grabbed the shooter by the throat and squeezed till the shooting stopped.

The van driver hit his brakes and looked back at the man in the black suit.

"Drive on, friend," Jon ordered calmly. "Follow your friends. Do it now."

The van driver hesitated and seemed to be frozen in fear.

"I'm not going to tell you again," Jon warned him.

This time the driver did as he was told. Two black vans left town at a high rate of speed. The third vehicle never moved from the house.

Those in the first van were unaware that Jon Crane was inside and in control of the second. Thus far, he had accomplished what he intended.

~

The sound of the exploding car was right on time for the other team members. Murray and Tim Spiegel broke through the windows on the far side and entered the house. Sheriff Wilbury kicked in a rear door and stormed in. They caught four men. All had moved away from the rooms where the captives were. A short gun-battle found the kidnappers to be outmatched. Three were killed and the other seriously wounded.

Grimes and Harel were found with their injured partner in the front room and Deputy Stallings was sitting up in a corner of the back bedroom. All were okay.

"What took you so long?" Grimes quipped as he tried to appear earnest.

"Wrong turn on the Interstate, boss," Spiegel fired back. "Let's get you guys out of here."

Wilson Farley was still unconscious and didn't look good.

"What all is wrong with him, do you know?" Spiegel asked his boss.

"Not sure. But be careful with his legs, they might be broken." Grimes was now leaning over his friend. "He didn't get out of the car before the blast. It threw him fifteen to twenty feet." He gently felt the length of the CIA Director's legs and found what he feared. "Yeah...this one." Pointing the right leg. "It's broken just above the ankle and the other at the thigh and just below the knee."

A large shadow appeared over them and then they heard a booming voice.

"This is Horace Wilbury of Brown County and Brownwood," the sheriff bellowed into his radio. "I need EMTs and backup in Rocksprings ASAP. Man down...I repeat... we've got an officer down."

Responses were immediate from authorities in Junction, some thirty-five miles away.

"Roger, Sheriff Wilbury. Air and ground support with ambulance on the way." The voice paused and then asked meekly, "Did you find Stallings, sir?"

Deputy Stallings walked out of the other bedroom, dusting himself off.

"Roger, Junction. Stallings is fine and back on duty." Wilbury did his best to sound official. Still, his voice choked up just a bit. He had found Stallings in the back room and untied his hands. He left the deputy to deal with his other bindings and stomped toward the front to support Murray and Spiegel. The cowboy and the Mossad leader ran to check the porch and outside.

"Can you give us your exact 'twenty,' Sheriff?" the dispatcher asked.

Stallings walking down the hall drew the sheriff's attention. As he looked, the flaming vehicle glowed through a side room window.

"Just get here in town," Wilbury affirmed. "You'll see us."

Yinon Harel and Murray returned from the porch and suggested they check for others. Then the Mossad leader looked around him.

"Where is Nava?" he asked. "Did you not find her?"

Spiegel heard him and stepped forward. "We got her, Yinon. She's hurt pretty bad, but she's in a hospital over in Tyler, Texas. Reiss is with her."

"Why there?" Harel looked confused.

"It's quiet and we can trust them. We're not sure who or what we can trust right now. That town came recommended by someone we do trust."

Murray turned to the Israeli leader. "I'll take you there, soon as we can, Okay? Right now, let's see who these people are that grabbed you."

They found more bodies strewn outside on two sides of the house, but no Jon.

"Well, he was definitely here," Murray said half joking. They looked through the abandoned van and found nothing. No sign of Jon Crane.

"Where is he?" Wilbury asked, his eyes more serious than normal.

Murray motioned with his hand to calm him down, "He's fine...I can assure you of that. Where he is...I don't rightly know just yet." He stepped to the road and looked toward where the vans had gone. There was no way to chase or even follow them. Murray heard a strange beeping sound from his pocket that he didn't recognize. Tim Spiegel stepped onto the porch and hollered at Murray.

"That's your cell phone, man," Spiegel told him.

"That's not now my phone rings," Murray argued.

"It's a text message, I'll bet you," The agent smiled.

Murray grabbed his phone and sure enough it read, "Message Received," in bright blue letters. He hit "ok" and the message came up.

"I'm fine. I'll catch up back in Caddo. Hope the others are Ok. I need to do this myself. J."

The cowboy looked up at his friends and nodded. "He's doing what he does." He told them. "He likes to work alone sometimes."

That comment struck Spiegel and his expression went blank. He seemed to accept what he had heard.

"I can understand that," he responded.

24

Sheri Shanahan was born in Rhode Island just over fifty-three years ago. Raised by her mother after her father left them, Sheri exhibited mistrust for men although she excelled in working with them. Her studies at Yale and Princeton led to a short teaching career at Stanford out on the west coast. While there she met Professor Steven Walden. His charismatic charm and attitude were magnetic. There, her interest in politics began.

Sheri never married although she claimed to have been engaged several times. Her features were pleasant and many found her to be attractive. Rumors about her sexuality would rise from time to time. She never worried or paid much attention to them. In her mind, she preferred men, but just didn't have the patience to put up with them.

Television appearances began while she was in her thirties and she was in demand for her outspoken manner. The heavily eastern European flavor of her political stances soon put Shanahan in a niche she could not get out of. She would proudly speak over other guests with a genuine smile plastered on her face. The tactic was great television, though it soon wore thin. Her positions on issues began to precede her and the offers for appearances dried up. She blamed men, those of the opposition party.

Shanahan and her mother moved to the south a dozen years ago where she found that practicing law, rather than the teaching of it, suited her. With oppressed victims cases in abundance, her business grew into one that drew national attention to her, yet again. The funds her firm earned came primarily from corporations. Businesses who would rather pay a settlement than fight embarrassing charges in open court. Be the charges true or unfounded, exposure in a public forum was more costly in the long run. Sheri understood which cases would be considered in this category, and chose her clients accordingly.

Her desire to affect change never left her. Offers to run for public office did not interest her. "Politics took too long," as she would quickly explain. Appointments to state and federal courts were also rejected. The possibility of being stuck in a non-effectual position frightened her.

There was one position she would accept, and one only. That position would afford her the power she sought and the ability to affect change to and around the document she found so deeply offensive, The Unites States Constitution.

The offer for that position had not happened quickly enough to suit attorney Shanahan. Alliances were necessary and she had begun to associate herself with people willing to operate under a quid-pro-quo situation. Her alliance now in position, she had started the wheels in motion that would end up with her gaining that ultimate prize.

~

By his watch they had been driving for four hours. *Even these large vans would need to gas up pretty soon,* he thought and looked over the drivers shoulder at the gauge. It showed a quarter of a tank.

"How much fuel do these things hold?" he asked the driver.

"Fifty-eight gallons," the man told him. "The range is about 750 miles."

They had made great time on the interstate. I-10 was nearly deserted this time of night and their speeds hit ninety miles per hour plus till they got onto the other four lane at Fort Stockton. US Highway 285 slowed them down to eighty except going through Roswell, New

Mexico. A short stretch of two-lane road took them under I-40 and north towards Las Vegas, New Mexico.

They had just gotten on I-25 North when Jon's phone beeped with the text tone. It was from Murray. <u>Call quick, 911.</u> That meant it was an emergency. Murray knew Jon was "busy," but something major was up.

Murray answered on the first ring.

"Hey, where are you, man?"

"Just north of Las Vegas, New Mexico," Jon replied. "Flying up I-25."

"You must be flying, listen...I just had a call from Barker. He and Phil picked up a bleep on the big radar screen in my safe room."

"Ok...what's that mean?" Jon asked.

"Means you might be in a heap of crap really quick. The bleeps look like small aircraft...Terry thinks drones... maybe. They came out of Abilene an hour ago and if you're where you say you are...they're coming right at you."

Jon looked to his right, toward the eastern sky. He could see the signs of daylight, but little else.

"Thanks, man," he told Murray. "I owe you one."

"You take it eas...." Murray got out before he realized Jon had hung up.

~

They say it's coldest just before the dawn. Lamar Jakes awoke to his own shaking from the morning chill. As his senses came to life, Lamar could tell he was not alone. The underpass had lured many other overnight guests. One sat nearby and stared at him.

Jakes sat up with a start and stared back. The other man did not flinch.

"You're not a regular, are you?" the man asked.

"Why? What business is that of yours?" Jakes fired back. He tried to show firmness while still shaking from the cold. It wasn't working.

"Your shoes aren't worn and they look fairly new. Your clothes are dirty, for sure, but they're not old either." The man stretched his legs out before him and leaned back on his arms. "What happened to you, kid?"

Kid? Jakes feared that meant he was in trouble now here as well. "I'm no kid," he answered. "I'm just lost."

"You're from one of the colleges, huh?"

The question startled Jakes, who responded with a give away answer. "How do you know that?"

"Look...kid..." The man lowered his chin and glared up at Jakes, his eyes seemed to be climbing into his eyebrows. "I've lived like this for years. You don't want this. Go home. Go back to school...whatever. Don't do this."

"I need a gun," the younger man spurted out.

The words shocked Jakes as he said them. His thoughts had just translated into spoken words without his permission. He didn't take it back, but he didn't add anything to it either.

The man threw his head back and seemed to laugh slightly. "A gun?" he repeated. "A gun can't help you. Who you gonna shoot?"

Lamar Jakes impulsively moved forward. His fear now overwhelmed by the instinct to survive.

Nearly face to face with the old timer, he spoke again. "There are bad people after me. Powerful, bad people and I know who's in charge."

Now the other man appeared concerned. Jakes sincerity matched his apparel. It was soiled, but real. After more than a full minute of staring at Jakes with a blank look, the man whispered.

"I know someone." Leaning closer he followed with, "Do you have money?"

Jakes hadn't thought about that. He grabbed for his wallet and it wasn't there. *They took it*, he remembered. He nearly panicked but then noticed his own wristwatch. Pulling it off, he held it out to the man.

"How much would this be worth?" he asked.

The man didn't touch it, but looked over closely in Jakes' hand. "That might do it," he said. And he began with instruction on how to find the person with the gun for sale.

Jakes rose and shivered again. He struggled to get hold of his shaking and thanked the man for his help.

"Just don't come back here, ok?" the man scolded.

"Never," Jakes told him as he headed down the abutment.

~

Jon told the driver to flash his lights like something was wrong.

"We're in the middle of nowhere," the driver protested.

The driver did not need for Jon to repeat himself. He flashed the lights until the lead van slowed and started down an off ramp at an exit named "Watrous." The lead van stopped and Jon told his man to stop about twenty feet back.

Jon grabbed the driver's neck and pinched it in a "sleeper hold" fashion and the man was out within seconds. Two men climbed from the front vehicle and started back toward Jon's. He quietly as possible let himself out the rear doors and fell down to look under the van.

As they reached the driver's door and the front passenger window, they could tell something was very wrong. The passenger was dead and the driver unconscious. One man yelled something that made no sense, yet Jon understood it clearly. The man at the driver's door started back toward Jon and the other man pulled the side door open.

Jon rose and leaned against the back of the truck. As the man stepped around from his right he was met by Jon's powered arm to his throat. Jon caught him before he hit the ground or made a noise. Then gently lowered him.

As he was still bent over, the other man appeared and drew a weapon.

"Who the hell are you?" his voice demanded.

Jon did not answer him, but slowly rose to his feet. As the armed man got a good look at Jon's suit, fear flashed in his eyes and he fired three shots. The final one bounced straight back into his own forehead.

The sound of doors opening on the lead van were followed by footsteps as two more men approached. Jon pulled his Glock and fired at one, hitting him in the leg. The last man turned and ran back toward the van.

In a reflective glance from Jon's right side, he saw something in the sky near the horizon. He grabbed the wounded man and carried him away from the van as he watched the other vehicle drive away. It didn't get far.

As Jon and his captive fell into a ditch, the first van exploded and flipped down the highway, end over end. Then within seconds, the van he had been riding in also blew sky high.

The unmanned drones had done their job and veered off in two directions. Jon looked down at the man with the wounded leg. He was conscious, but confused and scared.

"Who do you work for, friend?" Jon asked him.

Shaking and reaching for his leg, the man glared at Jon. "I'm not telling you anything."

Jon smiled at him, "Oh...but yes, you are," he corrected the man.

~

Ben had been awake since before dawn. He had packed a bag of his own and loaded it in the new Charger. He rarely drove the car and kept it in the upper garage. The 5.7-liter Hemi engine was far from a production vehicle. As with the 12-cylinder behemoth in Jon's Jaguar, driving was not to be taken lightly. He had, though, "learned" how to drive it. Jon made sure of that with lessons at a nearby track. But on the road, use was still limited.

Marsha was nervous about Ben's idea when he called her back to report what he had found. Yet reason dictated it was a necessary step. Ben had located where the bogus call to Marsha had come from. They needed to know "who" was behind it.

His plan was to go to Atlanta and check out this attorney he had learned about. Info on the Internet was vast, but really all the same. A radical, discontent lawyer who made waves when she could was always the bottom line. *But why was her office used for that phone call to Marsha?*

Ben knew he should let Jon know, but Jon had other issues he was working on. *Time to pull my own weight and be some help*, he thought as justification. Besides, *it's easier to gain forgiveness than permission.*

25

When local authorities arrived at the scene along Interstate 25, they found two badly burned and shattered vehicles. In and around the sections of what had been vans were the partial remains of four to five men. One victim was a puzzle to them. He lay some forty feet away from the closest blast site and showed no signs of burns, only horrific trauma. It appeared as though the blast concussion had dislocated nearly every major joint in his body. There was a gunshot wound to his leg, but the cause of death was the violence that caused him to be all but dismembered.

They say there's the exception to every rule. Those ordered to talk to Silas normally do so. This man had been the exception. Apparently he feared his employers more than the pain or even death. While he did not actually speak with words he did, in his own way, set Jon on the path he needed.

Receipts from a convenience store and other bits of documentation in his pockets all came from one area of the country. This man was from Denver, Colorado or nearby. That much Jon was sure of. He didn't know the name of his boss, but that would come.

Jon had walked deep into the southeast desert area from where the vans had been hit. Obscuring his footprints as he went, he had gone far enough from the site to feel safe from the investigation. It was from there he called Murray.

"Hey," he started the conversation. "I need a ride to Denver. Got any ideas?"

"Denver?" Murray repeated. "Lose your flying carpet, did ya?" When Jon didn't laugh he continued with, "Give me a second."

Murray walked over to Sheriff Wilbury. "Do you know anyone in New Mexico we can trust?"

While Wilbury pushed his huge hat back on his head to think, Deputy Stallings came up.

"New Mexico? You say," he threw in. "I've got a brother in Tucumcari."

"Where the hell's that?" Murray asked.

"Eastern side, maybe 150 miles from Albuquerque."

Murray reported to Jon who asked how close the brother was to Las Vegas.

"How 'bout Las Vegas...? That's the New Mexico one, I mean."

"Less than a hundred," Stalling told him.

Jon and Murray decided this might be the quickest and best chance.

"Can he go to a spot in the desert just off I-25 and pick up a friend of mine?"

"Sure...he's into four wheeling, big time," Stallings grinned.

"This friend might be dressed a bit funny," Murray said and went back to the phone for a minute. "How's your bag?" he asked Jon. "Gone, huh?" Looking back at Stallings he reiterated, "yeah...be sure he knows my friend dresses like a Ninja sometimes."

Stallings called his brother and the man said he would leave right away, and take Jon a change of clothes. The deputy's brother was the adventurous sort who loved any excuse to take his buggy out.

~

Sheri Shanahan walked the beach near her vacation home in Aruba. She had spent many memorable months down here seeking privacy and peace. Her visit this trip was much more "visible" than others had been. And for an important reason, it was her cover story.

Checking the time again, she determined it was close enough and pulled a cell phone from her Dior Panerea tote bag. The number she dialed was another cell phone, currently located in Washington, DC.

"Bogart, please," she requested to the person answering.

"One minute," was the short reply.

Shanahan continued her walk, her back to the rising sun, and held on.

"Grant here," the man's voice announced.

"I asked for Bogart," Sheri scolded him. "Don't do that."

"Sorry...it's early."

"Are the arrangements made for me?"

"Yeah...you leave at 10:30AM local on a tourist helicopter. It will take you to Haiti where you catch a flight into Miami under the name Laura Black. From there you're on United to Pueblo. The announcement about Denver should be out this morning."

"Ok...that's all fine. How do I get to the meeting?" she asked.

"A driver will pick you up in an unmarked car and take you to Denver. There won't be any questions, trust me."

"Trust?" she snickered. "I'm depending on you... 'trust' is what you need."

Cyrus Grant wasn't used to being talked to in this manner, but he quickly gathered himself and kept his cool.

"It will all be fine," he answered her challenge. "You have my assurances."

He waited for another response, but got another insult in its place. A blank tone meaning she had hung up.

~

Wilson Farley had been flown out by medical helicopter. The others were still in Rocksprings, Texas. Harel and Grimes both felt the news of their rescue should be kept quiet till they understood just "who" they were dealing with. Spiegel agreed and notified Barker back in Caddo Mills that they were being cautious.

The dead men from the house and the vans were checked for any ID or any information about what they were up to. Texas Rangers and local area police were going through everything they could find. The head of the Rangers was still upset with the feds over the handling of Ranger Garcia's shooting. He was onboard with the others in Rocksprings.

"I've been in law enforcement for over forty years. Never have I seen information handled and withheld from the public like this." He told Grimes over the phone.

Deputy Stallings sat near a front window, staring out into the surrounding area. He suddenly sat up straight and looked around for anyone who might be near. Tim Spiegel was in a doorway.

"Hey..." Stallings whispered and signaled with his hand. "Come here...look at this."

As Spiegel bent down to look out the window, Stallings cautiously pointed the man out. He was in the tall bushes across the street.

"Do you recognize that guy?" Stallings asked.

"What's wrong with him...I can't see much more than his head."

"He's been walking back and forth all morning," the deputy explained. "It's his clothes that don't fit. Those pants look like suit pants and his shoes are dress shoes...not boots. He looks to me like someone who got caught on the outside... and doesn't know just what to do now."

"Hmm..." The NCIS agent stood back and smiled. "Let's ask him about that."

The two men went out the back and split in opposite directions. Stallings went around the gas station and Spiegel had to take a longer track to stay under cover. When they had flanked the stranger, they closed in. The man in the bushes noticed Spiegel approaching first. There was not much in the way of cover, so he was the more visible.

At first the stranger simply froze and watched the approaching agent intently. When he knew for sure it was he the man was coming for, the stranger hastily pulled papers and a cell phone from his pockets.

He tore the papers into the smallest pieces he could and stomped on the cell phone before turning and running. He made it about fifty feet. There knelt Deputy Stallings, gun drawn and a very serious expression on his face.

Stallings did not offer a voice command. When the man stopped and threw his hands in the air. Stallings motioned with his service pistol for him to "get on the ground." Slowly, the stranger started that process until Spiegel came up and assisted him. The agent cuffed the man roughly and bent over him.

"Who the hell are you, fella?" Spiegel bellowed into his ear.

The man did not speak.

"You got him?" Stallings finally spoke.

"Yeah," Spiegel responded while pulling on the man's arm to lift him up.

The deputy jogged to the spot where the pieces of paper and the phone were. The paper was scattered through a couple of tall bushes and across the ground. He gathered up what he could find and stuffed them into one of his own pockets. Then the pieces of the cell phone were collected and put in another pocket.

Spiegel and the stranger were walking up as he finished and the agent looked at Stallings with a silent question.

"We got a jigsaw puzzle, couple of them actually." The deputy smiled, "I take it the cat got his tongue?"

"For now, yeah." Spiegel jerked on the man's arm. "We'll see about that, though. Won't we, friend?"

The three men walked directly across the street to the amusement of several of the other investigators.

"What you got there, Deputy?" one asked. "A peeping Tom?"

Stallings was not in a laughing mood.

"I need a clean, flat place to work on," he answered and offered little else.

~

Ben was having second thoughts about his trip to Atlanta. He could ask for forgiveness for taking the Charger, but it would have to be that. He had, kind of, promised he would let Jon know every time he planned to take it away from Dalton. It was just a security thing and he understood that. As he rolled the thought around in his head he became more uncomfortable with his original idea. But then he looked at the next-door stall and a smile broke out.

They never discussed the Jag.

~

A grey Ford sedan rolled slowly down the highway in front of the mountain mansion. The men inside looked it over and began to seek a spot to sit and watch it. They found a driveway across the road that seemed to head up an opposite hillside. Pulling into the drive and turning around, they heard the sound of a garage door opening.

Within a few seconds, a sleek Jaguar sedan roared down the mansion's driveway and onto the road. As it accelerated away, Jerry Blake pulled a folder from under his seat and looked through it quickly.

"That's him, by God," Blake proclaimed. "That's his car."

The Ford pulled back out onto the road and sped up to catch the Jaguar at first.

"No, no!" Blake told the driver. "Let's see where he's going first. Back off some."

They followed Ben out to the expressway and all the way to Atlanta.

~

As Deputy Stallings worked to reassemble the pieces of paper, Agent Spiegel looked at the busted cell phone.

"This thing's toast," he declared sourly.

"Is the SIM card in one piece?" Murray asked. "I know of a kid who can work with that."

Before he could respond, Spiegel's personal phone rang. It was Barker.

"Tim...I just got word from Director Scott back at MTAC. There's a full, complete, emergency evacuation of Denver, Colorado going on right now."

"Let me guess," Spiegel frowned.

"Yep, a top priority threat has been received," Barker confirmed. "The President has been given thirty-six hours to release the prisoners at GITMO or they blow the city."

"Where did he hear this?"

"It's on all the major stations, right now," Barker told him.

"Yeah...but you don't call me with a news bulletin. How did Scott find out?"

"Jason Shuck called him. He heard from Doyle. But the emergency had already been declared."

"So Homeland Security called the emergency?"

"Looks like it, yeah," Barker agreed.

"What did our boss say about it?"

"Nothin'...he just asked me to get the word to you quick as I could."

"Thanks, Terry. Keep your ears open, okay?"

"We'll be here...you guys are in the line of fire, you know."

"I've got some heavy duty experience with me here," Spiegel boasted. "Watch our backs and we'll get this puzzle figured out."

Barker was already concerned about the way his Director had sounded and now Spiegel, who was in the middle of it was also being purposely cryptic.

"Yeah, Tim...we've got your six, man."

26

Denver was in turmoil. Sirens were blaring all over and loud speakers screamed, advising everyone to complete all necessary business and leave the city. Electronic billboards flashed the same message at every corner.

Lamar Jakes was startled and suspicious. He had just completed a transaction for an old 38Cal revolver and was heading back to his campus.

This ain't right, he told himself. It had to be connected to the mess from last night. *Mithras is behind this.*

Cops were everywhere, loading people on buses and taxicabs. He needed to hide till this calmed down. Near the train tracks Jakes found a large, above ground sewer pipe that appeared dry. He climbed up and into it then scooted back far enough not to be seen. The sirens actually sounded worse from in there, but he covered his ears and hunkered down.

All he could think of was how he wanted his life back. But that seemed like a long way away right now.

Jon got the call from Spiegel while in Casper Stallings' dune rider. The steel cage vehicle had a V-8 engine and no body material what so ever, unless you counted the chassis pan. The vehicle featured one and two inch steel tubes wrapped around the frame and seats offering a clear, but sandy view of a terrain that required safety goggles.

Seventeen-inch wheels with wide rubber tires threw dirt and rocks in every direction. The ride was rough to say the least, but they were making good time.

"Say that again, Tim. It's a bit loud out here," Jon shouted into his phone.

Spiegel hollered back and Jon heard enough to reach out and grab the driver's arm and motion for him to stop. When he had the whole story about the evacuation, Jon did not commit to his next move.

"I need to think about this," he told the agent. "I'll call you back."

"Just what is going on?" The deputy's brother leaned back away from his steering wheel. "I'm all for a good adventure...but this is getting strange."

Jon and Casper talked about the situation and what they should and "could" do. They were about twelve miles from the Colorado border and some five miles off the beaten path. Casper said he had planned to use the sparsely traveled I-25 between Trinidad and Pueblo, but realized that would likely be going "up stream" at this point. Colorado opened both sides of the interstate for an evacuation so they would need to stay off road. Perhaps even further off, to remain unnoticed.

"We'll need to slip into Trinidad anyway to gas up and get a few supplies if we can," Casper advised Jon. "Then, if that works out, we can stay out in the desert right up to the outskirts of Denver."

"Sounds good," Jon agreed. At least that would offer him more time to think, even if it didn't work out completely as planned.

~

Congressman Fred Everett's phone rang at 7:30AM. He sat up on the couch he had slept on and had to think about where he was for a second. It wasn't often he spent the night in his office, but these were not usual times.

"Yeah, hello." He garbled into the phone.

"Boss...this is Jerry. We've got him. I mean we're on his tail right now."

"Take the bastard out," Everett almost shouted.

"Boss, we're in heavy traffic. We need to stay cool awhile. But we've got his ass and we won't let go. Soon as we get a clear shot, we're out of here."

"How long will that take?" the congressman wanted to know.

Blake stalled for a moment..."Not real sure yet. We're in the middle of downtown Atlanta and it's like an anthill with traffic and people."

Everett muttered an expletive that Blake understood full well.

"Boss, we don't need to get caught. That would come back on you, right? We'll get it done...just give us a bit of time."

As the boss hung up, Blake looked ahead in shock. "Where did he go?"

"I think he went down that parking tunnel for the hotel back there," the driver answered.

"Well, go around the block and follow him in, damn it."

Four minutes to go around the block and then take a ticket to enter the garage. They drove slowly down three levels, with panic about to set in. Then the man in the back seat screamed, "There it is."

They had found the Jaguar. But it was parked, locked and the alarm armed. All they could do now was wait. But there were no parking spots open on this level now. They drove around to near the exit and found a spot.

"This will have to do," Blake proclaimed.

~

Ben Shaw had walked out of the parking garage to the high-rise next door. The lobby directory showed an office for S. Shanahan on the twelfth floor. He rode up to that level and found the frosted glass door with a hand written sign.

"Offices Closed thru Next Week. For assistance, clerks will be on duty until 3:30 P.M. each weekday," it read.

Ben could see shadows moving inside the main office area so he moved with great caution. Taking a small cartridge from his coat pocket, he opened the end to form a shape that fit over the entire keyhole. Then squeezing the cartridge, a soft foam was injected into the keyhole and quickly hardened. When Ben pulled the form from the door, he had an exact copy of the key.

He wrapped it in a tissue and headed back for the elevator. There was time to kill, most of the morning and afternoon before he could use his new key and check out the offices.

Just before the elevator opened, his cell phone rang. Ben hurriedly stepped into the car and closed the doors, hoping the sound wasn't heard within the office. The shaft of the elevator cut off the reception to his phone, but it was still ringing when he walked back into the lobby. It was Jon...he was busted.

"Hello," Ben answered meekly.

"Hey, where are you? I tried the workshop phone and got nothing."

"Sorry, man. I kinda made a decision to check something out on my own."

"You what? Where are you?" Jon asked.

"Atlanta," Ben explained. He told Jon about the call to Marsha. He didn't want to, but now it wasn't a choice.

Jon mumbled something inaudible and then held the phone back where he could be understood. "Ben, I need you to look something up for me. I need you in the lab."

"Jon, I'm sorry. I got this lead on an attorney who might be mixed up in the case, you know...the nuclear stuff."

"Is Marsha Ok?" Jon's voice lowered.

"Yeah...the people who called her think they fooled her. She's fine."

"When can you get me what I need?" Jon was back on what he could control. "I'm approaching an area where the cell service may not be so good."

"Jon, have you tried the auto voice hook-up?"

Auto-voice was a company Jon had invested in several years ago. It was how he had made his money. Their program allowed voice operation of a system via microphone or even the phone lines. Ben had set it up in the new shop. Jon hadn't tried it yet.

"No... I count on you for this stuff, Ben." Jon was getting short with him.

"Tell me what you need and I'll see if I can access the system."

Rubbing his forehead with one hand, Jon decided to give it a try.

"I need sewer maps of Denver, Colorado with notations of passable sections that can be walked through."

Ben made notes and answered, "Ok, I can get that I think. You know they've evacuated Denver, right?"

"That's why I need the sewer routes to travel through. And Ben," Jon injected. "I need an access hole to them from the east side of town as far out as you can find. Got it?"

"Give me twenty minutes," Ben told him confidently and closed his phone.

He then looked around a found a coffee shop with G5 wireless access on the corner. He ordered a large coffee and sat with his back to the window.

As he worked, two men walked in and ordered three coffees and Danish to take back to their car. They noticed the young man with the small smart phone, but thought nothing of him.

Ben accessed the workshop system by voice and within fifteen minutes of voice commands he had downloaded maps of what Jon asked for. He just needed Jon to find a printer to send them to.

The two men got back to the car in the garage of the hotel.

"See anything?" Blake asked.

"Naw... I don't know where the guy went. I guess we just wait for the car to come out."

Blake rubbed his eyes. *I'm gonna need a nap*, he thought as he sipped his coffee.

27

In Trinidad, Colorado Casper Stallings found an open gas station. They were lucky. The traffic south on I-25 was now moving at about thirty-five miles per hour and bumper to bumper. The attendant told them there was no gas from Pueblo north and he was running low.

Jon noticed the station also held a small gun shop. He pulled his suit from under the seat and checked the Glock for ammo. *Six in the magazine and one chambered*. He knew he would need more.

Stallings walked up, paused for a second watching Jon and reached under his driver's seat. He pulled a Browning Hi Power, 9mm. It was fully loaded.

"I've got thirteen in the mag and one ready," he said while reaching back under the seat again. "Here's two more magazines," he looked them over and added. "One's full and the other looks like about eleven."

"I'll see if they'll sell me some 40's and some 9's." Jon winked at his new associate. He carried several credit cards in various names, all paid by his company account, and a Tennessee State Police ID under one of the names. He was way out of his area, but a cop on the job shouldn't have trouble buying ammo. He didn't.

The dune buggy held forty-five gallons in two tanks. The owner claimed it got twenty-three miles to the gallon so they should have a range of around a thousand miles. That also meant they were riding on a bomb. But...it was transportation, the kind they needed.

Jon walked out with his bags of ammunition and a smaller vehicle caught his eye. He went over to the go-cart and estimated the wheelbase and width. The tires were large enough to handle riding on the edges. Best of all, it was electric. Jon smiled as he went back into the store.

$475.00 later, he and Casper were tying the go-cart onto the top of the buggy.

"It's a bit of a long shot..." Jon grinned. "But heck...it might just work."

As they climbed back in the buggy, Jon's phone rang.

"Yeah, Ben," he answered. "You got it?"

"All I need is a printer to send it to."

Jon held a finger up at Stallings, "Give me another minute." And he ran back into the store. There on the back counter sat an old HP Wireless 8750, covered in dust.

"Does that thing still work?" he asked the attendant.

"It's supposed to," the man told him. "Two bucks a copy incoming."

Jon smiled, "Deal."

He held his phone near the printer and asked Ben if he could pick it up.

"Got it," Ben told him. "A HP 8000 model or thereabout, right?"

"You got it," Jon confirmed. "Let's go."

The dusty machine came to life. It whirled, spit and coughed, but then the paper tray reacted and pulled a piece into the rollers. After about three minutes, Jon had six color maps of the Denver sewer system with an opening marked near Parker, a suburb on the south side of the city.

"Good job, Ben...we'll talk about this other thing later. Just be careful."

"Oh, yeah. Everything's cool. I just have to wait a few more hours for the coast to be clear, that's all."

~

Back in Rocksprings, Deputy Stallings had many of the torn pieces put back together. The main item of interest appeared to be an ID card. With about two-thirds assembled, he stood up and called his boss over.

"What does that look like to you?" he asked.

"Wilbury leaned over and stared. "Looks like a seal of some sort."

Grimes walked up. It didn't take him long.

"It is a seal," he offered. "Homeland Security Seal. That name on there looks like Jeremy...Fletcher? Something like that."

He and Wilbury went into the room where the prisoner was being held.

"Well, Jeremy," Grimes started. "I can call you Jeremy, can't I?"

The man look sullen and frightened, but said nothing.

"You're in a heap of shit, son," Wilbury bellowed at him. "Those men you kidnapped are Federal agents. We can send your butt straight to Cuba, you understand that?"

The frightened man looked up and spoke in low tones. "I'm a Federal agent myself," he protested. "And my agency outranks all of you and yours."

Grimes threw his head back at the arrogance displayed. Then he knelt down next to the man and got right in his ear.

"That depends on what you were up to. You don't have 'carte blanche' to do whatever you clowns think is necessary." He stood back up and continued talking, "Just who sent you fellas here?"

"I'm not saying anything else till my boss gets here," the man snapped.

"Right after I shoot him." Wilbury stormed out of the room and looked back, "I'm coming back in here to shoot you."

Grimes smiled at the stubborn agent. "You're in way over your head." And he too left the room.

When he got back into the main room the others were in a small meeting. Grimes stepped into the middle of the pack and waited to be included.

"We think it's time to go," Spiegel told him. "It won't be safe here much longer."

"I agree," Grimes looked around as he spoke. "Where's the cowboy?"

"He went to get his copter," Spiegel answered.

"And Stallings and I are waiting for a ride back to Brownwood," Wilbury added.

"Do you think that's wise?" Harel asked the sheriff.

"I think better at home." Wilbury grinned a rare smile, "we can take care of ourselves."

~

The flight from Miami into Pueblo was forty minutes late. They had not considered the delays exiting traffic would cause other flights in the Colorado area. Shanahan was stoic, but not happy. To her, the lack of forethought was simply a screw up and those were not tolerated. Her intention to call Grant was headed off by a call she received from the Secretary of Homeland Security.

The Secretary position is a politically appointed cabinet post. In the years since this job had been created, cronies, hacks and figureheads held the position. The current occupant of the job was a holdover from the prior administration.

The new President was attempting to show outreach to the other side by retaining a high cabinet official from the other party. The man he chose was an easy pick.

Warren Ferris had been a war hero of some merit before coming home to run for congress. He was a popular figure to both sides of the country's battle over its own identity. An idealist in his thinking on social matters, Ferris could not help but be more pragmatic on financial concerns. He understood the need to control information. Though it left a bad taste in his mouth, he still supported the new Information Equality Act.

Ferris' main flaw was his justification for the steps being used to regain total control of the country. If allowed to vote their own convictions, the people would tend to lean in one direction more than the other. That, in his mind, prevented government from "taking care of its people." For their own good, they must be motivated to "vote" for those who perpetuate the social agenda at all cost.

The process was ugly. The first attempts seemed to go nowhere. But this latest plan might just work with lasting effects. It was an end that justified the means.

"We've found the female Israeli," the voice on Shanahan's phone said.

In response, the sarcastic attorney drew out a word as though it had multiple syllables.

"Really?" she mocked in a fake southern drawl.

Ferris bristled, but manage to hold his tongue for the moment.

"So you're letting me know you've had that taken care of, right?" Shanahan continued her taunting.

"What...No. Not yet. Is that what you want done?" The Secretary seemed thrown by the suggestion.

"I... don't make those decisions." Her voice was now lower and more pointed. "I have people who either do that for me or I replace them," Shanahan vamped. "Am I coming through to you?"

"You know, lady. I felt I had a dog in this fight for a while. But I'm really getting tired of your attitude."

"What a shame," she replied, her snarky attitude undiminished. "I have someone who can fix that for you. I'll have them stop by."

Again, Ferris attempted to bite his tongue. But his thoughts slipped through anyway.

"Right...that's your answer to everything," he heard himself say. "Threats."

The Secretary was losing his cool. He took a deep breath. His head felt light and his thoughts were swirling in rage.

This can't be the direction we go, he thought. Then, just as suddenly, he became calm.

"I guess I'll go ahead and mail this envelope then." His voice had lowered by two octaves and the attorney could hear resolve in it as he added. "Just in case...you know...I have an accident or something."

The game of "chicken" was turning in his favor.

"Look, Warren. It's been a long day and I still have much to do," she tried to smooth him over. "You know how it is to be in charge...you have to have a heavy hand or you'll lose control. I just get caught up sometimes. We're so close, now. Just weeks and we will have turned this big ship around forever."

"Don't threaten me again," the Secretary warned, his blood again rising in anger. "I'll take care of that situation we were talking about, but you learn how to talk to me...got it?"

"Oh...of course," she poured out. " Please...I hope you can accept my apology."

The Secretary took another bold step and simply hung up on her. Then, envelope in hand, he walked to a blue mailbox and slid the piece in.

"Apology, my ass," he muttered half out loud.

As he walked back toward his building, The Secretary pulled open his phone again and dialed the headquarters of NCIS. When the phone was answered he just said, "Get me Wilfred Scott."

"This is Scott," a voice said after the transfer.

"Will, do you know who this is?"

Taken back by the tone of his colleague's voice, Scott sat upright in his desk chair.

"Warren? Are you alright?"

"Listen close...I say this once and that's it.... You've got a Mossad agent in a hospital in Tyler, Texas. You have maybe six hours to get her out of there alive."

Director Scott gave him a second to add any more. When that didn't happen, he then answered, "Thanks, Will. Anything else?"

"Naw...you know that feeling like you just woke up... and wish you could go back for a do over?" His voice was tailing off now.

"I sure do, Will. Can I help?"

"Do your job...act on what I've told you," Secretary Ferris said firmly, like it was an order. "Oh...one more thing. Be watchful of Doyle, okay?"

"We know about him, Will. We know."

The Secretary of Homeland Security mumbled something unintelligible and hung up.

Scott laid his cell down and grabbed a phone on his desk.

"Get Grimes' first team up here, in my office, immediately," he barked. "And notify DOD the Secretary of HS might be in danger."

The agents assigned to Jerome Grimes were broken down into two groups. The second group was more cerebral and scientific. They operated mainly on forensics and statistics. Grimes called them his "geek squad."

The first team, which Scott had called for, was all ex-special forces or navy seals. They were front line operators who would break a few doors, or whatever, if need be.

With the team assembled in front of him, Scott gave one order.

"Nava Golan is injured in a hospital in Tyler, Texas. She is there alone at the moment except for a handful of local friendlies and we don't know who they are just yet." He looked at each man with a hard glare. "Get her out of there at whatever cost you may incur. Then find the others of her team."

The director then sat down. He had said all he needed to.

28

The desert between southern Colorado and the Denver area was a rolling plateau with dense, but low-lying vegetation. The off-road ride was bumpy at times, but Jon didn't seem to notice. He was going over the maps Ben had sent. Both he and Casper Stallings had been riding quietly for the last three hours.

"So," Casper turned and broke the silence. "Where in Denver are you going?"

"Don't know yet," Jon said without looking up.

The driver let that comment float a few minutes and then tried again.

"You know..." He said as if in the midst of a long conversation. "A guy I was talking to at the gas station said they had an incident in town last night. One that made the news." He glanced over at Jon who continued to study his maps. "In Denver, I mean."

"Yeah...I figured that's what you meant."

"They say it was radio-active stuff found near that ball stadium."

"I know," Jon answered.

"Now this new threat is claiming they got more."

"Yeah."

Stallings pushed on his brake. Not in a rush, but a steady, even stop. When the dust around them cleared, Jon put his maps down and looked over at the driver.

"What?" he asked the man.

"I don't get it...why do you want to go in there and risk the whole town going to smoke around you?"

"Because...I don't believe it will," Jon said with wide eyes and a slight smile.

"Then what in hell's bells is going on?" Stallings showed his growing frustration.

Jon handed the man his maps. "That's why I'm going in...to find out." He leaned over and pointed to some blue dots on the maps. "Those are manhole access points," he explained. "I can slip up and check every so often to see what I'm looking for."

"And just what is that?"

"Activity...any activity in the city. Somebody cleared the place out for a reason and I want to find out what that was."

"Well, then if you're so blamed sure it ain't going to blow up, I'll go with you."

Jon pulled his hands up in front of his face. Only the tips of his fingers and thumbs touched in a near prayer position. He lowered his head till his chin rested on the thumbs and forehead touched his forefingers.

"Casper... I owe you a great deal for your help," he said, raising his head and turning toward the man. "It's kind of weird that a guy like you would be here, available to get me where I'm going. But I learned long ago not to question fate, I just go with it."

Stallings stared at Jon. His look clearly indicated he had no idea what the man was talking about. But he stayed quiet nonetheless.

"If I am wrong," Jon said for effect. He didn't really believe he was. "And the whole place goes up. I need you to tell people who was here and that he tried to help." He lowered his hands and sat back against the seat. "You tell them Silas was here, okay?"

"Silas? You said your name was Jon."

"Can you do that for me, Casper?"

The driver put the buggy back in gear and revved the motor.

"Hell... I guess," he answered. "Still don't know what's going on," came out under his breath as they rode on.

~

The hour approached 3:00 P.M. and Ben had walked down the street to an electronics super store to browse and kill some time. A thought came to him that with the cat away; the mice might leave a bit early. Walking back toward the tall office building took him past a landmark hotel that had been in Atlanta for many years. It was there he had parked the Jaguar so he decided to check on it before going into the building.

A car with out-of-state tags caught his eye. Sitting near the check out booths, the car itself wasn't so odd. The fact that three men were in it... was. Two appeared to be asleep and the remaining one glanced at him as he walked by, but then continued with a paper he was reading.

Ben got to the floor where the Jag was parked and all appeared okay. Starting back out, he saw a door that led directly into the hotel's lobby so he took that, bypassing the walk through the garage check out. As the elevator doors opened on the main floor of the old Gas Light Building, four young people in business attire, carrying expensive looking leather cases, stepped off. Ben moved back to let them pass. None even pretended to notice him. With an inward smile, Ben got on the elevator and hit "twelve."

Stepping out of the elevator Ben could see the interior office lights were off. He took an item from his pocket. The trip to the electronics store wasn't totally a waste of time. He unfolded the electronic listening devise that could attach to walls, doors and other enclosures. Even the slightest noise would be picked up and amplified.

He listened at the door, through a smoked glass window at the far end and then the solid wall sections. All was quiet.

From another pocket he retrieved the key he had made earlier. It slid in fairly smoothly, and Ben felt the internal mechanisms of the lock gently begin to move. A firm pressure on the key rolled it a quarter turn and the door unlocked. Holding the door closed, Ben pulled the key and wrapping it carefully, put it back in his pocket. Then a strange looking, shallow box was drawn from a larger pocket. He pushed on a button inside the box and when it lit, he opened the door.

As expected, the office's alarm system sounded. Ben quickly looked around and found the control panel on an adjacent wall. Placing the box over the panel, he waited until the alarm stopped. The box had read the codes last used to unlock and re-entered them, disarming the alarm system.

The outer office was large, over twice as wide as it was deep. It held three desks, several bookcases and four large flat top tables with banker's lights on them. Different law books lay across the tables and it was clear they were used for research into the law pertaining to active cases. Everything was in good shape, not overly expensive or opulent by any standard. There was even some paint peeling in one corner of the back wall.

Ben took pictures of everything that drew his attention. Open books, plaques on the walls and even an odd picture made up of numerals in the shape of the star. Nothing reeked of incrimination or offered any answers as to why the call to Marsha would have come from here.

The door to the private office was closed and locked. Ben used a traditional lock pick and was inside in a manner of seconds. The view from there stopped him in his tracks.

The entire back, exterior wall was floor to ceiling plate glass. The attorney's huge mahogany desk sat centered in the large space.

The depth equaled the outer office, but seemed shorter on the left side. The difference was so obvious the eye automatically searched for a door or passage into another room or space beyond the end wall. But it appeared to be solid and covered with bookshelves.

What the outer area lacked in style and elegance was more than made up for in her private quarters.

This is nice; Ben smiled and stepped further into the space.

Large leather sofas sat on either side of the door and an ornate credenza lined up directly behind her desk. Nothing was out, no books left open as in the other space. It looked like a picture from Executive Design Magazine.

Ben took pictures of what he saw, even though they offered less than the nothing he found in the main office. The pictures were all abstract or landscapes. No family on her desk or anywhere else. As he focused on a picture set into the bookshelves, he stopped. Ben walked closer and noticed it was the same, or appeared to be, as the one in the outer office. Random numbers shaped as a star.

Weird, he thought, but he took the photo anyway.

The floor was carpeted and that caused Ben to notice something else. A section of the carpet in front of the bookcases looked rubbed and almost wrinkled. He felt all around the area, the shelves, the books and the photos in frames sitting within the shelves. When he finally found it, it seemed way too obvious. What seemed to be a leather cell phone case left on one shelf was not as it appeared. Ben reached for it and it slid back. An entire section of the bookshelves and the wall moved out two feet and then left.

As it opened, lights came on inside the space now exposed. Ben looked in and froze in place. Not from the blast of cooler air that escaped from the space, but from what he saw. He dropped the tools and the camera he had been holding. For a few seconds, he could not move.

206

29

While an eighteen-year-old boy was searching her offices, Sheri Shanahan arrived in Pueblo and was met by members of the Department of Homeland Security.

"Ma-am," the group's leader stepped forward. "Your transport to the meeting site has been changed."

"How so?" she asked, her nose raised and angled away from whom she addressed.

"Vehicle traffic still overwhelms the roads. We have a helicopter standing by."

Trying to remain aloof, the attorney waved the man away and began walking down the airport aisle. Another man in a dark suit walked up and told her, or rather asked her, to follow him.

The copter was a highly maintained Bell 430, the sleekest model of the commercial series. Shanahan climbed aboard and they took off almost immediately.

"Ma-am," the pilot said through his intercom. "We'll be traveling several miles to the right of the major highway system, not wanting to draw attention to our entering an evac-zone."

The passenger did not respond. She looked out her window in pure ignorance.

The dune buggy eased its way north just to the west of the Black Squirrel River. The sound of an approaching helicopter overpowered the engine noise of the buggy.

"We've got company," Casper announced.

Jon looked back and reached for his Glock. Casper Stallings had a better idea. Reaching down into a storage pocket beside his seat, he pulled out two caps. Handing Jon the baseball cap, he shouted, "Put this on...and tilt it sideways a bit."

"What?" Jon yelled back.

"Wear it like a kid...or a punk kid."

"Oh...I get it." And Jon Crane twisted the brim of the cap to his right and pulled it down. Casper pulled on a worn fishing hat and looked around. There was a large crested sand dune coming up on the left.

"Hang on good," the driver hollered.

The helicopter swooped low to check out the dune buggy. It wasn't supposed to be here.

Stallings turned sharply left and up the face of the sand dune till the buggy took air under all four wheels and flew. It landed some twenty feet away, rear wheels first and bounced hard.

Casper looked over at Jon. "You alright?"

"Yeah...that was different."

"Well, good. Here we go again." And he cut the wheels back to the right and flew another fifteen feet in the other direction.

Jon's stomach was beginning to have a mind of its own and his color was turning pink. As Casper started to turn for another jump he noticed the copter had seen enough. It sped away, at full throttle to the north and left them for the fools they appeared to be.

Jon pulled the cap off and held it in another position he thought might serve him better. But the queasiness relaxed and they settled back into their trip. After a couple miles Jon leaned over to Stallings.

"You know...that made me think of something I hadn't considered."

"What's that?" the driver asked.

208

"We've got to be getting close to Denver, right?"

"Yep...about forty miles, I'd say."

"Have you seen any blockade...of any kind?" Jon asked rhetorically.

"Damn...you're right," Stallings admitted. "Nothing."

"You'd think a quarantined city would be blocked off by now, wouldn't you."

'Like you said, man," Casper looked over at Jon. "There's something strange going on here."

~

The men at Caddo Mills had been busy themselves, monitoring the situation and also the national coverage of events.

"You know," Terry Barker sighed as he sat down at the big table. "How can stories like the border shoot-out go untold? Is the entire media in some huge conspiracy?"

Daniel looked up from his notebook. He laid his pen down and looked over at the agent. The comment stung Daniel as a professional, yet he clearly understood what the man was feeling.

"It seems that way, I know," the reporter tried to explain. "But it's not that simple."

Matt Turlock walked up, intrigued by the opening rounds of the discussion, and leaned against a doorframe to listen.

"Our profession doesn't make us immune from opinions. It's supposed to, but that's just naive. People tend to hire people who think like they do. Those folks ran the media and controlled the information for years. They were the final authority."

Daniel stopped for a moment, but Barker appeared to understand him and had no comment or question. Matt nodded for him to continue.

"Then 'talk radio' and that cable TV station came along. The national media was suddenly challenged. Its positions and commentary were now questioned."

Daniel was on a roll. His small audience listened intently.

"When those new information venues first started," he continued, "the mainstream media tried to ignore them. They figured this would be a flash in the pan, nothing to worry about. What they hadn't considered was the growth of the Internet."

The NCIS agent started to stir so Daniel quickly finished his thought. "The Internet allowed people to reach out and verify stories and facts they were hearing only on the new stations."

"But you can't believe everything you see on the Internet." Barker protested.

"No, you can't," Daniel agreed. "But there was enough that could be believed and further verified. That brought into question what the larger media was putting out." He leaned back, rubbing his head to where Matt almost jumped in to help. But before that could happen, Daniel spoke up again.

"What the main media reported wasn't so much untruthful, it was just highly selective. They offered stories that fit a certain philosophy and left out those that weren't helpful to their cause or agenda. That's what they got caught doing and in a big way."

"Yet this isn't a conspiracy?" Barker asked. "That's what I don't understand. How come they all say the same things?"

Daniel searched for an analogy. What he came up with was somewhat crude, but hopefully effective.

"If you hang around with people who don't like Polish jokes, you're not going to hear Polish jokes. And if you did hear one, you weren't likely to pass it on. Nobody has to tell you to do that, its just human nature."

Barker's expression showed he was skeptical at best. Daniel tried the same logic in another way.

"If you hear something you don't agree with; or worse, you believe it to be harmful, you're not likely to repeat it, much less pass it along."

Barker's eyebrows rose. That he could relate to.

Daniel finally noticed Matt standing there, his head nodding up and down in agreement. But Barker, the NCIS agent, didn't appear totally convinced.

"Add to that," Daniel went on. "The hatred stirred up against the detractors who were now getting more attention...it's a bad mix."

"But things are way beyond that," Barker came back. "Not reporting a simple story about politics is a far cry from men getting killed."

"I agree, it should be," the reporter nodded. "But when powerful people suggest those deaths could be misinterpreted by the public and hurt their overall cause, patriotism falls into a gray area."

A silence came over the table as Barker let it all soak in. Daniel looked inside himself for more to offer. That was when Matt Turlock spoke up.

"The pressure on those at the top is excruciating." Turlock began. "When a news outlet gets called down on a story they misreported or left on the newsroom floor, the first reaction is defense. The people in charge have their jobs and careers on the line. Decisions have to be made and too often, they've let those decisions come from their personal desires. What they 'want' to be the truth rather than what actually is."

"That's exactly right," Daniel added. "Too few of us have had leadership like I have...and I'm sure Matt offers to his people. They walk a fine line between giving in to the pressure and being forced out by it... it's quite a feat."

"Okay..." Barker sat straight like he had had a revelation. "But that dumb law they pushed through...you'd think they'd be happy about that."

"See there..." Daniel pointed at Barker. "You said it yourself. 'Dumb law.' That's how the people view it. In fact, it's been ruled unconstitutional in enough states that it's on the docket for the Supreme Court this fall."

"I haven't heard about that," Barker confessed.

"Exactly," Daniel threw himself back as though he had scored a winning goal.

The table got quiet for a moment until Matt started again.

"Think about what all has gone on. That bill was pushed through during the reversal of another bad law. The folks were up in protest everywhere..." he said.

Then Barker interrupted.

"But you know where I heard about it? Not the news, for Christ sake. I heard through the police network as different cities went on alert."

Anger clearly showed on his face as he continued.

"Alert for violence that never happened. The protestors were peaceful, but what did my TV say? It said the protestors were a threat to the well being of free speech..." Barker was sitting taller in his chair as he went on. "The right to free speech that the new 'Information Bill' would finally protect."

"I remember that," Daniel nodded.

"Then throw in those shootings," Barker added. "When congress people get hurt, the whole bunch of 'em gets sympathy. Not that they shouldn't, but I still don't know what or who was responsible for these shootings in Texas."

"That's how it works." Matt's tone was loaded with disgust.

"Well, you can't leave out what your boy was into, can you?" Barker said.

The room got still again, like all the air had been sucked from it. The NCIS agent looked around, but was not apologetic.

Then Daniel slowly leaned forward, his elbow on the table and his chin in his hand.

"You asking about Jon?" he mumbled loud enough to be heard.

"Of course," the agent said defensively. "You think I don't know who he is...and what he's done?"

Daniel carefully considered his next words.

"Let's pretend you're right." He stood as he spoke.

"Pretend? Aw...come on now." Barker shook his head in disbelief.

"Work with me for a minute, will ya?" Daniel began walking around the table, slowly. "I know what you think, and I understand it. But here's a question for you. What do you know about the supposed victims?"

"That doesn't matter..." Barker looked around for support that wasn't there. "They weren't tried... or convicted. We have a system to handle crimes like theirs."

"Right...we did have." Daniel had gotten to where the agent was sitting. He looked straight down at him to go on. "But these people had learned to hide within that system. The system couldn't and wouldn't touch them because of who they were."

"Still doesn't justify what he did," Barker maintained.

"How many more would have died if he hadn't?"

"You can't know that," the agent complained.

"Look into it deeper, my friend. None of us here know more than I about what Jon does." His face became even more serious as Daniel shared personal experience. "I wouldn't be here if not for him.

213

And the man responsible would still be out there and still in office...most likely."

The room again became silent. Phil Stone, who had been near the door, sat down across the table from Barker.

"I'm a law enforcement officer myself, son." Stone stared Barker down. "I get it. I know where you're coming from. But I too, believe in extraordinary times calling for extreme measures." He shook his head fiercely. "If you try to make me explain it, I can't. But I know I'm good with it." His eyes were wide and clear as he finished.

"So..." Barker asked as if in retreat from the discussion. "Just how many of the three mysterious deaths is he responsible for?"

"Three?" Daniel smiled. The others who were closer to the situation joined in with a slight grin. "I know of one."

"And I know of a couple." Stone added. "But don't try to get me to say that anywhere else." His grin turned to a grimace and he continued. "Back to the subject of now. These people, whoever they are, are bad folks and worse than that, they're powerful." He too, stood and pushed his fist into the tabletop.

"With control of the information, like we've seen demonstrated recently, these people could do anything. We're in a war, gentlemen, a war against the power of people who claim control over us."

He noticed Daniel had sat back down while he spoke. Stone acknowledged the respect with a nod and a smile. He took a deep breath and sat down himself. The police captain then finished what he had to say.

"It's not the first time people in this country have had to make tough decisions and take action." His tone was now sullen.

Barker looked at the group, one at a time. With the same confidence he started with, he asked one more, compound question.

"So...what are these folks up to, and how do we deal with it?"

"We wait till we hear from Jon," Daniel answered.

Barker's cell phone rang, breaking up the meeting.

~

Murray and the group from Rocksprings were almost half way to Caddo Mills when a call came in from Agent Barker. He needed to pass on the information he had received from Wilfred Scott.

"How far are you from Tyler, Texas," Barker asked the cowboy.

"I don't know..." Murray told him. "An hour, maybe hour and a half."

"Is Spiegel with you?" Barker asked.

"Yeah," his partner answered. "I'm here."

"Do you remember that officer or the pilot that brought us here?"

"What's going on?"

"There's a hit out for that Mossad girl. The whole town could be in the crossfire."

"Let me guess, Homeland Security?" Spiegel suggested.

"Bingo! That's going to be hard to deal with. We need to let them know and I don't want to talk to the wrong person...know what I mean?"

"Roger, that." Spiegel racked his brain. "The pilot's name was Spencer. Yeah...that's it. Try to reach Spencer at the local airport there."

"Will do, Tim." Barker signed off, "Watch your asses."

"Big 'roger' on that."

30

The creature raised its massive head and looked at Ben Shaw with total distain. Transfixed, the young man stared back in wonder more than fear. The beast remained unimpressed. It turned its head away and yawned, making only the slightest of sounds in doing so.

The enclosure was unlike anything Ben had ever heard about, much less seen. The floor for the habitat was elevated two to three feet from the other rooms' level. Ben assumed it was for mechanicals and other wiring. The temperature difference became uncomfortable as he stood there. A large thermostat on the interior wall read out digitally at 59 degrees.

The temperature range was critical for this animal. It was balanced for coolness to mimic its natural home, yet not cold enough to cause the animal discomfort.

"A Siberian Tiger," Ben said aloud and reflexively reached out to touch the glass wrapped steel bars separating him from the beast. Before his hand got to the barrier, the animal leapt to its defense.

Within a blur of movement the big cat now stood before the intruder, her head poised in a downward angle and its front shoulders protruding high above the line of her back. Middle toes of her six-inch wide paws hung through the bars and over the edge.

One large exhale surrounded Ben in the putrid smell of decaying meat. He staggered backward until bumping into the attorney's desk. It was not till then, that he brought his hand down from the position it had been in.

Ben noticed a silver chain hanging around the tiger's neck with a plate that said "Sasha" on it. Regaining his feet and composure, Ben returned the now completely interested gaze from the tiger.

"Sorry, Sasha," he muttered. "No offense... I assure you."

The huge cat appeared as though it was insulted by Ben's words. She lowered her head and turned her entire body with it.

She must be 500 to 600 hundred pounds, he thought watching her turn. It took several steps for her to return to where she had been resting. Once there, Sasha circled the spot three times before lying back down.

Ben tried to study what he had found without further disturbance to its occupant. *The cost of that cage*, it was more a full-blown enclosure, *had to be staggering,* he thought.

The interior had a fake mountainside, lush greenery on one end and a pool with running water. From the look of it, the water was filtered. Blocks of what had to be artificial ice sat around the pool. A barely noticeable glow within them gave away the coils circulating coolant through the blocks.

A door on the right opened to a passage hall near what should have been the exterior windows. Inside, there was access to an automatic freezer system. It kept 60 pound chunks of meat; he had no idea what kind, in separate chambers on a conveyor for freezing and then thawing before being dropped into the cage.

The world's biggest sand box sat in one corner and appeared to be mechanical as well.

Amazing, Ben kept saying to himself. Possession of such an exotic animal was completely illegal, but that did not seem to be an issue for this attorney.

Ben set about studying and documenting the details of the cage. Sasha appeared satisfied that she had issued her warning and returned to ignoring his presence.

~

The dune buggy drifted west as they approached the town of Parker, a normally sleepy suburb of well to do homes. It was risky, but necessary. Casper needed a passage into the urban areas that were now getting thick with buildings. The northbound lanes of highway number 83 were completely abandoned. Few vehicles were going south and those appeared to be looters with stolen goods hanging from every opening.

Jon pointed out a location from Ben's maps. It was just inside the perimeter road near Centennial. The area was an upscale industrial zone with architecture design to obscure such fundamental necessities, but Casper Stallings found the spot. The six-foot diameter pipe stood a foot above the ground and was covered with steel frame webbing.

"That doesn't look promising," the driver said.

"Pretty standard, really," Jon told him while digging into the pockets of the black suit. He pulled out four small blocks of what looked like putty and thin cord. The putty was wrapped around the corners of the gate and the cord strung to connect them.

"We need to back off a bit," Jon warned his friend as he hooked the end of the cord to a box with a tiny dial switch. Looking at Casper, Jon twisted the dial and the gate jumped off the pipe with sparks and smoke, but little noise.

"Can you help me with the cart?"

"Sure," Stallings answered. "Thought anymore about needing some help?"

"Man, you've already done more than anyone could expect. Really...get your tail back home and get word to your brother what I'm doing and where I went in."

Casper looked disappointed. Still, he stuck his hand out. When Jon pulled off his glove and returned the handshake Stallings said, "This has been a hoot."

They lifted and sat the go-cart into the pipe. The wheels sat even more flat than Jon had hoped for. It took a few more minutes to load his stuff and pull the black suit back on. Then he started the whiny engine on the cart and with a wave...he was gone into the dark of the pipe.

Casper Stallings shook his head and climbed back into his dune buggy.

~

After taking numerous pictures and making extensive notes on everything, Ben finally pulled the artificial phone case back and the enclosure sealed itself. The carpet in front of the bookshelves was pulled just a bit more, so he got down on his knees and tried to smooth it out.

With the interesting find behind the bookshelves, he took more care recording the other items lying around the room. Nothing else seemed to approach the tiger in significance, but maybe he could see something through the pictures later.

Ben checked for any disruption or signs of his being there. When satisfied, he stepped through the door and turned to pull it shut. It was then that he realized how long he had been watching and studying the tiger and its lair. The sun was going down. He looked at his watch, which read 7:35 P.M. It would be dark in just over an hour.

~

The aircraft hanger at Tyler Municipal Airport was noisy to begin with. The intercom seemed to screech and echo over the other sounds.

"Spencer...Lt. Walton Spencer, you've got a call...line four," bellowed through the building. The pilot heard the announcement, but it took a minute for him to realize it was for him. Spencer had no family, no girl friend or anybody he would expect to be calling him, especially at work. He grabbed a phone from the workbench and punched four.

"Yeah...this is Walton Spencer."

"Lt.," Barker began. "This is Agent Barker of the NCIS. I believe you gave me and my partner a ride earlier."

"Yeah, oh sure. Everything alright?"

"That's just it...not really."

"Hang on a sec." Spencer moved into an office and away from the main racket. "There...I can hear better. What did you say? Something's wrong?"

"That Mossad agent we brought in is in trouble. You guys need to move her quick... and watch yourselves."

"In trouble? From who?"

"This is where you have to just trust me, man. It's agents from Homeland Security or people they are using. They want to eliminate her."

"Ha. I think I recognize your voice, but this is silly. Do you guys punk everybody for gags or just when you're bored?"

"Spencer...this isn't a joke. You must know who you can trust around there. Move her! Just move her and if I'm wrong it won't matter."

"You are serious, aren't you?" the Lt. asked sullenly.

"Man...more than you can imagine. Stuff is getting weird all around the country. It's like stuff you read about from the revolutionary war."

"Alright, give me a number where I can reach you."

Barker gave one of the bunker's phone numbers. "Get moving, friend."

Spencer half ran and half walked to his car. As he pulled from the airport moving towards town he tried to think of those he knew and what side they might be on. His route passed a two-story VFW Building that by luck was surrounded by vehicles.

Spencer turned around and parked near the front door. The men inside were mainly sixty years or older, but there was a bunch of them. He got the attention of the post commander and asked to speak to the group. Trying to explain something he barely understood himself, Spencer asked for their help.

These men were not hard to convince. They were in attendance to support the case against the "Information Equity Act." Each man knew the news they were getting over the outlets sanctioned by the government was suspect at best, propaganda at worst.

"There's a young lady in our hospital who's in danger," he pleaded.

The men rose and began to go downstairs to the basement. From there they returned with rifles, shotguns and other weapons. The looks in their eyes were serious. Not overly confident or brash, just resolved to do what they could.

Spencer drove away from the building with a convoy of twenty-five trucks, cars and vans behind him. They set up a perimeter around the hospital and inside the front lobby.

The cop who had first met the NCIS agents when they arrived ran up to Spencer challenging what was happening. After a brief explanation, Officer Hillsboro, led Spencer to Nava Golan's room.

31

Sheri Shanahan's helicopter landed in the middle of highway 36. A limo and three vans for escort met the attorney and she was immediately driven north to the main campus of Boulder College of Philosophy.

They passed a practice field for the University that was occupied by men wearing black outfits. Shanahan watched the activity intently as they drove by. The men were in two distinct groups. Trainers appeared to be barking instructions that she could not hear, but knew full well what they were. She had written them.

Her meeting would be with a more select group, a smaller congregation of leadership who rarely planned to gather at one time. This was important. This was the big one. They were finally getting close to their goal.

Shanahan checked the time. She had an hour and a half before her meeting.

Steven Walden paced the pit of the amphitheater where this conclave would occur. All the leadership would be there, except Bogart. His appearance could not be arranged due to his other duties.

Walden too, understood the meaning of this meeting. Much was at stake and to be gained, but only guaranteed to a select few, a count that he was not among. These facts did not bother him at first. But as the prize became more real, so did his ambition. He had worked hard for the cause and risked much. Just compensation by way of title was surely not too much to ask.

At first the vibration in the pipe barely got his attention. But now it had been going on for over an hour and was getting stronger.

The pipe he was in was for storm drainage, not regular sewer piping that was much smaller. There had been no storms recently and the city was empty so the reason for the shaking was a mystery.

Lamar Jakes slowly crawled back to the opening to look out. It was not yet dark, yet all was quiet. No signs of life anywhere. The rumble within the pipe picked-up and he thought he saw a brief flash of light deep inside, but forced himself to laugh that off.

Nonetheless he climbed down and decided to move north above ground. It would be dark soon and he would have to choose whether to go on or not. The train tracks went through Boulder; in fact right by the College he was headed to, so he followed them.

Near the Westminster area, a cluster of abandoned vehicles clogged an intersection. Jakes found a small car with keys in it that he felt could be backed out and used. Some paint was shared with a couple other cars, but he got it free. A quick detour on the sidewalk and he found clear streets heading north.

~

Lt. Marsha Hurst's shift was over. She had not heard from Ben or anyone else throughout the day. Paperwork issues kept her at the precinct longer than normal, but she was finally on her way home.

She parked in the lot for the apartments where she lived and just sat in the car. *Should I call Jon?* she asked herself. What would she tell or ask him. She needed to hear from Ben. Flipping her phone open, she pushed the button for Ben. He answered on the third ring.

~

Ben stepped from the elevator and walked straight toward the parking garage. He moved around the gate guard for the exit and

223

almost stopped. Instincts kept him moving as he walked past the car he noticed much earlier in the day, still sitting there.

Now, one man stood leaning against the truck smoking as he approached. The man looked up at Ben with a disapproving stare and started to pull himself upright.

At that moment, Ben's cell phone rang. He fumbled around other gear he had in his pockets to find the phone. Just barely past the strange car he found his phone and answered.

"Yeah, Marsha. Hi," he said in a voice that carried in the confined space of the garage.

"Anything?" Marsha asked.

"Look...I may have something, not sure yet. Can I call you a bit later?"

That wasn't what she wanted to hear. More waiting. But she had little choice.

"Yeah, Okay," she told him. "Thanks."

~

Jerry Blake sat up from a nap to notice the young man walk by. He also saw his henchman react to the boy and then sit back down against the trunk. Blake opened his door and walked around to the back.

"What was up with the kid?" he asked.

"Aw...nothing. I thought he looked familiar, but I don't think so. He's just some kid talking to his girlfriend on the phone."

"Alright. Is the car still up there?"

"Haven't checked in a while, but it hasn't come out."

"Go see," Blake instructed. "Just to be sure."

~

Ben backed the Jaguar from its spot and slowly moved forward. He drove past the man walking toward him who was busy fumbling for his wallet and didn't really notice him.

The man stopped, mouth wide open and tried to look into the Jaguar, but the tinted glass obscured his view.

Turning the last curve to the exit, Ben had retrieved his wallet. He watched as the gate suddenly flung open to stay. A sign overhead stated the hours were 5:00 A.M. to 8:00 P.M.

What luck, he thought. *Great timing for once.*

He didn't notice the Ford crank up nor the man running behind him. The Jaguar passed by the other car and Ben turned right out onto busy Peachtree Street and headed north looking for access to the interstate.

Having to wait for the third man was just enough delay to put the Missouri trio two blocks behind the Jaguar, but they could still see it. Lady Luck continued in Ben's direction as red lights put him further ahead of the Ford. Casually, he turned left to reach the interstate junction and then back right onto the ramp entering the busy freeway.

The Ford jockeyed back and forth, trying to catch up. It was nearly a quarter mile behind when they got on I-75 north. Again, the Missouri crew darted in and out of lanes, slipping closer with each move.

Ben was unaware of being followed at first, but headlights did keep flashing in his rear view mirror making him look closer. When he finally noticed the car he realized he recognized it.

That's the car from the parking garage, his mind suddenly deciphered.

Ben began to mimic the actions of the Ford chasing him. He wove in and out of the lanes to gain space and move forward. He punched a couple of buttons on the Jag's dashboard and a small screen emerged. It was a rear view camera that focused on the Ford, zoomed in and got a picture of the front plate.

Missouri! He realized at once this wasn't about Washington. *It's the guys Jon was after over there. How the hell did they find me...in Atlanta?*

Ben hit the gas and felt the V-12 raise the entire platform of the vehicle and it leapt forward. He was swerving back and forth now and gaining distance from the other car.

He reached for his phone and tried to call Jon. No answer. The message said the called party was out a range at the moment.

"Damn," Ben muttered out loud. *How do I shake these guys?* he finished the thought in his head.

Interstate 75 North widened by several more lanes about two miles before the interchange at the perimeter, I-285. Ben could see the Ford swing out and speed up in his mirrors. He applied more pressure to the accelerator. The sound of his huge engine sent chill-like vibrations through him as the Jaguar nosed down and pulled away.

It was now getting darker and more difficult to keep an eye on the Ford. When traffic north of the interchange again backed up, he could see the lights straining around other vehicles. His threat was still there, still gaining.

~

A small convoy of late model sedans pulled into Tyler, Texas right at dusk. They seemed to be following GPS directions, which took them the long way around town to the hospital.

Lt. Spencer and two other local officers were inside the building, helping load Nava Golan onto a travel worthy gurney. Her intravenous tubes were connected to a small pumping unit so they could be lowered. Her doctor wasn't pleased with this effort, but when the situation was explained to him, he claimed to understand.

Twelve men in dark suits climbed from the sedans, that had parked illegally right in front of the hospital and moved toward the doors. The men of the VFW, who had spread out all around the building, came together. Fifty-three men, weapons in hand, stood together, blocking the doors when the surprised agents came up the steps.

"What is this?" he agent in-charge asked. "Stand aside, this is government business."

"Don't believe we can do that, mister," an old man near the middle offered back. As he spoke the sound of multiple rifles being cocked and readied overcame the moment.

"This is our town," the old man continued. "We'd like to know what that government's business is."

Then, the lead agent reached into his coat pocket, an action that led to some twenty men from either side of the blockage to aim their weapons at him. He stopped a second and then slowly pulled his ID and badge from the pocket.

"We're from the Homeland Security Department. We have information about a possible terrorist in this hospital," he tried to explain.

The old man spit within an inch of the agent's shoe and leveled his own western style 30-30 rifle. He leaned his wrinkled face toward the agent and glared into the man's eyes.

"Not what I hear," he replied. "That ain't why you're here at all, now is it?"

"Look here," the agent put his credentials away. "I don't know what's going on, but you need to step aside. This is serious."

"Mighty right it is," the old man bowed his back. "It's past serious."

32

Jon had stopped three times already to check his location and for any activity. From the maps he figured he was now on the north side of Denver proper and had not found anything going on. The piping from Coors Field was a private system that connected well past the stadium. Jon rode his cart right under the training exercises without knowing about them.

This time up he heard his phone beep. He'd missed a call.

The phone said it was Ben. *Ben, who was out running his own "Intel" mission without prior approval.* The thought made him grimace and shake his head. Jon climbed out of the manhole far enough to sit and gain a good signal for the phone.

"Yeah Ben," he said when the boy answered. "What's up now?"

"Jon...I'm in trouble." Ben told him while driving at over ninety miles per hour.

"What's the matter?"

"I've got a car following me. They came out of Atlanta on my tail. I can't shake 'em."

"First of all," Jon coached him. "Stay calm...you hear me?"

"Yeah."

"Do you remember your driving training?"

"Yes...I think so." Ben tried to sound assuring.

"Can you do a exit ramp shake off?"

"Where?" Ben thought out loud. "There's no place to do that around here."

"Where are you?"

"Just passed Acworth, going north on seventy-five."

Jon tried to picture the road coming up. He'd driven it thousands of times, it seemed. A spot came to mind.

"Ben," he almost shouted. "Can you make it to the Ga.20 exit?"

"Which one?"

"The Rome exit.... Highway twenty."

Traffic was thinning some, but still heavy. Ben wove his way in and out. A quick glance in his mirror showed the Ford's headlights were matching him.

"I think so," he told Jon.

"Do it there. You'll have to set it up, okay?"

"Yeah.... I remember."

"Alright," Jon went for calming tones again. "That should shake them. Now, should they still be on you when you approach the house...use the deer."

"You finished that?" Ben asked him.

"The button is that new one on your dash."

"Actually..." Ben stalled. "I'm in your car."

"My car?" Jon leaned over in surprise. "Which one?"

"The Jag," Ben admitted.

"Good choice," Jon smiled. "The button is the green one, far left on the dash. Do you see it?"

"Yeah, it's here."

"Just as you pass the house," Jon reminded him. "Now drive."

The men from Homeland Security were escorted back to their cars and watched closely as they drove back out of Tyler, Texas. The leader of the group called in to report the incident and ask for backup.

"No point," the voice said in response. "If they knew to stop you, they've moved her. We don't need a scene down there. Just clear out and let them think they've won."

"Got it," the leader answered. "Where to now."

"I've got an address outside the town of Caddo Mills I need you to check into."

~

Professor Walden met Sheri Shanahan just outside the amphitheater. He knew a VIP would be among the guests, but did not know who she was.

"Ms. Shanahan," he said with an outstretched hand. "Welcome to our seminar."

"Thank you, Mithras," she replied with a nasty, self-important smile. "You have served us well, that shall be rewarded."

Walden was stunned. He stepped back and looked at her awestruck. "Bogart?" he asked with due reverence.

"Heavens no," she laughed. "Bogart works for me."

Her host managed to remember what the evening was for. "Please...come in. Where would you like to sit?"

"Anywhere on the side. Just make it down front."

"Yes, ma-am." Walden bowed as he motioned her to enter. "Will you be speaking tonight?"

"No," she stated abruptly. "And don't refer to me or point me out in any way. Do you understand?"

"Certainly." His voice showed the confusion her last command caused, but she offered no explanation.

"How are things at the stadium?"

"Going quiet well, ma-am. I just left there a little while ago."

"Stop calling me that."

"What?"

"Ma-am...I'm not anybody's Ma-am. Is that clear?"

"Yes...Ms. Shanahan."

"How many do we have in total?" she asked him.

"There are twenty-four here and 150 at the stadium."

"Do they all check out?"

"Absolutely," Walden confirmed. "Over half those at the stadium came in during the diversion."

Shanahan looked like she didn't know what he meant.

"The shootout at the border...all those cops we killed."

"Aw...yes. The lid stayed on that nicely. Accomplished two things with one event on that one."

"Yes Ma...I mean, Ms. Shanahan. The news has the public so confused, they don't know who or what to believe anymore. Better yet...most don't even care. The programming on the networks has them glued to their TVs. Reality this and that. It's grown so since the teens, it's hard to believe. The shows are twenty-four-seven now."

"The plan requires we go very fast and like clockwork, don't you agree, Professor?"

"I do." Walden smiled wide, "and get a turn for this country that has taken too long to happen."

"Yes," she agreed halfheartedly. "Wonderful for the country."

"It's about time," he said. "Let me go bring them in."

"Please...I can't wait to see my soldiers."

~

Lamar Jakes drove to within three blocks of the campus amphitheater. He parked the small car and checked his gun. The light ahead told him that was where he should go. Slinking through the trees and shrubs, he got to the edge of the courtyard surrounding the building. He caught a figure moving out of the corner of his eye and crouched low.

It appeared to be a man, dressed all in black. He too was almost low crawling on his approach.

Who the heck is this, Jakes thought. He continued to watch as the man slipped into a side door and disappeared. Lamar moved to follow the shadowy figure, his curiosity having gotten the better of him.

~

Jon let himself in a side door after hearing voices inside the building, many voices. The cart had carried him to within a half mile of this place. He assumed he was on a college campus. It had all the trappings, just too few signs.

The interior hall led to a ladder attached to the brick wall. It went to the lighting baffle catwalk over an open theater style classroom. Jon quietly climbed to the catwalk and watched as two groups of men filed into the room. He noticed one man in a plaid sport coat standing near the front. A woman, dressed to the nines, sat alone to one side.

He could not see her face from where he was so he checked the walkway for stability. It was narrow, but steady. The pathway was covered in cords and cables so the steps were taken with care. On the far side he settled down. The noise of the men entering had ceased so he had to be quiet. Sliding out his phone camera, Jon set it for maximum zoom and snapped pictures of the primaries down front and then the gallery itself. The man in the sport coat stood, raised his arms and began to speak.

Jon touched the record button on the phone and listened to the meeting.

33

Ben drove through the Cartersville area of I-75 at speeds over 110 miles per hour. The big car held the road like there was glue on its tires. His pursuers began to fall behind, but they were still there.

Punching the GPS system to locate the Ga. Highway 20 exit, he knew he needed to start reeling in his plan. The exit was only a few miles to the north.

He would need some other traffic around them, and he had to let the Ford get closer. That was the part he didn't care for, but the plan wouldn't work otherwise. A group of vehicles appeared to be about five miles ahead when the road straightened enough to see the taillights. At the rate he was going he would overtake them too quickly.

Ben let off the Jag's gas pedal and slowed to ninety miles per hours. It was only a guess, but he figured the cars up front were likely doing seventy or eighty, tops. His mirror showed the headlights of the Ford getting larger. He lectured himself to stay calm.

At the lower speed, Ben opened the center console to see if Jon had a Glock in there. *Nothing,* he sighed. *Jon keeps his gun on his person.*

The headlights were really getting closer now, ten or twelve cars lengths back and closing. The GPS showed they were about three miles from the exit. He let the Ford get a bit closer and than punched the gas again. The Jaguar launched forward as though it been at a standstill.

The group of other traffic was still together, just ahead. There was a large, slow curve to the right just before the exit. The surface changed from concrete to blacktop on the exit that dipped sharply down hill right after you left the highway. The exit was also abnormally long, almost a quarter-mile to the stoplight at the bottom. It was the perfect spot to try the ruse.

The Ford was now right on Ben's rear bumper as they entered the long curve. Ben went to the far inside, left lane as he passed the first of the slower traffic. With the Ford on his butt, Ben looked for a pair of cars with the gap he needed.

There they were, he screamed inside his head. Two cars about a length and a half apart were running in the right hand lane.

Ben slowed again, just a bit. He let the Ford almost touch his bumper. Then as the curve straightened, Ben hit the accelerator and pulled hard on the wheel. The Jag whipped across the expressway, in front of an approaching tractor-trailer and between the cars in the right lane. Steering back to forward and foot off the gas, Ben felt the Jaguar grab the asphalt of the exit. He lightly tapped the brakes to slow his speed down the exit ramp.

The Ford braked as hard as he could. Smoke rose from its tires, but they still flew past the exit, stuck in the inside lane. The Jaguar had disappeared down the ramp and the men from Missouri had no choice but to go forward. They had no idea whether their prey would now take another route or what?

"Slow it down a little," Blake told the driver. "Somebody might call that little trick he pulled into the cops. We don't need to draw attention to ourselves if they come looking."

Blake ordered that they head for the big house in Dalton and wait there.

~

Lucy touched down at Caddo Mills and was met by Agent Barker running up from the hanger.

"Just heard from Scott again," He started. "Somebody in Homeland Security knows about this place. They're likely on the way now."

Murray didn't hesitate. He tossed a set of keys from his pocket to Barker and pointed to his old pick-up parked next to the house.

"Would you drive that thing out to the highway and turn right. About five miles up I've got a place I can hide Lucy."

Spiegel was helping Harel and Grimes from the helicopter. He looked at Barker and asked. "Did they get to the Israeli at the hospital?"

Harel's attention turned to Barker with that question.

"No," the NCIS agent smiled. "Spencer got her out of there. It's a cute story, I'll tell you later."

"How is she?" her boss asked.

"No real report on that, sir. I don't think she's regained consciousness."

They moved away from the fling-wing and Murray lifted her up and away.

"I need to go I guess." Barker began to run toward the truck. "Daniel will let you guys in."

Murray climbed higher than necessary just to look around. At 4000 feet he could see no headlights coming from any direction.

Doesn't mean they ain't coming, he told himself.

~

Lamar Jakes had used the same entry point as Jon. He looked around, but could not locate him once inside. Being familiar with the building, he worked his way to the stairs going to the balcony level. The lights remained off there, so he felt safe in moving forward.

In a crouched position, Jakes low-crawled to the front row of the balcony and carefully looked over the edge. The two sets of men in their black suits had just walked in and taken seats. Professor Walden was standing and preparing to address them.

Jakes blood boiled and he began to shiver as he stared down at the man who had tried to have him killed, for nothing. Reaching into his pocket, he pulled the revolver and checked the cylinder for cartridges. Then barely reaching over the railing, he aimed at his nemesis...and pulled the trigger.

The click was hardly audible, even to Jakes and little else happened other than that. He pulled the gun down to look at it closer. The futility of that set in quick, what he knew about guns he had already used up.

He leaned over the rail and tried again. Still nothing.

Sitting behind the short barrier wall, Lamar Jakes drew his knees up onto a near fetal position. He stared now at the gun that had failed him. *All this ...for nothing,* kept repeating in his mind.

~

An agent stuck his head inside the boss's door. Normally NCIS Director Wilfred Scott would have it closed, but he'd gotten caught up in his plans.

"Director, sir," the agent spoke without knocking. "Metro police pulled a floater out of the Potomac."

"Yeah," Scott replied, not really thinking. "What does that have to do with...." The director leaned back and turned toward the door, a sullen look on his face, "no...don't tell me."

"It's Homeland Security Secretary Ferris, sir."

Scott put his elbows on his desk and cupped his face in his hands.

"Was he a friend of yours, sir?" the agent asked.

"I knew him a long time...or thought I did," Scott answered. "Signs of foul play?"

"Not according to the newspapers. They're saying he'd been depressed the last few months. Feeling slighted and lacking support from the current administration."

"Newspapers?" Scott stood in surprise. "When did they find him?"

"About two hours ago, sir."

"Two hours... and it's in what papers already?" the director's voice elevated.

"The local rag and the one in New York, sir."

"They're getting down right sloppy, aren't they?" Scott smirked through his anger.

"Yes, sir. Looks like it. That's kind of quick to be on the street with a story."

"Well..." The director paused for a second. "There's no one to point that out anymore. They pretty well do and say what they want lately."

"There is some good news though, sir," the agent continued.

Scott looked at him without speaking. The agent knew to go on.

"They got that girl, the Mossad agent, out of the hospital. She's okay and into hiding."

"That is good news." Scott stood back up. "How did they do it?"

"Locals...a bunch of old vets with hunting rifles held off twelve to fifteen HS operatives."

"You're kidding," the director beamed. "They stood up to them?"

"Ran them off, actually."

237

"Where's the girl?"

"They have her in safe keeping, they say...till they know who they can trust."

"Where are the rest of team 'B'?" Scott asked him.

The agent looked back out through the door. "They should be getting back any minute."

"Have them all up here soon as they do."

"Yes, sir," the agent snapped back and pulled the door closed behind him.

34

The address by Professor Steven Walden had really just begun. He had welcomed the members of the media, both print and broadcast, who were in attendance. Not by name, but in generalities. Then he recognized, again anonymously, celebrities from Hollywood and New York, a few district court judges and some former members of congress who had hopes to be so again.

They were all dressed in the same unisex black pants and loose fitting jacket, which made it difficult to determine men from women, much less anything else.

That was likely the point of the attire, Jon thought. *Even if they happen to be photographed, identities would be impossible.*

It was about this point that Jon's attention was drawn to a sudden movement below him. He watched the area closely and it occurred again. Someone leaned over the balcony wall with what looked like a gun. But nothing else happened.

Not needing any amateur interference, Jon quickly looked for a route to that level. He climbed off the catwalk and tiptoed along a narrow ledge on the circular back wall. It was a heavy molding strip and it ended near some two-inch roping. The cord hung down to the rear of the balcony level. Jon slowly and quietly lowered himself by the rope till he was at the back of the darkened seating area.

The figure was still there, down front where he had been, curled into a sitting ball and gently rocking himself. Jon stayed low and crawled down the center aisle. From there he slid himself with a kick, landing right next to the figure. He grabbed the man by the back of his neck with the right hand and covered the figure's mouth with his left.

Then pulling the balled up man's face right up to his own, Jon released the back of his neck and placed that hand's forefinger straight up, over his own lips.

The unnerved figure was obviously a young man, not much older than Ben. But he presented a problem. He couldn't be allowed to make a scene and be noticed.

Lamar Jakes nodded that he understood the "quiet" signal the man crouching over him was giving. The man slowly removed his hand from the kid's mouth and whispered,

"Can you stay quiet?"

Jakes nodded again.

Jon took his recorder out and began listening again to the speech being given below. What he had missed appeared to be just more acknowledgements of those in attendance, and Walden was getting into the meat of his presentation.

Setting the recorder on the ledge, Jon sat down next to the young man and again looked toward him. The frightened face stayed silent, but looked like it could erupt at any second. Jon again put his finger to his own lips, touching the tip of his nose.

Lamar Jakes again nodded that he understood.

Murray had landed Lucy beyond a sand ridge, but she would still show, especially in daylight. He got out and checked the position his Bell 407 was in. Satisfied, he walked over the ridge and when he was clear, pushed a button on a remote he held.

Two small rockets fired up and over Lucy at slight angles away from each other. They each carried one corner of a camouflage netting that draped over the helicopter gently. Barker drove up in the truck as this was happening and smiled in approval.

"Is there anything you haven't planned for?" the agent asked him grinning.

"Burn me once," Murray said seriously. "Shame on you."

"So you've had trouble here before," Barker figured.

Murray climbed in on the passenger side of the pick-up.

"You could say that," he answered. "Not gonna be that easy next time."

They pulled the truck next to the new house and walked to the hanger.

"Have you guys heard from Jon?" Murray asked.

"Nope, nothing."

"How about Ben?"

"The kid? Nope, not a word from him either. We got HS agents, we believe, on the way here. But that's about it."

"HS?" Murray had to think a minute.

"Homeland Security," Barker said in disgust. "Never trust the new kids."

~

Ben sat through the red light at the bottom of the exit. The thought that came over him there swept away everything else. The fear...the excitement...even the adrenaline rush from the chase simply smoothed out. *I'm fine. I'm in control of this.*

He lifted his right hand from the steering wheel and studied it. There was no shaking.

The sound of the horn behind him drew his eyes to a rearview mirror. Headlights in the mirror glared and the horn blasted again. Ben then looked forward to the traffic signal. The light was now green. He felt the smile that stretched across his face and his hand again grasped the wheel. Easing down on the accelerator, the Jaguar lurched forward like a big cat. He briefly thought of Sasha.

Jon had often told him, "You never know how you'll react to a situation till you're in it." As the powerful vehicle crossed the intersection and roared up the entrance ramp, Ben realized he now understood what Jon meant.

Courage isn't the lack of fear. It's how you deal with it. But that thought was quickly followed by the warning his mentor had also offered. *"Don't count on its consistency."*

The traffic on I-75 north was still light. Ben looked ahead and to the southbound lanes for the Ford. After several miles and no contact with his pursuers, another thought came to him.

They didn't find me in Atlanta...they followed me from Dalton to Atlanta. They know about the house.

"Okay," he heard himself say out loud. *Now what?*

His thoughts turned to a plan to get home without falling into their trap. They would be waiting for him.

Jon sat, crouched down with his back against the short wall and looked over at the young man next to him. He didn't appear frightened. Jon sensed more frustration and pure anger from him.

In his lap, the young man held the gun that had failed him. Jon reached over and gently took it. It was an old, in fact very old, Targus model 94, .22caliber revolver. The hammer was cocked halfway back, which is the "safety" position.

Leaning over to the youth's ear, Jon whispered, "You don't know too much about guns, huh?"

Jakes looked back at the man dressed all in black rubber with a stare of complete indignation. Jon pulled the hammer back to full and whispered again.

"You had it on safety."

Lamar Jakes face went flush with color. Not embarrassment, but livid anger.

Jon feared the young man might speak out in his rage so he again raised his finger to the tip of his nose. Jakes took a shallow breath and seemed to relax.

Jon repositioned the gun's hammer to "safety" and set it down by his side and opposite from the kid who had tried to use it. Then leaning back against the wall, Jon attempted to listen to the address being given below. It sounded like the introductions were about over.

"Our dreams of a just and fair government are nearing fulfillment," the voice stated with loud, cheerful pride. "It has been one step forward and then two in reverse for some time, but through your efforts... the people now hear what they need to hear. Not that, which only confuses them."

The crowd erupted in brief applause.

"I know you say the courts will soon take away our rightful advantage. Once again allowing those naysayer's to pollute the airwaves and cable with lies and petitions paid for by the greedy, opulent rich." He waited for another applause that didn't happen.

"The position of the Court is thought to be secure by those who would undo our work yet again." Mithras then spun on his heel and walked to the opposite side of the arena. His reference was to the repeal of the Health Care takeover after the country stood up against it.

"But as you have witnessed here...in this town, now empty save for us, our troopers openly train for their missions in the baseball stadium. Our power is strong."

He looked to the ground as though his next words were written there.

"This power will change the course of events leading to this October and the convening of the Court. Our law shall not fall or fail. The control of information will continue to be ours. The hateful, divisive rhetoric that served only to separate us from those who had not yet grasped the enlightened message is now silent. That venomous flow of lies against how we all must live together in this world shall not return. The law now in place, which protects our message from those detractors, will not fall."

Jon frowned at the young man sitting beside him.

"What's he talking about?" he asked in another whisper.

Jakes tilted forward and to Jon's ear. "The Information Equity Act."

"But that's going down in flames, isn't it?" Jon peeked over the wall to make sure they weren't being heard. "Seems like every state has sued against it."

"They've got some big plan in the works. I don't know exactly what," Jakes told him. "How are we going to get out of here?"

"Patience," Jon assured him. "I want to find out what they're up to first."

Professor Walden continued his presentation.

"The actions that are currently in the works... will have a profound impact on how this nation thinks and acts for decades to come. Your parts of this, your duties are not yet over. We asked that you continue to keep the faith and protect our movement from those who might damage it." He walked again from one side to the other.

"Those voices who promised the people self-control are now silent. Their lack of understanding, of how the people must be led to the proper way of thinking, has finally been corralled."

This applause line hit its mark and the crowd erupted.

"And...that line of thinking shall stay off the public airwaves." He added through the cheers and many who stood to raise their arms in the air. Walden paused to let the adoration wind down on its own. He looked toward the floor and lifted his right arm; fist closed in a sign of solidarity. Many in the crowd quietly joined him.

Having peeked again, Jon sat back with a puzzled look and whispered yet again,

"Who are these people?"

"Media types...Hollywood celebrities...the usual suspects, like me," Jakes answered, staring straight ahead.

"You?" Jon grinned. "You're part of this? That's hard to believe." He raised the gun up for Jakes to see.

The young man mumbled softly, "I was a believer...damn near became a martyr for the cause. Against my will."

There was no response to that from Jon. He studied the sullen expression on the kid's face and then leaned back against the wall.

Details can come later, he thought.

The professor had gone over the laundry lists of complaints they had about the information stream the IEA had cut off. He called it "lies," "distortions," and threw in a few racial accusations for good measure. Then he seemed to calm down dramatically and changed his tone from lecture to appeal.

"The points we hope you shall echo will be obvious to you." He turned his head like a lighthouse, staring out at the crowd as individuals. "The truth, as you know it, may be stretched from time to time, but that is for the common good. Some facts cause only division and we have no time or patience for division. You will know what to do and what to say, just as you have all along."

Mithras moved to the center of the audience and reached out with both arms.

"You, my friends have brought us all great distances. The work that comes will be messy. Be strong and of good faith. Know that what you see happening is for the best. The final efforts shall take place soon and give new meaning to our time of celebration."

Jakes turned to Jon, "The Fourth of July is in three weeks."

"That quick?" Jon questioned.

"That day." The young man seemed positive.

Jon peeked over another time. "Who's the woman sitting down there by herself?" he asked.

"I have no idea...I didn't notice her."

"Must be somebody special." Jon slumped back down. "Not saying a word or even acting like she's into what's going on."

"My colleagues," Walden started up again. "Within the hour I shall travel across town to view the training of our stalwarts. Those recruited and brought in for these very important jobs. This too is an example of what we can accomplish with misdirection and subterfuge. Those we brought in came through undetected. In mass numbers while attention was drawn to the eastern side of the Texas border. Your accounting of," he paused to emphasize what came next. "And just as important, if not more so...the omission of certain details, has allowed for the acquisition of our troops."

The assembled rose to give themselves a big hand over that statement. All except the woman who sat in solitude. Walden carefully glanced in her direction and was relieved to see that she was, at least, smiling.

"Truth...is what you make of it." Mithras smiled broadly and yelled over the applause, "and how you use it."

Again, they roared with approval.

"Troops? Is that what he means by 'others in a baseball stadium'?" Jon whispered.

"Coors' Field," Jakes answered with blunt frankness.

"How do you know that?"

"I kinda was there the other night. They wanted to use my body parts to decorate the place and make a statement."

Jon didn't ask for a follow-up right then. He looked at the sour faced young man and figured the explanation would be best served up... in other than whispers.

The remainder of Walden's talk was platitudes and individual mention for some who had gone beyond what they had been asked. The crowd remained standing and when directed to, found their way out through the rear.

Walden stood, front and center until the last had walked up the aisle. Sheri Shanahan was still seated. The professor stepped towards her and she stood, face down at first, and then looked up to stare him in the face.

"I understand now how you do so well in recruiting," she offered smugly. "Bogart did well to choose you, Mithras."

Walden silently bowed...and with an arm, pointed the way to the side exit. Shanahan turned and walked out. The smiling Mithras followed close behind.

As it ended, Jon retrieved his recorder-phone and noticed Jakes attempting to get up. He reached out, held him down and again motioned for him to remain quiet.

They would let the others leave the building before trying to escape themselves.

"It's the only way," Jon cautioned him. "Just sit tight."

35

Lt. Walton Spencer and several members of the Tyler, Texas VFW had Nava Golan hidden in the home of a VFW member's widow. Kate Griffin wasn't even on the books. If they came to search member's homes, she wouldn't be listed. Her husband had been dead for seven years.

"Don loved the James Bond movies," she grinned. "He would have gotten a real kick out of this."

"Thanks, Sara." Spencer hugged her. "Charles is just across the street if you need him, okay?"

"We'll be fine. Is this all the medicine she's taking?"

"Doc says that's it. She should sleep most of the time."

"Alright...now git. I do want you to tell me what this was all about, when you find out yourself," she hollered after him.

"I'll do that..." Walton yelled back. "Maybe we'll both enjoy the story."

He knew this wasn't the end of it. They would be back, and in force next time. He again dialed the number Agent Barker had called from.

"I'm getting out of here for a few days," he told Barker. "If they haul me in, who knows, I might tell 'em everything I know."

"Come on, man. You're tougher than that. Hell... I can judge people."

"Yeah...maybe so. But there's too much riding on this. If they figure out how much you guys already know about them...they could change everything up." The Texas lawman knew what he said made sense. "Right now, they just think a bunch of old rednecks got their backs up over government interference."

"You're sure Golan is safe?" Barker insisted.

"They don't come any tougher or meaner than Kate Griffin. And there's no reason they should suspect her."

"Where are you going?"

"Ha! That I don't know yet. I'll figure it out."

Phil Stone was listening in. He shook Barker's shoulder and spoke up.

"Tell him to go the Shreveport. Park his bird at the police lot. I'll fix it for him. He can stay in the dorm there with the squad."

"Did you get that?" Barker followed.

"Yeah...thanks man." Spencer didn't know what else to say. "I appreciate that."

~

Ben Shaw got off the expressway an exit earlier than usual. He drove into downtown Dalton to the old warehouse district. Jon normally would leave at least one vehicle there and Ben thought a swap would be in order. Then he could drive right past the bad guys and they'd never be aware.

The only problem was... there was no other car in the warehouse. His main plan having evaporated, Ben strained to come up with another. That new button on the Jaguar's dash caught his eye, the one Jon told him about.

That could work if they were the right distance behind me, he convinced himself.

The Jag rolled back onto the streets and Ben headed to the far end of the old highway, Highway 71. He figured they would be expecting him to come as he had left, and then try to cut him off before he got to the house. What he needed to have happen was another chase. The entrance to the old gas station was too close to just go in through there. They might notice and then that would be busted.

As he turned up the road and past the gas station, Ben floored the Jaguar. It's pipes roared and she ripped past the house and the Ford, which was waiting near the driveway. Ben led them on a chase back out to the expressway overpass and turned around.

Now he was in position. The Jag led the way back toward the house with the Ford about four car lengths back. Ben cornered onto Highway 71 with a fishtail slide and again screamed past the house. He reached over and pushed the green button.

The Ford came around the corner and picked up speed. Then it just appeared out of nowhere. A full-grown, twelve point buck stood in the middle of the road, right at the driveway to the house. The driver of the Ford stood on his brakes and steered hard left. The Ford slipped loose at its rear wheels, spinning out of control. First bouncing off the hard rocks to the left it then twisted off the pavement into the heavy brush on the other side.

The hologram generated buck vanished as quickly as it had appeared. No one in the Ford noticed the Jaguar make it's left turn into the gas station and disappear. The driver struggled to bring it under control. As the Ford came back on the pavement, the right rear wheel collapsed and the back quarter panel dug into the dirt. The Missouri car rolled over several times.

When it had ceased rolling and came to a complete stop, two of the passengers were still inside the smoldering vehicle.

~

Some ten minutes after the speaker and the woman had left, Jon carefully led the young man out of the amphitheater. He was surprised to find a complete lack of security. The over-confidence of this group was amazing.

In the light of the street lamp overhead, Lamar Jakes got his first good look at the man with him. He knew the guy was in some black colored outfit, but this thing blew his mind.

"What are you, anyway?" he asked Jon. "A Seal or something?"

Jon smiled. He watched as Jakes reached out to touch an arm of the suit.

"Something like that, I guess," he answered.

"Who are you?" was the youth's next question.

Jon had about gotten used to this one, especially when it came from strangers.

"Call me Silas."

"You don't look like a Silas."

Jon just grinned. Before he could think of what to say to that, his phone buzzed and shook in his pocket. The vibration was due to the "quiet" mode. Caller ID showed it was Ben. Jon was relieved, big time.

"Hey," he answered. "Tell me you got home okay."

"Well, yeah," Ben started. "I'm fine. The car is great, man. I mean, I love that thing."

"What is the other side of this story?" Jon could tell there was more.

"The deer did its job, but I think the guys chasing me were going a bit faster than you anticipated for its use."

"Wrecked 'em, huh?"

"Oh, man. Did it ever."

"Did you call Gil?" Jon asked. Gil was Sgt. Gil Gartner of the Dalton police.

"He's here now. There's a bunch of them outside. It's a mess Jon."

"Could you ID who they were?"

"Yeah," Ben told him while he grabbed his notes. "The car is registered to a Gerald Blake of Missouri. The other two worked with him."

"Gerald or maybe Jerry Blake?"

"Sure, that's a nickname they use a lot."

"I don't even have to look him up. He works for Everett. I remember the name."

"Well...you won't get anything out of him. From Gil's description, Blake got thrown out ahead of the car as it rolled. Then the thing caught up with him. He ain't with us any more."

"The others?"

"Unconscious is all I know. They took them to Hamilton Medical."

"Who all knows they were chasing you?"

"Just Gil."

"Good." Jon was pleased with that. "Let George know what's going on."

"Will do... Hey...I've got something more you need to know. Two things really."

Jon looked over at the young man standing there with him. Lamar Jakes was obviously taking it all in, but so far had not interrupted.

"Go ahead."

"When I got in the house I had an urgent message from Dr. Webster."

"Who?"

"Dr. Webster...from Fernbank. Anyway, he said he located the nuclear stuff from the Texas incident. The stuff that was loaded up on the truck and then foamed."

"I heard something about it, yeah." Jon was wondering where this was headed.

"Well, debris of that nature has a fingerprint. A reading the gamma rays and isotopes give off. It's not perfectly unique, but readings are hardly ever exactly the same."

"Okay," Jon wanted the bottom line of this. "What of it?"

"He says it's a perfect match to the debris found at Coors' Field in Denver."

Jon looked again at Jakes who could hear most of what was being said. The man's eyebrows had slung down over his eyes, but he shrugged his shoulders.

"So," Jon asked. "It's from similar stuff."

"No, that's just it. It is the same exact stuff. Somebody broke into the foamed truck and took some of it to use in Denver. They wanted it to look like it could have been a bomb."

Then Ben started with the tale of Marsha's phone call. He explained all that had transpired and her call to him about it.

"That's why I went to Atlanta, Jon."

"Is she alright?"

"Yes. I've talked with her since I got in. So...what have you been doing?"

Jon smiled and slowly shook his head.

"I'm standing here with a young man who knows about Coors' Field. We haven't really had a chance to talk about it yet."

"Where are you?"

"Not going to say right now, just in case. Let Marsha, Murray and those guys know I'm good, okay?"

"Sure. You know they could have traced you by now if they're listening."

"Yeah...but we're gone from here...right now." And he closed the phone.

Jon looked at Jakes and said, "Looks like you're coming with me for now. You got a problem with that?"

253

"Not really... Jon," Jakes grinned. "I told you, you didn't look like a Silas."

Jon tried to lead him in one direction. Jakes pulled back and pointed,

"I've got a car over here."

The go-cart was in a drain pipe about two hundred yards away, but a car made more sense. Besides, he could get the information from this kid on the way.

"Alright, lead the way," Jon told him. "I want to hear what happened to you anyway. Who that guy is and why you wanted to kill him."

"Fine, I'll tell you the whole story, but... he's still mine, okay?"

Jon looked at him like he didn't understand.

"Walden, Mithras... or whatever he calls himself," Jakes declared. "He's mine."

"We'll see," Jon assured him. "I like a man with strong motivation. Can't wait to hear about it."

The two slipped around the lights toward the small car. The trip to Coors' Field would help with some major pieces to the puzzle as Jon began to put it all together.

36

Sheriff Horace Wilbury had spent the last couple of days with mixed emotions. His niece's husband, Ranger Neal Garcia was doing better. So he had been told.

Wilbury had not yet made the trip to go see him or his niece. Garcia had been stabilized in Junction, Texas and moved to Abilene for better hospital facilities. His care was the best one could ask for, both inside the hospital and out.

Abilene Regional was guarded 24/7 by the Texas Rangers. Some sixty members strong rotated watch duties using their off-time hours. There were no less than twenty-five on site at any given time. Agents from the various federal departments were being turned away. Not knowing whom they could trust, the Rangers trusted no one.

Sheriff Wilbury was also on the "guarded list." Much to his feigned displeasure, there were six Rangers alternating shifts in and around Brownwood. Wilbury pretended to complain to Irv Stallings, his deputy.

"If the Rangers want you protected," Irv simply smiled and lamented. "You get protected. Relax boss, it's an honor bestowed to your niece."

"So...your idea is... we just sit here?" the sheriff argued, but really didn't mean it. He knew his place and what they should do, as well as Stallings.

"Yes sir." The deputy turned to go outside. From the door he paused and looked back at his boss. "Sheriff, I don't know just what it will be...but they're gonna need us at some point. If we ain't here when that happens... we're no good to anybody."

Wilbury half grunted and slouched back into his chair. He pulled the huge hat off his head and laid it on the desk. Then with a look that couldn't be distinguished between a grimace and a smile, he shouted back.

"Oh yeah...really? That's what you think, huh?" Leaning forward now, arms stretched across the desk he exhaled loudly and continued. "Guess that's why I keep you around."

"Could be, sir." Stallings grinned and tipped his hat. Then went on outside to check with one of the Rangers about any news.

~

The ride from the campus in Boulder to central Denver took close to thirty minutes. The distance wasn't that far. Jakes had driven a "round about" course to be sure they weren't seen.

Jon forwarded the pictures he had taken on to Ben and listened to Jakes. The story the young man told was convincing and credible. Jon thought of the small Koran Murray and the deputy had found near the SUV wreck.

"So, were you converting?" he asked Jakes.

"To what?"

"To Muslim."

"You mean Islam," Jakes corrected him.

"Ok, whatever...did this Mithras guy give you a bible...I mean a Koran?"

"Yeah, everybody got one. They took conversion as a good sign they could trust you. A westerner going over to the faith was a big step. Meant a lot to Mithras."

"Is he Muslim...or Islam?" Jon tried to clarify.

"I don't know." Jake had never thought about that before. "Didn't seem to matter what he was. He was the leader...that's all that mattered, really."

"So, you let them think you were converting, huh?"

"Yeah, I guess so. I never was too religious anyway. Suppose I did let them think what they wanted." Jakes slowed down and turned into an empty lot. He pointed straight ahead to a large stream of lights glowing skyward from a structure.

"We're here," he said then put the car in park and shut it off.

They walked the three blocks to the main parking lot that surrounded the stadium. Jon picked a padlock on the gate and they were in. Semi-circular ramps led from one level to the next. No guards were apparent, anywhere.

They crisscrossed back and forth till Jon could hear voices. The two ducked into an alcove as the voices passed and then walked further down before ascending any higher.

Along the third base line were writer's boxes. Another quick lock pick and they were in. Jakes pulled back the large glass window that slid the width of the enclosure and they could now hear what was happening down on the field.

The assembled masses were in what looked like five distinct groups. There were labels on tall sticks, like you'd see at the Olympics, but they were too far to read.

"Come with me." Jakes waved at Jon as he went back out onto the concourse. Several yards down was a door marked "Concessions."

"Can you get in here?" he asked Jon.

"I believe so," the man answered and within less than a minute the door was open. "OK, what are we looking for in here?"

"They sell those little binoculars for the games. I'm hoping there's some in here."

Back in the press box with their plastic spyglasses, they could now read the signs labeling the groups.

There was "Cleveland," "St. Louis," "Tampa," "Pendleton," and "Wichita."

Jakes looked at Jon and asked, "Any of that mean anything to you?"

Jon shook his head. "Not yet it doesn't. But it will, I promise you that." He tried to make a picture, but they were so far away from the field he doubted anything would make any sense. As he lined up another shot, the phone again vibrated forcefully.

"Yeah?" he answered.

"Jon." Ben sounded excited. "Those pictures you sent. That woman sitting there by herself...I know who she is."

"Great, found out that fast. Good work, Ben."

"Not the way it happened," Ben told him. "Remember I told you I went to check out a lawyer's office in Atlanta?"

"Right."

"It's her."

"Who?"

"The lady in your pictures is the attorney I went to check out. Somebody called Marsha from her office."

"Are you sure?"

"Positive. There were pictures of her all over the place in there," Ben nearly shouted.

All Jon could reason from it at the moment was that Marsha was in danger. Ben had figured that much out as well.

"This lady is weird, Jon," he cautioned. "She has the strangest pet...you won't believe it."

"Call Marsha and warn her and let Murray...no, I'll call Murray now. This thing is getting stranger and I found out they have some big finale set for July Fourth."

"What should I tell Marsha you want her to do?"

"Tell her to go to a land line and text me the last four digits."

"Got it," Ben responded and hung up.

Jon knew the area code and prefix for the phones in Marsha's part of town. With those last four numbers he could call on a number she could then walk away from. Trace or no trace.

He immediately called Murray back at Caddo Mills and brought them up to date. The attorney from Atlanta, the cities listed below on the field and the big training camp going on. Murray explained about the Secretary of Homeland Security and the mystery around his death. He told him that Grimes and Barker's boss suggested they not trust anyone from DHS till further notice.

"Sounds reasonable to me," Jon agreed. "I'll tell Marsha the same. I'm hoping to be home day after tomorrow, have to stop along the way and take care of something."

"Ok, partner. You stay safe."

"Will do. Oh...if that list of cities makes sense to anyone there...how about letting me know."

"Yep...oh man! Speak of the devil," Murray muttered suddenly.

"What's going on?" Jon asked.

"We were warned about a visit from that agency."

"They're there, huh?"

"Oh yeah...about twelve vehicles worth," Murray said while he and the others watched the monitors. "Problem for them is...we're all underground and I hid Lucy. We look like nobody's home."

"Good. And good luck! I'll let you go." Jon didn't want any traceable signal being emitted from the safe room in Caddo Mills, so he hung up. Jon rubbed his chin and looked at Lamar Jakes.

"This is starting to look like a war," he told him.

The young man said nothing.

37

The phone call between Jon and Marsha was short. Still, she understood everything. There was no time for sweetness and light in this conversation. The situation was getting way out of hand.

"Where are you?" she tried.

"Can't say just now. I'm good though," he replied and she let it go. They covered the facts and what needed to be done...and then were through with the call.

Within twenty minutes of her talk with Jon, Marsha received a radio message from the precinct. It was the duty sergeant and he was not speaking in his normally loud tone.

"Listen Hurst, stay clear for awhile," he uttered softly. "The captain has guests who are looking for you."

"Can I call you on a land line?" she asked.

The sergeant gave her a secure number and waited.

"What's going on?" she started with.

"It's DHS, about three of them and six more with ICE jackets on."

"Immigration?" Marsha was stunned.

"Look here," the sergeant got serious. "I heard the captain tell them you were transporting a prisoner to Winston-Salem. He doesn't want you coming near here... got it?"

Marsha realized what she was hearing. Her eyes widened and her posture slacked.

"Thank him for me," she told the sergeant. "I'll be in touch."

Marsha immediately called Ben. She needed transportation out of the area. After a couple minutes discussing the situation, Ben asked her if she could get to the Greenville- Spartanburg airport.

"Sure," she answered. "What do you have in mind?"

"I've already got the G5 on alert to go get Jon, but that's not until late tomorrow. I'll see if he can pick you up in Spartanburg since they'll be watching Charlotte airport."

"Wish I could go get some clothes from home first," she lamented.

"I wouldn't chance that. Besides, you've got stuff here, right?"

"Well...yeah. I almost forgot."

"Okay then...head for South Carolina. I'll call with his arrival time soon as we work it out."

~

Jon and his new traveling companion would be about five hours out of Denver when Marsha called again. The night before had been spent jockeying for a better and closer spot to find out what was going on down on the field. The press box turned out to be the best place so most of their time was spent there.

Jon documented approximately how many were in each group, but could not tell any details of what they were talking about. Around 2:00AM Jon decided it was time to leave.

Back at the small car Jakes had found, Jon looked around and said, "no...let's take that one. It'll be more comfortable for the ride."

There was an awkward moment following that. Jon finally looked at the young man and said, "what am I going to do with you?"

"What... does that mean?" Jakes challenged.

"You're coming with me for now."

"Oh...no. I've got things to do here, man," Jakes argued.

Jon lowered his head and shook it slightly.

"I can't let you stay here right now. It could mess everything up."

"Why? You think I can't handle it?"

"Doesn't matter," Jon shot back forcefully. "Kill him or get caught and killed yourself. Either way you spook 'em and they change their plans."

Jakes spun away and grabbed the door of the little car. "He's mine, damn it. You can't take that from me."

Jon stepped up and grabbed his arm, applying just enough pressure from the suit to make his point. "Think a minute, will you?" He turned Jakes toward him.

"That can still be your job. Now is just not the time." He kept his grip on the youth's arm and gave him a chance to consider it.

"Ok," Jakes reluctantly gave in. "But what are we doing till then?"

"Come with me and you'll learn. I've an unrelated thing in Missouri to deal with and then there are plans to make about this thing." Jon turned loose of Jakes' arm and pointed back to the stadium, "This is bigger than you think it is. Be patient."

Half way into their ten-hour trip was Marsha's call. It had been fairly quiet up to that point.

"Is everything alright with your lady?" Jakes inquired.

Jon glanced over at him and then looked back at the highway. He had been working out his plan for Missouri. His mind concentrated on the question.

"She's a cop. In North Carolina." Jon stated staring straight ahead. "We have people who give us information," he took one hand from the steering wheel and waved it in a circle as he tried to come up with the right words. "You know, about what I do."

Jakes leaned hard against the seat back and focused on Jon's face.

"I don't know what it is that you do," he reminded Jon.

"Preemptive vengeance," Jon smirked. "I guess that's what you'd call it." He allowed his words to hang for a moment, and then continued. "There are some powerful people out there who hurt others just because they can." Jon turned sternly toward Jakes, "I verify it...and then stop it."

"Congress people, right?"

"Started that way," Jon affirmed without looking over.

"Oh, shit!" Jakes complexion lost most of his color. He slammed a fist into the door panel. "You're for real?"

Not sure if that was a question or not, Jon didn't offer a response. As the young man recovered, he leaned forward and tried to regulate his breathing.

"They call you...the Son. Is that right?"

"I prefer Silas."

"Are you gonna kill me?" his mouth asked before his brain thought about it.

Pausing at the inference of that question, Jon drew his own deep breath before answering with another question.

"Do you kill people to stay in power?"

"Hell, no," Jakes spit out nervously

"Well... there you go." Jon smiled. "You're not on the list, then."

Satisfied for the moment, Jakes again became quiet. Jon went back to planning for Missouri while they drove on.

As they approached Kansas City, Jon said he would need to stop to pick up a few things.

"Like clothes?" Jakes managed a grin.

Jon looked down at the black suit he still wore.

"Among other things," he said with a blank stare. Then Jon picked up a cell phone and punched a button.

Ben Shaw answered from the Hamilton Medical Center in Dalton, Georgia.

"Ben, do you have ID's on those other two guys yet?"

"Yeah, Stinson Wallace and Tom Yates. Both of Springfield, Mo."

"What kind of shape are they in?"

"Doc says they'll make it just fine. Bruises and a concussion, one has a broken arm."

"I need you to set up a monitor and sound receiver they can hear for later, can you do that?"

"Sure, Jon." Ben was getting out a notepad to write it down. "How do you plan to transmit?"

"I'll probably stream it from my phone to yours. You can hook it up from there, right?"

"Sure, just give me a couple hours to set it up."

"You'll have more than that. I'll call you when I'm ready."

Hanging up Jon noticed an odd look on Jakes' face.

"What?" he asked his passenger.

"How many people work for you in this deal?"

"More than I planned on."

They pulled into a shopping center on the outskirts of Kansas City. Jon parked the car near a men's shop and looked for a certain credit card. He handed it to Jakes and said,

"Pants 33" X 32", Belt 36", shirt X-large or 17" neck...pullover if they got one. Shoes 10 ½ medium."

Lamar Jakes nodded his understanding and opened the car door.

"If you don't come back," Jon said flatly. "You know I'll find you."

"Yeah," Jakes answered. "I bet you would."

As the young man disappeared into the store, Jon looked at a large sign advertising other shops in the mall. Earhardt Electronics and Games was listed.

That'll be my next stop, he thought.

38

Agents Spiegel and Barker joined Murray topside. They conducted an inspection of the property after last evening's guests had left. The DVD recordings showed at least twenty-five men, some wearing DHS on their backs. But most wore the initials ICE for Immigration Customs and Enforcement, a unit directly reporting to the Homeland Security people.

The barn had been searched, though not disrupted. Several tables and a cabinet were pulled over in the hanger.

"Think they had an idea where we were?" Barker asked.

"They were definitely looking for something," Murray laughed as he picked up his belongings. "I'd like to know who I could bill for this mess."

"Out here!" Spiegel hollered from near the house. When the others got over there, he had pulled down a paper. It was a notice that was left by the visitors. Spiegel handed it to Murray saying, "looks like we got you into some big trouble."

Murray looked over the paper and wadded it up.

"Confiscate my house for aiding and abetting illegals?" he laughed. "Not today, guys."

"They're really starting to play hard ball over this. If my sense is right, people are going to start getting hurt." Barker kicked the dirt as he spoke, "hell...where do we go to stop this?"

"We start by studying what we can find out about those five cities Jon gave us. There's some connection...some reason they're cited," Murray suggested.

"But again...who do we trust?" Barker asked. "Who can we talk to?"

"Grimes will know," Spiegel nodded. "He'll know who's clean and who's not."

"Let's see what they did inside the house and get back down underground," Murray said taking the lead. "Hell, they could be watching us."

"You got ammo hidden in the house?" Barker asked.

"Good idea," Murray smiled. "I sure do. Won't be much good up here, will it?"

They checked and secured the house as well as they could. Gathered up the weapons and ammunition from hidden storage areas and took everything back into the underground bunker.

Grimes, Phil Stone and Yinon Harel were waiting for them.

"Reiss got a call through just now," Grimes told them. "This town, Tyler, Texas, is doing their best to hold out. Those ICE goons are threatening to tear each house apart in their search."

"Can she travel?" Murray asked.

"She'll have to." Grimes looked at Harel for confirmation. The Mossad leader nodded once.

"Then let's go get her," Murray offered.

"You are a real cowboy, aren't you?" Barker laughed. "You don't just go in and get her. Hell...that town's under siege."

"Listen up..."Grimes stepped in. "If you're willing to risk going, here's how we'll do it. Reiss can get them to a junction on Interstate 20 called Sand Flat. They'll hide under the overpass till you get there."

"I know Sand Flat," Murray said. "Nothing there except the overpass."

"Ok, at the same time we need to make a bunch of noise to the south of town, like we made an escape that direction," Grimes continued. "They have to believe we got them out of that town or those people will pay a price."

"Let me call Wilbury," Murray offered. "He might be able to get some Rangers to create that noise we need."

~

Lamar Jakes did well in his selection of clothes for Jon. Tan pants and a white pullover shirt that looked like they came from his closet at home. Jon changed in the car and went shopping himself at the electronics store.

"This place is unreal," Jakes said. He had never been in a gaming store before. The selection of toys was beyond anything he had imagined.

Jon found the gadgets he needed and bought a few additional cell phones. At the checkout a thought came to him on how he could make his plan work.

"You're on the team now, right?" he asked Jakes.

"Do you pay by the hour?" the youth teased him.

"Good," Jon nodded. He liked the cocky attitude. "You'll do fine."

As they drove on toward Poplar Bluff, Jon introduced Lamar Jakes to their prey. A man who had caused the deaths of many children with his drug business and murdered others who had gotten in his way.

Congressman Fred Everett managed to keep himself separated from his dirty dealing by the use of others. It was time for that to stop. Jakes' part in the plan was simple enough. It really didn't put him in any immediate danger. But, if the plan worked, it would make another corrupt federal official go away.

~

Horace Wilbury called into Rangers temporary headquarters in Waco. The main HQ building in Austin was closed because of the nuclear scare. He spoke with Senior Captain Lance Gilroy and explained the situation in Tyler.

"I've got...maybe twelve men in that area," Gilroy said, while thinking as he spoke. "Let me see if we can't make something happen with six or eight of them."

"Captain that would great," Wilbury thanked him. "Can we coordinate the timing, our boys are trying to pull off an escape while ya'll do that."

"Certainly, Sheriff," the top ranger assured him. "Give me a couple hours to work this out. You know...here we are plotting, for the right reasons, against agents of our own country. How the hell did we get to this?"

"That I don't know. What's even scarier is that most of the folks in this country have no idea what's going on. Cause there ain't no one telling 'em about it."

The Captain paused for second, and then replied. "I used to get aggravated with that cable station...the one they shut down. I thought they just mainly kept things stirred up, you know. But now I remember the one thing they never did."

"What's that?" Wilbury asked.

"Demand the other stations be shut off."

"That's true, Captain. The folks have to pay attention to everything and then figure it out for themselves."

"I hope this thing, whatever's going on, can be stopped before too many more people get hurt."

Wilbury grunted at that thought. "You know, people get what they got coming."

"Horace," Captain Gilroy closed with. "I'll be back to you shortly old friend.".

269

"Thank you, Lance. Be waiting to hear from you."

~

Marsha met the G5 at Spartanburg's Greenville-Spartanburg airport. She knew and recognized the pilot so they were back on their way in minutes. The trip would go first to Dalton, Georgia to pick up the gear Jon needed and then on to Poplar Bluff, Mo.

Marsha's plan was to go on to Missouri, but she would clear that with Jon first. The plane lifted from Spartanburg and Marsha Hurst wondered about her contact. The man if it was a man, that tipped her about the Mossad coming in.

Had they already found and dealt with him? she thought. *Strange business. You don't even know who it is you're worried about. Did he have a family? Is he a government employee?*

So much going on she didn't know who exactly to trust other than Jon and Ben. Like the others she wondered most of all, *how could this be happening?*

~

Jon stopped again, this time at a costume store in Poplar Bluff.

"You need a ball cap and some glasses. Geek you up a bit," he told Jakes.

For himself, he picked a dignified looking fake moustache, a stick-on neck tattoo and a wig of blond hair. There were some "place and stick" moles on the checkout counter, three for the price of one.

"One's probably enough," he said looking at his chin in a mirror there.

Jakes watched and tried to figure what this man was up to. But Jon only told him he would stand outside a building and look nervous.

That wouldn't be hard, he told himself.

Back in the car, Jon pulled on the wig and secured the moustache. He put the mole off to one side on his chin and made sure it was stuck good. He then got out the more important items, the ones from the electronics store.

Jon set two microphones on his person, one in the wig and the other on his belt buckle. The camera he already had. But he attached a new item to it, a remote lens about the size of a button. The camera went into his pants pocket and the wire from the lens ran up through the shirt and stuck to a button near the top of his chest.

He moved around, climbed out of and back into the car to make sure everything would stay in place. Then Jon looked at Jakes.

"Get your hat on, will ya?" and he cranked the car. They drove to the downtown area along North Main until they reached the corner with West Pine. Jon parked a half block from an old two-story retail building. Pointing in that direction, he told Jakes to wait in the car till, "this pager goes off."

He handed his accomplice the modified relic. This unit operated by remote up to a certain distance. Jon hit the remote clicker and the pager beeped.

"When you hear that beep again...go to the front of that building and do your thing."

Jon then got out of the car and walked to a fast food shop across from the building. He ordered a coffee and sat near the windows.

Looking back at the car, Jon dialed the number for Everett's office from one of the new phones he had purchased. A man answered on the third ring.

"Congressman Fred Everett's office, how can I help you?"

"I need to speak with Everett," Jon said sternly.

"He's quite busy at the moment. I'm sure I can help," the voice said calmly.

"Oh really?" Jon did his best to sound sinister. "Can you help about Blake?"

"Who?"

"Jerry Blake, dumb ass. Don't play games with me."

"One minute, please," the voice said and he was on hold, but not for long.

"This is Fred Everett. Who is this?" the new voice asked.

"You can call me Silas. I'm an old friend of Jerry's."

"He never mentioned a Silas... What's this about?"

"Well...it's about him being dead and his helpers banged up on that job of yours over in Georgia."

The line became very quiet. Jon almost feared the man had hung up. Then the voice spoke again.

"Who did you say you were?"

"Look man. The job went bust. You know it and I know you know it. Your boys are going to roll over on you any time now. Plus you got other problems."

"What other problems?" Everett was on the hook now.

"That kid your boys were chasing. He's not one to mess with, if you understand. I need to talk in person if you want the rest. Oh...I can help shut up those mutts in the hospital, too."

"I don't talk directly...I mean, I usually go through others."

"You ain't got time, friend. Now or reap the whirlwind, as they say."

"Where...where do you want to meet?"

"Right across the street, man. Come have a burger and some fries. It might just save your life."

Jon could see a man come to the window on the second floor and stare down at the food shop. The phone went dead and now all Jon could do was wait and see what happened.

Within five minutes, the man came out the front door of the building, looked all around and headed across the street. As he entered the store Jon spoke out,

"A burger and fries, today?"

Everett slid into the booth across from him.

"Make this quick," he demanded.

"Patience, friend. One must have patience." Jon looked up at him.

Everett slid himself forward and looked around the inside of the store, then out through the window.

"You have more to tell me?" he asked.

"Yeah. That kid is pissed, man. Word is he left Georgia two days ago to come see about you."

"See about me? How does he know about me?"

"He got to the boys before the cops showed up. Seems twisting a broken arm is a great motivator. Yates gave you up, like that." Jon snapped his fingers in the man's face.

Yet more of Everett's color drained. Now this man used another correct name.

"Yates?" he tried to play dumb.

"Yeah...Yates and Stinson Wallace. You want to play like you don't know 'em? Fine...I'll be on my way then cause they can't... hurt... you, can they?"

Jon started to get up, but Everett raised both hands, "No. Wait a second." He could hardly speak he was now trembling so. "You heard they were talking?"

"Talking...singing hell, even dancing for the local Leos and the feds."

"Then it's too late anyway."

"They ain't signed nothing and the drugs won't make the recording any good in court. Word I got was they need another week to get well enough to say it again, where it's useful."

"Can you shut them up?"

"Sure, I trade favors. What you got for me?"

"Twenty-five thousand. Clean bills."

"Huh? That's per guy, right?"

Everett threw himself back against the seat. "Yeah, whatever...each."

"Ok...consider it done. Oh, and you don't want to stiff me over this either. That wouldn't do at all, got it?"

"Yeah, I got it. You bring me back proof they aren't going to talk and you'll get paid." Everett was feeling more in control as he slid out from the booth. He headed for the door and Jon pushed the pager button.

Jakes climbed from the car and walked toward the building as Everett pushed the food shop door open and began walking across the street. He was looking back to be sure that man in the store wasn't following. Not watching where he was going.

Jon had dialed his phone and waited till Ben answered. "Did you get that?"

"Every word," Ben said.

"How about the boys?"

"Oh yeah, they saw and heard the whole thing. They're giving up everything they know as we speak."

"Can George get the Missouri State police here pretty quick?"

"He..." then Ben laughed. "You know George. He had 'em on stand-by. They should be right around the corner."

At about the middle of the road the congressman looked forward. Jon looked up at Everett as he noticed the young man walking near his building. He froze in the middle of the lanes of traffic and just stood there glaring at the young stranger. Jakes played his part well, looking nervous and his hand in one pocket for extra suspense.

Everett turned on one foot to go back to the food shop as sirens blared around the corner. Six Missouri State police units pulled up all around the congressman. Everett began pointing toward a young man who was now walking toward a Mercury sedan.

Four officers surrounded Everett and the rest, with warrants in hand, entered his office building. Jon stepped from the burger joint and walked directly to his car, as Everett was being handcuffed and patted down.

"I thought you were gonna kill him," Jakes said as Jon climbed in on the driver's side.

"You disappointed?" Jon asked.

"Kind of," the kid admitted. Glancing down at the floorboard, he added, "Why this?" and then looked back up at Jon.

"Needed him off my plate... and this seemed to be a good idea." Jon cranked up and pulled away from the curb. "If he beats the charges or gets out...we'll see... I'll deal with that when it happens. For now, we have bigger problems and that creep is off the street."

Lamar Jakes looked like he was in a trance. He sat back, chin resting on his chest and said nothing more.

"So...did you learn anything?" Jon smiled and asked him as they drove toward the edge of town.

"Doesn't seem like it," the young man frowned. "Not yet anyway."

"Someday you'll get it," Jon assured him. "Just remember what happened here."

39

A squad of twelve Texas Rangers rode into the south side of Tyler, Texas right at dusk. Radio communication directed them to the VFW hall just inside the city limits. They were in three cars with six motorcycle escorts.

Five blocks over Reiss was getting Nava ready to go and thanking Kate Griffin for her help.

"We shall not forget your kindness," he told his host.

"Young man," Kate smiled a broad grin. "It was my full pleasure, I assure you."

"Spencer said he would call here, right?" Reiss asked again.

"He'll call. Soon as they're ready."

The VFW members were loading three vehicles with covered gurneys, two pick-up trucks and an SUV. A lookout on the roof noticed movement several streets over. It was the ICE people and this time they had ATF trucks with them.

"Let's move out," Spencer hollered and signaled with his arm.

The VFW members drove away in separate directions, each vehicle with a Texas Ranger escort of one car and two motorcycles. The federal vehicles were on them in mere minutes, but did not know what to do with the Rangers in such obvious proximity.

They split up and followed the caravans while the leader of the ICE operation radioed in for instructions.

"What do mean there's three of them?" the commander heard back in his ear.

"We have three separate possible targets with local law enforcement escorts, Sir."

"Are they armed?"

"Hell, Sir. I would have to say 'yes' to that."

"Stay close while I get clearance to engage."

"Roger, that."

The VFW teams picked up speed and Spencer, in the group headed due south dialed his cell phone. Kate Griffin answered.

"Great day for a drive, don't you think?" Spencer asked her.

"I can't right now. Got company coming and need to fix dinner," she responded while nodding to Reiss. "My car's in the shop anyway."

"Well, maybe next time," Spencer told her.

Reiss had his wounded friend strapped into the back seat and stepped toward the house. Kate was now on the porch.

"God speed, my friends," she offered. "Just leave the car. Don't worry about it."

Reiss suddenly stood at full attention and saluted his benefactor.

"My husband would be very proud of that." Kate covered her heart with one hand and wiped a tear with the other.

She stood and watched her car quietly leave the yard and head north toward the freeway.

Jon sat silently making notes in his small book. Lamar Jakes walked around the car in nervous anticipation.

"You have a jet?" he spun and asked with some sarcasm in his voice.

Jon looked up and considered his answer.

"It's an arrangement." He told the kid.

"And it's coming here to get us?" Jakes cross-examined him.

"Relax...." Jon leaned back against the Mercury's hood. "He had to make a stop in Georgia first. They'll be here."

The airport in Poplar Bluff was busy that evening. It was getting dark now and the lights of air traffic filled the sky. Some planes making their approach came within yards of where they stood. The lack of daylight made them seem much closer than before.

Jon's cell phone rang. It was Marsha.

"Is that you sitting at the end of number six?" she asked.

"Yeah... that's us. You got everything?"

"I've got what Ben sent," she answered.

Jon looked up and watched as the G-5 glided overhead and touched down softly. He said something else into the phone that Jakes could not hear and hung up. Gathering his notebook, he climbed in the car and cranked it.

"You coming?" he asked Jakes.

The young man got in and pulled the door to sharply.

"Am I going home now?" he questioned.

"Texas first." Jon was nearly out of patience with this kid's attitude. "Home later."

They drove toward the terminal and parked near the rear. Jon grabbed his belongings and motioned for Jake to follow him. They walked around the building rather than through it and quickly found the G-5 rolling to its berth. The pilot went in to complete his paperwork and file a flight plan for the next leg of his trip. Jakes noticed the pretty woman waiting at the steps of the plane.

Jon hugged her before introducing them.

"My new accomplice." He smiled while pointing toward Jakes.

The young man nodded respectfully and they all climbed aboard. The interior of the world's best business class, personal aircraft was overwhelming to the kid.

"You're kidding me," came out of him as he grinned and walked to the rear of the cabin.

"Make yourself comfortable," Jon told him. "We'll be leaving in a minute."

Jon and Marsha sat in front facing seats for what little privacy they could get. He took her hand and squeezed it gently.

The pilot opened the door to the cabin area and stepped inside. His look was of concern.

"Something wrong?" Jon asked instantly.

"I don't know," the man replied with doubt ringing in his voice. "We're all set to go to Dallas, but a guy sitting near the flight plan table kept staring at me." Rubbing his face, the pilot then continued.

"That gave me the creeps. I was ready to pass it off as paranoia when it got worse."

"What do mean by that?"

"When I walked away from the desk, I turned back a second and caught that guy calling somebody...and still giving me the stink-eye."

Jon stood and offered his most assuring tone.

"Go ahead and take off like all is well. I'll check into what we can do about this, alright?"

"Yeah...sure," the pilot nodded and turned toward his flight deck.

Jon reached out as a thought came to him and asked, "How much room do you need to land this thing?"

The man stopped and slowly turned back to Jon. He clearly understood what Jon was thinking and wasn't sure he liked it.

"About 3,000 feet," he answered.

"Ok, thanks."

"I'll need twice that to get back up," the pilot threw in emphatically.

"A full mile?"

"Unless you've got a catapult handy, yeah. That and then some."

Jon's eyebrows climbed high on his forehead. He smiled at his trusted pilot, nodded and just said, "Thanks."

Sitting back down next to Marsha, he pulled his phone from a pocket.

"Everything alright?" she asked him.

"Yeah...if I remember correctly. I just need to check something with Murray."

~

The call found Bogart in his Washington office. Congressman Grant wasn't pleased.

"What do mean Texas Rangers are interfering?" he demanded.

The caller explained the details of events in Tyler, Texas and Grant stood, his face flush in anger.

"Do we take them out?" the caller asked.

Grant paused. That would be a big step. A challenge to keep quiet like the other incidents, yet what were they to do? It occurred to him that some organized resistance had formed.

But who were they? he thought.

"Sir?" the caller asked again. "Our guys need to know what to do."

"How did they get involved anyway?" the Speaker of the House pleaded.

"Some Sheriff over in Brownwood called them. That's all I know."

"Call me back in thirty minutes," Bogart snapped at him. "I'll let you know then."

Grant needed to get Shanahan in on this. This was the whole ballgame. It would be her call.

His bottom desk drawer held several "burn" cell phones, lines that couldn't be traced. He grabbed one and punched in her number.

~

Lucy descended to just 400 feet as they reached I-20 north of Tyler. Murray swung out wide so they could see under the overpasses.

"That must be Sand Flat," he hollered while pointing. "See the car under there?"

Yinon Harel agreed and they sat down just north of the expressway. Murray found a high spot for the landing to keep Lucy's blade tips out of harms way. He would not shut her down for this stop.

Reiss jumped from the vehicle and opened the rear door as Harel got to him. They pulled their injured comrade from the car and carried her to the helicopter.

Within minutes they were back in the air and heading west.

"How is she?" the Mossad leader asked.

"She spoke this morning," Reiss answered. "I think she's doing better."

A blue light flashed above Murray's head. It was a signal he had installed to let him know if his cell phone rang. It was patched into Lucy's internal communications system.

"Hey, Jon," he answered almost gleefully. "We've got the lady Mossad agent and all is good. You on the way to Dallas?"

"That's why I'm calling, Murray," Jon explained. "We may have some folks aware of us."

"Aware?"

"Yeah...aware and tracking us."

Murray understood that if that was so, whoever they were...they were powerful. He keyed his microphone and asked Jon what he had in mind.

"How much straight highway is that road out from your house?"

"How straight?" Murray quizzed.

"Enough to land on..."

Murray understood the question and considered his answer. Again, he keyed in.

"That thing will need close to a mile, right?"

"You're good, flyboy," Jon teased to easy the tension.

"About two miles northeast of the house...start the approach there. The road is pretty good till just past my place."

"Ok, Murray." Jon paused a few moments. "If my pilot is okay with this idea, we'll be there in less than an hour, I figure. If you don't hear back from me...watch for us out there."

"Your man is good, Jon. He can handle it, I'm sure," Murray tried to sound convincing. He waited for a response, but Jon was already off the line.

Lucy nosed down a few degrees as Murray picked up speed.

"Something wrong?" Harel asked.

"Naw...we just need to get home. Company's coming."

40

Sheri Shanahan did not hear her cell phone. She was in the area with Sasha, checking the feeding equipment and air filtration system. The noise wasn't bad, but just enough to conceal the ringing. Shanahan would not learn of the decision made in her absence until hours later.

Cyrus Grant threw his phone at the still open desk drawer. It missed.

"Damn," he muttered louder than he intended. The hard plastic unit bounced and slid along the floor. It came to rest under a sofa, beyond Grant's reach.

Staring out his office window for several minutes, his "Bogart" persona began to "feel his oats," and the power of his position. He inhaled deeply and turned back toward his desk. The phone used by the ICE agents was still lying there. Grant picked it up and hit callback.

"Yeah," the man answered harshly. "What do we do?"

"Take 'em out. All of them," Grant said forcefully.

"We'll do what we can, Sir," came back through the phone.

"What does that mean?" the boss demanded.

"Hell, man. They're scattered all over Texas by now. They left in three different directions."

"I don't need them talking to anyone. Run them down and take care of this."

"How about that sheriff over in Brownwood?" the agent asked.

"Send a drone," Grant heard himself say. The sound of it scared even him. He stiffened up and followed that with, "Messy, I know. We'll make it look like a cartel hit."

"You sure about all this?" the voice on the other end asked.

"Too close to back off now," Grant said softly. "Just do it."

~

Murray approached home with added caution. The two-lane blacktop road lay between County Road 66 and Market Road 6. He took Lucy low to check the condition of the pavement and his memory of its layout.

"What are you doing?" Harel asked with some concern.

"My friends are going to land a jet on that road in a few minutes," Murray stated bluntly and then turned to look at the Israeli. "I'm checking for holes or problems."

Harel looked surprised, "Didn't we just go over an airport back there?"

"They want to slip in unnoticed...like we are."

Harel understood. He nodded once and began studying the road himself. He heard Murray on the radio again.

"Lucy to B1, over."

"Hey...I mean B1, go ahead." It was Phil Stone on the other end.

"Setting down outside the hanger in three, over."

"Roger that, Lucy. Good to have you home."

As he lowered the Bell 407 Murray caught a glimpse of the G5 screeching down the roadway and coming to a stop just beyond his driveway.

Phil Stone and Tim Spiegel ran from inside the hanger to help with the injured Israeli agent. Murray jumped down from his copter and ran to his pick-up truck. He was down his driveway and at the road in two minutes.

"Greased that nicely," he yelled to the pilot who signaled with a thumb up, but hadn't heard a word.

The cabin door swung down before the plane had completely stopped. Its three passengers climbed out and jogged to the truck. A brief introduction of Lamar Jakes was met with a puzzled look, but no comment. Jon and Murray went back to the plane and helped it turn 180 degrees. The pilot revved its engines and watched for his helpers to clear the area. With a smile and another hand gesture, he then rolled the G5 up the road.

When the bird finally arched up into the darkening sky, Murray clapped once and grinned. Jon nodded his approval. The G5 would go on to Dallas and find out who was possibly waiting for it.

"I still need to hide Lucy," Murray told his friend and pulled on his arm for them to go.

They drove back to the hanger in a strange silence. They were all together now, except for Ben, who was in Dalton.

What do they do now? was the unspoken thought on everyone's mind.

Murray climbed into his helicopter and lifted off. Tim Spiegel took over the truck. He knew the drill and would meet Murray at the low spot up the road.

Jon and the others went down into the shelter where there were handshakes all around, except for Daniel Seay. He sat on the sofa, one of the phones in his hand and his face turning ashen.

Jon stepped over to him.

"What is it?" he asked.

"Ben just got a call from that professor who's been monitoring the southern Texas area," Ben said before he even looked up. "There's been a large explosion in Brownwood."

"Brownwood?" Jon didn't yet understand.

"The whole block around Wilbury's office. It's gone."

The room fell quiet. Agent Terry Barker suddenly ran to the phones and asked rhetorically, "Has anyone heard from Spencer?"

Barker fumbled for a note with the cop's number and dialed frantically. The message informed that the number was "not in service."

The NCIS agent looked at Jon, "Wilbury arranged the Texas Ranger escort for the boys in Tyler," he explained to the newcomer in the hideout. "How do we find out what's happened over there?"

Grimes had his cell phone opened. "I can't get a signal," he proclaimed.

"You won't in here," Daniel told him. "Use one of these."

Barker handed his boss the phone he had used and Grimes called the offices of his boss and friend, Wilfred Scott.

"Will, I can't disclose my location so please don't ask. I need to know about any off the chart activity south of Tyler, Texas."

"How do you know about that?" the NCIS Director was confused. "We don't even know what's going on down there."

"What do you know?" Grimes pushed.

"Three separate incidents, attacks on civilians being escorted by Rangers. From what we can figure, two were ground attacks and one was from the damned air."

"What do you know about Brownwood?" Grimes followed up.

"Is that involved with this?" Scott asked. "That was a city block blown up. How... we don't know yet."

Murray and agent Spiegel had stepped into the underground room. Murray spoke up, his face pale from what he had heard and grabbed Grimes arm.

"Ask about drones...predator drones," he ordered.

Grimes stared at Murray in disbelief, but asked the question anyway.

"Radar picked up something in both locations." The man paused while he processed everything he was learning. "If they're using predators... they've got juice and they're desperate."

Both ends of the line became silent until the director in Washington spoke again.

"Jerry, I need what you know. I can't help without it," he said as his voice trailed off.

"We've got to add it all up first, boss," Grimes responded.

"We?" his boss asked.

"I'll get back to you soon as I can," Grimes told him and hung up.

Murray, Daniel Seay and Phil Stone were heading for the door. Jon stepped in front of them.

"Just where you going?"

"Wilbury needs help," Murray muttered.

"Man, if he's in any shape to receive help, we can only do it from here, right now," Jon pleaded. "We need to sit down and combine what we know...figure out what we're up against."

The men looked at each other and back to Jon. That was the first time he had directed any leadership at most of them. And they knew he was right.

The group assembled around the sofa, chairs and a small table. It was Murray Bilstock, Daniel Seay, Matt Turlock, Marsha Hurst, Phil Stone, Spiegel, Barker and Grimes of NCIS, Harel and Reiss of the Israeli Mossad and Jon. Nava Golan was there, still heavily sedated and sleeping.

Ben Shaw was in Dalton. Jon called him and put him on speaker.

Lamar Jakes sat in the corner, eyes wide and witnessing an event he didn't understand. Neither did he realize at that moment, the information he held would be of critical importance.

They all sat except for one. The speaking began with Daniel Seay and all eyes turned toward him as Jon slowly paced the room, listening intently.

41

It was a rare occasion for Mithras to call Bogart directly. The first time he actually answered and spoke himself. But the stakes were getting higher and time was short.

"We got him," the man in Colorado bragged.

"You sure?"

"Absolutely. They placed a call to him just before the release. He was in there."

"Alright," Bogart sounded satisfied.

"What about the other mess?"

"The girl wasn't with any of them."

"Any? What do you mean by that?" Mithras asked.

"They played us. Three directions and none of them was her."

"Where the hell did she go?"

"Look...if I knew that, this would all be different." Grant was frustrated and angry. "We have no idea where she was being held or where she went. None of them will say a word."

"They didn't kill everybody?"

"You don't learn much from dead people, Stephen."

"We don't use names, remember?"

"Oh, screw you. Get off my phone. I need to think." Grant tossed the phone at his desk and walked to a window. Washington could be pretty at night, but Cyrus Grant saw no beauty this night. He wondered when Shanahan would call and what he would say to her. They were so close. Too close to quit. The main plans were already in motion.

Hang in there, he told himself. *This will all be over soon.*

~

News on the main networks began to mention Brownwood, Texas. The stories were muted compared to the reality of the damage. A Mexican drug cartel was blamed for what the news called a revenge bombing. There were three suspected casualties, the stories said. None identified at the time.

~

The meeting at Caddo Mills was now well into its second hour of fact sharing. The reporters had told of how the incidents were manipulated from the start. The media either didn't mention or misreported each event beginning with the border attacks.

"How is that possible?" Phil Stone asked. "Are you saying the media controls what we know and when we know it?"

"If you ever know about it at all...yes," Matt responded. "I would say we were back to the days of the Pony Express rider." The Louisiana editor leaned back in his chair. "Except those riders were just late with the news, they didn't alter it."

"I don't know, Matt," Stone added defiantly. "The size of a conspiracy like that would be mind-boggling. Someone would talk for sure."

Daniel Seay leaned over the table and looked directly at Phil.

"It's not the normal 'conspiracy' you're used to dealing with. These are 'like minded' reactionaries who believe they are doing right." He paused after that and glanced around. "They are not ordered or even asked to do what they do."

Matt picked up again.

"Subtle suggestions are offered by people they agree with," he threw in. "Right up to party officials they share agendas with."

289

"This stuff is too important, I mean...really? They just keep it from us and we know no different?" Stone was still not convinced.

"It's been going on for a while," Daniel assured him. "Just not at this level. They even did it when there was that other network calling them out on it everyday."

"The one that was shut down by the information law?"

"Yes," Daniel confirmed with nearly animated gestures. "Now with them and the radio guys out of the way...they can tell us anything they want."

The table became quiet. Each one there thought of stories they personally knew about that didn't get attention in the media. Murray immediately thought of the border attacks and Sheriff Wilbury's Ranger relative.

That was just a diversion to get people and vehicles in further up the border. he said to himself. *All those sheriffs and ranchers killed...for a damned diversion.*

"The Austin threat was completely misrepresented," Daniel picked up again. "The truck carrying the residue, where our Mossad friend got hurt, was never told at all."

"The Denver scare and evacuation," Matt injected. "Was all a hoax. They were just set ups to insure the proper reaction for later diversions."

Lamar Jakes was prodded to speak up and tell his story about being inside the Denver situation and who his contact had been.

"Professor Walden is Mithras," He explained along with details of how he and others were recruited and tempted with promises of an Islamic Jihad that never was to be.

Yinon Harel spoke up at that point.

"We were asked to come and assist with the possible Islamic uprising and invasion." He glanced around the room and leaned back against the sofa. "I must tell you, this is all domestic. It is internal to your country. Those responsible are powerful and they have the support of most of the media...but they are your people."

Daniel and Matt nodded in uncomfortable agreement.

Jon remained quiet. He had given each person there a list of the cities he saw marked at the Denver training camp.

Phil Stone looked like he wanted to talk, but kept staring at the list in silence.

Marsha brought up her contacts and the people who were after her.

"The same ones who were after Nava and Reiss in Tyler, I'm sure," she added.

Ben, through the speakerphone, offered his knowledge of Sheri Shanahan and how he believed she was involved. That part of the story didn't make much sense to anyone else. Yet it was undeniable that she was somehow part of all this.

"The cities are the key," Matt blurted out.

Jerome Grimes looked up like a light had gone off in his head.

"The President is from Wichita," he threw out. "He likes to go home for major holidays."

"Isn't the VP from Tampa?" Marsha asked.

Several others nodded and everyone started sitting up a little straighter.

Tim Spiegel spoke for the first time. "The VP is supposed to be in St. Louis on July Fourth, some special dedication. Our office was going to help back up the Secret Service," he recalled.

Grimes nearly stood. "That's right. And though POTUS likes to go home on holidays, he's scheduled to be in Cleveland to honor some former senator who turning ninety that day."

"So what is this about Oregon?" Daniel asked, referring to last city on the list, Pendleton.

Grimes jumped up, "Excuse me a minute," He said and grabbed a phone. Calling his office, the NCIS agent could be heard asking someone to look up an answer for him. Within a minute he had hung up and came back to the group.

"Pendleton, Oregon is the safe house city for that week," he beamed as he spoke. "Today is Monroeville, Alabama. Next week is Beulah, North Dakota and the week of the fourth is Pendleton.

Many of the others looked confused.

"If everything goes to shit..." he started. "Some major attack, threat or natural catastrophe, there's a safe place designated to take the President and the VP for safe keeping. It changes every week and only certain people know the schedule."

The room was still quiet.

"Somebody with a high clearance is in on this deal." Grimes shouted that time.

"Assassination," Phil Stone muttered at first. Then he got louder as the group looked over at him. "It's an assassination, both of them."

"Both?" Matt Turlock nearly stood in his chair.

"The President and the VP, both of them," Phil reiterated.

"A coup?" Barker leaned in to ask.

"Kind of... A domestic coup, if you will," the cop from Shreveport explained. "Wasn't there a supreme court justice who died this spring?"

"Yeah...but that was covered in all the papers and on TV," Daniel offered.

"Nobody said they stepped on all the news," Phil said in a much lower voice.

"It's not out yet, but the President is going to name Foster. He's the same as Wofford in philosophy and rule of law," Marsha piped in. She looked around somewhat sheepishly and then added. "My contact in Washington told me that three weeks ago."

"If there's a different president the nomination could be very different, couldn't it?" The cop was on a roll.

"Well, yeah, Phil. But this is a lot of trouble over one appointment," Daniel surmised.

"Who's third in line?" Stone asked in rhetorical fashion, "Grant." He had answered his own question. "That would change everything, wouldn't it?"

Marsha looked up at Jon. He had not uttered a sound himself through the entire discussion. He stood; now back against the wall, listening to every word and idea.

"Why? Why all this to gain the presidency, now?" Matt asked. "Even for a supreme court appointment."

"Do you like that Information Equity Act that's on the books?" Stone sarcastically threw out.

"Why...no. The Supreme Court is going to..........." Matt stopped himself.

"Not if they get a new justice appointed by Grant they won't." Phil leaned back in self-satisfaction.

It was then that Ben's voice was heard over the speakers.

"Shanahan," he said.

42

Bogart's phone rang. The one he had thrown across the room. He could hear it, but couldn't find it. Knowing the caller had to be Shanahan, he grabbed another from the desk drawer and dialed her.

"What's wrong with your phone?" she asked.

"It's here," he admitted. "I just can't put my hands on it right now."

"I saw that you called earlier."

"Its been taken care of," Grant said as forcefully as he dared.

"And what would that be?"

"There were too many people meddling in our business, being in our way. I ordered a pair of hits."

"You ordered?"

"Yes...I took care of it. You weren't available...so I did it."

Shanahan could feel her face flush with anger, but she didn't let it come through in her voice. She began pushing keys on the keyboard in front of her.

"Tell me what you've done and I'll see if I can get a lid on the reporting," she said.

Grant explained the Rangers interference with the Mossad agent and how the Brownwood sheriff was involved.

"That town is already on some news stations." She rubbed her forehead as she thought. "I'll offer a gas line explosion and tell 'em we need this quiet for national security."

"How can you do that?" Grant exclaimed. "After the fact, I mean?"

"Homeland Security called me about it half an hour ago, asking what to put out. I didn't know it was our mess at that time.

They're on board with the cause. You know that... they'll do what we need."

"And the Rangers?" Grant tried to reminder her.

"Haven't heard anything about that...must be small potatoes."

"Have you heard from the team leaders?" Grant had turned to thinking ahead. The team leaders were those in charge of the physical acts for the Independence Day coup.

"Everyone is in place. Huh...its less than two weeks from now, isn't it?"

"I'll be glad when it's over."

"Just don't forget your first duty. I'd hate to have to replace you before you get moved in good."

"Not funny," Grant snapped. "I know what this is about and I won't forget. We keep that law on the books and the control stays in our hands. There won't be any stopping us."

"Just keep your head on straight till then, okay?" She cleared one screen on her computer and silently went to another.

"Yeah," he told her. "I can do that."

"Good," she replied with a detached tone that sent a chill through the congressman. "I have something you need to take care of." Her inflection was partially caused by the distracting images on her computer. So unnerving was the information she stared at that Shanahan threw herself against the back of her chair and rubbed her temples with both hands. A gesture Grant did not see and would never be aware of.

The Speaker of the House hesitated in his response and the air between the phones became quiet. Shanahan didn't wait long. His silence seemed to give her focus.

"I've been trying to get information on a police officer in North Carolina. She seems to be at the center of some sort of network."

"What kind of network?" Grant's curiosity clicked in.

"News about us. Not by name of course, but information I'm not comfortable with people knowing."

"You say, 'she.' Who is this person?"

"Her name is Marsha Hurst. Have you ever heard of her?" she challenged.

Grant's eidetic memory spun and pulled up an answer.

"Yes... yes," he nearly shouted. "She was involved in that drug cartel thing late last year. She got hurt. Pretty badly I understand, but recovered."

"That's her," Shanahan responded, still in calm monotone.

"You need me to check into her?" Grant assumed.

"No...I know what I need to about her, she's off the grid right now anyway. And her office is covering for her."

Bogart listened silently.

"It's her boyfriend I need you to find out about. He's the key to this."

"Boyfriend?" Grant left his question open.

"Jonathan Crane, the millionaire, businessman and philanthropist. He lives in North Georgia somewhere."

"That name...shit!" Grant reacted with a jolt. "He was rumored to be tied to that killer... 'The Son'... or whatever."

"That's right...the one who kills congressmen." Shanahan almost giggled as she spoke, "what's your day job again?"

Grant didn't find that funny either.

The lawyer rolled out what she knew and continued scrolling through different pages on her web connection. "I'm not far from Dalton. I'll send a team to check out the house."

"You're sure he's her boyfriend? A cop and a killer?"

"Sure as I can be... now the rest is up to you," she threw at him.

"What am I supposed to do?" Grant asked.

"Find out who his other associates are, where he's been, what he's been up to. I need something to draw him out before he gets on to us."

"You really believe he's a threat then?"

"Enough that he needs to be stopped." Shanahan answered quickly while staring at information the congressman could not see, "either way...we don't need to chance it."

"And the girl...the cop?"

"When she raises her head...kill her."

The Speaker of the House looked around his office as if for witnesses to what was just said.

"Killing a cop is bad business," he whispered. "You know that as well as I do."

"What quicker way to draw him out?" Her words were sharp and threatening. "Don't forget the larger picture here. A cop's death will all blow over in the aftermath of the big plan."

Grant sat down behind his desk without a response to that. He spun around in his huge chair and looked out the window.

Shanahan frowned again at the computer screen in her Atlanta office. After another silent indication of frustration she changed the subject. Offering yet more orders to Bogart.

"Tell Mithras to cool it with those drones," she said without equivocation.

This caught Grant off guard yet he kept his reaction to it somewhat muted. His eyes closed in an extended blink as he took a shallow breath and then softly exhaled.

"The drones? They don't leave any sign. Why is that a problem...?" he tried to ask.

"My information comes in at all times," she cut him off. "Even as we speak."

Her arrogance was always thick, but this was just showing off. A contact at Homeland Security just posted a "watch" for persons tracking drones flights through satellite imagery. Someone was on to them and being nosey.

"There's been too much use of those...and in too little time," she directed. "Besides, that sheriff had connections to our boy."

"Crane?" Grant asked.

"Or The Son, as it were." Shanahan now scolded with her tone, "through that dead senator's son."

"You're not serious," Grant exclaimed.

"I am *nothing* if not serious, Bogart." Her voice now would cut stone. "I found it, you prove it...and deal with it."

It made sense to him actually. *Should have thought of that myself,* his mind shouted inside itself. He blinked hard again while seeking composure.

"This is all getting a lot messier than we thought," the man finally muttered.

"Buck up, will you?" the lawyer shot back. "Grow a pair and get moving. Time is short already."

As Bogart started to answer he heard the faint click. The call was over, she had hung up.

After several minutes of staring at clouds, the Speaker of the House spun in his chair and reached for his Rolodex. It was old fashioned compared to today's electronics, but it was what he was comfortable with. He rubbed the case with his fingers before pulling the index lever down to the letter he sought. With a deep breath this time, he pushed the lever to open.

~

Ben Shaw had asked Jon to step away from the others for a minute.

"I have some odd news from Dr. Franklin at Fernbank," Ben explained. "I just want to run it by you first."

Jon walked to a far corner of the room and slid down against the wall.

"Okay, I'm clear," he said once he got situated. "What is it?"

"The bodies of the three Muslims who had been hauling the bomb stuff," he started.

"Well," Jon corrected him. "We don't know that they were Muslims, but I know who you are talking about."

Ben winced at the castigation, but let it go.

"The field exam of the bodies showed heavy radiation sickness." He waited a second before he added, "but it wasn't from the materials in the truck."

"What?" Jon didn't understand.

"It was radiation poisoning, for sure. It's just that they were injected with it. The exposure didn't kill them. But it didn't help the guy in the back of the truck, Doc says. He believes that one likely died first."

"How does the doctor know this?" Jon was standing back up now. "The bodies were blown all to pieces by whatever hit them."

"From pictures and readings the techs took on site." Ben went on, "the bodies had a radiation signature quite different from the materials taken from the truck. Knowing what we do now about this entire deal... the doc says he thinks he sees puncture marks on the bodies."

"Get to it, Ben."

"They were given shots. They probably thought it was potassium iodine to protect them from the exposure."

Jon was quiet for a few moments as it all gathered into a conclusive thought for him.

"It was all a big sales job," he finally announced. "That... Denver and Austin. Just making some things appear to be more than they were."

"That's Dr. Webster's feeling about it."

"Call him and thank him for me, Ben. You can tell him I believe he's got it figured. Just don't tell him the other stuff we're working on, okay?"

"Well, sure...but why? He's like one of the team."

"The team is too big already." Jon cautioned. "Too many people in jeopardy because of what and who they know."

"They just want to help, Jon."

"Then look at it this way, Ben." He uncharacteristically pleaded. "We don't need it getting out, to anyone, that we're on to this. The more involved, the bigger the risk."

"Got it." Ben agreed. "Oh...Jon."

"Yeah?"

"They *were* Muslims."

Jon shook his head.

"I'm going back to the meeting." He said and as he hit the speaker button on the phone he added, "And so are you."

43

Brownwood, Texas was in total chaos. Irv Stallings had walked down the block a half hour before the blast hit. No one knew what had happened. Sheriff Wilbury was not to be found.

"Get in there and dig!" Stallings screamed at the volunteer firemen. "He might be under something."

Two of the men held the deputy back from trying himself. The condition of the rumble left little doubt of the complete devastation within the office.

Two of the Rangers were being treated for injuries. The others were unaccounted for. Austin had been called and more units were on the way. A small crowd began to gather. They were kept two blocks back and appeared stunned by what they saw. Some stared, but most hardly spoke. Even to each other. Nothing like this had ever occurred in or near Brownwood before.

"Come on, Deputy. Please go with the paramedics," the fireman coaxed. "You're obviously in shock, man."

Stallings looked at the man trying to help him with a blank gaze. He turned his head back to where the building had stood and took and deep, deep breath.

"He'll go with you now, won't you Irv?" the man said to the medics.

They took the deputy by the arms and gently led him to their van.

~

"Immigration Customs and Enforcement," the voice answered. "Yes, Sir. Right away, Sir." The clerk then transferred the call.

The office that had answered Bogart's call was in Oklahoma.

Moore, Oklahoma to be exact, a suburban, bedroom community south of Oklahoma City. It was quiet there most of the time and it was close to the local airport. The Director of the regional office liked it there.

"Yes, Mr. Speaker," the director said as he picked up his phone. "I was told I might hear from you."

"Your phones are secured?" the caller asked.

The director flinched at the question. "Why, of course. All our lines here are."

"You understand the gravity and sensitivity of this call?" Bogart asked.

"Certainly," the man responded. "We're on board completely."

"We?"

"Well, I mean... I am, Sir," he stuttered a bit. "I understand the cause."

Bogart let the man stew a moment, then continued.

"The OTG Program you've been developing. It is ready for an operational test?"

The director stiffened his back with pride. His office had been working on the Observation, Tracking and Gathering platform for seven months. It was Top Secret, off budget and his personal pride and joy.

"What do you need checked on, Sir?" he asked the caller.

"Not what... who. It's a person of interest to national security. I need this done quickly and without exposure."

"What do you have for me to go on, Sir? A SS number, or just a name?"

"Right now just the name and where he's from."

"That should be plenty."

"It's Jonathan Crane of Georgia. A town called Dalton."

"Jonathan Crane?" The director paused sounding a bit confused. "The millionaire investor?"

"That was quick," Grant said before thinking.

"No, no Sir. I haven't done anything...I mean, not just now."

"Damn it, man. Make some sense will you?"

"I started a file on him three months ago, DHS was investigating him so I used him as a test subject."

"What did Homeland Security want with him? I never knew about it."

"One of his companies bought a closed plant in Oklahoma City. He had taken options on three offices in buildings in Shreveport, La. and then walked away six weeks later. Within a month he was looking around here. DHS wanted to know what he was up to."

"And?" Grant prodded.

"They set up some heavy duty loom in an old tool and die factory. There are twelve people working for him. No big deal."

"Is that all you have on him?"

"He's an interesting guy. Stayed in Shreveport, very hush, hush... at a time the Russian mob thing went down. No connection to him, though. Pure coincidence."

"Why do say it was hush, hush?"

"He came in very quietly. Private jet." The director was accessing information as he spoke. "We tracked him to a police captain's home at one point, looks like he stayed there."

"Who was this captain?"

"Phillip Stone of homicide division," the director answered and quickly added, "clean as the driven snow, that one."

~

Ben Shaw's attention to the discussion going on in Texas was disturbed by an alarm. A contact sensor on the garage triggered the system, which alerted the home's occupants and locked down the exterior perimeter instantly.

Sliding across the second sub-basement floor, Ben turned on a monitor that automatically displayed cameras in the area of the disturbance. What he saw caused him to lean back in the rolling office chair and whisper.

"Jon."

There was too much activity in the Caddo Mills hideout for Jon to hear, so Ben needed to speak louder.

"Jon," he repeated. "Man, I need to tell you something."

Crane put a hand over his empty ear to better focus on the ear bud connected to his phone.

"What is it, Ben?"

"I've got company."

Before Jon could respond, the lights in the underground hideout blinked and a monitor screen lit up on the wall. The discussions stopped and all eyes in the room turned to the screen. It flashed different images, four seconds at a time, from all around Murray's ranch. Vehicles were roaring in from the highway, surrounding the house and the hanger.

"Stay still, everyone," Jon called out.

The men above ground could not have heard a shouting match in the hideaway, but it was better that the room settled down.

The vehicles, fifteen or sixteen in all, were sedans, SUVs and three extended vans. Men climbed out and began to swarm over the property, too many to count from the camera images.

"Ben," Jon asked into the phone. "Are you alright?"

"Yeah," the boy replied. "I've got ten or twelve trying to get in." he had also activated a monitor showing Caddo Mills. "You've got a small army crawling on you there."

"Just sit tight," Jon cautioned his charge back in Georgia. "Don't use any deterrents. Not yet anyway. Let 'em think you're not there."

"I'm good," Ben said calmly. "I can wait them out. This is kinda odd, though," he added. "Hitting us both at the same time, don't you think?"

"I don't know for sure what I think, yet." Jon took a shallow breath as he walked to the monitor flashing pictures. "I know I don't like this."

Phil Stone stood from his chair, his color draining. "I need to call Sara," he declared firmly. "I need to check on her."

Murray looked to Jon. He was more familiar with the systems here. Jon had ordered them. His friend nodded and Murray led Phil to one of the phones.

"Tell her to go a friend's house for a few days," Jon suggested. "Don't scare her. We just have to be sure how big this thing is."

Phil's color was returning and going straight to red. His expression was all the response Jon needed.

"Who else has family at home?" he asked.

The NCIS agents sat in silence. The Mossad team also remained mum. Daniel and Matt Turlock looked at each other and then stood at the same time.

"Matt, I'll get Sara to go by your house and take her to Wilda's," Phil announced, speaking of Matt's wife.

Turlock turned toward his old friend. He closed his eyes, nodded slightly in agreement and sat back down. More a pile of clothes than a person, he rested his head on his hand.

"Lori is going to freak," Daniel mumbled as he paced to a phone. "Will this shit ever really end?"

The comment was subdued and Daniel never realized anyone had heard it. No one in the room reacted outwardly. Though the thought was already hanging heavily over Jon Crane.

Daniel's frustrated words drove it home like a blow to the solar plexus.

Lamar Jakes noticed the transition without understanding what it was. Watching Jon's every move and expression during the crisis, Jakes had been impressed by the calm nature this man maintained. With Daniel's words came a subtle mood swing that Jakes witnessed, but instantly discounted. Jon's outward gesture did not register to him as important. He saw the man's eyes tighten as his head pulled close to his chest. His right hand made a tight fist that he held for several moments. Jakes saw the change, but didn't recognize it for what it was.

Silas had stepped forward.

44

A ringing phone awakened the occupant of room 212. The sound was wrong and sunlight peaking into the room added to his confusion. It was not his cell. The harsh tone was the room's landline phone.

The man sat up and struggled to remember where he was. It was the Rugged Country Inn outside of Pendleton, Oregon. The phone screamed again.

Damn! The man half thought and half yelled as he rolled to answer it.

"Yeah," He answered, falling back against the pillows.

"This is Mithras."

The man was really confused now.

"How did you find me? You were supposed to use the cell." He challenged.

"We know what we need to, don't worry yourself as to how." Mithras scolded. "Do you have three Ultimates on your team?"

"Yeah," the man told him. "The vests aren't here yet."

"That's alright," Mithras replied firmly. "It's the commitment I'm interested in."

"Well, they're all ready." The man paused as he lay back across his bed, "looking forward to those virgins, I guess."

" Don't disparage them, not even in the least. Is your entire team there already?

"No," the man countered. "Some are in Washington State and some in Idaho."

" I need one of the Ultimates to come here for reassignment. You pick."

"My plan requires for three here, Mithras." The team leader reminded him. "I can't insure success without all of them."

"You can...and you must." His boss smiled an unseen grin. "Call me at the regular number with your decision. I need him here in two days."

~

The assailants in Dalton spent twenty minutes pulling, prying and some cases beating on the mansion's exterior. Their jackets were black with the lettering obscured. Ben took remote pictures and enhanced the images.

"They say 'ATF', but it's marked out." He reported to Jon.

"Our guys jumpsuits say "DEA" and 'ICE'," Jon responded. "There's a few in plain suits."

Then Silas realized they were not using the hideouts full abilities. Jon stepped over to Murray.

"Where's the audio panel we had put in?"

Murray's eyes flashed like a light had gone off inside his head.

"Over here!" he half shouted and led Jon to what looked like a fuse panel. Opening the flat metal door exposed old fashioned round fuses, or what seemed to be. Murray dialed a red one clock-wise and a speaker came to life.

"Anything...any sign of them at all?" one of the plain suits asked in a loud voice.

"No sir," replied a jumpsuit.

"Go over everything again," the suit ordered. "Somebody's here...I can feel it."

Jon looked around the room. All eyes were on him.

"We keep waiting," he told them.

"Jon." Ben's voice crackled through the phone again.

"Yeah?"

"Dalton's finest are just about here," Ben said with a distinct smirk in his voice. "Gil must have got the alarm."

"What are your guests doing?"

"Oh, they're bugging out. Guess they must not have their warrant with 'em."

"Probably not." Jon joked with him. "Listen...don't open the house yet. Just talk to Gil over the phone. Let him know you're okay. Just don't open the house."

"Might be a straggler hanging back, huh?" Ben inferred.

"Just keep it locked down for a bit longer."

"Will do."

Murray pointed to the monitor. The man in the suit was dialing a cell phone.

"Ben...there's a guy using a cell phone right above us. Can you track it?"

"Give me two shakes," came back in response.

Jon and Murray watched and tried to listen in, but the man wasn't close enough to a microphone to be heard.

"Jon," Ben broke in. "The call is to a number in Colorado. Your guy there referred to the other man as Mithras."

Lamar Jakes straightened up from his leaning position against a wall and moved closer. Jon raised one finger towards the young man and then turned back to the phone.

"What are they talking about, Ben?"

"They're looking for Murray. They haven't found the copter and they think he's away."

"Just Murray?"

Ben was silent a few seconds as he listened to more of the conversation from ground level in Caddo Mills.

"They were hoping you were there, too," Ben announced. "And they mentioned Marsha."

~

The attacks south of the city had left Tyler, Texas, in turmoil. Local citizens and Texas Rangers had been killed in three separate locations. Word of mouth accounts by survivors were quite different from the news stories outside the immediate Tyler area.

"Drug raids gone bad, my hairy butt!" Kate Griffin exclaimed at her television.

The local news was a mere blurb. Blink and you missed it reporting and even that was factually incorrect. Initial reports failed to mention the deaths and offered that three mobile drug labs had exploded during high-speed chases in the area.

Reality spread through Tyler like a wildfire. Within hours, residents were calling relatives and friends in other cities and other states attempting to get the truth out.

"There's more to this..." they tried. "We're not being told the truth."

Some believed, but many others wrote them off as zealots. The message from the tube and on the written pages had more weight, and there was no one in that arena to counter that message.

The injured had been taken to the hospital, the walking wounded were patched up and held temporarily in the Tyler detention facility. The Chief of Police protested, but he was overruled by order of Homeland Security.

Lt. Walton Spencer, the helicopter pilot who led the rescue effort, was among those severely wounded. He lay in silence, in a hospital bed, surrounded by Government Officials trying to ask him questions.

310

As Kate Griffin walked past his door, Spencer recognized her and muttered as loud as he could, "Mama."

She stopped and looked at who was calling and, of course, the officials all looked to see who he had called to.

Mrs. Griffin was not related to Lt. Spencer, but she did know who he was.

The injured man blinked rapidly at her, stopped and then blinked again as hard as he could. Kate caught on and rushed into the room.

"Oh, my poor baby," she cried.

The officials stepped back to give her room. Spencer's glare communicated to her as well as words.

"Can't I have some privacy with my boy?" Kate yelled and looked all around the room with a scowl. "Git, I said!" she screamed at them.

The reluctant men moved toward the door and into the hallway. Kate leaned over the Lieutenant who whispered into her ear. "Call this number...tell them we need help," and he called off a phone number he remembered as Agent Barker's.

Sara Griffin looked back at the door. Men were still menacing the hallway. She repeated the number to assure Spencer that she had it.

"Son, I'll go see what the doctor says." Leaning forward, she kissed his cheek. "I'll be back directly."

In the stairwell at the end of the hall, Kate dialed the number on her cell phone. The other end rang in a hideout in Caddo Mills.

Agent Barker looked as surprised as anyone when the phone rang. Only Jon's cell phone had a signal down here, or so they thought.

"What model is that?" Murray asked. "It ain't supposed to work down here."

Barker grabbed the unit, "I forgot," he said. "It's a Nokia...just over six watts."

"Cell phones are less than .010 watts," Daniel chimed in.

"Not our Global units," Barker acknowledged. "They can burn deeper than this." He flipped the phone open and answered, "Yes?"

Sara Griffin had no idea who she was calling.

"This is Kate, Kate Griffin in Tyler. Lt. Spencer asked me to call this number."

"Yes, Mrs. Griffin..." Barker responded. "This is Agent Barker, NCIS. How is Spencer?"

"Hurt bad," she told him. "He and nine others are in the hospital here. He said they need help and quick."

Barker looked at his boss who nodded before the question was asked.

"Mrs. Griffin."

"Yes."

"Can you get back in to see Spencer?"

"I think so, yes," she said, her voice trembling now.

"Mrs. Griffin...I need you to... Spencer needs you to hold together. Okay, can you do that?"

She took a loud, deep breath and responded, "yes."

"Tell Spencer the FBI is coming. And he can trust them...you got it?"

"I got it," she answered with more authority in her voice now. "FBI... he can trust the FBI."

"Go tell him that...and thank you for all you've done."

"You're welcome young man," Kate said in her best Texas accent. "Oh...and get these assholes out of my town, will you?"

"Working on it, Ma-am."

Jerome Grimes was already on one of the wired phones. He dialed directly into Jason Shuck's office, the Operation Director of the FBI.

When Shuck answered, Grimes didn't waste time or words.

"Mr. Director I'm Special Agent Grimes, NCIS. I'm calling on behalf of our director, Wilfred Scott."

"Yes, Agent Grimes...we've met. What do you need?"

Grimes explained the situation in Tyler and the urgency. He was put on hold, but only for a minute.

"Special Agent, if you're in contact with anyone there at the hospital, let 'em know four teams from Dallas are on the way. Two by air and two by convoy."

"Thank you, Sir. They already know."

"Say again?"

"Knew I could count on you, Sir."

"What's your sit-rep, Agent?"

"We're 'ok' for now, but it's getting thick. We'll be in touch...you can count on it."

45

In her high-rise office overlooking downtown Atlanta, Georgia, Sheri Shanahan had finished checking all her reports on her computer. Before closing everything down, she hit a keystroke that went to a camera within the closed cage beside her office.

Sasha was lying on her back, twisting her spine. Shanahan smiled and pushed the button to power down her system. She was not aware that every site she had visited, every keystroke she had made was being recorded on a computer located in a second level sub-basement, in Dalton, Georgia.

~

Matt Turlock leaned into Phil Stone to ask a question.

"You reached Sara?"

"Yes... I should have told you right away," Phil apologized. "She's on her way to your house right now."

"She reacted quickly!" Matt tried to smile.

"We've been through..." Phil caught himself and paused to consider his comment. "We've been through tough situations before. Sara knows what to do."

The group in hiding settled down, somewhat. The monitor still showed activity above ground, but the men in jumpsuits began to walk toward their leaders. They raised their hands from their sides in a gesture that meant, *what now*?

Grimes, Spiegel and Barker led the way back to the table. Then Harel and Reiss followed and soon the places were again full. Marsha sat with Daniel who was near Matt and Phil.

Murray Bilstock stood at the monitor, his gaze locked in on the intruders above him. Lamar Jakes had not moved. He continued to lean with one foot against the wall. A position he appeared comfortable in.

Jon had found a corner, out of the way, where he leaned back and slid down until his rear end touched the carpet.

Phil Stone took over the conversation as though no interruption had occurred.

"Ok," He started. "We know what they're up to...how do we stop them?"

There was quiet all around for several minutes. Finally Jerome Grimes spoke up.

"We need to call the dance," He said cryptically.

Neither those who understood nor those who did not questioned the comment. Everyone knew he would follow up, and he did.

"There are too many places to prepare for. I'll guarantee you, they are not making big plans for every possibility."

"Okay...I understand we have limited resources," Phil agreed. "But what can we do to control things without them knowing we're on to 'em?"

"We take away their options," Grimes answered. "Force their hand toward one target. One we can defend or be the aggressor in."

"Jerry," Harel spoke up. "You know I respect you, but think further, my friend."

The room turned to the Mossad leader and waited.

"We know this...they have brought men and equipment in through the Mexican border. They used decoys to accomplish it."

"Right...your point is?" Grimes asked.

"One of the possible locations is in Oregon, correct?"

Grimes' eyes lit up, but he said nothing.

"How many men and how much in supplies have come in through the northern border? We haven't even considered that."

Phil Stone leaned back hard and rubbed his eyes with both hands.

"It's all about the numbers," he said in frustration. "The man's absolutely right. We have no idea how many men they've got invested in this. They've been wasting them left and right just to throw everybody off."

"Can't fight an army you can't see," Grimes said while staring at the tabletop. "Or don't know exists."

"Why can't we just tell the President there's a threat?" Matt asked.

"He won't back down from a threat," Harel pronounced firmly. "It would be a sign of weakness. There's no evidence to show him and the agencies sworn to protect him...hell, half of 'em are suspect."

Murray turned to the table and shouted, "They're leaving."

The assembled turned, as they needed to, to see the screen.

"Think they're gone this time?" Daniel asked rhetorically. No one answered.

"I'm going up to check on my stuff," Murray announced and he looked toward Jon in his corner. Rather than get up to go with him, Jon simply nodded his approval.

Terry Barker stood and pulled his Glock 23 from its holster. He ejected the magazine to check it.

"Think I could stretch my legs a bit," he declared as he popped the magazine back into the grip and chambered a round.

Murray looked at Barker, squinted back toward Jon and then nodded to the NCIS agent. "Sure... come on."

Dust was still in the air from the vehicles when Murray and Barker stepped into the hanger from the cabinet. They came into view on the monitor and Marsha rose to walk around the table. She watched the two men and the area very carefully.

"So..." Phil Stone said loudly. "Where were we?"

Daniel Seay brought the meeting back to speed. "We were talking about how the President wouldn't back down from a simple threat."

Grimes spoke without looking up, "We have to turn the threat on them," he said firmly. "Make them feel the need to change plans."

Tim Spiegel pushed back from the table and uttered his first words of the discussion.

"It's still the numbers...the numbers we don't have. How can we intimidate a force that may be larger than we considered?"

Ideas were raised and discussed, but each fell short of agreement.

Spiegel spoke again, this time changing the subject.

"We know we can trust the FBI." He looked at his boss as he said that. Grimes nodded silently in agreement.

"And I believe the CIA is on our side," Spiegel continued. Again Grimes agreed.

"Side?" Phil asked sarcastically. "What are the sides? Just what are we up against, some foreign power? Ourselves?" He searched the room, but no one responded. "Hell, how do we know who the people would support? They're being fed information that isn't true. How deep does that go?"

"It's like the revolution all over again, isn't it?" Marsha Hurst threw in without looking away from the monitor.

"What?" Phil was confused by her comment, and he wasn't alone.

"We're experiencing the revolution in our own time." She turned to the table and went on. "Adams, Washington,

Revere...Thomas Jefferson, they were all radicals. They weren't sure how the public would react to them either."

She checked the monitor while her statement soaked in to the others. Murray and Terry were on their way back. Marsha smiled a self-satisfied smile and deliberately looked at each of the others there, including Jon.

"All they could do was what they believed in. What they thought was right. And let the chips fall where they may." She was nearly preaching now.

As Murray and Terry stepped back into the room, they found it quiet, with Marsha standing to one side and commanding everyone's attention.

"Okay...." the cowboy quipped. "I got a feeling I missed something."

Marsha bowed her head and didn't respond. Phil spoke for her.

"Our friend was just explaining to us why this is so important, Murray," he said. "The 'hows' were getting so bogged down... that the 'why' nearly got lost."

"It's very basic, really," Daniel added. "It's born in us all."

"Fundamental to our being," Matt Turlock joined in.

Others nodded and muttered agreements. The spirits in the room appeared to be lifted as they continued talks on just what they should do.

In his corner, Jon didn't miss a word. He quietly turned the phone over and pushed the "speaker" button, turning that function off. He raised the phone to his ear.

"Ben, you still there?" he asked softly.

"The whole time," Ben replied.

"How does the radar look around Murray's ranch?"

"It's clear...they're gone and out of the area."

318

"Does that include the highway out front?"

"You mean your landing strip?" Ben countered without flinching.

Jon smiled and paused a minute.

"You're thinking ahead of me, huh?" he finally asked his assistance.

"Always, boss," Ben assured him. "And yes, it's clear and the G5 has been alerted. I could tell some time back you would call for it soon."

"What's his ETA?"

"Just under two hours if he hauls ass."

"Ask him to come on...I need to come home for a bit...Oh, a couple more things."

"Yes, sir."

"Call that pizza place in town. I think they have a unit in Caddo Mills. I want ten large pizzas with bread sticks and drinks delivered to Murray's ranch, but make sure they do this."

"Okay...what?"

"Have the records, computer and otherwise, show the order going to an address in town. That's very important and there's an extra hundred in it if they will."

"Got it. I'm sure they can handle that. Say...how bout' me?"

"I'll bring you a piece. How's that?"

"Thanks," Ben replied with a smirk in his voice. "And the other thing?"

Jon lifted his gaze to the young man now standing across the room. Lamar Jakes was intently listening to the conversation that crossed the table. He had not spent much time with people like this. What he had imagined of them was quite different.

"Yeah," Jon added. "I'll be bringing a guest. He's not much older than you. Gather up some clothes he can use...he's about your size, I figure."

"Another straggler?"

"One that's real lucky to be alive," Jon told him. "I'm putting you back on speaker now."

46

Preparations across five states were down to the logistics of moving people into place. The efforts would be coordinated, but by no means simultaneous. Shanahan's plan was to drive the President and Vice President to Oregon in the midst of chaos.

Besides the soldiers they had recruited, the group needed volunteers to help with the set up. Suggestions and funding for travel were sent to union groups. They were told that the coming holiday time would be the best to demonstrate against the court's overturning of the Information Equity Act.

The thousands who would protest had no real idea of the full plan they would be party to. Their knowledge wasn't necessary. When the artificial threats of nuclear attack were to be deployed, that lack of knowledge would be helpful to the plot. Some in the crowds may be killed in the ensuing panic, but that was the cost of revolution.

Prof. Steven Walden sat in his office, gazing at the ceiling and running those plans over and over through his mind.

Beautiful, he told himself, *simply beautiful*. Everything had gone well, with the minor exception of whoever was fooling around in Texas.

We'll find 'em, he thought, *and when we do*. He didn't finish the thought. It wasn't necessary. His mind had gone on to the current day's needs. It was now ten days until July Fourth. Tomorrow the unions should be notified to begin plans for their protests in Ohio, Missouri, Florida and Kansas. That job was up to him, but not until Bogart ordered it.

~

The lawyer Shanahan was scheduled to make a speech in her hometown on July 3rd. In her address, she would proclaim her love of the judicial process. The speech would appear to have one meaning that day, yet take on a terribly different meaning within the days following.

She stopped at the Krispy Kreme along her route home that evening.

"Evening Ms. Attorney, ma'am." The counter clerk greeted her like an old friend, or maybe a regular customer. "What shall it be tonight?" he asked.

"Half dozen fancy...you know what I like Charles, and the other half in regular Krispy Kremes."

As the man walked away she called after him.

"Now that "Hot" sign is on out there. Don't try to send those older ones home with me," she teased.

"Oh, no ma'am," Charles smiled a huge grin. "Wouldn't do no such a thing."

Most people needed to shy away from such treats, but Shanahan's metabolism burned the calories quickly. She never had an issue with her weight in her entire life. Besides, tomorrow the dominoes would begin to fall into place. Tonight was a time of celebration.

~

Cyrus Grant remained in his office in the capitol building until after 9:30 P.M. He stared at a map of the continental United States that stretched over six feet of the opposite wall. His mind was not at ease.

The actions he had ordered in Texas were of little or no consequence. The media helped with that. The agencies they could count on were now tested and true. Those loyal to the government should not be aware or have time to react once things began.

The phrase "*if it seems too easy, it may well be,*" kept running through his mind as he stared at the map.

That's my country, he repeated to himself. *Mine to do with as I wish.*

No matter how often he told himself that...he wasn't convinced.

Cyrus Grant stood and walked to his window. Looking up at the stars he uttered what he considered to be a prayer.

"God...if you're up there, please do not judge me for what I am about to do." He broke his gaze from the window and looked down to the floor. "Judge me by what I do after."

The man who believed that within ten days he would be the next President of the United States stood and looked at the floor for several more minutes.

~

More than another hour of discussions had not moved the group any closer to a consensus. The pizzas had arrived and that took up some of the time, but talks really continued through dinner.

The Caddo Mills group had tried several scenarios, but each had issues.

"We need to find out how they plan to hit Oregon, if that is what their plan is." Phil pounded the table with his fist. Not hard...just enough to have an effect.

Checking his watch, Jon saw this as "as good a time as any." He slowly stood from his corner and all eyes turned to him.

"It's about time," said Daniel Seay, leaning back. "Everyone has spoken except you."

"Yeah," Murray chimed in. "What's in your head?"

Marsha's expression became one of concern. She had seen the look he bore before.

Jon stepped toward the table and looked at each one there.

"Before I start, I want to be very clear on one thing." He let that hang there for everyone to consider before going on. "I am, if nothing else in this life, extremely proud of being part of this group. Do not ever forget that, regardless of what comes next."

No one mocked his statement, though to some it may have appeared a bit lofty and assuming. Murray, Daniel, Marsha, and others who knew him best, became just a bit pale in color. Murray even sat down.

"I've listened as closely as I could to everything that's been said here." All eyes were intently on him now. "It's my opinion that you are correct to believe you must force the location on them. Do not allow them too many options. You can't cover them all."

The group showed no real emotion to that. Phil made a note and Jon could see Daniel rubbing his chin. He knew that meant his friend was apprehensive about what may come next.

"There's one crucial area that I am convinced we do not have time to correct." He took a deep breath and considered his next words. "We don't know just how they plan to do this. Through diversion, like they used to set everything up, or direct use of the nuclear materials they have."

Some stirring began around the table, yet everyone stayed basically quiet.

"We don't know their numbers, the extent of their plan or even exactly when they plan to strike."

"I thought we determined it was the Fourth of July," Phil finally spoke up.

"That holiday can be over several days the way people celebrate. And they could use more 'set-ups' just to direct things. In fact, I'm sure they will to some extent. Just like you figured out...they must control the actual location of the hit, or hits as well."

"That sounds like you don't think we can stop it," Matt Turlock challenged.

"Not in the way you're thinking, no. We don't have enough information."

"We know who, what and all the possible wheres," Phil insisted. "So we lack a couple of details...we have to act on what we know. The information we have."

"No, the information we lack is vital. We all know who the major players are in this plot, the leaders. If we don't stop them, we haven't stopped anything." Jon turned and pointed to Phil Stone. "Is there enough evidence on anyone... for you to make an arrest?" Though speaking to Phil, his glance also sought out Marsha, who said nothing.

"I could sure give 'em a good talking to," Phil blustered. "Scare the crap out of 'em. That works more than you might think."

"An arrest, Phil... Could you make one that would stick?" Jon pounded the point.

The long time officer of the law gritted his teeth and said no more.

Jon looked over at Grimes, Barker and his old rescuer, Spiegel. Each had years of experience with law as well. None said a word. They knew where he was going.

"There are three we know to be the leaders," Jon's voice was a bit louder now. "We also know that they believe we cannot touch them legally."

"Now, Jon..." Daniel started.

"Please, my friend," Silas' tone cut him off. "Let me finish."

Jon began to walk around the table.

"Without these leaders in place...their plan, their coup, would evaporate." He leaned forward and touched the table with one finger. "They must be removed from the picture."

"You're standing here... telling us... you're about to commit major crimes?" Matt asked with nervous anger in his voice.

"I've said no such thing," Jon answered calmly. He straightened back up and walked toward the wall. "What I am telling you is this. I would hope you'd spend your time on getting the word out, the best you can. It may not work, but if enough people caught on...that too could stop this. For now."

Jon stopped in front of Lamar Jakes and said for only him to hear, "You're coming with me, okay?"

Jakes nodded.

Jon turned back to the others. He noticed Murray stand up again, and move toward the monitors.

"I'm leaving in just a few minutes," Jon told them. "Jakes... is going with me. What I do from here is up to me.... If you don't approve and can prove anything...go for it." He looked around once more, meeting each one with direct eye contact.

"I will only say again, your focus on these leaders will be a waste of time." Jon paused, taking a deep breath. "And time you do not have. Leave that alone. Concentrate on what you can do. Get the word out, organize the best defense you can and by all means...stay safe."

Murray caught the glimpse of a blip on the radar screen and monitor.

"Something's coming in," he alerted the group.

"That's my ride," Jon said calmly.

He walked over to Marsha and leaned into her forehead gently.

"You have to trust me... Can you do that?" he asked her.

Marsha hugged his neck, saying nothing.

"I'll take that as a 'yes'," Jon pulled back and smiled at her. "Will you stay here with Nava till it's time to move her?"

Marsha nodded and managed to get, "of course," out of her mouth.

Walking toward the exit with Jakes in tow, Jon bumped into Murray intentionally and whispered, "I'll be in touch and soon. Just going home right now."

Without moving, Murray muttered back, "You'd better."

Jon and Lamar Jakes walked to the road. The G5's lights were lighting the roadway as it came down. When the pair reached the road, the plane was already turning around.

In only minutes they were on board. The Gulfstream Jet screamed down the highway and lifted. Jon took the cell phone, connected to Ben, off speaker again.

"Ben, we're on our way," he said.

"Roger, that," Ben replied.

"I'll get home with the Mercury. Remember; please...keep the house locked tight. Don't open anything till I get there."

"Got it. See ya soon," and Ben hung up.

Jon noticed Lamar Jakes staring as he hung up.

"What?" he asked the kid.

"Another Mercury?" Jakes smiled. "Seriously?"

47

Luther Brooks had been an FBI agent for thirty-six years. The last seven were as District Special Agent in Charge of the Eastern District of Texas.

When Brook's hybrid-chopper landed in Tyler, Texas he had two other Bell-Boeing V-22 Ospreys and seventeen heavily armed agents with him. A vehicle convoy of six trucks with an additional seventy-two National Guard troops from the Dallas area were on their way.

The Ospreys landed on a youth ball field just one block from the hospital.

"Move it!" Brooks called out and he and the contingent double-timed to the rear doors of the hospital. Once inside, Brooks was confronted by an old acquaintance.

"Luther, what's the big show all about?" Charlie Gunn asked. He and several of his DHS men stood, blocking the hallway. "We've got this."

"That's the problem, Chuck," Luther smiled. "You're not welcome here. The Governor asked us to look in on things."

"I'm under orders from the acting Secretary of Homeland Security!" Gunn barked and arched his back defiantly.

"Still like sticking your nose in the air, huh Chuck?" Brooks chuckled. "I heard the Secretary had an accident. So now it's Doyle, huh? You guys are so screwed."

"Luther, don't push me...this is a matter of national security."

"Yeah, yeah. The Texas Rangers were smuggling drugs. I heard that ridiculous cover story your new boss put out."

"Well... tell it to the acting Secretary."

"You tell him he still owes me money from a poker game in Virginia."

Brooks held one finger up over his shoulder and then pointed forward. He and his men moved ahead, pushing Gunn's people aside.

"You have your acting secretary call the Attorney General, Chuck. And until then...you attempt to obstruct me or my mission again and there will be casualties. Am I clear on that?"

Gunn backed up against the wall. He pulled his cell phone from a vest pocket while the FBI moved past him and his people.

"Boss, I've got trouble here," he said into the phone. The response was short and sweet.

"Back off...we'll let the media handle it. Don't make anything worse than it is," the voice ordered him.

Gunn answered sharply, but respectfully and then slammed his phone closed.

"Come on," he called to his men. "We're relieved."

And handle it they did. By the evening news of that day, the major networks all covered the story in Tyler, Texas.

"Abbott and Costello Revived in Texas Town," was the lead-in.

"Who's on first?" the smiling on-air host asked. "The current administration can't seem to decide who they want to handle a simple drug bust."

Pictures of the FBI arriving at the Tyler Hospital were narrated with, "In the apparent invasion by an agency known to be more 'loyal' to the administration and more acceptable to the locals of that area, the questions are outnumbering the answers."

The on screen image changes to a young woman with a guitar. The same narrator's voice now declares, "Should American Idol winners be liable for federal taxes on their prize money? Our viewers vote next. Stay tuned, right after Sports."

~

Ben Shaw was not wasting time while the G5 was enroute. Jon had not issued specific orders other than "keep the house locked down." But some things didn't require orders. Ben just knew.

He walked across the sub-basement floor to a bank of computers sitting in a cool, dark corner. They were monitoring different aspects of this case, as best he knew to watch. Two were wirelessly ghosting Sheri Shanahan's office and two were monitoring calls to and from the Capitol Office Complex and Atlanta.

Another surveyed the University library computers in Boulder, Colorado. Jakes revelation as to how messages were transmitted to Mithras broke the stalemate on that issue.

The only one with any new information was the personal desktop of lawyer Shanahan. Ben sat in amazement as he watched the replay of her trip through all the top-secret sites her system had access to.

As the pictures flew by, Ben lurched and reached out for the pause key. He then backed up the imagery to what he thought he had seen.

"Damn..." he heard himself mutter. "That's the hospital in Tyler, Texas." He moved to another frame and recognized a series of shots of the Brownwood sheriff's office, before and after. Next came the ones that stopped him, a group of pictures of the house.

"This house."

Ben ran through the eight different photos and then back again. He noticed spots that didn't belong. Focus and close-up rendering exposed what he found.

"Jon was right." He slumped into his chair, "there's two men on the roof."

330

Printouts were made as he wondered where those cameras could be.

"They're not ours," he said out loud and as the words cleared his mouth his eyes lit up. "Satellites." He unconsciously snapped his fingers. "She has access to satellite photographs." Then the total reality hit him. "And she can control what they look at...damn."

He finally moved the recorded screen shots forward and found another of great importance. There on the screen was Sasha, the white tiger.

"She can check on the cat without opening the wall."

The change of subject matter reminded him of another program he had running. Quickly spinning around and awakening the monitor there, Ben keyed in his request for results. The building permits for all work on the Gas Light Building in the last ten years.

The list was intensive, but what he sought stood out clearly. The plans and permits for the tiger's cage, including the external elevator, separate air handler and the automated feeding system.

He printed out everything and organized it according to category.

48

Reports of the news from Tyler, Texas did not ease the mind of Mithras. He was concerned that it drew any attention at all.

Attention only leads to discovery, he heard rattling within his thoughts. *Did someone tell me that, or did I just make it up?* He wondered.

Either way, *this wasn't good.* The professor sat at his desk and unlocked a drawer. It was really a drawer within a drawer. Not totally secret agent stuff, but it added security.

Inside he kept a wooden box and a stack of papers. Setting the box to one side on the desktop, he leaned back to study the papers. They were lists, names of recruits who had not measured up completely. Many were still students at the university, and all had been placed in "sleeper" status.

A quick count of those still in Boulder, Colorado came to twelve. *That would have to do,* he thought and quickly made a new list of those names. While replacing the papers and reaching for the wooden box he paused, staring at the box. It had been a gift from Bogart, many years ago. How the speaker had come to have it was never disclosed.

Placing it in his lap, Steven Walden raised the lid and exposed the contents. A soft cloth, fringe lined, mini blanket lay over a somewhat dull finished German Luger pistol. This wasn't just any Luger. The weapon was extremely unique. It carried the serial number "One."

Early in the twentieth century, around 1906 it is told, the U.S. Army sent 5000 .45 caliber cartridges to the Frankford arsenal that were then transferred to the Luger plant. The famously reliable pistol was manufactured as a 9mm in Germany. The United States wanted to have one that fired their more popular .45 cartridges.

In 1907, two units were shipped to the Springfield Armory for testing. The results did not lead to a contract and one of the pistols went unaccounted for following the tests. Records for Serial number "One" were simply lost. Though fired several times, some notes referred to it being damaged while others called the testing abusive and claimed the pistol was destroyed in the process.

Luger Number "Two" is in a museum in Washington, D.C. Serial number "One," along with a magazine containing six rounds, lay in the lap of a man known as Mithras.

~

Lucy rose from her hiding place and landed at the front of the hanger. The NCIS agents would be the first to leave Caddo Mills. Rather than go to Dallas, they asked Murray to take them to Tyler. Grimes wanted to coordinate with the FBI and find out just who in D.C could still be trusted.

"We will wait till Nava can travel with us," her Mossad leader said stoically as he shook his old friends hand. "You take care my friend. Jerry, you and I, we must meet again."

"Sorry we got you guys into this," Grimes contritely offered in his good-byes. "We really didn't know what we had here."

"It can be prevented, stopped I mean. Now that you know what they would do."

"Yeah...we'll stop it. It's only a matter of body count, I fear."

Marsha called to the agent as Nava leaned up and tried to speak. "She wants to say something."

"I could hear the man, the one you call 'Jon,' talk through my sleep," Nava said to Grimes. "He is good. He's a strong leader. I could feel it in his words."

Agent Spiegel smiled at her. "You don't know the half of it."

His boss and the Mossad team all looked at him strangely.

"I'll tell the whole story one day...over beers, okay?" Spiegel nodded.

"I like that idea." Nava smiled and lay back against her pillow. "Making plans means there's a future."

"Let's call it a date," Spiegel added and then they left with the cowboy.

Daniel had walked over to see if Marsha needed anything. Before he could ask, Matt called to him. A phone was in his hand.

"Daniel...we've got work to do,'" he nearly shouted across the room. "The news is starting to smear Jon."

"What?" Daniel knew what he'd heard. He just didn't understand. "Smear him how?"

"They're saying a rich industrialist is behind the attacks using nuclear weapons. One went so far as to name him and tie him to 'The Son'."

"They were on me in Charlotte," Marsha told them. "That's one reason I'm here. My boss didn't like the way the DEA was snooping into my business. He tipped me off and told me to get lost, literally."

"The channels are lining up pretty clearly. From Homeland Security down is working with these insurrection types. The FBI is more old school," Matt explained.

"I heard the Secretary of HS was found dead. My people think he was killed by insiders," Daniel said as he came back to the phone location.

Matt handed him a line and added softly, "Ferris was a good man...caught in a political nightmare. He may have done himself."

Matt and Daniel reached out through their own networks to find papers willing to counter the accusations thrown at Jonathan Crane. Some tried, some declined to "get involved." The power of the press was strong, but a far cry from what it had been.

~

He had to stop and remind himself from time to time, but the Speaker of the House was a congressman from the state of Virginia. Seldom did he go there now, except for re-election speeches and photo-ops.

Grant was born into a coal mining family in the eastern mountains of Kentucky. The town of Cumberland, in the county of Harlan, was home. He kept a secluded cabin there near the top of Black Mountain. There were to be festivities in Richmond for the Fourth of July holiday, but he would spend the week prior in the thin air of Kentucky.

"Staley," he called to an aide. "Check my schedule. I want to get out of this town by Thursday."

"Sir, I can reschedule anything past that date if you like."

Thursday was two days away. Staley's suggestion made him ask himself, *why wait?*

"Change of plans, Staley," he hollered.

"Yes, sir?"

"I'm leaving just before close of business tomorrow, nothing after 4:00 P.M. Let 'em know I'm off to Virginia."

"Not a problem, sir." The aide stepped into the office, appointment book in hand, "I'll make it happen."

"Thank you, Staley, a good holiday to you and your family. Good things seem to come around this holiday. Let's hope for some this year."

Closing the large book, Staley replied, "May that be the case, sir."

49

The trip from Dalton's airport to Highway 71 took under twenty minutes. Few words were exchanged along the way. Lamar Jakes' eyes were open, but hardly focused on the dimly lit view.

"So...this is where you live, huh?" he asked the driver.

"Yep."

Jakes then looked around the interior of the Mercury Marquis as though he had just become aware of it.

"I pictured you in a fancier ride."

"You don't like my car?" Jon grinned.

"It's fine. If you get tried of driving you can stop and play some soccer in here."

"You never told me where you're from," Jon broke in.

The younger man was taken aback. He had lost control of the conversation.

"You never asked," he muttered toward the floorboard.

"I'm guessing California." Jon took a quick look to his right as he spoke.

"Close..." Jakes answered. "Sparks, Nevada. It's near Reno."

"Ah. Okay." Jon sounded satisfied and justified in the same breath.

"Okay?" Jakes was offended, but not sure why.

"Yeah...Okay." Jon turned onto a two-lane side street, "and this is where I'm from, okay?"

The next turn would be onto Highway 71. As the Mercury approached it, Jon's tone changed dramatically.

"Put your head down between your knees," he barked.

"Excuse me?"

"Close your eyes and put your head between your knees...it's not that hard to do."

Jakes slowly bent forward and placed his head below the dashboard level. The Mercury passed the mansion and drove on toward the gas station.

"Stay down now...I'm serious," Jon repeated his order.

The car slowed and swung to the right before turning left. Jakes felt the slight bump as they entered the tunnel, but had no idea where he was.

"Just another minute," Jon proclaimed, sounding more assuring this time, but still quite serious.

There was the sound of a large motor and then a thump behind them. As he tried to imagine what that could be, Jakes realized they had stopped.

"Okay...you can get up now," Jon announced as he opened the car door.

Through the windshield lay surroundings that totally disoriented him. Jakes undid his seatbelt and opened the door. He was now inside a solid rock structure with bright lighting. Stalls lined one side with cars and trucks carefully parked.

"What the...?" slipped through his lips. But it was not loud enough to be heard. "What is this place?" came out with more volume.

Jon didn't bother to answer the question. A small door opened at the far end of the expanse and another young man stepped out.

As Ben walked toward them, Jon motioned for Jakes to "come along."

"Ben..." he began. "This is Lamar Jakes of Sparks, Nevada." Jon then turned to Jakes, whose eyes were still attempting to digest what they were seeing.

"Jakes, this is Ben Shaw. Ben is my associate and technical advisor."

Ben reacted to that with surprise and a slight grin. Jon sheepishly cocked his head and smiled back.

"Never had to introduce you before," he explained with a grin.

"Hey...I'll take it... Hi, Lamar," Ben shot back as he extended his hand to the guest. "Nice to meet you."

Jakes returned the handshake, but all he could think to say was a question.

"How many cars are in here?"

"Five right now," Ben told him. "Each has a special purpose." He pointed to the pick-up truck and headed that direction. "Would you like a closer look?"

Jon watched as Ben began the tour then nodded and moved forward.

"I'll be up in the lab area," he yelled out and stepped into the elevator.

~

Sheri Shanahan stood at her living room window with a glass of red wine. She wasn't yet sure whether red or white was best with donuts, but the testing was fun.

Her thoughts this evening were focused on the plan. It was set in stone now. No way to stop it or change it really, the time nigh.

At least I'm disconnected from it. She raised her glass toward her own reflection in a toast. *No ties to me until it's all done.* Her self-serving smile stared back at her.

Walking back to her desk, where the draft of the speech laid spread out, she thought again about the double entendres. References to her "love of our system" and how "the law stood above all else." *Were any too obvious?*

She realized that several were only there for her own enjoyment. This was far too important for any lingering ideas or questions from her audience of that night. She began editing her work and left only a few comments with lingering vagueness.

~

"Luther, good to see you again." Jerome Grimes reached for his old friend's hand.

Special Agent Brooks had just left the room of Lt. Spencer. As the team leaders shook hands, Agent Barker excused himself to go in to visit Spencer.

"Jerry?" Brooks faked confusion. "What brings you here?"

"Yeah, right." Grimes grinned and introduced his other accompanying agent, "Luther, this is Agent Tim Spiegel of our New Orleans office."

"The interest in all this seems to be wide spread. New Orleans? Really?"

"I needed people I could trust implicitly." Grimes leaned against the wall and glanced down the hallways. "Who do you trust in D.C. these days?"

"Jerry, a question like that could be tough on someone's career." Brooks sounded skeptical.

"Jason is working with Scott on this," Grimes alluded to his Director, Wilfred Scott and the Head of FBI Field Operations, Jason Shuck. "We don't have time to play cat and mouse, Luther. What do you know?"

Brooks hesitated again, but only for a few seconds.

"Jerry..." he started and rubbed his face with one hand. "I've seen agencies be un-cooperative before...but this is something else. It looks like there are two distinct tracks. One down from HS and the other starting with us, we only figured it out a few days ago."

Grimes slightly nodded. He did not comment or interrupt him.

"You know Ferris is dead?" Brook asked, meaning the former Secretary of Homeland Security who had been found in the river a day ago.

"Yeah," Jerry affirmed. "We heard."

"That leaves Doyle running the show and I'm frankly not sure what his agenda is."

"Where does the CIA stand right now?" Grimes asked. "Farley was with us in Texas. He got hurt there. Who's running that operation now?"

"So that's where he was." The FBI Agent grimaced and rocked his head back. "That answers your other question. They put out that he was involved in espionage with the Israelis."

"Is he alright?" Grimes pushed.

"Far as I know. He's in the hospital at Langley." Brooks studied his old colleague's expression and didn't like what he saw. "Don't tell me it's true." He went on. "Were you guys working with Mossad behind our backs?"

"Doyle was in the meeting." Grimes looked Brooks straight in the eyes. "We thought we had Al Qaeda pulling something. Farley and Scott called in a team to help us."

"Mossad?" Brooks was stunned. "Are they still here?"

"I told you, Luther. You're being played. Darin Doyle knows all about it. He's most likely the leak that has caused our casualties in this investigation."

"Is that kid in there... Mossad?" Brook pointed to Spencer's room.

"No," Spiegel spoke up. "He's a local cop. But he and the town's VFW members risked their lives to help us get her out of here."

341

"Her?" Brooks spun on his heel in disbelief. "There's a woman Mossad agent out there?" His eyes grew wider. "With no credentials to be here?"

"Look...Luther, there's a coup attempt in process in this country, a double assassination. It ain't Al Qaeda, its not even foreigners...it's domestic." Grimes leaned into his friend, nose to nose and finished with, "Do you want to help us stop it, or not?"

50

The worktable had been organized for him. Jon found neat stacks of printouts, charts and diagrams. The largest pile about the lawyer, Shanahan.

Clear blueprints and drawings of the high-rise office complex grabbed Jon's attention. The extra-ordinary permits, proposals and actual building plans were all public record or accessible through Ben's computer prowess.

"Fascinating," Jon reacted out loud. From simply going through the papers one time, the manner to get to her practically wrote itself. He would study everything again, and in much deeper detail. The path was there and laid out for him.

He found the disturbing, yet not unexpected copies of several news releases. Ben had printed them out and laid them to one side. One of the major T.V. Networks had accused Jon of espionage. Two front-page newspaper stories questioned his associates, including Marsha, suggesting they were harboring him. The innuendo was weak and lacked any balance. Still the charges in the stories were damaging.

Jon carefully placed those papers back where they had been and sat perfectly still for several minutes.

They are attacking and endangering my friends, he thought. *I never really asked for friends...and again, they are in danger because of me.*

His trance like state continued until he heard the elevator door open. Reaching out for the smallest stack of papers, merely half a dozen in total, Jon picked it up and spun around to greet the two young men.

"Is this all you found on the Speaker of the House?" he asked in a tone full of sarcasm.

Ben didn't respond verbally. He knew Jon well enough to know when something was wrong. With the news reports he had left for him, Ben knew this was one of those times.

Reaching down, Ben pulled open a drawer on the two high, file box sitting under the table. The drawer was nearly full, separated by indexes showing dates. All of it was about Cyrus Grant.

"I see," Jon acknowledged. He flipped through and pulled out a random section. "Any weaknesses in here?"

"Not much. He's a scary guy," Ben finally spoke.

"Family?"

"No...wife died in a car crash over sixteen years ago, he never remarried. Used the sympathy to his advantage for at least three re-elections. By then he was set as the unbeatable incumbent."

"Kids?" Jon continued his inquisition.

"No," Ben replied. "None."

"Then you're exactly right." Jon turned to look at Ben approvingly, "a man with nothing to lose. He's one scary dude, for sure."

Ben pointed at the drawer, "we never had him on our radar, but there's enough in there to qualify him without involvement in this plot."

"Qualify?" Jakes asked. "Why so cryptic?"

Jon stood and took a step towards the guest.

"Don't ask about things that don't concern you," he said. "We'll deal with what he's into now. That's more than enough."

"Did you see the stack on Walden yet?" Ben asked changing the subject.

"Naw. Is there anything we can use?"

"Not really. He's a different type of case."

"How's that?" Jon walked to the table again and picked up the stack labeled "Mithras."

"He's been a flake so long, he's off the scope. No one has paid him any serious attention in years."

"He's a killer," Jakes let slip out.

Jon stared him down, but the youth stood resilient. Neither said a word.

"A college professor," Ben stepped in again, "with a history of making radical statements, in and out of class. He's almost bullet proof just from being a jerk."

Jon broke off his low intensity glare at Jakes and sat down at the table.

"The school hasn't tried to get rid of him?"

"Sure...many times. But he's tenured and the media loves him."

Jon turned to Jakes who stayed quiet that time.

"Better," he consoled him. "I know what this guy means to you, I really do. And I plan to take you with me when I handle him. Just how I'm going to do that...I'm not sure of yet."

"I want to be the one," Jakes said almost as a request more than statement.

"I'm sure you do. I would if I were you."

Ben saw it was time to break up the conference and let Jon do what he needed to do.

"How 'bout I take Lamar up and show him his room?" he asked.

Jon nodded and started to turn away. He spun back to them quickly.

"Ben," he called out. "Do we still have the keys to the little house in town?"

"Yeah, both of them...yours and Mom's"

345

"I'm going to go there in the morning to think this through for a day or two. I believe my old 'safe room' will be a comfort to me."

"Sure, I'll dig up the key." Ben smiled, but this was new. "What's the deal?" he questioned.

"I just need to get back to basics for a bit. Don't sweat it."

Ben nodded though something about this made him nervous. He turned to lead Jakes upstairs.

"Oh...Ben." Jon raised his hand. "One more thing. Have one of our companies buy my old house and put it in...I'll get the name to you when I decide, okay?"

Stranger yet, Ben thought. He decided to just go with it.

"Yeah and that reminds me." Ben half grinned and changed the subject, "you were right."

"About what?"

"Not unlocking the house." He pointed straight up with one finger. "We had company up there...on the roof."

"You got a location for me?"

Ben leaned over the table and pulled up the satellite pictures he took off Shanahan's computer.

"They were right there," he said.

"Good work, Ben." Jon smiled again. "Is my suit ready?"

"Yes, sir."

"You guys go ahead. I'll see what our other guests were up to."

~

It was 10:00 PM on the east coast when the cell phone rang. Noise in the bar was intense. Though he could barely hear it, the sound of the phone was what he was waiting for.

Those who would describe him to authorities later used words like scraggly and unkempt. His long black beard and deep-set eyes caused many to say he was a Muslim. Only the bartender had noticed him cross himself right after looking at the phone.

"He didn't answer it?" the cop would ask.

"Naw...he just looked at it and turned it off."

"Then what did he do?"

"He reached into his pocket, you know...those big outside pockets on overcoats."

"He wore an overcoat...in Florida...in June?"

"Hey, I don't question the patrons about their attire, okay?"

The cop stepped back away from the bar and the stool where the mysterious man had been.

"Get somebody in here with a geiger counter, quick."

The readings would be fairly low, but enough to confirm the call that police received at 10:06 PM. It was a bomb threat to the hotel across the street from the bar. Not just an ordinary bomb threat...a dirty bomb threat.

Other police teams in the hotel lobby were hearing similar tales of the shabby man with the long bread. A trail of radiation from 1 to 2.1Gy came from the elevator to the exterior doors. Anything over 2Gy was considered moderate, yet serious exposure.

"Call the Mayor," the officer in charge barked to his assistant. "Tampa is in shut down with a nuclear threat."

The trail would show that the man went to a second floor bathroom, shaved in the sink and left through the back stairwell. A total search of the building began immediately.

The man was, by 11:30 PM, in a late model Ford sedan traveling south on Interstate 75. He was now vomiting slightly, but it was not as bad as he thought it would be.

The next morning, someone would have to call the Vice President and tell him his hometown would be closed until well after the Fourth of July.

~

Jon found the redesigned suits hanging in a closet near the elevator. One was subtlety marked "M" and the other "J." The material was the same in appearance while being fifty percent stronger against high velocity penetration. The right side now had a channel that ran up from the ankle area, around the armpit and down the arm.

Jon felt the channel and found it was a specially constructed magazine holding over 200 rounds of .40 caliber ammunition. The flap at the wrist curled to connect with the bottom of the Glock. The rounds were fed hydraulically up through the magazine.

"That's pretty neat," Jon said out loud. "But the gun would melt down way before firing that many rounds."

Then he saw the boxes on the floor of the closet. Each contained a modified version of the Glock 23. Not thinner like Jon's original custom pocket gun, these were thicker along the slides. Slides that had special holes cut to move air rapidly as the slide chambered a new round. The barrel was not obvious at first glance. It was quite different, made of high-grade tungsten steel with an outer shell half again as thick as the standard. A note in the box explained that the weapon had been tested to 300 rounds continuous firing.

That's what he meant by more firepower. Jon smiled to himself. The new Glock had an external holster with a chase built into it, allowing room for the magazine.

He pulled the suit on and found it weighed only four additional pounds over the last model. Another feature to the long magazine was that the weapon could dangle from his wrist, freeing the hand for use on other things.

Fully suited up, Jon went to the third level basement and drove the pick-up out through the gas station. Instead of turning right toward the house, he went left and circled around to a dirt back road up the rear of the mountain. The walk from the end of that road was short and he found another vehicle already there. It was only fifty yards to his house and the rooftop.

51

The control of information has been key to holding power for centuries. Some have done so through use of force and others rely on like-minded brethren in the media.

Those currently seeking to wrestle power away from the elected have long enjoyed the support of many media outlets. Even before the Sponsor's failed attempts to affect change by using mindless gangs and violence.

This most recent campaign received supportive reporting in the operational area, with one exception.

"Why can't we get a handle on that paper?" Bogart would harangue Mithras each time a contradictory story would appear.

"The editor won't budge. He's one of them."

"When it comes to time, he needs to be brought in line or silenced."

"I understand," Mithras had assured his boss. That was weeks ago. It was time to take corrective action.

The "ultimate" that had been culled out for special assignment was a young man named Carlos Martin. He did not meet directly with Mithras upon receiving his orders to leave Washington State. The newly converted Muslim zealot picked up his package and left for Louisiana as requested.

"Your equipment will be waiting for you in a bus station in Oil City. The key to your locker there is in the package," Mithras told him by phone. "What you do will assure the strike against the great Satan to be successful."

"Ali Akbar," Martin bellowed in response.

"Yes, my son. Ali Akbar indeed," Mithras continued. "Your target is the newspaper in Shreveport. Get inside the offices, deep as you can, before you commit. Do you understand?"

"I do, Mithras. Ali Akbar."

"You journey should take four days. Pick up your equipment and then take two days to plan your way in." The professor paused to allow comprehension. "I should hear of your bravery one week from today."

"As you command," Martin promised as Mithras hung up his phone.

~

Large bolts held down the heavy metal roof material on the backside of the mansion. Their pattern allowed for footing on the steep surface and the roof melted into the mountain so access was simple.

Jon crept up to one ridgeline and across the top. He noticed a small box tied to the chimneystack. The unit held a dish for transmission of whatever it was there to pick up.

Jon pulled a cell phone and hit intercom.

"Yeah, Jon?" Ben answered.

"Are you picking up any frequencies that penetrated into the house?"

"Frequencies?"

"Are we being bugged, Ben?"

"Oh...hang on a sec."

He checked a scanner set up just for that type of invasive signal.

"Nope...we're clear," Ben reported. "Nothing getting through."

"Okay," Jon responded and pulled the box free from its mounting.

Didn't think anything could get through this material...its nice to know that's true, he smiled as he thought.

Climbing back down, he brought the transmitter with him.

Ben might enjoy looking at it, he told himself. *He can see if it collected anything we didn't detect.*

~

An envelope arrived at the offices of the Wichita Eagle newspaper. It would be opened in the morning and sent to the managing editor shortly after that.

In cryptic verse, put together by cut out letters from magazines and other printed materials, a message warned of massive demonstrations. The timing was set for the national holiday and the location was because of Wichita's stature as birthplace of the current President.

Union members from all government services and major private businesses were to converge in a statement against the nominee to replace Justice Clarence Wofford. The fact that the nominee was not yet named didn't seem to matter.

The effects of this announcement were simple.

"I understand," the aide said bluntly over the phone. "We can't allow him to take that chance. Wichita is out for the holiday celebration."

"I thought they said he was going to Cleveland for Senator Wilson's birthday anyway," the caller reminded him.

"Well..." the aide confided. "He is now, for sure."

"Oh...did you hear about Tampa?"

"Yeah. Threats everywhere it seems. The burden of public life, I guess," the aide surmised. "You can't even go home for a holiday."

52

Daniel, Phil and Matt were ready to leave Caddo Mills. Everything appeared safe topside. Murray had been to Tyler, Texas to drop off the NCIS crew. The uninvited visitors had not been back. Apparently satisfied the ranch was vacant.

"I've got a flight scheduled out of Shreveport to Pittsburgh," Daniel told Murray.

"You sure flying commercial is safe for you?" the cowboy asked.

"Couple days ago I would have had doubts. The plot seems to have moved on now. They're not worried as much about us as they are getting things started."

"That's for sure," Matt chimed in. "Two cities have been squeezed out already. Their idea is to force things in the direction the plotters want this to go."

"Have you talked to your man in Washington, yet?" Murray asked Matt.

"No. Couldn't get through. I'm sure it's a mess rescheduling the plans."

"It's looking more and more like Pendleton, isn't it?" Daniel enquired.

The three nodded in agreement and Murray looked over at Marsha. She was listening and when she caught his glimpse, she too nodded.

"Has anyone heard from Jon?" Murray asked.

"Nope." Marsha spoke softly to not disturb Nava, "don't expect to for a while. Not after what he said." She stood and walked over to the men. "I know we'll hear *of* what he's up to. Probably sooner than later... if I don't miss my guess."

"Will you folks be alright while I take these guys to Shreveport?"

"Harel and Reiss are up top, taking a walk and looking around." Looking back to the wounded Mossad agent, Marsha continued. "She's better. Her rest is more eased...less stressful. They'll be ready to get out of here before long."

"Yeah, well...I don't know about that," Murray grinned. "It might be best if they stay here till everything cools off. Some agencies are looking for them as spies."

Marsha acknowledged Murray's concern. "I'll try to talk to them all when the guys get back down here."

"Ok," Murray snapped as he looked to the newspapermen. "Got your stuff together?"

Daniel gave Marsha a hug and he and Matt headed toward the exit.

Phil Stone had been sitting in deep thought at the table.

"You coming, or what?" Matt called to him.

Phil's face was drawn with concern, yet he said nothing. Nodding to Marsha, he stood and joined the others.

"Are you alright?" Daniel asked him.

"Yeah...let's go," the police captain responded.

"Be back quick as I can." Murray winked at Marsha and they were gone.

~

The basement safe room was a bit moldy, but the smell dissipated quickly. Jon's studies were mainly on the lawyer and her office set up. The more he learned about her, the more convinced he became. *She was not a candidate for rehab.* The office complex, with its massive elevators and feeding system fascinated him.

The delivery guys don't even have to come upstairs, he said to himself. From the street level, they load frozen meat into separate compartments marked with dates. The dates at ground level were some two weeks out.

What a system. He offered praise for the design and operation. By the time the meat gets there, it is thawed and drops into the cage when ready. *Not touched again by human hands.*

The mechanical system and timer set up captured his attention the most. *This can be useful,* he thought.

"This could work," he said out loud. He made several notes to himself about items he would need. Number one on the list was several hours alone in that office.

Steven Walden was a quick review for Jon. *Bad guy, no redemption value, too many people killed by him or on his word.* His notes on this target started with "first." The tactics would be direct.

Include Jakes to some degree. He scribbled out in bold letters. *He deserves it...he* told himself. *Actually, both of them do.*

The Speaker of the House would be the real challenge. *More info needed for sure,* he thought and wrote down. Ben's material included the man's home state of Kentucky, but he spends much of his time in Virginia as well. *May catch him there,* he wrote.

"Call Swanson" he wrote near the bottom of the page. Sharon Swanson was now a Major in the Kentucky State police. Promoted after the Russians incident, she was really still healing from the injuries sustained in that attack.

Jon considered her an equal to Phil and Marsha. He respected her courage and law enforcement professionalism. *If there's anything I need to know about Grant and Kentucky, she'll know it,* he thought as he wrote.

~

Cyrus Grant picked up his interoffice phone and called for his aide.

"Come in here a minute, please?"

"Right away, Sir."

Marvin Staley entered the office, appointment book in hand.

"Close the door, will you?"

Staley deliberately closed the heavy door and walked toward the Speaker's desk. He stood, waiting for his instructions.

"Marvin...have you announced where I will be for the next week?"

"No, Sir."

"I don't want to be bothered this time. The press release said I would be near the beach in Virginia, right?" He watched as his long time assistant made a note and nodded affirmatively. "I will, in fact, be at the cabin in Kentucky. But only you will know that, clear?"

"I understand, Sir. I hope you can get some peace and quiet. You need the rest."

"Thank you, Marv." Grant closed his own book and stood. "I think I'm gonna go ahead and leave right after lunch," he declared. "If I need anything, I'll call you."

"Certainly," Staley nodded almost to the point of bowing and stepped backwards to the door. "See you after the holiday, Sir."

Grant flew by helicopter from Andrews to Richmond, Va. His Secret Service team escorted the Speaker to the plane scheduled for the private flight to Cape Charles, Virginia.

The Secret Service agents were relieved at that point.

"Thank you, gentlemen." He shook hands with each member of the detail. "See you in a few days. Have a great holiday."

"Thank you, Sir," the team leader responded. "Looking forward to your return."

Grant found that choice of words to be ironic.

My return will be under quite different conditions. The Speaker thought as he smiled at the men.

The detail accompanied him to his scheduled flight, but they would not be required to follow. Budgets cuts had altered the rules in place since the September 11, 2001 attack. They would pick up the security again at Andrews AFB on his way back to Washington.

That charter jet left on time, it just went without him. As soon as the escort team signed off, Grant left the plane and was taken by car to another private helicopter. The ride to Harlan County Kentucky and the Black Mountain cabin took less than two hours.

His private two-man security team had a fire waiting in the stone fireplace and cold beer in the refrigerator.

"Hey boys," he greeted them cheerfully. "Are the fish biting?"

~

The doughnuts were half gone. So was the wine. Sheri Shanahan found herself splayed across an oversized chair in her living room.

Undignified, she scolded herself internally, *unladylike at best.*

The first attempt to stand caused her to catch herself against the large arm of the chair. The hand she used to steady herself trembled as it grasped the leather chair arm.

Disgust more than fear shot through her as she willed the arm to behave. Getting to her feet, the normally stoic lawyer walked directly to a hanging mirror. Her eyes squinted at the face in the glass. Again she reached for something solid and again the hand shook.

"Could this be nerves?" her voice asked the mirror. The eyes in the glass opened wide now. "Nonsense," she uttered and pulled the hand away from the wall.

But her body was not through shaking. Fighting the urge to steady herself yet again, she turned and walked toward the window. Unfamiliarity with the sense of being nervous didn't make it any easier. The unconscious mind, primed with enough wine, had frightened itself as the reality of the coming days set in.

Opening the window's lower sash allowed a cooling breeze to enter. Shanahan gathered herself quickly in the sobering wind.

"I need to get away," she declared boldly. "Just for a few days."

She had no plans for the time prior to her speech. Hadn't really thought about it. Her time and concentration were all focused on the plot.

"Aruba was too far," she said aloud. Besides, she needed to stay in the states in case things got locked down. "Must be somewhere I can go." Again, speaking out loud to no one. Then an idea struck her. Her late father's estate had a condominium in Florida. Near Panama City or Destin, she couldn't remember which. They used it now for rental property.

"I'll go there," she declared, again to no one, but herself.

Her still slightly inebriated state did not allow for clear thinking. She would learn in the morning that rental agreements are binding contracts, regardless of how powerful you think you are. The estate's unit was in fact rented the entire month of June.

"Find me something else, then," she would demand of the real estate agent. "I want to go to Florida."

She left by private plane from Peachtree-DeKalb Airport in the early afternoon of that next day.

53

Jon emerged from the little house's basement after two and half days in seclusion. He had talked with one person while there, Major Sharon Swanson of the Kentucky State Police. Within the thirty minute conversation Jon got the information he needed.

"Can you get me the coordinates for that cabin?" he asked near the end of the call.

"Sure. What else can the Kentucky State Police do for you today?" she teased."

"Keep everybody away from there for a few days."

"You got it." Swanson was still considering how she would do that as she answered, "been wantin' to close that mountain off for some time."

"Just give me a few days first," Jon added. "I've got a couple other details to take care of."

Driving out the short driveway, Jon called Ben.

"Have Jakes get ready. Packed and ready...we're leaving in the morning."

"Say, Jon..." Ben interrupted. "You asked about when Shanahan would be away."

"Yeah?"

"She's gone. Out of state. Not sure for how long, but she left by plane yesterday."

"Good man." Jon liked what he heard and showed it. "Tell Jakes our trip will be delayed just a bit. But still get him ready."

"Yes, Sir." Ben then asked, "you coming here?"

"On my way."

Half way to the mansion, a thought came to Jon. He pulled over to the side of the road and grabbed a cell phone.

"Well, hey. *There* you are," Murray answered zealously.

"I need you to do something for me," Jon asked bluntly.

"Sure...what?"

"Get with those NCIS boys. I need you to get next to the President to warn him about what's going on."

"Me?" Murray half laughed. "How in the hell...?"

"Tell that Jerome fella, he needs to pull every string he has and make this happen."

"But, Jon..." Murray reached for words that weren't there.

"They say the man is stubborn. If it comes from someone he knows he'll just dig his heels in. It must come from an outsider."

"You expect the President to listen to a dirt kicking cowboy?"

"That's the tricky part, my friend," Jon eased into this.

"Trickier than what?"

"You remember what happened in Columbia?"

"A bunch happened in Columbia, Jon." Murray's patience was wearing. "You're starting to worry me a little."

"Lendono thought we were both me."

"Come again?"

"The President might just listen to an outsider who owns a ton of businesses."

"Then you do it," Murray quipped.

"I need to be in two places at once, Murray."

The cowboy suddenly realized what Jon was asking. He stood in total silence, trying to rationalize this idea.

Jon gave him a few seconds and then started up again.

"I need you to trust me on this, Murray," he pleaded. "Cause I need you to pretend to be me."

~

The paranoia of Steven Walden grew with each moment. Bogart and the lawyer had gone into hiding. He had nowhere to go. Though much of his ongoing legal defense cost were paid by donations, his personal finances stayed nearly depleted. Far below what might be needed to rent a getaway home, much less own one.

The additional "sleeper" volunteers were staged into groups to guard his offices. His home was "too conspicuous" he figured.

I'll just sleep here till this is over, he convinced himself. The new guards could blend into other student activities and not draw attention.

Mithras found an old roll of duct tape and used a piece to attach the Luger pistol under his center desk drawer. Not in it...but under it.

He had taken each round from the rusted magazine and wiped the mold and rust stains from them. The magazine itself was washed and blow-dried with a hair dryer. Then the internal spring was lubricated with some 3-in-one oil. He'd kept a can in his desk for years. He'd just forgotten why.

With the rounds cleaned and the magazine washed and oiled, he slid the old ammunition back into its holder. Slowly, he put the mag back into the pistol before taping it into place. He was ready now. In a strange way, having the gun there comforted him.

A knock at his door startled him.

"Yes," Walden half stammered. "Who is it?"

"Got your dinner here, Professor."

It was one of his guard troops with a big bag from Half Fast Subs. He opened the door and took the delivery.

"Did you get a diet drink this time?" he impugned.

"Yeah...sorry about that," the young man assured him. "They had what you wanted."

Walden sat down at his desk. With elbows on the desktop he ate his sandwich angrily. Every few minutes he would lift a knee to feel the gun taped under there. A slight smile would appear as he did this, but his smiles were more camouflage than confidence. They were weak and never lasted too long.

The bites of his meal became smaller as he continued through the motions.

"Just over a week to go," he heard himself mutter. "It'll be over soon."

~

Lucy touched down at the police airport in Shreveport. The flight had been a quiet one. Murray didn't mention his conversation with Jon, but the others could tell something was up.

The handlers and service techs quickly surrounded the copter and checked her every bolt, nut and reservoir.

"You don't have to do that," Murray called to Phil as the gas trucks rolled up.

"Hey...its fine," Phil answered. "My city thanks you for your service," he smiled.

"You guys be careful." The cowboy put on a stern look as he spoke. They each knew how serious the situation was.

"Murray, good seeing you again, my friend," Daniel declared. "You take care, too."

Matt and Phil had already stepped beyond the rotating propellers. They turned and waved to Murray as he climbed back aboard his craft. As he pulled his seat harness tight and leaned back, he noticed Phil and the service crew. They were all standing at attention, saluting.

Instinctively, he stiffened his back and sharply returned their gesture. Emotions swelled up in him. He took in a deep breath and checked all around. Hollering "Clear," Murray eased back on Lucy's stick.

He flew east at first. Then swung hard, back around a full 180 degrees. Dropping down, he ripped over the airfield low and fast. Lucy rocked back and forth as she roared past Phil Stone and the others, blasting her way toward Texas.

~

Jerome Grimes answered the cell call while still at the hospital in Tyler.

"Yeah, Murray." He almost sounded dismissive. "What is it?"

The tone came through, even with Lucy's engine racing and the outside air whistling past. Murray happened to notice the crack in the windshield from his first encounter with the unknown assailants. It helped him regain his focus.

"Look Mr. NCIS. I've got a message from Jon and instructions of what he wants us to do...emphasis the word 'us.' Do you copy?"

Grimes straightened up and looked around in silence. Finding what appeared to be an empty room, he signaled to Barker and Spiegel to follow and stepped into the more private area. Once inside, Grimes pushed the "conference call" button on his phone.

"Ok, Cowboy." His voice was much more respectful this time. "We're listening."

"Jon has this idea that you should get me in to speak with the President."

The NCIS leader grimaced. Looking at his men there with him, he abruptly cut Murray off.

"Say there, Cowboy..." He nearly yelled into the phone. "We should talk about this in person...you copy that? Seriously not a conversation for anyone else to hear."

Murray didn't react to the tone this time. It was the words. They made sense to him.

"Roger that, I copy five by five." He thought a second and then added, "you still at the hospital?"

"Affirmative." The communications were becoming brief statements.

"Must check in with friends left behind," Murray said cryptically. "Then will reconnect with you."

Knowing who the "friends left behind" were, Grimes countered, "I'll talk to Yinon. You come on. We need to connect ASAP."

Murray checked his current position.

"That considered," he replied. "I'm ten minutes out."

"Use the police field, copy that?" Grimes instructed. "We are in route."

"Roger...see you in ten."

54

Jon's time at the mansion was a near windmill of activity. He emerged from his lab area with a small bag and brushed right by Ben and Jakes going to a file cabinet.

"These are signed and executable," he said placing the file into Ben's hand. It read across the top, <u>In the Event of my Death or Disappearance.</u>

"Whoa!" Ben cried out. "What the hell is this?"

"Some of it you're already working on," Jon said flatly. "Steps one and two you've got going already." He grabbed two "ready bags," one with the street clothes arm and the other with the black suit. "The rest you can handle if need be."

Ben was paging through the instructions. "Those to notify," he read. "Notify about what?"

"Ben, you'll know what to do...and when if it need be."

Jon then handed Ben a remote control and offered yet more instructions verbally.

"Shanahan has a speech scheduled for July 3rd, around eight o'clock that night, I believe." He stopped moving and got right into Ben's face. "When she leaves there to go home, hit this remote. Then go to her house and scare her out of there."

"What?"

"Make her leave...she'll run to her office. That's all you need to do."

Ben sat the remote on his desk as Jon walked toward the elevator.

"Don't lose that," Jon said turning back to them. "And Jakes, be ready...we leave soon as I get back tonight."

As he got near the Mercury, Silas made him gravitate in that direction. But he overruled the thought. *The Jaguar would be less conspicuous in this case*, he explained to Silas in silence.

The trip to town took just over an hour and a half, his work inside the office less than an hour. Jon had studied Ben's notes and the schematics of the cage and feeding system. Setting the conveyor belt to obey the remotes command, he closed the sliding bookcases carefully and made one additional adjustment to them.

As he left the inner office, Jon noticed the picture Ben had mentioned. The odd star shaped design made of numbers. There was a picture of it in Ben's file.

I see why it interested him, he thought. *I'll ponder it later.*

In the elevator going down, Jon changed into a maintenance uniform, one that was non-descriptive. Its intent was to draw less attention to someone working on the external feeding system from the street level.

Spraying a quick drying resin into the padlock, he rocked the hardening material until it had set up firm. Then a quick turn and the lock snapped open. He withdrew the material and sprayed a cleaner on and into the lock.

The open access door showed a conveyor belt with sections of beef. The diagram on the door panel showed sections were marked one through fourteen. They supplied daily food drops that would cover a two-week period. Only three drawers were visible. Those were marked eight, nine and ten. Cranking the carriage forward, Jon could tell that meat had just been delivered the day before.

This was perfect, he thought. He then cranked the unit backwards; passed where it had been and selected a drawer marked "six." By July 3rd that slot would be within two positions of delivery to the cat. He injected that meat with two syringes he had brought with him.

Closing the access panel, he replaced the padlock and walked back to the Jaguar. The coveralls were slipped off and tossed into the trunk with his bag. Jon then casually looked around and walked away. He took an easy stroll around the block before returning to his car. That should confuse any cameras that might be watching. He took twenty minutes before returning to the car.

Driving back to Dalton allowed time to organize the next part of his extended plan. He did call Ben with one request.

"Would you ask the pilot to be ready in about two hours?"

"Sure," Ben replied. "How did it go?"

"You're nearly set," Jon answered. "I have something for you when I get back."

"Oh... Jon?" Ben added.

"Yep?"

"I've got Dr. Webster on stand-by at Fernbank. In case we need satellite surveillance or whatever."

Jon smiled. "That's not a bad idea at all. Nice thinking."

"Just don't want you getting hurt." He said as he looked down at the papers in his hand.

~

The hideout at Caddo Mills was low lit and nearly quiet. Mossad agent Reiss was up at ground level watching for Murray or anything else. Yinon Harel, the Mossad leader, had just hung up from a call from his old NCIS friend, Jerome Grimes.

He walked softly over to a sofa where Marsha Hurst was napping. Most of her time was spent checking on Nava Golan, the injured agent who was with the Mossad team.

"Lieutenant," Harel whispered. "Lt. Hurst."

Marsha awoke, sat straight up and tossed a small blanket to the side.

"Yes?" she responded, still half asleep and rubbing her eyes.

"Things are starting to warm up." Yinon Harel was blunt.

"How's that?" Marsha stood so they could step further away to talk.

"I just got off the phone with Jerry." He stepped back toward the table. "Our cowboy is not coming back here right away. It seems Jon has asked him to do something that Agent Grimes needs help with."

"Did he say what that was?" she asked.

"Murray is going to reach out to the main man, personally."

"The President?" Marsha seemed as surprised as everyone else in the loop. "How...what...? I don't understand."

"I don't have any details, I don't believe Jerry has a full idea of 'what' either just yet. They'll let us know."

Marsha walked toward the exit and stopped.

"This Jon," Harel began. "There is much more to him than it first appears, yes?"

Marsha looked back at the veteran fighter.

"Much," she confirmed. "And to some degree, the same with Murray."

"You have faith in them then?"

Nodding gently, she replied. "You will, too. If we all survive this."

"Ah...I see." Harel smiled and stepped towards her. "What would you say our chances of that are?"

Marsha reached out and grabbed the man's upper arm. Looking him straight in the eyes she proclaimed firmly. "Better than you might think."

~

Daniel Seay had been back in Pittsburgh for one day. Lori was still in hiding, but Daniel felt he needed to go back to the office. Copies of stories about Jon were piling up on his desk.

"Can't we stop this crap?" he asked his boss from the door of the editor's office.

"Nice to see you, too." Bill White hardly looked up.

"Seriously...they're tarring him and anyone who has ever dealt with him, with no evidence at all."

"Including you, huh?" White now looked at Daniel.

"You don't believe any of that... I know it."

"That's the problem...it don't really matter what I believe. Hell, it don't matter what the damn truth is long as there's only one thing being said."

Daniel walked closer and sat down in front of his boss's desk.

"What can we do?"

"Wait it out...hope for the best. The people thought they wanted this, well...enough of them thought so anyway. Now they're not so sure...even those way over on the far side of what we believe in."

"But what if something happens and things don't change back?"

"I don't like the way you asked that." White leaned hard against his chair back.

"You shouldn't." Daniel blurted out. "He's working to stop it."

"He?" The editor now leaned forward and frowned.

"Yeah...he."

"Like Columbia?"

"Boss...we don't know what happened down there, except the drug community is short one crime family."

"This isn't Columbia, Daniel. The press, or should I say the populist media, will defend the bad guys no matter what."

"I need you to approve some stories."

Bill White sat way back again, folding his hands in his lap and staring at Daniel. He finally shook his head and muttered, "Bring 'em to me."

"Thanks, Boss." Daniel jumped up and headed for the door.

"Thanks, nothing," White called after him. "If he goes down...you go down... and then me by association. I'm just trying to save my ass."

"There's more to it than that, Boss!" Daniel hollered as he jogged down the hall.

55

Jon Crane pulled back into the third level basement where Ben and Lamar Jakes met him.

"The plane is waiting for you," Ben announced.

"Good. I need to get just one more thing for you, well two actually, before I go."

They all went up one floor and to Jon's lab.

"Stay here, please." Jon never allowed anyone in his laboratory. He came out with a small box in one hand and a mask in the other.

"What's this?" Ben asked.

"On the night the lawyer makes her speech, while that office is empty, you will make one last visit there," Jon spoke mysteriously.

He handed Ben the mask. "I want you to put this on before you open the box."

"Now?"

"No...when you are in the office. Don't open it till then...at all."

"What is in the box?" Ben knew, but was asking just to be sure.

Jon gave him a look rather than an answer.

"You will find a notch cut into the bottom of the bookcase, three feet from the seam of the opening, to the left." He explained. "The notch should be obscured by the carpet so you will need to feel for it."

Ben listened with intent. Jakes appeared completely puzzled.

"There's a vial in this box...do not open it until that night and you are in that office with the mask on...do you understand?"

"Yes, Sir." Ben smiled at the responsibility being placed on him.

"Carefully ease the vial from this box into that notch and smooth out the carpet pile to cover it."

"Got it."

"Ben...I don't like leaving this to you. It is something I should handle myself." The pause was unavoidable, "I won't be here."

"Where will you be?"

"Seeing to Bogart." He answered then looked Ben right in the eyes. "What you do will clean the slate."

Ben felt a cold chill run through him. It was something in the way Jon spoke.

"Yes, Sir." He heard come from his lips as if in third person.

"You have the remote?" Jon asked.

"Yes," his voice answered.

"You remember what to do after her speech?"

"I do."

Ben wanted to say much more, but he didn't...or couldn't. He fought off the look of concern he knew was coming through. Then Jon glanced down for a second and turned. He looked at Jakes and sternly asked him, "You ready?"

"Sure...yeah, let's go," the other young man responded.

They checked the travel kit one last time and loaded it into the Mercury. Jon looked over at Jakes and tilted his head.

"You know the drill," he told him.

"Man...not again," Jakes complained.

"It's for your own safety," Jon assured him. "The less you know, the better for you."

Jakes leaned forward and lowered his head below the dashboard. Jon pushed a button and the sequence started. They rolled down the tunnel and with a clear view of the street, the Mercury turned hard right and roared up past the mansion and on toward the airport.

~

Murray finished explaining Jon's instructions to the NCIS crew. He was shocked by their reaction. They listened closely in the small office at the Tyler Police Air Station. When he was through, they didn't stay quiet for long.

"Could work!" Spiegel pronounced with a hand slap on the table.

"I don't see any other way," Barker added. "With the limited time we have."

"Now hang on." Grimes assumed control of the room. "The President might just listen to someone like Jon Crane, sure." He pointed to the cowboy. "But this ain't him."

"I won't try to carry the ruse further than when we get in to see him," Murray spoke up. "Not toward him anyway. It's just important that the press think its Jon from there on. We just have to sell the President that we know what we're doing."

Grimes sighed deeply. "Worth a shot," he said. "My credibility with him won't matter if this doesn't work."

He stood and pointed to Lucy.

"Can that thing get us to Washington, DC?" he asked.

"Not in one hop, no."

"Make arrangements for a flight outta here then," Grimes ordered. "And soon."

Murray found an old Lockheed L188C cargo plane parked near the rear of the airfield.

"Can this thing fly?" he asked the ground crew there."

"Hell, yeah," a man with a rag in his hand answered. "Where do you need to go?"

"You the pilot?"

The man pointed to the corner of the hanger.

"That's him over there."

"Get her airworthy and ready to go. National security." Murray barked.

"I heard that!" The ragman grinned. "How far's she going?"

"Washington, DC." Murray bellowed as he walked toward the man in the corner.

~

The G5 glided into Denver's airport and taxied to the private arrival's terminal.

"Can you stay and wait for us?" Jon asked the pilot. "This will be a fairly quick turn around."

"Sure," the pilot smiled and added. "You know they charge for parking this thing, right?"

"I get it." Jon shook his hand. "But I do need you to wait if you will."

As the other man was beginning to speak, Jon's phone rang.

"Go ahead," the pilot assured him. "I'll gas up and be waiting."

Jon nodded, gave the thumbs up and raised the phone to his ear.

"Hey, Major. Thanks for getting back to me."

"I've got those coordinates," she told him. "And some news you might could use."

"Okay..."

"He's here... Now," Major Swanson announced.

"The papers said he was in Virginia this week," Jon recalled.

"Apparently that's his cover. He is here and an aide bought enough groceries and beer for nearly a week at the local market this morning."

"Interesting." Jon was thinking as he spoke. "Thanks, Major. You say you have the air coordinates for that cabin?"

"Yeah...I'll text them to you when we're done."

"I owe the State of Kentucky a favor."

"And we keep good records," she teased him. "Come see us."

"Might be sooner than you think. Thanks again."

Jon turned to see Jakes standing there, well within listening range.

"You spying on me?" he asked the young man.

"On you?" Jakes laughed. "No, sir. I just want to see Professor Walden... again."

"Follow my lead and you'll have your chance at him," Jon said while digging into the travel bag. He pulled out what looked like a heavy tee shirt and tossed it at Jakes.

"Put this on," he instructed.

"Damn...this thing is heavy for a tee shirt."

"Just put it on. It's Kevlar." He looked around and saw a rest room sign. "Wait for me here, I'll be right back."

When he returned, Jon had on the khaki pants, white pullover shirt and light tan jacket.

"It is June, you know," Jakes told him.

"Yeah, but the mile high altitude allows for a jacket. Let's go."

The rental car was a Ford Taurus. The drive to Boulder and the campus took thirty minutes. Traffic was returning to normal slowly in Denver. The scare had left some residents unsure about coming home. The campus seemed busier than town.

Jakes pointed out the building housing Walden's office.

"You can park over there." He pointed to a line of marked spaces just below an incline.

As they climbed the four steps from the parking area, Jakes grabbed Jon's arm and pulled him to one side. He quickly sat on a bench and looked away from the building.

"See those guys right there?" he asked Jon, his face beginning to flush.

"Where?"

"At the foot of the stairs going into the building."

"Okay...I got 'em."

"Well, I know them." Jakes' color was now going pale. "When I first joined the group and converted, they sent us to Koran classes. Those guys were in the class with me."

Jon's head tilted to one side.

"Nice catch," he said and sat down next to Jakes. "Do you see any others you recognize?"

"I don't know."

"Take your time...if we know where they are, we have the upper hand."

Jakes scanned the area while holding a hand in front of his face, rubbing his forehead.

"Up on the porch, near the door," he said. Then a moment later he added, "and to the left at the corner."

"Good." Jon declared calmly. "Now are you okay? Can you work with me?"

"Yeah. I'm fine," the nervous youth replied.

"Here's what I want you to do," Jon spoke slowly and resolutely. "Stay directly behind me and close. They won't be able to see you if you stay behind me, got it?"

"Yeah."

Jon reached inside his jacket and pulled a Glock 23, the full sized one. Handing it to Jakes, he asked him.

"Can you handle this? The safety is off... so be careful."

376

Jakes nodded as Jon stood.

"Alright then, here we go... If anything happens, you take out that guy at the corner."

They walked toward the building and Jon powered up the right arm. As they passed the first two, he lined them up. Altering his path to move in closer to the men, he made eye contact with the one nearest and swung the arm hard.

Jon's forearm caught the man flat across his chest. The blow lifted him from the ground and propelled his body backwards, immediately slamming into the other man only three feet away. They both went through a large set of boxwood shrubs before anyone could notice.

Stepping up his pace, Jon climbed the stairs and reached the top just as the man there noticed his friends were missing. Jon grabbed his throat, raised him off his feet and carried him into the brick wall. He pulled back slightly and popped the man's head against the bricks.

While holding his victim steady he glanced to his left to see the other man standing in place and slowly raising his arms. Jakes had the drop on the guy. The Glock pointed at him with one hand, the other with one finger held against his own lips in the "hush" signal.

Jon stepped over to that man, disarmed him and tapped him against the wall as well. The two unconscious men on the porch were propped up in sitting positions, heads down and knees up, as if napping.

Looking around the campus to see if any attention had been drawn to them, Jon and Jakes were surprised to see everything calm. The few people within viewing range were all absorbed in reading from either books or text messages on their phones.

A slight motion from Jon's head signaled Jakes they needed to move to the doorway. The double doors stood open leading to a lobby.

"Don't expect that to be all of them," Jon warned as they moved through the door.

The lobby area was empty except for two wooden bench seats. Other doors offered access to three hallways.

"His office is where?" Jon whispered.

Jakes pointed to the left and they opened that door.

A man stood from a chair just beyond the door and challenged them.

"How'd you get in here?"

Jon put his left hand forefinger to his lips and softly said, "...quiet."

This confused the man for a second. Which was long enough for the right arm to reach the man's chin and mouth area. Again, Jon used the nearby wall as a weapon. He sat the man back into his chair and followed Jakes to a closed door on the right side of the hall.

Painted letters on the glass proclaimed the occupant to be Professor Steven Walden. A shadow seen through the frosted glass exposed a man standing to the left side of the door.

Jon signaled for Jakes to be quiet and step back.

"Watch out here for a couple minutes," he ordered then grabbed the doorknob and twisted it. The simple lock mechanism gave way to the power of the arm and Jon stepped into the room. The shocked man at the door was overpowered and tossed against the baseboard.

Walden, who had been sitting at his desk, stood wide eyed with his mouth hanging open.

"Professor Walden," Jon addressed him. "My name is Silas." He glared at the man behind the desk. "I don't have an appointment... but we need to talk."

56

The Lockheed cargo plane from Tyler, Texas landed at Andrews AFB under special clearance from the White House. Jerome Grimes had served in the Marines with a current member of the President's advisory staff. The man knew his friend would not abuse the friendship or trust that went with it.

Marine Two, one of the official helicopters used by the President, waited for them. Within an hour, the NCIS agents and Murray Bilstock were on the lawn at the White House.

The President and another man approached them from an overhang nearby.

"Mr. President," The senior advisor began his introductions. "This is Special Agent Jerome Grimes of the Headquarters NCIS office."

"Agent Grimes." The President extended his hand.

"And these are Agents Spiegel and Barker. They have been working on a case with Jerry that needs your immediate attention, Sir."

"Agents..." The President dipped his head toward them. "Please...what is this case? All this...mystery you bring me?"

Grimes stepped forward and spoke.

"Sir...Mr. President. There's no simple way to say this. We have credible evidence of a massive plot to assassinate you sometime before the July Fourth holiday."

The President was not shaken. He was though, clearly interested.

"Really?" he asked with a touch of skepticism. "We have channels to handle such things. Do we not, Agent Grimes?"

"Sir," Grimes begged. "This is more than an assassination. It is a coup attempt. I hate to say this, but it involves several agencies of the government."

The President stared Grimes down for several seconds before speaking again. He lowered his head then drew his eyes back up to meet Grimes'.

"Warren Ferris was a good man," he said softly. "His death didn't pass the smell test to me."

"You're on it, Sir," Grimes replied with respect. "The HLS appears to be neck deep in all this."

"How do you figure the breakdown runs?" the President asked.

"I have faith in Wilson Farley, Jason Shuck and Wilfred Scott. Beyond that, I'm not sure."

"So...the CIA, FBI and your boss. How is Farley?"

"Doing better I am told, Sir."

"So that's all we have for 'our' side?" the President asked.

"No, Sir," Grimes answered and reached back for Murray. "We have Jonathan Crane."

"I heard he was coming..."The President looked Murray over. "But that's not Jonathan Crane."

"No, Sir," Murray said. "I'm not. But to protect you, it's important that I appear to be Jon... to the press in particular."

"Who are you, son?"

"My name is Murray Bilstock, Sir."

"Bilstock?" The leader's eyes flashed. "That's a rather unusual name." His stare became more intense. "You from Texas?"

"He was my father, Sir." Murray raised his chin and continued, "I know what he did."

"Wasn't this... 'Son' character thought to be responsible for his death?" the President asked directly.

"That was the speculation, yes," Murray admitted.

"I've read Jonathan Crane's name associated with this 'Son.' What do you know about that?"

"You can trust Jon Crane with your life, Sir," Murray asserted.

The President looked at his trusted advisor, then Grimes and back to Murray.

"Seems that's what I must do, then," he said with conviction. "Let's move inside."

As the President turned and started to move, Murray noticed what before had gone unseen. Six marines, in camouflage, lowered their weapons and stepped from behind trees and other cover.

The President motioned to a guard at the door and pointed at Murray.

"Sign this man in as Jonathan Crane," he instructed. "The others have their credentials."

~

Daniel's first editorial was on the streets in Pittsburgh, but found little support from other publications. There had been no mention at all on local television.

The Danger From False or Incomplete News hit the major media outlets hard. It included facts that Daniel had witnessed himself. Incidents that had gone unreported or misreported.

Bill White had shaken his head when he signed off on it.

"Man...this could fall in on us in a hurry. You know that, right?" he had cautioned.

"If Jon is unsuccessful..." Daniel responded. "That really won't matter in the scheme of things."

He told about the conversations he'd had with the reporter from Austin, the lack of coverage on the attack against the sheriffs at the very beginning...or what they thought was the beginning.

He told of investigations conducted by private individuals with the help of some official agencies and the forceful discouragement from others.

Daniel told what he knew and could expose without endangering others.

Some in Pittsburgh took notice. They called relatives or friends in other areas of the country. But at this rate, the word would hardly spread in time to help.

In Shreveport, Matt Turlock was doing the same thing, with basically the same results. Papers in Dalton, Georgia and Burlington, Iowa were contacted. Dalton helped and joined in, Burlington did not.

"The boss won't touch it," Earl Johnstone from Iowa told Daniel. "The pressure is on."

One local Dallas, Texas TV station did a report with film, of the men in black crawling all over Murray's ranch. It ran only once and the film was confiscated for "national security" reasons.

Still the truth eked its way out. The effects were not instant, yet truth has a power all to itself. It does not stay down forever.

~

"Look, whoever you are," Walden mustered all his courage to bow his back and confront the man in his office. "I'm tenured here. The media will support me and you can't prove a thing...whatever you think you know, you're wasting your time."

Jon caught himself laughing. His look of disgust grew more intense and he stepped closer to the desk.

"I have all the proof I need...Mithras." He glared at the professor.

Walden stiffened even more and backed away.

"You stay away from me. I don't know any Mithras," he proclaimed while feeling his way along the wall, into a corner. "You're out of your mind." He quivered, his words barely audible.

Jon moved closer still and looked down at the desk blotter. The word "Shreveport" stuck out. Near it in the same color ink was the word "Ultimate."

"There are some facts I know you can help me with," Jon continued and stalked the man into his corner. "You're going to give me details. Details I need to close this situation and shut it down."

"You can't close anything," Walden spit back defiantly.

"What is an Ultimate?" Jon asked in a sudden change.

The professor's eyes flashed to his desk and back, widening as they moved.

"Someone willing to give their all for the cause," came his automatic response.

"There is no cause, you creep. It's already over Walden. The plot is done."

"Heh...so you think." The shaking man frowned at Jon with reddening eyes. "We have a 'failsafe.' You can't stop it."

"I need you to tell me about this 'failsafe,'" Jon coaxed him.

"So...you don't really know it all... do you, huh?"

"Not right this minute..." Jon sneered at him and leaned into his face. "But within the next few... I promise you, I will."

Mustering what courage and audacity he could Walden bowed up again.

"I don't know who you think you are...but you don't have the authority to come in here." Mithras took a deep breath, and then snarled at his tormentor. "Much less to ask me these impertinent questions."

"The only thing I don't have...is time to waste on you." It was Silas speaking this time. He grabbed a section of window casing near

Walden's head. The powered arm squeezed the solid wood into dust as Walden watched in horror.

"I can do that to every bone in your body... You won't die for hours."

Mithras stared at him in disbelief. His eyes outgrew their sockets.

"We know the locations you picked," Jon shouted. "Which one is it?"

"Ha!" the madman screamed at him in surprise. "You know nothing!" Fear overrode his ability to think and he continued as if bragging. "The location doesn't really matter." His voice was defiant and deliberate with each word.

"Doesn't matter?" Now Jon was confused. "What do you mean... it doesn't matter?"

The powered arm menaced the professor, pushing against his chin as Jon crowded him.

"Kill me, then!" Walden defied him. "You're going to anyway."

Without breaking eye contact, Jon reached into the professor's lower chest and grabbed the tenth rib on his left side. The pressure applied between the thumb and forefinger first broke and then crushed the flat bone.

Walden's eyes rolled back... blinked and then refocused as he struggled for his breath. Blood seeped from the corner of his mouth. He had bitten his tongue.

Jon methodically moved to the next level of his rib cage and the man gasped.

"No..."

"Don't waste my time," Jon warned. "Talk to me, now."

"Tracking signals!" Walden screamed as he glanced down at the arm. "Fail safes... two of them." He looked down and shook his head. Through his pain a sly grin appeared for a second. "Wherever they go, the President..." he coughed. "And VP are dead already. They just don't know it yet."

"What kind of signal?" Jon asked as he took hold of Walden's upper arm. "Signals to what?"

"Tracking signals... for the drones if we need them."

Jon leaned back as the realization came over him.

"Predator Drones?"

"Yeah...you can't stop this," Walden answered with a small bit of vitriol he still had left in him. "We'll get them on the ground or in the air."

A slight pressure applied to his upper arm brought Walden's concentration back in line.

"No, please..." he begged and trembled.

"Where are these tracking devises?" Jon demanded and squeezed harder.

"With them..." Walden cried out and spat blood. "They're on them."

"And the bomber?"

"Bomber?" Walden seemed confused by the change of subject.

"Your suicide bomber...Shreveport, you remember?"

"Shreveport must be punished...That's done as well. He's there already."

Jon released the man's arm and walked toward the door. He needed to inform Murray and the others.

Hunched over and holding his side with his right arm, Walden raised his head.

"That's it?" He spit out blood and attempted to wipe his chin.

Jon opened the door and waved for Jakes.

"No...not nearly. I brought an old friend of yours who wants to say 'hi.'"

Lamar Jakes entered the room and Walden's face went straight to crimson as he clearly recognized Jakes.

Time accelerated at that point. Everything seemed to shift into a higher gear. Mithras stumbled to his desk as Jakes closed in on him. Leaning against the desktop with his left arm, Walden reached down and came up with the Luger. Strands of duct tape hung from weapon like ribbon as he leveled and pointed it at the kid's face.

Jakes stopped within inches of the weapon, but the professor did not. He pulled hard on the trigger.

The firing pin of Luger No.1 impacted the ancient .45 caliber round and a spark ignited. The old casing could not contain the explosion of the decaying gunpowder. Flash and fire erupted the breechblock in one solid piece, tearing through the ejector housing and sending the barrel tumbling forward. The lead slug turned sideways inside the barrel, ripping a gash in it.

The pistol's body frame separated as the heat and concussion reached the magazine. The next two rounds at the top of the magazine exploded, tearing the grip and Walden's hand apart. The rear toggle pin and magazine catch flew back into the professor's forehead and did not stop until they hit the rear wall behind him.

The instant this all took... was less than a second, and not over yet. Jagged sections of barrel flew forward striking Jakes just above the right eye. Blood erupted wildly as the impact sent him into a spinning fall. Jon's movement toward him had begun as the kid landed, face down on the floor.

The flames from the explosion of the remaining rounds singed Walden's now dead face. Slugs flew at random into the ceiling, walls and furniture. Two bounced off Jon's jacket, another grazed his arm.

Like an imploded building, Walden's body, minus a hand, fell in a heap behind the desk. Flames on his shirt collar flared and flickered out. He did not move after that.

Jon reached the young man and gently rolled him over. The wound was fierce.

"Is he dead?" Jakes asked from his delusional, semi-conscious state.

"He's gone, kid. You got him," Jon assured him and tried to stop the bleeding with his hand. "Hang on," he coached as life seeped out of the youth's body. The weight on his arm became limp and Jake's undamaged eye opened blindly and locked in place.

Jon felt rage building and the urge to scream welled up in him. Even Silas was in disbelief. It had only taken a second. Stiffening up more than standing, he looked down at the young man. Silas struggled to gather and restore Jon's composure.

That could be Ben...or Daniel or even Marsha...My God...it could be any of them and just as quick, he realized and it frightened him.

Jon's mind focused and began to concentrate on one thing. *This has to stop.*

Walking from the office, he pulled down a drapery to wipe his hand. Jon left the building and threw the drape into the bushes. His trance like steps took time he did not later remember. At the car, he climbed inside and silently watched the commotion build until the authorities began to react. Only then did he calmly crank the Ford and back away from the parking spot.

The suddenness of Lamar Jakes' death had hit him hard. He was half way back to the airport before clear thinking returned.

*I have to call Murray...*His mind spun. *Warn them about the failsafe. And Shreveport! Oh my God, Shreveport.* He remembered Shreveport and the Ultimate. *There's a suicide bomber in Shreveport.*

Jon grabbed his phone and dialed.

57

"Shreveport is a big target, Jon," the voice demanded more information. "Do you have anything specific?" The call to Murray did not go through, so he had called Phil.

Still wired and frustrated, Jon fired back. "Think a minute, will you? What from your city has been a thorn in their side?"

It didn't take Phil long that time. "Matt's newspaper."

"That's my guess," Jon snapped in confirmation.

"Ok...I'll put 24 / 7 surveillance on the building. They're still not staying at their home, so that's not an issue." The cop hesitated a minute. "Damn... this is fast."

"What?"

"There's an APB out on you from Denver."

"You're kidding."

"The funny thing is, a report came out two hours ago about you meeting with the President in Washington, DC. Their fancy news network has you in two places at once."

"Murray did his job well."

"Yeah...until the President decides you used him as cover for a murder."

"That's also Murray's job. I can't worry about that right now."

"Hope you know what you're doing, Jon."

"Listen...I am on my way to Washington. Just pulled into the airport so we should be in the air within the hour."

"Jon...this APB has you as an accessory. The story claims the kid killed Walden and then the Campus police killed him. Is that kid dead, Jon?"

"Some gun Mithras pulled exploded on him. The kid was too close."

"Damn."

"Look, Phil. I can't really think about that right now. The plot has a facet we didn't consider. It could still happen."

Jon explained the "drone" concern to Phil.

"Can you think of a way we could detect such a devise?" the cop asked.

"I'm betting Ben can. Or he'll know someone who can."

"The latest word is the VP is still going to St. Louis and the President to Cleveland," Phil told him.

"There's still Pendleton, but none of the locations mean that much anymore. It's the trip we have to be concerned about."

When the call ended, Phil Stone called across the river to his friend at Barksdale AFB.

"Colonel Meyers, this is Phil Stone of the Shreveport police. Yeah, I'm a friend of Matt's.

Phil asked about the Predators and if it were possible to intercept targeting radio signals.

The Colonel explained that the frequencies used by the Predators had an unlimited range. The ground control frequencies were secure and difficult to intercept. The communications frequencies, on the other hand, were open and a simple "signal hopping" receiver could pick those up. Targeting was done through communication frequencies.

"So, we could tell what the target was?" Phil asked.

"Theoretically, yeah" the Colonel told him. "You want to tell me what's going on?"

"I'd love to, but I'm afraid you might think I'm nuts."

"After this conversation that wouldn't be too much of a stretch," the Colonel quipped.

"Let's just say it's big. Bigger than that deal you helped Matt with last year."

"Cartels, again?"

"Worse."

The Colonel got quiet. "Okay...let me know what you can and if you need these facilities...call me."

"You sound like you have an idea," Phil queried.

"The Air Force ain't no vacuum, Captain." The Colonel's voice was very serious. "I'm afraid I know too well what your man is in to."

"You do?"

"Several of the units you were asking about, drones, have been misused in recent weeks. Every investigation we start ends with orders to 'stand down.' Those things aren't toys and testing is usually fairly open. Something's going on."

"Yes, Sir. I'd say you have a pretty good idea of what we're up against," Capt. Stone confirmed.

~

A phone rang in a Kentucky mountain cabin. The owner froze and just stared at it for a few seconds. It wasn't supposed to ring...except in dire emergences. The phone was a "burn" phone. It didn't use caller ID or any frills. *Could be a wrong number*, the owner hoped.

"Yeah," Cyrus Grant answered, trying his best to disguise his voice.

"Boss, have you seen the news?" The caller was Marvin Staley.

"No..." Grant expelled with a deep breath, his frustration clear.

"Professor Walden is dead," Staley just threw out.

Grant's face cringed. He replayed the words in his mind, but they still did not make sense.

"Dead?" he challenged. "Walden...in Colorado...dead how?"

"Some kid...a student they say, shot him. But there's more."

"More what?"

"His guards describe a man with the kid. It sounds like Crane...or, you know, that 'Son' character."

Grant sat on his thick leather sofa and rubbed his head.

"Okay...okay, I understand your concern. Does anyone know where I am?"

"No, Sir."

"Re-enforce that. Put out a press release, nothing to do with Walden...think of something I might comment on and be sure to say I'm in Virginia."

"Yes, Sir."

"And toss that phone you're on. I'll do the same. Use set number three next time if needed."

"Got it. Sorry to bother you, Sir."

"No...you did the right thing. I needed to know. That 'Son' fella is a threat to all of us in congress."

"Right," Staley said and then heard the click.

~

Jon found the G5 and banged on the door. The pilot saw the blood and immediately asked, "Are you hurt?"

"No...it's not me."

The pilot looked beyond Jon and saw nothing. He pulled his bosses' arm, helping him in and stared at his eyes.

"Not the kid?"

"I'm afraid so," Jon answered. "We need to go."

"Didn't really get to know him," he said turning back and slumping into the left seat.

"Me either, really," Jon said. "I would have liked to."

"I filed to go back to Dalton."

"We have to get to DC," Jon corrected him. "Can you change that in the air?"

"Sure, I don't know about fuel though."

"Do the best you can." Jon stepped into the lavatory to clean up. "Just do the best you can."

Coming out from the lavatory, Jon noticed a compartment marked "PGS." The compartment door was locked. He went to the pilot to ask what it was.

"That's a last resort escape mode," the pilot grinned.

"Okay?"

"You strap it on, belt style...skydive away from the aircraft and throw the packet out, far as you can."

"Does it work?" Jon's mind became intrigued with the idea.

"I've never tried it," the pilot said flatly. "I'm chute certified. Just not sure about that thing."

"So, it's a parasail without a motor?"

"Basically, yeah."

Jon's interest grew. "Can I look at it?"

The pilot pulled down a visor and found a small key. "Sure," he said and handed off the key.

Its size surprised Jon. The "packet" the pilot told him about was the size of a softball, with a CO2 cartridge attached. The ropes and belt material appeared to be the same as the ropes Ben had bought last year. Those were nearly impervious to any cut or break, he figured these must be as well. The color of the casing was black, belt included.

Like it was made for me, Jon thought. *Could blend in with the suit just fine.*

He put the paraglider unit in his bag with the black suit. Leaning back in the plush leather seat he tried to concentrate on the task ahead. Visions of Jakes flashed in his mind, returning fears of what his growing exposure has caused those around him.

Digging back into the bag, Jon found three lipstick cameras and two sound transmitters. His thoughts made him pause as he held the cameras. Then he stood, looking around the cabin for places to set them. An idea was forming.

58

Spiegel and Barker looked at each other from oppossing four cushion sofas. Both men were impressed by the room, it really was oval. The heavy tan leather couches were laid out across from each other. Angled in a funnel shape yet parallel to the desk. The position was set so that each guest had an unobstructed view of his host.

"Mr. Bilstock," The President started and then waved his arm slowly towards the others there. "And I assume, you gentlemen as well..." he continued. "Have solid evidence that there's some national plot to overthrow this government. Is that about right?"

Murray looked around to see he was left to answer the question.

"Yes, Sir. We've been living with, and in, those facts for over a week now." He felt strength growing in his voice as he spoke. "People have been hurt and killed. Some not even knowing what is going on."

"I haven't heard of any incidents that could be tied to anything like this."

"Sir," Murray struggled to explain. "What we know to be true...and what has been reported in the media are two different things."

The President understood, but offered little more than a disgusted look in return.

"And the end game is me?" he asked.

"Actually, Sir. With all due respect...no." Murray glanced toward Grimes to see if he wanted to step in with the details. The NCIS agent stood and stepped forward.

"Mr. President, the ultimate target is the nomination to the high court," he shared. "The desired result, we believe... is to defend the Information Bill that is coming before the court this fall."

A squint came to the President's eyes.

"So you mean Dan would be killed, too?"

"Yes, Sir. The Vice President is also a target."

"That would leave it to..." The President looked to his aide who was standing in a corner and changed subjects abruptly. "Where is Grant, right now?"

"At his condo in Virginia, Mr. President," the man said right from the hip.

"I see." Ever so lightly, the president pounded the desktop with a fist. The look on his face showed thoughts were changing in mid-stream. "Is Dan still in Florida?"

"Yes, Sir," the aide responded. "Till the 3rd."

"You're telling me," both hands were now on the desktop, "that this plot is joined by officials of the government?" He was glaring directly at Grimes.

"Sir," Grimes reminded him. "We've already mentioned the agencies involved."

"I'm aware of the lack of certain loyalties at the departments you suspect. But," the president argued. "You can't corrupt an entire agency."

"But Sir, those people react to orders and the information they're given."

Somehow that simple statement seemed to resonate with the President.

"Pretty audacious undertaking, don't you think?" He looked back at Jerome Grimes.

A knock at the main doors interrupted Grimes before he could answer. Another aide entered the room carrying a note. It was handed to the President.

As he read the note his expression became more of a blank stare. The leader of the free world had read something he clearly didn't like. Sitting back against the heavy tuffs of his chair, he glared at Murray and then Grimes.

"Gentlemen...one of the things I must always be vigilant to and aware of... is the political nature of this office." He stood up and crushed the note in his hand. Turning his back and staring out a window, he spoke to his own reflection in the glass. "I must be careful how I react... and... what I react to."

The President's stare continued and after a momentary pause he added, "Those who would discredit me are constantly watching."

Grimes leaned forward. "Sir, has something happened?"

The President turned back around. His face displayed a desire for confrontation.

"A college professor in Colorado has been killed by a student." He watched them for their reactions. "This professor has been an agitator and a 'shit-stirrer' for years. Just a radical, country-hating, west coast academic type."

The men on the sofas sat in silence. Murray rolled his eyes and squirmed. He was beginning to get a bad feeling in his gut.

"So what's the big deal, you ask?" the President continued in an oddly sarcastic tone. "Well...witnesses put the real Jonathan Crane at the scene with the student who killed this man."

Grimes' hand went to his forehead. Spiegel and Barker stared at the floor.

Murray, having figured it out a second ahead, stood to speak. He raised a finger and looked toward the President.

"Sir...was that professor's name Walden?" he asked.

"Young man...I demand to know, right now. Is this thing real... or am I being set up in some partisan sting?"

"No, Sir...this is real."

"You said it was vital to my safety that you appear to be Crane, did you not?"

"Is the professor Steven Walden, Sir?" Murray repeated.

"Yes...that's his name... and you know this...how?"

"He is known in the conspiracy as 'Mithras'," Grimes jumped in.

The President's reaction to that name was transparent though not interpretative. Something registered, but he didn't offer what. He did however, become less agitated.

"The name 'Mithras' was part of the attempt to kill me?" His voice was much lower now.

"He was a major player, Sir."

The President sat back down and adjusted a pen and notebook on the desk. A gesture that allowed him time to think before he spoke again.

"This is how you deal with a threat?" He looked at them all. "You kill them?"

The question was more an inquiry than a challenge.

"Jon went out there to get information from Walden. I don't know what else happened." Murray tried to convince him. "Walden took his orders from Cyrus Grant. We know this...we just can't legally prove it."

Another knock at the doors again broke the conversation. The aide stuck his head in and said, "Sir, there's a call from Jonathan Crane being patched through on line four."

~

Grant had tried to contact Shanahan, but again she was out of reach. Spending her days bullying attendants at the pool of the high rise in Panama City Beach, Florida. She found that time went by faster if she maintained a certain level of insobriety. That task had become her job and she would see to it for three more days.

After the third unsuccessful call, Grant thumbed through his private, coded file. The names Icarus 1 and Icarus 2 were listed with odd-looking numbers after them. The code wasn't all that fancy, but it was effective. The first four numbers were actually the phone number's last digits in correct order. The last six digits were in reverse order making it somewhat of a puzzle, yet easy enough for him to remember.

Grant dialed the first number and a voice answered in code.

"Challenger here."

"Initiate Icarus option," he ordered as Bogart. "Effective as of the second."

"Roger... Icarus option on two of seven," the voice acknowledged.

The same message was given to the other recipient with the same results.

The men on the other end would begin carrying two mini-radio devises, one a receiver, the other a transmitter. When the first began to lightly vibrate, on or after July 2nd, they were to turn on their transmitter.

These signals would lead the drones to their targets.

~

Capt. Phil Stone placed a special detail in and around the offices of the Shreveport Times. The twelve men included three sharpshooters.

"Is this really necessary, Phil," Matt complained. "You're scaring the staff half to death."

"According to Jon, they should be." Phil Stone adjusted his belt and sharply nodded at his old friend before leaving his office.

"Do you even know what or who you're looking for?" the editor called after him.

"A guy with a fuse hanging out of his butt," Stone barked without looking back. He knew Matt trusted him and he knew his friend understood the situation. The newspaperman just hated being fussed over.

Matt sat back down to review the information on his desk. The stories were getting worse by the hour. Jonathan Crane was being accused of high crimes and terrorism. The names of those who had associated with Crane were also being tainted, including his own.

No evidence or standard of proof was offered, only accusations relayed in the most emotional ways possible.

"Hold our front section," Matt hollered while pushing a button on his desk. "I've got a headline I want to go this afternoon."

A voice from the box replied, "thirty minutes, boss. That's all we got."

Matt Turlock didn't respond to that comment. He was already banging away on his computer.

59

"Mr. President...Jonathan Crane here, Sir," the speaker box proclaimed to the room.

"Mr. Crane, this situation is beginning to take time I'm not sure it deserves. Are you in a position to make sense of it?"

"Sir, it's clear to me. The judgment is up to you and I know your reputation for bravery precedes you." The words could have been a butt-kiss, yet Jon made them sound sincere. "This is bigger than you...you and your friend, the Vice President. An attorney from Atlanta seeks to be on the Supreme Court, She..."

"She?" the President interrupted.

"Yes, Sir...she," Jon restated. "Has worked at this through other means before. By means of a group calling themselves the 'Sponsors' that attempted assassinations at lower levels to weaken your administration. That effort having failed, she now has gone more direct."

"So far, Mr. Crane, this is a well crafted fantasy."

"No fantasy, Mr. President. The Austin nuclear threat that feigned a street collapse as a cover up, the nuclear materials being stolen from a transport, the death of your Homeland Security Secretary as well as many other Texas sheriffs and citizens...knowledge of the safe house city for next week..."

The President perked up at the suggestion they knew about that.

"Pendleton, Oregon," Grimes said calmly from the couch.

The President leaned back.

"But it turns out, " Jon continued. "Even that is not really a necessity."

"There's no reason to go to Pendleton... or any safe house," the President offered.

"But there will be, Sir. And when that happens you need to disregard it," Jon told him.

"It's procedure...if the situation calls for it, I really have no say."

"This time you must, Sir." Jon was emphatic. "Pendleton will be where they are strongest. We don't have time to prepare against that."

"But you say they have a fall back plan."

"Yes, Mr. President. I believe they do."

"What is your proposal then, Mr. Crane?"

"When the situation occurs, stay with your plan to go to Cleveland...or at least say you are."

"Ok. I'm listening."

"Sir, we need electronic surveillance on both you and the Vice President starting immediately."

"For what?"

"A transmitter, Sir. A tracking transmitter."

"What have you learned now, Jon?" It was Murray asking this time.

"They do have a fall back plan...Walden called it a failsafe. It involves Predator drones."

"Domestic use of the drones is prohibited," the president said strongly.

"So is killing you, Sir," Jon quipped back.

The room became quiet after that remark and stayed so for a couple of minutes. Jon finally broke the silence.

"Mr. President...my pilot tells me we must stop to refuel. I can still be there in about four hours."

401

"No..." The president answered quickly. "Today is the 29ᵗʰ. I will stay here and have Dan stay in Florida until the first. I need time to think. Come here then, on the first."

"Increase your security and be careful who you use," Grimes consoled.

"Who do you suggest?" the President threw back at him.

"I'll leave Spiegel to head a team here and Barker can go to Florida tonight."

"My Secret Service?" the President pointed out. "I have them."

"They can stay, but make sure my men are in charge."

"They won't like that..." the president said and then Jon stepped in.

"Not a good idea," he offered. "The President is right. We don't know who all the players are. Let the Secret Service believe it's their game. Don't change anything just yet. Just don't share the details."

The room became animated as the guests stood to leave. The president ignored all that and leaned onto his desk.

"Did you kill him?" he asked point blank into the speaker.

"Walden?" Jon responded.

"Yes," the president repeated. "Did you kill him?"

"No...but I wish I had."

"What does that *even* mean?"

"Walden pulled some weapon on the young man who was there with me. They had history. Bad history."

They could hear Jon's voice crack a bit and he took a second before continuing. "The weapon blew up in Walden's face. It killed them both."

"I'm to believe this... story, just like that?" the President challenged him.

"Sir, like everything else in this...that's entirely up to you." Jon then took charge. "I will call you again in two days. You tell me then... what you've decided."

~

Monitors let Ben know the Mercury was back, but he didn't go to the third sub-level. He stayed at his desk. It had been a busy three hours since last talking to Jon.

The elevator door opened and Jon headed straight for Ben's work area. He did not smile.

"I've talked to Phil," Ben said without getting up from his chair. "The frequencies you need to monitor have been programmed into this." He laid a small unit, similar to a digital wristwatch on the desk.

"Whoa...you're a bit ahead of me," Jon answered and picked up the devise. "What frequencies?"

"You haven't talked to Capt. Stone again, have you?"

Jon started to understand what had transpired between Ben and his police Captain friend.

"He told you about the drones and the signals, right?"

"Yeah," Ben responded. "The control signals will be in the range this monitor tracks. You will be able to tell when the drone is coming."

"So...you figure I plan to be there?"

"Aren't you?"

"Well, I hope to be. That's really up to the President."

"What's up to him," Ben offered in a wry tone, "is if he knows about it... or not." He didn't look up, fully expecting a comeback from Jon. That didn't happen.

"Okay...this is good," Jon did say while putting the unit in his pocket. He opened another desk drawer. "Is this where you keep the other electronic stuff?"

"What do you need?" Ben slid his chair that way while asking.

"A transponder. One I can set to a specific signal."

Ben pulled a small key like item from the drawer and flipped open its lid. " What frequency do you want it set to?" he asked.

"Just show me how, okay?" Jon looked his assistant in the eye. "I'll set it later."

"I won't be able to find you if I don't know the signal you've set," Ben told him.

"Don't worry about it, I'll handle it...Now...What else is going on?"

Ben leaned back and stared at Jon. He knew better than to argue, not yet anyway.

"You gonna tell me about Jakes?" He asked.

Jon stopped and lowered his head. He took a deep breath and on the exhale said,

"Not now."

"You've got to tell me sometime, Jon."

"In due time...just not right now. I asked you what else was going on."

Sliding back along the huge work desk area, Ben stopped himself at a spot piled high with documents.

"News stories are flying everywhere." He grabbed a stack of printouts and handed them to Jon. "Daniel and Matt have tried to issue contradictions. But the heavy, national coverage has you, or 'The Son,' as the bad guy and our friends as accomplices."

Jon shook his head as he glanced through the stories.

"Is this it?" he asked.

"The feds have a warrant out for Marsha."

"For what?" Jon's face showed its first emotions.

"They claim she's harboring fugitive terrorists."

"The Israelis."

"Yeah...is she still with them in Texas?"

"It's best they stay there till this is done," Jon proclaimed.
"How about the lawyer?"

"Still in Florida. I'm having her watched and the airport in
Panama City, Florida will let me know when she leaves."

"Ben, I need you to ship Murray's suit to him, overnight
express. Use Phil Stone's address in Shreveport."

"It's pretty late," Ben reminded him.

"I called the office we own. The manager is there, waiting for
you."

"It's good to be the boss, huh?" Ben cracked.

"I just need that suit to get to Louisiana by tomorrow."

Ben got up and went to the closet.

60

Murray Bilstock's flight to Shreveport had taken an hour longer than he'd expected. Phil was waiting for him. Murray thought it was to take him to get Lucy, so he could go home.

"Jon wants you to stay here, if you will," Phil explained.

Not taken aback too much by that, Murray smiled.

"Ok...more role playing? I'm not real good at that... as it turns out."

"Well, he disagrees," Stone grinned. "He says you did perfect in DC."

"I didn't fool anyone, especially the president," Murray snapped at him.

"Maybe not, but you made the news people look like fools. They still can't decide where Jon really was." Phil smiled and grabbed Murray's bag from the airline's carousel. "That's all Jon wanted out of it. Just a crack in their armor."

"He should thank the 'big man' for that. He went along with it."

"There's a package coming to my house for you. Should be here by mid-day."

"Package?" Murray asked.

"That's all I know." Phil told him as they loaded into the police cruiser sitting at the curb. "He said you'd understand when you got it."

"Sara's good?" the cowboy asked him tenatively.

"A little nervous...but she's good... yeah."

~

The heat and humidity of Louisiana was difficult for Carlos Martin to get used to. Colorado's air was much lighter and cooler. He had spent nearly two days walking the streets around the Shreveport Times, learning the terrain and understanding why Mithras wanted him there early.

That morning Carlos left the air conditioning in his room set lower as he dressed in his best suit. The vest was laced up under his coat. His sweat was less profuse.

The vest held six blocks of C4 and a detonator cap attached to a hand held switch. The vest itself was slim and would allow him to go as far into the building as he could, undetected. When he reached his target, he would then set it, and himself, off.

Carlos did not know his boss was dead. He knew of Mithras, not Steven Walden, so the news of the professor's death was not a concern to him. As the clock on the motel room wall read 9:35 A.M. he checked the mirror one last time and left the room. He didn't bother checking out, it was in an assumed name anyway. No one would ever know who had destroyed the "evil voice of capitalism."

Martin parked his rental car on Lake Street near Marshall. The walk to the newspaper building was only a block from there. His watch said 10:00 A.M. as he took the trigger switch from his pocket and curled it into his right hand.

~

Matt Turlock's office was on the second floor. He had meetings that morning with members of the Special Olympics team of Shreveport. Their gala dinner and awards ceremony was scheduled for that evening and Matt wanted to interview the group's leaders. They brought with them four members of the girl's wheelchair basketball team.

"Come in, please," Matt directed as he swung his door wide. His guests, all eight of them, filed into the office and found places to sit or park.

"Thank you for seeing us," the head coach smiled and said to Matt. He had just taken the man's hand when all "hell" broke loose.

~

The plain-clothes detective assigned to the editor's hallway noticed Carlos as he came in. Working too hard to look "cool" was the giveaway. When the bomber stopped outside Matt's office and raised his hand holding the trigger, the veteran officer stepped toward him.

"Do not flinch... Do not move one muscle," he said in a firm voice. Pulling his revolver from under his coat, the detective leveled it at the man.

Carlos was trained to push the button if confronted, but what he saw in the office gave him pause. The girls in wheelchairs made him freeze for just a second.

The group in Matt's office heard the shouting and saw the strange man with his arm held up. They became upset and the panic quickly spread. Screams began to echo through the hallway as other employees ducked into doors where they could. Carlos Martin turned toward the officer with the gun and glared at him.

"Back off, fool," he yelled. "You shoot me... this whole building goes up." Martin held his hand and the trigger higher.

The detective did not move. His hands fixed solidly to his handgun, and his eyes on Martin's hand, holding the bomb trigger.

The officer then noticed a red, laser dot appear on the man's chin.

"Drop what you're holding," he ordered Martin. "Do it, now!"

"You have one more second to back-off...I'm telling you," Carlos threatened.

The officer loosened his stance slightly, still aiming at the threat. He touched a switch on his shirt, quietly opening a microphone Carlos could not see.

"There's a spot in your neck..." The officer proclaimed to both the bomber and now the sniper across the street. "That when broken, you can't and won't... move another muscle...ever."

Carlos Martin knew about the C2 vertebra, the stories were legendary. If that spot on the neck were severed, the muscles of the body would shut down instantly. A shot like that from where the officer stood was impossible.

"Ha!" Martin nervously scoffed at him. "There's no way you can...."

The next sound was of breaking glass, a muffled thud and a few screams.

The shot came in from across the street, a parking deck ledge some three hundred yards away. Martin's mouth stopped, as did his eyes. A splash of red matter hit the wall behind him. The would-be bomber stood like a statue for a full second before his body collapsed. It landed face first just inside Matt's office.

Screams picked up even louder as the detective rushed to the body. He grabbed the wrist of the man's right hand and turned it over. The thumb rested above a button on the control, but the thumb had not moved.

Matt Turlock was now standing over him as well. He didn't speak except to try to calm the people in his office. He hollered for an assistant to open a side door where the guests could leave without stepping over the body.

Grasping Martin's thumb with his left hand, the officer pulled the devise away with his right. He then looked at Martin's face. A small hole was in his chin, dead center and right below the lip. A rather jagged and much larger wound had opened the back of the man's neck. A blood pool reached out and grew from it.

"Perfect shot," the detective said, over and over. "Perfect shot."

Phil Stone was on the scene within thirty minutes, Murray Bilstock in tow. Phil congratulated his team on a "job well done," while Murray called Georgia.

"They got him, Jon. He could have taken out this whole building. They got him."

Jonathan Crane sat down near Ben's desk. The relief and joy one would expect was not there. He saw it as another example of the danger his friends were in, because of him.

"Thank the officers for me," Jon asked Murray. "I'll talk to you later this afternoon."

And then he hung up.

Murray was stunned. *This was a great victory*, he thought. *Phil's people stopped this guy right in his tracks and Jon hangs up? What is up with that?*

~

"I'm going upstairs to make a call," Jon announced and stood.

"Am I in the way here?" Ben countered.

"No." He stopped and reached into a pocket. "These are the serial numbers of cameras I installed on the G5. See if you can activate them and tell me what altitude you can receive images from."

Ben looked at the note he'd been handed. "Sure."

After two steps, Jon pivoted and raised his finger.

"Did you handle those papers I asked you to process?"

Ben stood himself, "Yeah. What are you up to?" he demanded forcefully.

"Ducks in a row, Ben." Jon climbed into the elevator and looked back. " Putting ducks in rows."

61

Jerome Grimes' call reached Jon before he could get to the kitchen.

"Cleveland has been compromised" he said. "We got word ten minutes ago, it'll be in the news within the hour."

"What is it?" Jon asked.

"Nuclear threat, just like the others."

Jon thought a second. "Sir, call this number and ask for Ben, he's my assistant. Tell him I want him to give you the details of the trace signature the material has been leaving. It's all from the same small sample stolen a few weeks back."

"And then...?"

"Release it to the press, all of 'em."

"Undermine the claim, I get it," Grimes said.

"The president needs to go to Cleveland tomorrow, not Pendleton."

"Have you called him yet?"

"Naw...and I can't wait much longer. Getting ready to in a few minutes."

"One other thing..." Grimes threw in. "My daddy's name was 'Sir.' I work for a living."

Jon laughed and hung up.

Murray got the package and found his black suit. A note Jon had stuck inside said simply, "Barksdale." He looked up at the police captain.

"Can you get me into Barksdale Air Force Base?" he asked Phil.

"Matt can." The answer was more a reflex, and then his tone changed. "When do you need to go...and why?"

"Not sure yet. I have a feeling it'll all be obvious when the time comes."

~

The box had been hidden under a stack of firewood since April. He really hoped it would not come into play, but Cyrus Grant was now sitting and studying it.

It was fifteen inches long and about nine inches wide. The depth varied inside because of the switches, gauges and knobs. With the lid closed it stood about five inches tall. The insides were what Grant now studied.

Closing speed, he read. The gauge was a digital readout he assumed would be important. He clearly understood the two toggles in the right hand corner. "Arm" and "Fire" were marked and stood out from the others.

The largest knob was marked "A-B and Both." Should the targets be traveling separately or together, the controls were there.

The one marked "signal ready" didn't make sense at first, it was simply a lamp that would light in the correct conditions. Next to that was a switch reading, "send." His hand written notes from months ago explained what all this meant. That switch would send a radio signal out for the tracking devise to lock on to. Then it could offer its location and become the target.

Grant rubbed his face with both hands. He didn't like having personal involvement in the act, but with Walden dead and no word that the Cleveland ruse had worked, he had to be sure. He would handle the weapons himself.

Setting the box to one side, he pushed a button on a cell phone.

"Yeah, have you heard anymore about Cleveland?" he asked the man on the other end. The response was negative.

"Then I need you personally involved," he ordered.

The man complained, saying he had important things he still needed to do.

Grant chastised him. "You have a crew there, just to be sure. If this doesn't work out, you're dead anyway. We all are."

The voice continued to protest, but in a much weaker tone. His words were cut off.

"You can and will be there," Grant demanded. "You knew there was this chance. Do you understand me?" This time he received an affirmative answer.

"Good," he told the man. "You call me as you leave."

~

Niko Fogarty excused himself from the table. The luncheon was for new Secret Service agents assigned to the POTUS detail. He stopped at the drink table and appeared to be getting another cup of coffee. There was more to it than that.

Fogarty placed a small plastic bag under the saucer and held it in place with one finger. As he walked back to the table, he pretended to almost trip near his boss and POTUS detail chief, Charles Haggers.

Grabbing the back of Haggers' chair with his left hand for balance, Fogarty's right hand, with the coffee cup, hovered over his boss's iced tea glass for only a moment. With a firm squeeze against the plastic bag, it broke. The contents ran down into the glass.

All attention and accompanying ridicule was directed at Fogarty, not his right hand.

"Sorry, boss," he offered through the laughs of the others as Haggers reached out to steady him.

"You okay, there?" the chief asked him.

"Yeah...this rug tried to bite me, that's all." Fogarty grinned and continued on to his seat. The boss took a large sip from his iced tea and then tapped on the glass for attention.

"Ok, listen up," Haggers started. "This has been fun, but it's time to get back to work." He unfolded a piece of paper and began to read from it. "Duty for the POTUS trip tomorrow shall be myself. Stand-by will be my back up agent, Niko Fogarty, who's already had one trip tonight." He couldn't resist the joke.

The assembled agents all had a good laugh once again and Niko simply raised his glass to them. He smiled and looked at each one there, glass held high.

Ali Akbar, he said to himself, *to the new beginning.*

Yinon Harel heard the beeping first. Murray's security system at Caddo Mills was unique and impressive even to a veteran Israeli agent. He stood and walked to the large flat screen monitor that had focused on one camera image. Marsha sat up, and laid her book down. She watched the goings on at the surface while her feet searched for her shoes.

"Where is Reiss?" she asked softly. Sound in the underground bunker carried well, but did not echo. Still, they tried not to disturb their colleague. The injured Nava Golan was better. Undisturbed rest was what she needed so they tried to remain quiet.

Harel looked back at Marsha and pointed up.

"He's up top, somewhere."

Marsha rose from the sofa and stepped to the screen.

"Who are they?" she asked, pointing to the images.

"There's four of them. One black SUV," Harel whispered. "They went up on the porch of the main house."

"You're sure Reiss is up there?"

"Yes. He doesn't do well below ground. Not for extended periods anyway."

"But where is he?"

"I don't know that."

The monitor screen again became active. Four men emerged from the house and spread out around the property. Two moved toward the hanger. The motion sensor cameras suddenly changed viewpoint. One had picked up Reiss moving away from the barn. In a low crouch, he was running toward a sand drift near the far side of the hanger.

"I've got to go up top," Harel said with urgency. He checked his weapon and extra magazines. Then, after glancing back toward Marsha and Nava, he silently stepped into the exit.

Marsha went to the gun closet and found several handguns mounted on the back wall. Her training and experience told her they weren't right for this application. Sitting against one corner was a Heckler & Koch MP5. The 6 pound, 9mm machine gun was fitted with a 30 round magazine. It was a weapon Marsha was familiar with.

More motion from the monitor caught her eye and attention. She turned to see a fleeting, blurred image. It was two of the uninvited guests rushing past the opening of the hanger.

As she started to turn back, Yinon Harel appeared in the same frame. He was moving toward the hanger-opening... weapon in hand.

"I've got to help," she heard herself say. Pulling the MP5 from the wall of the closet, Marsha lunged toward the exit slapping the bottom of the magazine as she ran.

62

The President of the United States sat alone in his office. He had spoken to his Vice President once about the decision. They were in agreement. Whatever he decided was what they would do. His old friend had every confidence in his decision-making.

The large desk was layered in papers. Newspaper articles and tapes of broadcasts had been reviewed. His instincts were to be skeptical of what he saw as "radicals" on either side of an argument.

The press would love to skewer me, he thought. *And their hate goes beyond facts.* Facts were a casualty of an administration some years back. The media sold itself out for a cause and agenda they seemed to believe in, enough to alter the truth when necessary to defend that cause.

"Sir," the speakerphone announced. "It's the Homeland Security Secretary, I mean acting secretary... on line six."

"Thank you," the president responded. "Tell him I'll be with him in a minute."

Leaning back and rocking in the big leather chair, he asked himself, *what's this all about, now?* His trust for the stand-in secretary was not as it should be to start with.

"Yes, Darin," he answered. "Kinda busy today. Can you make it quick?"

"Sir, I hope to," Doyle responded. "Our agents need your approval to plan for the safe house."

"Haven't made that choice yet."

"Sir, with all due respect. The other locations are compromised beyond any level that I can authorize travel."

"You authorize?"

"Sir, you know what I mean." Doyle knew he was close to a line he didn't want to cross. "It's my job and the Secret Service looks to me for leadership in this."

"When I've decided where I will go, Darin," he paused and gathered his building anger. "You'll be one of the first to know." After a short, but pointed pause, he concluded, "am I clear on that?"

"Sir, I will be traveling with you in this case. Just to be sure."

"I'll try to give you time to know how to pack." And the president popped the button on the phone set. Doyle's insistence on knowing the plans was the last straw. He would go along with this man from Georgia and pray he knew what he was talking about.

Pushing the intercom button, he asked for an aide to come in the office.

"Sir," the man came in and stood near the door.

"Get Crane on the phone."

"Didn't he say he would call?"

"You know... he did," the president answered, cocking his head to one side. "Try to get him anyway before I change my mind."

"You don't usually change your mind, Sir," the aide teased him.

Rocking back into the chair again, he looked up at the trusted assistant, "No... I don't... do I?"

Clean up in the offices of the Shreveport Times was not complete and Matt Turlock was still deeply involved. The editor's concentration was broken when he heard the question Murray asked. He and Phil had just come in and walked straight back to where Matt was working.

Matt took him by the arm and pulled him into an interview room.

"Why do you want to get into Barksdale?" he asked the cowboy.

"To be honest...I don't exactly know just yet." Murray's face was as serious as Matt had ever known it to be. "Jon sent me a message. All it said was 'Barksdale.' Is that place big enough for a 747 to land?"

"The big jet? Absolutely," Matt responded and his expression changed as he spoke. He quickly added, "You don't think?"

"Yeah...it's got to be in the plan. We have to be ready in any event. Can you get me in there?"

"But from Andrews to here...that's quite a bit off course."

"Not Air Force One..." Murray corrected his friend's thinking. "Jon has that handled. But Air Force Two. The VP is still in Florida, right?"

At that moment Phil Stone came in...unannounced.

"Just heard from Grimes. He's still in Tyler with the FBI guys." His expression was grave. "They've heard a rather disturbing rumor through their home office."

Phil had their attention with that. Matt slowly asked, "What?"

"Warrants have supposedly been issued, but dated tomorrow."

"Warrants? Who this time?" Murray begged to know.

Phil pointed at Matt and spoke slowly.

"You," he said." And me... Marsha and Daniel Seay."

"For what?" Matt and Murray asked simultaneously.

"Treason," Phil answered bluntly.

"That's a broad charge isn't it?" Matt asked him.

"That's what makes it so serious. They can be as creative as they want with that one."

"They're throwing charges around like kids playing cops," Murray scoffed.

"Yeah, that's two for Marsha, now." Phil pointed out. "The heat is on."

The cowboy rubbed his chin. He almost didn't want to ask his next question.

"You didn't mention me," Murray pointed out, "or Jon, did you?"

"Yeah...that's the worse part." Phil took a breath.

"Worse than treason?"

"It's just a rumor...keep that in mind." Motioning with his hands as though he were pushing down something unseen, he continued, "they say...the word is... there's a hit contract out for you two."

"Does Jon know?" Murray asked without hesitation.

"I just talked to Ben before I came in here."

Matt looked back toward his office, still being cleaned from the bomb attempt.

"But I'm on the list...and they still tried to kill me?" the newspaperman wondered out loud.

"Doesn't make sense, does it?" Phil agreed. "Somebody didn't get the word."

Murray straightened up and stared at Matt.

"Or Walden was going off on his own." The cowboy's fists curled into knots and he headed for the exit. With his eyes focused on the floor as he walked, Murray muttered under his breath.

"This is getting interesting."

~

The cabinet door was open. Marsha could tell the instant the passageway door swung back. This cabinet sat at the rear of the hanger. It was actually the secret entrance to the underground hideout.

With the mini machine gun at ready position, she leaned toward the opening to look out into the hanger bay. It was clear.

Marsha eased along the inner walls of the building, moving to her left and then up the sidewall toward the front. She could hear voices. They seemed to be outside, on the left.

At the hanger's main opening, Marsha slid to the exterior corner and peeked around. Yinon and Reiss stood about thirty feet back, facing the side of the hanger. With hands in the air, they stared towards the hanger at their captors.

Marsha held her back against the aluminum and slowly craned her neck to look down the side. There, standing only feet from the side wall, were the the four intruders.

Three were holding guns on the Israelis and the other was on his cell phone.

"Who are you, guys?" he demanded of the silent Israelis. "Where is Bilstock?"

Marsha could tell that Reiss had spotted her though he didn't move. She rolled back along the wall and into the hanger. Pushing with her finger against the aluminum sidewalls, she guessed the material was fairly thin. *It better be,* she thought.

There were no windows along that side, but she could now make out what was being said through the aluminum.

"He ain't here, boss. These guys must be those Mossad fellas. What should we do with them?"

Marsha didn't like what she was hearing. She stepped back about six feet from the wall and strained to listen.

"The boss says 'take 'em out.'" She heard the man say.

Marsha raised the MP5 over her head with both hands. Angling the barrel downward she sprayed the wall from right to left and then back again. About twenty-five of her thirty rounds were fired in a matter of seconds, piercing the aluminum as though it were paper.

She turned and held her breath, pointing the weapon to the hanger opening until she heard Yinon call to her.

"Marsha...Marsha!"

Harel and Reiss appeared at the big door and she lowered her gun. The Isreali team leader looked back at the bodies outside and then to Marsha. Reiss, dumbfounded by her quick actions, approached Marsha smiling from ear to ear.

"That was amazing!" Reiss proclaimed. "You got them all." He grabbed her shoulders and gently shook her as his boss came up beside them. Marsha looked at them both and managed a slight smile.

Harel pointed to the entrance through the cabinet.

"We have to let the others know," he ordered. "This is getting rough." But he then headed back outside.

"Where are you going?" Marsha asked.

"To check those guys for I.D. They were going to kill us...not arrest us." His expression then changed from potential victim back to hardened military specialists. "Reiss, do you have a camera phone on you?"

"Yeah," he pulled it from his pocket.

"Go with Marsha," Harel said as he took the phone. "I'll be down in a few minutes."

63

Jon stepped off the elevator and into the second sub-level laboratory.

"You've missed a couple of phone calls," Ben announced without really looking at him. He was leaning back, as far as the rolling office chair would allow, rubbing his eyes with both hands.

"Yeah?" Jon grabbed another chair for himself. "Been on the phone myself."

Ben uttered softly without moving, "Really?"

"Worked out a plan with the President. He's a hard sell, but we're together on it now."

He had also been on a call to Kentucky working out serious details for his plan. He would discuss that with Ben later.

There was no reaction from his young assistant. Jon realized the situation was taking its toll on the boy.

"What's going on, Ben?" he asked.

"Everybody is okay...so far, but there's been an attempt on Matt Turlock and four guys hit Caddo Mills looking for Murray." Ben sat upright and turned his chair in Jon's direction.

"Marsha's fine?"

"She's a hero according to Reiss." The weight of everything was beginning to show on Ben. His breathing was shallow and rapid. It made talking difficult.

"One more day, Ben." Jon's voice was calm and reassuring. "This will be over soon enough." He didn't ask the boy for details. He knew they would come as soon as Ben relaxed a bit.

"Harel believes the guys were there to kill Murray...not arrest him...kill him."

Not too surprised, Jon listened without interrupting him.

"A suicide bomber walked right into the newspaper offices in Shreveport." Ben had changed gears. "Capt. Stone's people took him out," he said excitedly. "No real damage, nobody else hurt."

Jon nodded heavily in approval of what he had heard.

"There's more," Ben said with a blank stare. "The FBI says there are warrants to be issued tomorrow for Daniel, Capt. Stone, Matt Turlock and Marsha...for treason."

The obvious absence registered with Jon right away.

"Not Murray?"

"The guys at Caddo Mills...that was a contract hit."

"Murray's not even in Texas."

"I know, Jon," Ben cut in. "The point is...it's a contract. And there's one on you, too."

Jon's eyebrows rose, but only slightly. He leaned back, looking around at all the monitors in the area.

"Anything show up yet? I mean since those guys the other night?"

"No. It's been quiet."

"Well, I don't have time to wait for 'em." His mind formulating a plan as he spoke, Jon stood. "Where is the Jag?"

"In the garage upstairs."

"Perfect," he smiled. "You enjoyed driving it, right?"

Ben didn't respond, except with a grin that Jon enjoyed seeing. The tension was loosened by the possibility of hit men outside.

"Take a drive around the mountain," he told the boy. "See if you pick up a tail."

Ben opened a drawer and grabbed a set of keys.

"You have your own keys to my Jaguar?" Jon teased.

Ben didn't say anything. He walked quickly to the elevator as Jon called after him.

"Call my cell the minute you're in the car. And keep the line open the whole time."

"Got it," Ben shouted back.

Jon went to his weapons closet and then, when the elevator came back, he rode to the third level basement.

"Dan, I've given my word to this man. I trust him...I seriously do." The President of the United States was convincing his VP to go along with the plan.

"Mr. President, you know how much I respect you, and your judgment, but what you suggest I do is beyond any protocol."

"That's why it just might work, Dan. I remember you saying you would go with my lead on this."

The line became quiet. His boss's words hit home with the Vice President. They had discussed privately the conditions they were up against. The public was not being told what actually was going on in their country, but rather a version of facts suited to those telling the tale.

"I had planned to take my family on this trip," the VP finally said, breaking the silence. "I think I may have them follow along, later."

"I definitely agree, Dan." The President paused and then added, "There's no one I would rather have on my side in this. You know that, don't you?"

"Sir...it's going to be fine," his friend told him. "I'll keep a channel open on the plane."

"God's speed, Dan."

Yinon Harel entered the hideout carrying several black wallets.

"Figure out who they are?" Marsha asked him.

"They're not who this says they are." He threw the IDs on the table and turned on the camera. "Doesn't take much of a detective to see these pictures don't match the faces on the identifications."

Marsha and Reiss looked at the pictures Harel had taken and those in the wallets.

"Send those pictures to Ben. He can run them and find out who they are."

"I'm sure he could, but does it matter? We know what is going on." The Mossad leader walked over to his injured team member. "It is just as well she can't travel yet. We need to wait this out. Here...in hiding."

"What did you do with the bodies?" Reiss asked.

"I covered them with a tarp...put some rocks on the corners to hold it down."

"That won't take long to start drawing critters," Marsha warned.

"You're right," Harel agreed. "After dark, we'll find a shovel and get them below ground."

64

Ben picked up some followers shortly after making the right turn. They stayed back at first, then after the next turn they sped up and closed to within a few feet of the Jaguar.

"Jon, they're here. Black SUV. All over my bumper."

The cell phone was on "speaker," lying on the seat.

"Take 'em the long way around. Drive fast as you're comfortable with," Jon recommended. "That'll make sure they're really after you."

"We gonna use the 'deer' again?"

"No...just bring them back past the gas station and the house. I'll be there."

Jon was sliding into his black suit, but without the parasail. He had stopped at the Mercury to retrieve the suit, but didn't pick the sedan for this ride. Keys to the old pick-up truck were in his hand. He put the carry bag back into the Mercury and climbed into the pick-up. It cranked on the first try and Jon pulled slowly from its parking slot. Activating the tunnel access, he drove down into the gas station. With the truck beyond the wall, he kept the motor running and waited.

"Turning up 71 now," Ben called out and within a minute the Jaguar flew by the old gas station. Close on his rear bumper was the black SUV.

"I'm with you, Ben," Jon told him and pulled out onto the highway in the old truck. Its weight kept it from gaining on them. In fact...they were pulling away.

"Go around again, Ben. And slow it down to under fifty."

"Roger that!" Ben hollered out. "Fifty it is!"

As the pick-up made the first right turn Jon had them in his sights again. The truck hit seventy-five miles per hour and he was tight against the SUV before they noticed him.

"Go, Ben!" Jon yelled as his front bumper almost touched the SUV. "Floor it!"

Jon had activated the hydraulic extenders on the trucks bumper. The air powered shocks that would send the bumper flying forward nearly three feet. Sensors would trigger them automatically just prior to impact with another object.

As the Jaguar pulled away, Jon hit the gas on the pick-up and closed the distance to the assailants. At less than a second to impact, the bumper shocks fired. The heavy steel and chrome jumped ahead, propelling into the SUV. The hit lifted the car's back end, careening it forward on only its front tires. Steering was rendered impossible for the driver. When the rear end and tires of the big vehicle again touched the ground, the front wheels were turned sharply to the right.

The driving force of the rear wheels landing on the pavement pushed the SUV out of control. Jerking right, it bounced like a billiard ball off the side of the mountain. Then ricocheting back onto the road, the SUV wobbled back and forth before finally rolling over one complete cycle.

The pick-up skidded and squealed to stop only feet from the wrinkled vehicle. Jon was out of his truck and standing at the SUV before the men inside could react. He used the strength of the powered arm to pull the rear right door from the car. Hinges bent and all but pulled loose from the chassis. Weapons lay everywhere within the big SUV's interior. Shaken loose by the rollover, the guns were now in the floor, on the seats and some had broken through the side windows.

Jon reached inside and grabbed the man sitting closest. He yanked him from the car. Adjusting his grip to the man's collar, he pulled him up with the arm and glared directly into his face. Blood ran from man's nostril and mouth, but his eyes blinked and opened.

"Who are you?" Jon demanded through clenched teeth. His voice more a growl than spoken words.

The eyes of the face in front of him had barely focused. The mouth slowly opened, but it did not speak. Four high-powered rounds from an AK-47 abruptly ripped through its body. The bullets were not slowed by the obstruction and slammed directly into Jon's suit. He could feel their impact, but none penetrated.

Dropping the now dead body, Jon stared at the gunman only four feet away. The assault rifle flamed and barked again. More rounds bounced off Jon's armor. He stepped with one stride into the gunman and grabbed him by the throat. The weapon fell from his hands as his feet left the ground. Fear swelled in the man's eyes. He kicked and flailed, trying to reach the pavement again without success.

Jon held him steady. Looking up into face, he repeated the same basic question.

"Who are you people?"

More gunfire came, now from his left side, striking Jon's arm, shoulder and rib cage. Still, the projectiles ricocheted harmlessly away.

In an instant, Jon threw the man he was holding against the car, perhaps a bit too hard. He jumped, and in one motion traveled nearly ten feet to the other man who was still firing at him. The suit's powered legs had never been tried before in an actual situation. They worked just fine. Jon's hand impacted the man's head as he came down, leaving the gunman out cold.

After subduing this man, Jon looked for the fourth. Ripping the driver's door open, he found that body slumped in its seatbelt, neck clearly broken. The large rolling car had dealt with him. In all, three were dead. One was badly shaken, bruised and unconscious.

Ben had turned the Jaguar around and was pulling up to the scene. As he opened his door, Jon stuck out his arm and hollered, "No...stay there."

Jon gathered the ID information from all four. None matched the person carrying it. He handed the wallets to Ben who stood in silence behind the Jaguar's door.

"Call George," Jon instructed him calmly. "Have him send some men and a few ambulances."

Ben reached into the car and picked up his phone...released the call he'd been on and dialed.

~

Murray entered Barksdale AFB at around 9:30 PM that night. Matt had arranged for him to stay there overnight and the cowboy was given clearance, under the name Francis Marion, to be on the flightline.

His phone rang at just before 10 PM.

"Yeah, Ben," he answered.

Ben explained the plan and what Jon was expecting.

"If we're right...and the signal does come on," Ben told him. "I'll call you right away."

"Alright," the cowboy replied.

"If we're wrong...I don't really know. I don't have a plan for being wrong."

Murray chuckled a little. He liked that attitude.

"When should they be here?" he asked.

"Not till tomorrow evening. Guess you have some time to wait."

"That's cool," Murray quipped. "I always did like Air Force food."

430

~

Sheri Shanahan checked her cell phone that evening before dinner. It registered the calls Grant had attempted to her.

"Not now," she scoffed and deleted them. Looking into the hall mirror of the condo, she ran fingers through a section of her hair and straightened her neckline. "Can't be bothered with crap now. We either win or we don't."

Her plan was to return to Georgia in the morning and go over her speech for that night. Tonight...was for fun and a bit more wine.

~

Cyrus Grant was feeling more comfortable. He had verified that the world believed he was in North Carolina. His cabin on Black Mountain in Harlan County Kentucky was secure and he was again familiar with the control box he had been studying.

His notice, that the President was on the move, would come through a group broadcast email. It would simply say, "Red Ryder rides." That message alerted all secret service agents along the president's proposed route. It was supposed to be a precaution.

In this case it would also tell Bogart that all was ready.

65

Jon Crane spent the morning going over instructions with Ben. Some were to do with the mission, others Ben did not like or understand.

"Are you sure about this?" he asked again and again.

"Ben, I need you to support me in this, it's the only way."

The instructions were specific and very detailed. Including what to do when Major Swanson called from Kentucky.

"You call Marsha first," Jon emphasized.

As for the mission, Ben had a huge role in that. He was to monitor the airwaves for the appearance of a radio signal while also watching the cameras secretly filming inside the G5 cabin.

He would feed information to both Jon and Murray. Information they needed to save the two highest elected officials in the country from murder.

"Any word on Shanahan?"

Ben spun around and brought up a message system monitor.

"She's booked to fly out of Panama City early tomorrow."

On-line papers and TV news shows that morning were an onslaught of critical stories, mostly aimed at the President.

"Cowboy Politician Demonstrates Lack of Judgment," and "President Plunges Headlong into the Deadly Area for Holiday" were basic headlines and lead-ins to stories on the morning news shows. People in the Cleveland area knew this wasn't true, but were powerless in getting any contradictory word out.

"They're really on his case this morning, huh?" Ben commented.

"Today is the day...or so they think."

"You believe the media is in on this?"

"Not in a conscious, rational way...no. But they're so blinded by their agenda, the truth just doesn't matter to them anymore. To some of them, its even an obstruction."

"If you're successful, will that change?" Ben's question was wishful.

"I don't know...what do you call success? They'll jump to the right side of the discussion for a while, sure. There won't be any choice for them... It just won't last."

"So it won't really change until that law is overturned."

"That'll be the start. Getting both sides out to the public again is our only hope. If they choose correctly in what they believe, if they verify stuff before they believe it..." Jon shrugged his shoulders. "Truth is like the horse and the water story. You can lead them to it, you just can't make 'em drink."

"They've had a good taste of one-sided, dishonest news. Maybe they will think about it," Ben added.

"None of this mess we're in now could have ever happened... if the media were honest." Jon bowed up in anger. "It would never have gotten this far."

~

The President prepared for his trip in Washington, as did the VP in Florida. The Washington prep included a ten-minute phone call from the president to the pilot of Air Force One.

In Tampa, the Vice President met with his pilot and briefed him on the possibilities and what to expect.

The flights were to leave at approximately the same time. Air Force One to Cleveland, Air Force Two was scheduled for St. Louis.

433

~

When Yinon Harel awoke that morning, he saw Nava Golan sitting upright on the sofa.

"Agent Golan," He asked quite officially. "How do you feel?"

The voice woke Reiss and Marsha Hurst. Marsha felt Nava's forehead and looked to Harel.

"Doesn't feel warm at all," she smiled. "I think her fever has broken."

Reiss had grabbed her hand and patted it in his own joy. The injured agent looked around at her surroundings. Her confusion showed through blinking eyes as she tried to organize her questions.

"I have been listening for what seems like days." She said, her first words in over a week. "We are still in Texas, yes?"

"We are, agent," her boss answered with a smile. "What all do you remember?"

She blinked and reached deep for memories. Her eyes changed their expression several times until she finally spoke again.

"I remember the truck and the foam. Then I dreamed about a helicopter and a hospital." She looked at Marsha with a quizzical stare. "I dreamed I watched her on TV, shooting a machine gun through a wall."

Reiss laughed. He sat down next to Nava and hugged her around the shoulders.

"No dream there, agent," he told her. "Lt. Hurst here is our hero. She saved our lives."

"That was real?"

They pointed to the huge monitor on the wall.

"We should have this system," Harel joked.

"Why are we still here?" she asked seriously. "Can't we go home?"

"Not just yet." Harel shook his head. "Soon...but it's not over yet."

~

Bogart had slept in that morning. He didn't mean to, but staying up too late studying the controls in the box got to him.

An aide, one of two there with him, had left a pot of coffee outside his door. He opted to go downstairs for breakfast. The news stories pleased him.

"Who could sympathize with a man who won't take precautions?" he said, addressing the small TV more than anyone else. Grant checked his watch.

Eight hours, he thought and smiled slightly. *This should be over in eight hours.*

~

Murray Bilstock was walking a taxiway some hundred yards off the main runway at Barksdale AFB. He had been exercising his legs and his mind. Going through ideas and the different ways to look at situations he had learned by being around Jon.

A small wooden box, some four feet square, sat beside the taxiway. Murray bent down and looked it over. There was a door, locked with a big padlock. Next to that was a metal pipe protruding from the box at an angle, going into the ground. The cowboy clicked on a radio the ground crew had given him.

"What is this box?" he asked.

"Controls for the runway lights, Mr. Marion," came the answer. "If something goes out, the crew can tell from the panel inside...where the trouble is."

"That pipe...it's pretty secure, then?"

"Yeah...I'd say so. Don't think you could pull it out, if that's what you mean."

Murray nodded and thanked him. That was exactly what he had in mind. He smiled at being called "Mr. Marion." The name Matt chose for him was of the revolutionary hero known as "The Swamp Fox." Murray liked that and he knew Jon would as well.

66

Ben and Jon had tried to lure out any other hit teams three more times that day. Satisfied none were there, they parked the Jag and the pick-up back in the sub-level garage.

Jon checked his gear and he and Ben went over his duties, one more time.

"Don't forget Shanahan tomorrow," Jon said firmly. "No matter what happens."

"I got it."

Jon loaded the Mercury he would drive to the local airport and turned to Ben with his hand out. Ben hugged his friend instead.

"Think about this, will ya?" he begged.

"I have Ben, it's for the best," Jon assured him. "Everybody will be fine once this is done. The heat should be off."

Ben didn't respond. He watched his mentor climb into the Mercury and open the garage doors. The tunnel lights came on, following in the direction he would go. He stepped back as the sedan pulled into the tunnel and then disappeared.

It was 5:30 P.M.

The entourage from the White House to Andrews consisted of three helicopters, Marine One and two other escort-decoys and a team of secret service agents. The team leader was hospitalized with what was thought to be food poisoning, and his replacement was on the scene.

Niko Fogarty would be the agent assigned to fly with the president and with him was the acting secretary of Homeland Security, Darin Doyle.

In Florida, Air Force Two was loaded and on the runway. The Vice President and his secret service agent were strapped in and ready to go.

"Jon, do you read me?" The voice in his ear was Ben.

"Roger, Ben. I got you."

"There's an unknown signal emitting now from the plane in Tampa, nothing as yet from Andrews."

"Got it, Ben. Stay on top of it."

Jon went to the cockpit of the G5 and handed the pilot a note.

"Here are those coordinates we talked about. When we get within range you'll pull the maneuver, right?"

"Will do, Sir. Good luck to you. I sure hope this works."

"It will. I really appreciate your help," Jon told him and leaned on his shoulder.

"Anytime... you know that," the pilot answered.

Jon stepped back into the cabin area of the G5. Just passed the entry area, he closed a set of curtains the pilot had installed. They broke the view from the cabin area into that section.

"We're starting our approach, sir," the pilot announced over the speaker system. Jon sat down and strapped in. He could see the huge jet from his window.

Air Force One was loaded and moving to the runway.

"The Vice president is in the air, Sir," Doyle reported.

"Thank you, Mr. Secretary," the president answered and buckled himself in.

Marine One and the escorts were airborne and on their way back to Washington. The huge Pratt-Whitney 6204 Turbine engines roared and shook the body of the big aircraft.

"Cross check for take-off," The pilot advised on the intercom.

On approach, the G5 called the tower.

"N55DB private," the pilot called to the tower. "Requesting emergency clearance, Alpha-Tango-Bravo per instructions, over."

"Your clearance is verified, N55DB private. Proceed on course to runway four west."

"Roger, tower," the G5 pilot acknowledged.

Air Force One began his sprint down the runway, slowly at first. The huge jet gathered speed with each foot traveled.

"Jon...signal now emitting from plane at Andrews," Ben announced.

"Got it," Jon replied.

After some six hundred yards, the Air Force One pilot reversed the engines and hit his brakes. The aircraft nosed downward and slowed rapidly.

"Takeoff aborted!" the pilot declared. "Emergency traffic on the runway."

Doyle and Fogarty looked out their windows and at each other.

The president, in his private compartment, stared out his window at the small plane landing nearby.

"Jon," Ben shouted this time. "That signal from Andrews has stopped. Repeat...the signal has stopped."

Jon was surprised, but not shocked.

"Good, Ben," he assured the youth. "Good job...keep an eye on it and watch this interior cabin, closely."

The huge plane rolled to a stop near the end of the runway. The small G5 rolled up to within fifty feet and stopped itself.

The President emerged from his compartment, carrying his overnight bag.

"Change of plans, Darin," he declared. "I'm going with them."

"What?" The secretary was nearing ghost-like coloring in his face. "You can't do that."

"How do you plan to stop me, Darin?" The President walked right past them and to the door, which was already opening. An emergency chute flew down and the president jumped into it. Doyle and Fogarty quickly followed and as they stood up, Jon was there with the president.

"This way, Sir," Jon pointed.

"Whoa...who is this?" Doyle demanded. "What's going on here?"

"These are my precautions, Doyle," the president referred to him by his last name only. "You coming, or not?"

The secret service agent started to draw his weapon, but a look from Jon gave him second thoughts about it. The men climbed into the G5 and Jon pulled up the ramp-door. They were moving within two minutes.

"You guys can sit there." Jon pointed to seats near the back. "Mr. President, your area is here." And he pulled the curtain back closing off the entry.

"I'd buckle up quick, if I were you," Jon warned the other two. "This pilot jumps off the tarmac."

He joined the President in his area. The high backed seats blocked vision to and from the rear. As they also buckled up, Jon's earpiece spoke again.

"Jon...the signal's back. It's coming from your plane now."

Whispering carefully, Jon asked, "Are you sure?"

"Yes...I'm sure. There's more. The secret service agent put his hand into his coat just before it started back up."

Jon looked at the president and then the curtain behind them. The president grabbed his arm and whispered, "what?"

Jon put a finger to his own lips and whispered back.

"I need you to trust me. Can you do that?"

"Jon..." the earpiece spoke again. "Did you hear me?"

"Yes, Ben," he said with his hand over his mouth. "I got it."

Jon took his narrow Glock from his pants pocket. The president's eyes got bigger. He handed the weapon to the president, asking.

"Can you handle this?"

The man released the safety, turned it over in his hand and put the safety back on.

"So you're good?" Jon acknowledged.

The president shook his head and placed the handgun by his side.

"I'll be right back," Jon told him and went up to the cockpit.

Darin Doyle stood and stepped toward the president.

"Are you alright, Sir?" he asked.

"I'm fine, Mr. Secretary. You can retake your seat."

Doyle looked angered, but had little choice in the matter. Walking back to his seat, he looked at Fogarty as though to ask a question. Fogarty nodded his head and smiled.

In the cockpit area where he could speak, Jon gave the pilot his final instructions and inquired about altitude over mountains.

"Will the decompression throw you, too badly?" he asked.

"The mountain will come up to meet us. It's about 6300 feet where you plan to go. I can re-fire and snap the door closed in plenty of time. Just hang on to something."

"If I understood what you said, I'd be scared," Jon smiled.

"Just as well," the pilot smiled back. "I made most of it up."

Jon held up his phone and got Ben's attention.

"Look, contact Murray and Air Force two," he ordered. "Tell them to implement the diversion to Barksdale. Make sure Murray knows the Secret Service agent is the suspect."

"Will do," Ben replied.

Looking at the pilot, Jon asked him. "How will I know when we're close?"

"I'll flash the cabin lights, twice."

Jon nodded and went back into the entry area. Staying behind the curtain, he opened a compartment door and quietly removed his bag.

67

Cyrus Grant sat on the edge of his bed and stared into the box. Both lights were on, letting him know the targets were ready. With a flick of a switch, two Predator drones were launched. One from outside the old Turner Air Force Base near Albany, Georgia and the other from a small airfield near Winston-Salem, North Carolina.

The reading indicated Air Force One would be in range in twenty minutes and the Vice President's plane in eighteen.

The instructions were to arm the weapons at the five-minute mark, meaning estimated time to the target, and fire at ten seconds to contact.

He leaned over the box, mesmerized by the dials and digital readouts.

It's still daylight, he thought. *But it would be dark before any rescue missions could be launched.* Nervously he rubbed the edge of the box as he waited and watched.

Murray knew he had less than twenty minutes to prepare. The big jet would be there soon. He had to separate the targeting transmitter from the plane. The light control box came to mind.

"Can you stop the jet anywhere along that runway?" he asked the controller.

"Long as it had time and space to stop, yeah."

"How about near that box?"

"Probably," the controller guessed.

"How quick can they move the plane away?"

"That's another matter. That takes a bit of time."

"Ok, then. Can I get a cart out there, say a hundred yards from the box?"

"Sure."

"Do that please, and try to stop the plane short of the cart. I'll do the rest."

Murray ran downstairs and a ground crew member met him with a "mule." The large motorized cart would normally pull several luggage trailers.

"Lever forward is 'go,' pull back to stop. Reverse is here, but don't use it. Just make a wide turn."

"Thanks, man," Murray told him and jumped onto the unit. He drove out to a spot about one hundred yards past the box and stopped to wait.

~

Jon had changed into his black suit and secured the parasail in place. The president was used to Seal Team gear, but was impressed by Jon's outfit.

"Stay strapped in tight, Sir." Jon spoke softly, "I am going to open the door up there for a few minutes. The cabin will decompress."

"Navy pilot," the President smiled. "I'll be fine."

The cabin lights blinked twice and Jon knew it was time. He rose and the president grabbed his arm on the way by.

"Good Luck, son."

Jon nodded and pushed his way to the rear.

Doyle noticed him first.

"What the..." he tried to say as Jon held him in place, a hand on his shoulder. Fogarty went for his gun, but Jon leveled the full size Glock between his eyes.

444

"Step with me." he ordered the Secret Service agent. Then looking at Doyle, Silas cautioned firmly, "Stay... I mean it."

The acting Secretary of HLS pushed back against his seat, eyes wide with fear.

Fogarty stood and moved in the direction Jon motioned. As they passed the president, Fogarty glared at him. At the pressurized entry door, Jon stepped into the secret service agent and grabbed him around the neck with his left arm. The powered right arm pulled the door release and they waited.

Fogarty flinched and tried to pull away.

"Move again and I'll break your neck," Jon warned him.

Within a few seconds, the pilot killed both engines and the plane felt as if a huge parachute had been deployed. He then nosed the jet upward to further slow it down. Jon pushed on the door with his powered arm and it fell away, open to the darkening sky.

Lights flashed, sirens screamed and air rushed out through the door like a hurricane. Holding Fogarty with both arms now, Jon launched himself out with the agent's scream rising above the noise of the air.

When they had cleared the aircraft, Jon heard the engines start up. The G5 rolled hard to port, a complete barrel roll that rocked the open door and pulled it shut.

Jon and Fogarty tumbled for nearly a minute and the mountainside was closing fast. Jon looked around and through the dim twilight could make out the roofline of a cabin. He leaned that direction with his body and Fogarty's. They slowly moved toward the cabin with their freefall.

~

The other 747 had landed in an "emergency equipment situation" at Barksdale Air Force Base. As the door opened,

Murray called for the secret service agent to assist him with the crisis.

"What's going on?" the agent demanded while climbing down.

"Just this," Murray stepped out from under the stairs and stuck a chrome plated .45 in the man's ribs. "Come with me," he ordered.

They rode the mule out to the wooden box. Murray disarmed the man and cuffed him to the pipe.

"If you're still here in ten minutes," Murray smiled at him. "I'll come get you."

The man struggled desperately with the cuff, but it wouldn't budge. As Murray drove away, he watched the man reaching inside his coat for something. The man was right handed and Murray had cuffed that arm, so it was little use to him.

Finally, the agent came out from his pocket with a small, flat card. He reached back and threw it as hard as he could, with his left hand. It didn't go far.

Murray heard the buzz, or thought he did. He looked up to see a flash as the drone launched its missile. He leaned forward on the mule and kept the pedal down. He was about seventy-five yards away when it hit.

Ground erupted all around the wooden box. Fire of all colors flashed and dirt rose from the earth in a ball. The mule was pushed by the blast and nearly fell over. Murray could feel the heat from the fireball run up his back.

Stopping the mule, Murray climbed under it while debris fell all around him.

When the smoke and dust cleared there was a large hole in the grass. No wooden box. No secret service agent.

~

Darin Doyle couldn't believe his eyes. As the interior pressure evened out he started to stand. Doyle realized he needed to act and fast. He stood and pulled himself to the front, reaching for his gun. The president was standing in the aisle, with Jon's Glock pointed at Doyle's midsection.

"Have you got cuffs, Darin?" he asked quite calmly.

"Sir, what is this?" Doyle tried.

"Don't even go there, son. I know everything. Where are your cuffs?"

Hesitantly, the acting Secretary of Homeland Secure nodded and reached for them.

"Put your gun down here first," the President ordered. "And then cuff yourself to your seat. I wouldn't mind shooting you. Not one bit... You choose."

The pilot came over the speaker system.

"Sir, are you alright?"

"I am, son."

The pilot realized who was speaking.

"Sir, where's Jon. Mr. Crane?"

"He went out the door, son. He's gone."

Jon waited as long as he could. He hoped they were over the cabin.

Pulling up his legs, he placed both feet in Fogarty's chest and kicked the man out away from him. The agent appeared to have been shot from a cannon. His body flew, mouth open in a now silent scream, and fell directly toward the cabin's roof.

The impact was just below the ridgeline. Wooden shingles and plywood decking gave way, leaving a large gaping hole as the man's body disappeared from view.

Jon remembered his beacon transmitter and flicked the switch to start its signal. Catching a glimpse of the drone from his right side, he pulled the parasail from its pouch and threw it out in front of him.

Cyrus Grant sat on the edge of his bed and watched the light come on in the control box. He hit the "fire" button for the second missile.

Within that same microsecond, Fogarty's body crashed through his bedroom ceiling. It landed broken and twisted just inside the bedroom door.

Bogart didn't have time to even reason what was happening. The missile followed Fogarty into the cabin.

The streaking missile was so fast that Jon could hardly turn away from it. The entire cabin exploded in a huge flash and pieces of logs, timbers and other materials were suddenly rushing at Jon in the cloud of fire.

He twisted his head as far as possible, looking away. Still, he began to be pummeled by the flying fragments. He saw treetops just under him. The parasail was ripped by debris and tore away. Thick smoke blinded him and then the world went black.

68

She had heard the news that morning, but tried to avoid it. The TV in the lobby was turned up loud and surrounded by other guests and passers-by. Sheri Shanahan heard enough while walking to her cab to know it wasn't good news. Not for her anyway.

Her attempts to ignore the subject were dealt yet another blow by the paper lying on the seat of the cab.

"ASSASSINATION ATTEMPT FOILED," the headline screamed in the largest type possible. "Massive Plot Uncovered" and "House Speaker Sought_for Questioning," were smaller parts of the story. At the bottom of the front page was still another sub-text story, "Billionaire Industrialist Hero Missing."

Though her plan was now dust, she had no concerns about herself. The lawyer had been overly careful to insulate her name from any of it. Grant and Walden knew who she was, but Walden was dead and Grant discredited. His word alone wouldn't be enough if he did try to involve her. She pulled a copy of her speech for that evening to make a few subtle changes. Calmly, Shanahan also picked up her personal voice recorder and hit the record button.

"Initiate Plan C and gather list of possible team members by July 6th."

Putting the recorder down and laying her head back against the seat for minute, she allowed herself a thought. *It'll take longer now, but it can still be done. I just need to work harder.*

~

"It's very faint, Major. But I have a signal," the trooper said into his radio. He stood at the 3900-foot mark on the wooded side of Black Mountain in eastern Kentucky.

449

"The cabin was at 5700 feet," Swanson replied to him. "He's somewhere between you and there." The major thought a second and keyed her radio again.

"Is the signal moving at all?" she asked.

"Naw...seems to be stagnant. It ain't moving."

Sharon Swanson didn't like that answer, but at least he would be easier to locate than if he were stirring about.

"Carry on," she ordered. "And watch yourselves up there."

~

Murray had called Ben five times since last night. He was now back in Caddo Mills to get Marsha and the others. A team of Texas Rangers and FBI from Dallas were there to offer guarded escort.

Members of the Homeland Security, DEA, ICE and Secret Service were all undergoing deep interrogation and screening. Darin Doyle was in custody in Cleveland, awaiting transport back the Virginia.

"The president is giving a speech this afternoon," Marsha informed the cowboy.

"Still no word from Jon?" he asked in reply.

"No...we just don't know."

"Why?" Murray let loose. "Why did he leave that plane? All he had to do was throw that jerk out. We were home free at that point."

"Murray...we're home free because of it," Marsha asserted.

"Because of what? Him jumping?"

"Jon is still wanted for questioning about some of the congressional deaths, we are not." She grabbed Murray's arm and forced him to look at her. "Our involvement was as accessories, based on association with him. That's all gone now. There is no association to talk about. Jon is not here to speak of it."

"That doesn't make any sense to me at all," the cowboy complained. "If they think we were involved, they'll arrest us just the same."

"No...not in this case. Without him there's nothing. We can't be accused of aiding a man... who's not there," she paused as those words hit her. "To defend that he even did anything."

"Who told you this?"

"Jon did." She wiped her eye and continued with her head down. "He looked into it."

"I don't know...." Murray was still a skeptic.

"Have you been detained at all? Has anyone asked you about anything...other than what you did last night?"

Murray shook his head. "I...I just don't believe all this."

"Ben wants to see all of us at the mansion this weekend," Marsha told him. "He has some notes for us that Jon left."

~

At thirty minutes past one o'clock on the afternoon of July 3ʳᵈ the President of the United States addressed the nation from a small podium in Cleveland, Ohio.

"My original reasons for being here, as important as they are, have been overshadowed by the acts of some in our government and private citizens that came together in events last evening.

Charges are pending a thorough investigation, so I will not speak to specifics. What I can talk about, is that some elements within our government." He stopped to measure his words. "Apparently conspired with others in an effort to ultimately transform this country through an appointment to the Supreme Court."

The crowd around him gasped and spoke out loud causing him to raise his hands for quiet.

"A major issue to be before the court this fall, is that of the current Information Equity Act... which has so divided our country that a vast majority of states have sued to have it overturned."

The President stared directly into the television cameras.

"To that point...I will say this."

He gestured to the skyline behind him.

"I stand before you in the city of Cleveland. A city besmirched by stories of a nuclear attack rendering it unsafe. The people of Cleveland, and the surrounding areas, knew this was not true. Yet the national stories persisted. The reason for this senseless act is a part of the case, so no further speculation shall be offered here. As you can clearly see, the news stories were without merit. They were and are, untrue."

The president took a drink of water before continuing.

"I want to officially thank, and asked the congress to consider accommodations for two civilians who were instrumental in saving both my life and the life of the Vice President through their actions, Mr. Francis Marion of Louisiana and Mr. Jonathan Crane of Dalton, Georgia. I asked further for your prayers of safe recovery for Mr. Crane who has been missing since the actions he took last evening."

Immediately, the members of the media began to yell out questions.

"Mr. President," the winner of the hollering contest asked. "If you say Mr. Crane was with you, who then was this Francis Marion? People on the scene at Barksdale described him as possibly being 'The Son'."

"That man also did a brave service to our country," the President responded. "Whoever he is."

"But, Sir. Really? That name is taken from the history books. Francis Marion was from South Carolina, a Revolutionary War hero. This is an an obvious fraud."

"I cannot speak to that. Whoever was there, I can assure you of this. Mr. Crane was in the plane with me, and he saved my life."

"Mr. President," came the next question. "Have you spoken to Speaker Grant?"

Expecting more about Crane, the President was puzzled by the change of course.

"I have not," he squinted and told the reporter.

The follow-up to that was, "if anyone had?"

"We would all very much like to talk with the Speaker, as soon as possible."

"Our sources say he was not in Virginia. Can you explain that?"

"What is for me to explain about that?" the President shot back. "It's a holiday. He had the right to be wherever he chose. Next question."

"Jonathan Crane has long been suspected to be the Son?" was shouted from the crowd.

There it was, the one he was waiting for.

"Mr. Crane took direct actions that saved my life... the details will be available to you all later...after the investigation." The president laid his arm on the podium and leaned slightly forward. "You tell me that people in Louisiana identified 'the Son' as having been *there*. I don't see how a man can be in two places at the same time, do you?"

"What of the charges against Mr. Crane?" was bellowed from the rear.

"There are many unfounded charges against him and those who worked with him. As I've told you, high-ranking officials in several federal agencies are being investigated in relation to this plot. Any charges they issued, which stemmed from that plot, are obviously null and void."

"But Sir," a voice rang out. "Crane was already a suspect in past murders...was he not?"

"Jonathan Crane is missing, and for all we know may be dead," the President answered. "Speculation about his past activities is now only that. He is not here to answer charges or to defend himself."

"Are you issuing a pardon for him then?" came from the floor.

"Mr. Crane is due my 'thanks.' He requires only that."

~

Shanahan watched the speech from her home in Atlanta. She pulled the SIM cards from all the cell phones in her special stash. They were placed into a blender on the kitchen counter that already contained about a cup of vinegar. After the 'puree' cycle had run for nearly thirty seconds, the slushy mixture was poured down the sink.

She calmly washed the blender's jar and continued watching the president's speech. When it was over, she went to her desk to look over her own address for that evening, yet once again. And then took a nap.

~

"Marsha is on her way here. Murray is back in Texas and I just spoke with Captain Stone in Shreveport." Ben aimed his voice toward the speakerphone while pacing the floor in the lab. "They're all asking me if Jon has called."

"No one has heard anything from him then?

"That's all I know, Daniel," Ben told him. "I'm waiting like everyone else."

"I understand... Is that it then?"

"No...Can you come down this weekend?" Ben asked him.

"Where? Dalton?"

"Yeah...here at the big house. We need a meeting."

"You can't tell me what it is over the phone?"

"He asked that you come down...just for the day."

"Jon asked?" Daniel's curiosity peeked. "What's going on, Ben?"

"He left instructions and a request before he left."

"Are you saying he knew this would happen?

"Maybe he thought it could...I'm not sure."

"I'll be there," Daniel relented and exhaled heavily.

He hung up the phone and looked at Lori, sitting by his side. She held his hand in hers.

"They'll find him, Danny," she leaned in and whispered. "He'll be alright."

Daniel didn't respond. His gut told him something was wrong. He just didn't know what.

"I'm going to Dalton this weekend," he confirmed in subdued tones. His stare crossed the room without focus or purpose.

Lori didn't question that or the reason for it.

"Do you want me to come with you?" she asked softly.

Daniel squeezed her hand back, "Yeah...I do."

~

Matt Turlock called Phil Stone at home.

"Did you see that?" he asked about the President's address.

"Yeah...it's all over," Phil surmised. "The man as good as said that... If they find him, the heat is back on. If not...that's the end of it."

"Do you think Jon knew that... going into this?"

"You think there's anyway he didn't?"

69

Ben left the house mid-afternoon, heading for Atlanta. The lawyer's speech would be downtown, at the Centennial Olympic Park. The timing of all this was important, but not to the exact minute.

Every vehicle there was available to him, but Ben found himself thinking like Jon. He passed up the Jaguar and even his new Charger in favor of the older Ford 500.

Don't need to attract attention, he heard himself say.

The container with the special vial was in the trunk. He respected it to the point of fear and took extra care in packing it. The other items in his "tool kit" were on the seat next to him.

Arriving at the Gas Light Building's parking lot, he found it mostly empty and the gates in the up position. He parked on the third level to be out of sight and made a trial run to the floor of her offices to check it out.

The doors were locked and the offices appeared to be unoccupied. Taking his time, Ben went out to the car, moved it to another spot in the deck, and then went back in. His work there took less than fifteen minutes. The key worked perfectly. The switch Jon had left him lit up, and he could hear the mechanized feeding belt move forward inside the cage.

Sasha was at first not impressed with the additional meal falling into her bowl. She rolled her eyes in near disgust at the intrusion, stretched her jaw in a fake yawn, but that was about it.

Jon had considered the possibility. Not only was the meat injected with Acepromazine and Xylazine, 30mg/50mg, it was also permeated with Nepeta Cataria, commonly known as catnip.

The huge Siberian Tiger got the first whiff of the substance and wrinkled her nose. She soon became enthralled by the smell coming from the meat. Licking it and then rolling it around the cage, she finally devoured the twenty-six pound hunk of beef in four mighty bites.

Ben did not witness this. He was busy feeling along the bottom edge of the bookcase for the small notch Jon had left him.

"There it is," he mumbled as his fingers located the half-round slot.

As Jon had told him, it was three feet from the joint where the bookcase would open. Ben pulled the mask from his pocket and adjusted it on his face. Then carefully, he raised the top of the case holding the vial.

Easing it from the box, his nervous hand reached toward the bookcase, pulling the carpet fibers back slightly. With his other hand, Ben slid the glass tube into the notch. The vial fit like a glove and when Ben re-fluffed the carpet, it virtually disappeared.

Though he wore gloves, he took no chances. Slowly and methodically wiping every surface he had touched. Ben stopped on the way out to look again at the odd art work on her wall. The star made of numerals. He had studied his photos of it back at the lab, but the mystery remained just that.

Doesn't make any sense, he told himself.

With extra caution, he then locked the two doors and went back to his car.

Sasha, the tiger, was walking around her cage, shaking her head and yawning. When she finally settled down, the beast was nearly out of camera range. The monitor would only show Sasha's nose and her tongue protruding through the huge incisors.

Ben pulled the Ford 500 out onto Peachtree Road and headed toward Shanahan's home.

~

Murray Bilstock had contacted the G5 pilot asking for the coordinates where Jon had left the plane.

"Kentucky?" he said looking up from his chart map.

"Black Mountain area to be exact," the pilot answered into his phone.

"My chopper can't make it that far on one hop. Could you come get me? I'd like to fly over the area...just look around."

"I don't mind, but it costs money," the man explained. "I can't authorize it myself."

"I'll get Ben to pay for it...there won't be a problem," Murray assured him.

"You at that ranch house... with the long road out front?"

"That's me."

"I'm on my way."

The cowboy collected his night vision goggles and binoculars. Trying to think what all he might need, he looked at a box of flares.

Too dry in the mountains this time of year, that's not a good idea. He opted for a parachute instead. *If I see anything, I'm going down there.*

~

The lawyer's speech came off without a hitch. She spoke of patriotism and loyalty and got several ovations that made her stop for a minute or more. There was no sign of her true feelings about the country's leadership. Or that she had just failed in a coup attempt.

Even if Grant were found alive, he couldn't hurt her.

He has no proof, she reminded herself over and over. Nearly to the point where she realized it was herself she was trying to convince. A few drinks and handshakes followed her address and then it was time to leave.

Driving home she headed up Peachtree Street toward Ponce de Leon Avenue. Something, some thought along the way, made her decide to go to the office.

What had happened to Grant? That question was bothering her. She had computers at the office that could offer information on Grant and what had happened.

Sheri Shanahan got to the high-rise at 10:42 P.M. and turned on her monitor. It had been left on the screen showing Sasha's cage. The vision of her beloved cat rattled her. In an imprudent rush, the attorney jumped to the bookcase and pushed the release button.

The cabinet rolled and the glass vial was crushed. Toxic gases engulfed her within microseconds.

~

Ben Shaw waited outside Shanahan's home for nearly three hours. He allowed that she might have gone for drinks with friends after the speech, or perhaps even dinner.

He was supposed to insure that she left the house and hopefully went to her office. At 1:10 AM he decided to drive back to the high-rise office building. As he came close to the towering building he could see lights on in what appeared to be her floor. Driving past her marked parking spot; he felt relief, noticing her car was there.

It was late. His being caught there now would lead to many unanswerable questions. But Ben went back into the building and up to her floor.

The elevator doors opened and he could see it was definitely the lawyer's offices that were lit up. He stood at the outer door with his formed key in hand, but thought better of using it. Instead, he listened. There were no sounds, nothing coming from inside.

Should I go in to be sure? he thought. *What if the substance hasn't dissipated yet?* It was simply too risky on all levels to go in.

He finally put the key in his pocket and returned to the car. The hour was very late. There was nothing to do now, except go home.

The drive back to Dalton would take over two hours. Along the way, somewhere north of the perimeter highway, he tossed the key out along I-75.

Daniel Seay was up early that morning. He scanned the Internet for word of the lawyer Shanahan's speech or any other news about her.

She's one of the details. Jon won't let a detail go unaddressed, he said to himself.

But there was nothing. Sheri Shanahan wasn't big news to start with. With all the news of the assassination attempts, the missing House Speaker and the billionaire hero, nobody cared about her speech.

Lori came into the kitchen where Daniel sat with his computer.

"Any word from Jon?" she asked.

"No," he answered. "Still nothing."

"Happy Independence Day, honey." She hugged his shoulders. "You know you played a role in keeping it so."

Daniel looked up at her and smiled. He couldn't think of any words for that.

The FBI, with help from state police in Washington and Oregon, had set up traffic stops along all highways near Pendleton, Oregon.

Some cars and vans tried to turn around and run. Others gave up with little resistance. In all, over 400 illegals were taken into custody. Many of them wearing fake DEA or ICE jackets and carrying false IDs.

The hit teams were not carrying the weapons they had planned to use. Without final instructions they were left clueless and just abandoned the mission.

The authorities estimated that some 300 others had managed to escape into Canada. The attack in Pendleton would have been massive and messy. Local police collected weapons that had been thrown away for months after.

Across the country, agency officials from Homeland Security and down were being questioned. Military bases, where predator drones were stationed, had emergency inspections and inventories taken. In all, eight unauthorized flights were disclosed and arrests made. Members of Mithras' militia were rounded up throughout the southwest.

70

"We've got to be close," Murray said looking out the co-pilot's window. "That's smoke on the side of the mountain."

It was now the day following the holiday. Still no word on the missing and the world was just getting a few details of the plot against the government.

Murray and the pilot had left Shreveport that morning. Their attempt to go to the area earlier had been stalled by search teams on the mountain. They traveled to Louisiana to meet with Phil and wait for clearance.

"Just about..." the pilot leaned the jet right a few degrees. "Ok, this is about it."

"Can you circle around? I thought I saw the outline of a structure down there."

"You probably did. There was a cabin."

"A cabin? You knew this?" Murray challenged him.

"Well, yeah. The grid map shows any structures in the flight path. It was a pretty nice one, too."

"Whose was it? Do you know?"

"Private listing. I don't know if Jon was aware or not. This is definitely where he wanted to come. And where he dropped the bad guy off."

"You didn't know he was planning to jump, too?"

The pilot got quiet for a moment. He breathed in and held it, then continued after exhaling.

"I had a pretty good idea from the way he was acting. But he never said. I just wasn't all that surprised."

"What do you mean?" Murray asked as they flew back over the demolished cabin.

"He took a parasail from the plane last week. Said he'd replace it later."

"Could someone jump from a plane like this with a parasail?"

"We'll have to ask Mr. Crane. It hadn't ever been done before...not that I know of."

"I don't see any search teams down there."

"You know, you're right. They're not only away from here:..they're not anywhere... Hang on a minute."

The pilot swooped down toward the base of Black Mountain. There were a few cars, but certainly no search effort being staged.

"They either found what they wanted," he told Murray. "Or they've given up."

"Will my phone work from here?" Murray asked him.

"Naw..." the pilot pulled up and banked left. "Let me get clear of these mountains."

"Ok...tell me when. I need to talk with Ben."

~

Ben Shaw was in the lab area, glued to the TV monitor. Local breaking news that morning from downtown Atlanta was wall to wall on every station.

"A nationally known, local civil rights and labor attorney, Sheri Shanahan was found dead in her downtown office this morning by cleaning crews." The voice was over pictures of the building and corridor outside her offices. The report was quite specific.

"How she died was still under investigation, but sources on the scene describe a grisly mess. The attorney apparently collapsed while checking on her 1200-pound Siberian Tiger in its specially designed cage adjacent to her office area. Somehow, Ms. Shanahan fell with her arm through the cage's glass encased bars."

The reporter took an obvious pause to convey to his audience the disturbing nature of what he would say next.

"The large predator, apparently used her arm to drag her body half-way into the cage." The reporter then looked into the camera, "I'm not going to describe what happened in the days till she was found." He took off his glasses and laid them on the desk. "We just hope her death preceded it."

"Damn," Ben muttered. That was more than he had expected. "But she's not gonna plan anything else...that's for sure."

The cell phone rang, so he turned the TV off.

"Yeah, Murray. You coming tomorrow?" he answered it with.

"What time?"

"When everybody gets here."

"Alright. Say..." he threw in. "Do me a favor?"

"Absolutely."

"There used to be a cabin at these coordinates on the side of Black Mountain." He then called off the particulars. "Find out who owns that land, would ya?"

"I'll see what I can do."

"Thanks, man," Murray said. "Are you ok? I mean are you doing alright?"

"Yes, Sir. I'm ok I guess," Ben told him.

"Well...I don't like it. Not one bit. I feel like I'm being left out of something, you know?"

"I don't like it either, Murray. I keep hoping Jon will show up."

"Did the Israelis make their flight?"

"Yep. A quick, secret stop by the White House first. The President wanted to thank them. They are now about half way across the Atlantic."

"Good," the cowboy replied. "Brave people."

"Like Jon," Ben added.

Murray didn't say anything to that. He let the air hang dead for half a minute and then closed out the call. "I'll see you guys tomorrow."

~

Murray's phone rang again before he could put it down.

"Hey, cowboy." The voice was NCIS agent Barker.

"Yeah, Terry," he answered with a subdued tone.

"Still no word, huh?"

"No. It's not looking good."

"Well...I'm on my way back to LA. Spiegel is back in New Orleans and the boss is helping reorganize stuff in DC. I just wanted to let you know...if there's anything we can do. Just ask, okay?"

"Thank you...all of you. He's a pretty resourceful guy. If there's a way out of this, he'll find it... he may already have."

"Say again?"

"Nothing...tell the others we all appreciate the support."

~

Daniel and Lori were the last to arrive. Marsha had come in the night before and Murray early that morning. They met in the living room of the house.

Ben started the meeting.

"I apologize for the cryptic way I had to handle this. It's all Jon's orders and I wanted to follow them. This is not what he wanted, but he told me it was the only way we could all be free from the suspicions that surrounded him."

They all stared at him in silence.

"He knew what he was doing was risky and he made these provisions in the event he didn't come back." Ben then opened an envelope and began reading.

"Crane Investments is doing quite well. The assets grow daily and he wanted that business to continue to grow and provide for all our needs. In his absence, Jon asks Daniel Seay to run the day-to-day end of Crane Investments as Operations Manager. He'll have full authority to buy, sell or move assets as he sees fit. He shall pay himself an annual salary of $950,000 per year for these services."

Ben looked at Daniel. The man was trying to absorb what he just heard. Lori grabbed her husband's hand reassuringly while Ben handed him some papers to sign. Not waiting for a reply, Ben flipped through his papers to another section.

"Murray Bilstock is to receive a taxes paid grant from C.I. in the amount of 135 million dollars. The only instructions left, in the form of a requests, are that he 'buy Lucy a faster sister,' and continue looking out for those in this room 'as though he were me.'"

The cowboy was struck silent. When words did form in his head, he chose to keep them to himself, for now.

Ben looked around the room and pointed out,

"Captain Phil and Matt are not here, but Jon wanted this read to each of you."

He unfolded another paper and began.

"Captain Phil Stone is to receive two million in cash, taxes paid, for him and Sara to retire on."

Ben turned the page over, "Matt Turlock will find that Crane Investments has purchased the Shreveport Times and is naming him Editor and Publisher for life. A salary commensurate with such duties is to accompany the title."

Ben then looked at Marsha.

"Marsha Hurst and Benjamin Shaw shall be named co-trustees of the corporation and shall share in its assets as they see fit. The mountain house shall always be home for either or both, as they choose. Ben shall provide for whatever needs his mother and her husband should have or develop, at Ben's discretion."

He then opened the last folded document.

"My trusted G5 pilot, Harold Foster, shall be placed on full-time retainer at the rate of $350,000 per year, should needs of any in this room come up. The corporation shall cover any and all expenses for flights deemed necessary by anyone mentioned in this request."

Ben folded the papers he still held and sat down.

"Is this a will?" Murray asked.

"No," Ben quickly replied to that. "If Jon is missing for the appropriate number of years to be declared dead, seven I think it is, there is a will. These are just operational instructions he wants carried out should he go missing."

"So, he doesn't plan to come back," Murray spoke again. "This is how he thinks he's saving us."

"I can't argue with that last part," Ben shared. "You may be exactly right, that may well be what he thinks. All we can do now, is what he asked or go our own way."

Each one there sat in silence for several minutes, stunned by what had happened and its impact on their lives. Ben broke the silence one last time that day.

"Last, but not least," he announced. "We're all supposed to go to dinner."

71

It was Thursday of that next week when Sharon Swanson called Ben.

"Mr. Shaw, do you know who I am?"

"Jon mentioned you several times, Captain, yes."

"Well, it's Major now..."

"Sorry."

"Not a problem...look...I'm calling because Mr. Crane asked me to do him a favor a few weeks ago."

"Yes, Ma-am?" Ben perked up with anticipation.

"And I managed to do it." Then she paused... "We found him, so to speak."

"Is he dead?" The words came from Ben as though pushed out by fear.

"That's the way it looks."

"I don't understand, major." Ben's voice was cracking. "Looks like, what?"

"He said you would understand...I'm bringing what I found back to you, tomorrow. One box, not to be opened except by you and Ms. Hurst...understood?"

"Yes, Ma-am."

"I'll be coming in on a Kentucky State Police C-130 at your Dalton airport. Will you meet us there?"

"Yes ma-am."

"Alright then." And she ended the call.

Ben called Marsha in Charlotte.

~

As the large cargo plane landed a group of combined high school bands played America the Beautiful. An honor guard from the local National Guard station helped unload the large, coffin like, box into the hearse for the trip to the house.

Plenty of locals were on hand. George Vincent, Doris and Gil Gartner were there. But other members of Jon's group were not in attendance.

At the house, Ben asked that he and Marsha be accorded some time alone with the remains before others came in to show their respects. The coffin like box was placed in the front room.

They took about twenty minutes with it and then opened the doors. The county coroner came in first. He looked at the contents of the box and quickly ruled it was insufficient to declare Jon dead. His watch, bits of the armored suit and a few pieces of what could be bone were all that was there.

With no confirmation of death, no funeral was planned or held. Instead a memorial service honored Jon's service to the community and a message from the President was read to the assembled crowd.

~

Word spread about the cabin in Kentucky. Grant's aide, Marvin Staley, came forward telling authorities he "believed" his long-time boss might have gone to Kentucky, rather than Virginia.

His body was never found, but enough DNA was recovered to conclude Grant had been present at the time of the cabin explosion.

Rumors became facts and the once powerful Speaker of the House was soon named in the coup attempt. Darin Doyle talked and his close associates in Homeland Security were rounded up and questioned. The proud agency would serve under a cloud of suspicion for years, monitored closely by the FBI.

The Secret Service was revamped from the top down. Monthly screening of agents was established to restore integrity.

The plot was unraveled, exposed and in time, the country moved on. The roles played by the NCIS and the Israeli Mossad agents were kept quiet. Francis Marion was never located and the search for Jonathan Crane continued. As the days that followed came and went, things fell into order and life went on.

~

Three months passed quickly. Summer drifted by with few remembrances. The leaves changing colors seemed to return the awareness of time. Then finally, mid and late October began to feel like fall in the north Georgia Mountains.

The U.S. Supreme Court had taken only three days of evidentiary hearings before declaring the Information Equity Act unconstitutional and void. The decision was six to two with one abstention.

National coverage of this event varied from no mention at all; to opinion pieces lamenting the throwback to days of "junk news." Some decried the lack of integrity by those who would now return to the airwaves. The public, who paid little attention to the major networks, was notified more by the changes that took place. Some of those were almost instantaneous.

Dormant radio stations flickered back to life and the cable news station reappeared, if only with minimal programming at first. They were soon swamped with offers for sponsorships as they brought their schedule back to full speed.

That's when the entire story of the law, its impact and ultimate defeat were finally told.

One major T.V. network announced the dismissal of its entire news department. Replacing them with journalists of old school morals and disciplines. With all this happening, the story of the plot, and Jon's involvement to derail it, was not emphasized or heavily broadcasted. This had been part of the agreement between the President and Jonathan Crane.

Life in Dalton, as in the rest of the country, slowly regained its routine. Those in congress, who took advantage of their positions, continued to do so. Rumors of the demise of "the Son" gave new life to their ventures.

Computers, on the second sub level of the mountain mansion, continued to offer suspects from across the country. Candidates for "removal," as Jon had always called them. Ben and Marsha would now do the preliminary research on-line and through other contacts. It all felt the same, yet it was all quite different.

72

Evening began to fall on the mansion as Ben Shaw sat, staring at the elm tree out front. It was fine, despite the newly carved letters in its trunk.

They had shown up overnight several weeks before. "HW" "LJ" and "JC" were carefully inscribed in the bark.

Sheriff Wilbury, Lamar Jakes and Jonathan Crane were now memorialized on the tree.

A small plaque was also set into the ground at its base. The size did not diminish its message.

"This tree honors the New Sons of Liberty everywhere" It proclaimed.

Ben liked it. He kept the plaque polished and the ground cover neat.

The garage door opened. It was Marsha looking for him.

"Ben, there's been another call about Mississippi," she called out.

"Same guy?" Ben asked without looking up.

"The same."

"He looks like a bad one for sure."

"Yeah... I think its time for a road trip."

The young man thought for a minute. "It has been long enough," he agreed. "I think you're right." Ben then stood and dusted himself. "I'll go."

"No, that's alright, I'll go. Just wanted you to know first."

She went back in and through the house. Upstairs, she walked through the hall and into the master bedroom. Marsha Hurst then climbed into the elevator and went to the second sub-level.

A single light glared over one of the worktables. She approached the figure sitting there, staring at a computer monitor.

"The call you wanted to know about has come in." She paused for a moment... "It's Mississippi. Looks like he's going to need action."

"Thank you, Marsha," the figure said and continued with his study.

"Look... Jon..." she said without thinking.

At that, the man turned sharply and threw his finger up in front of his nose. Even in the low light she could see his face flush at her words.

Glaring her down, he muttered, "shush."

"I mean...Silas," she corrected herself. "Look...isn't it time we let the others know?"

"Marsha, all is going just fine. Daniel is doing a good job running the business...everything is getting back to normal, or at least close to it."

"Then we should tell them."

"Not yet, Marsha. In due time, just not now." He turned back, typing on the keyboard as he spoke again.

"They're safe now... *You're* safe now. My operation is back to its fundamental roots."

Marsha stood shaking her head. She desperately needed to cry out at him, but didn't want to interrupt his thoughts.

Still staring at his keyboard, Silas leaned back and continued.

"Nothing, but the rules... the basic rules," he said turning toward her. " If I follow those rules, no one gets hurt as a result of what I do."

"You put too much store in that, Silas," she pleaded.

"No...please," he turned away again. "Work with me."

"I am!" she demanded. "You know that... and so is Ben."

She then gathered her courage and blurted out a revelation she had kept from him till now.

"Murray still calls... three times a week... asking if we've heard from you."

Silas' head tilted back and he rubbed his forehead. Looking at her once more, he sought direct eye contact.

"Murray is a good friend," he said, his voice trailing off. "He's out of danger, too. He deserves his peace for now."

The man stood and stepped more into the light. Marsha could see his healing injuries. Her hand brushed his hair back as she leaned in and kissed him.

Jon emerged from within and scanned her through Silas' eyes.

"I do love you...you know that?" he said as a matter of fact.

Her gentle, affirmative nod shook loose a tear, and it startled him.

The stern gaze on his face turned into wonder. He cupped the side of her face with his right hand, softly brushing away the tear with his thumb.

"Don't cry. Not about me...not ever," he implored.

Marsha pushed herself against him and looked up at his face.

"Will you do something for me?" she purred.

"If I can... of course."

"Then talk to Murray," she tried once more.

Silas leaned back. Stone faced yet again, he stepped toward the elevator. Marsha turned her body slightly as he moved passed her.

"I will... when the time is right," Silas turned back to answer her. "I promise."

Not wanting the conversation to end there, Marsha squeezed into the elevator with him. Resigned to his will for the time being, she changed the subject on the ride down.

"You are moving your arm much smoother. How does your face feel?"

"Better," he said, wanting to assure her. "Much better now. The grafts are healing well."

The short ride was over and as they walked into the garage area Jon turned, twisting his left arm and right ankle as a demonstration.

"Those breaks have healed nicely, too," he declared.

"That suit saved your life," she managed with a smile.

Another change of expression brought Silas forward again. He shrugged his shoulders, gazing trance-like at the floor.

"I never thought about hitting the trees like that..." He paused, then raised his head adding, " I was really, very lucky."

"You still need to be careful." Her soft voice lectured.

"I will..." Silas claimed, looking soberly toward the Mercury. "It's time for me to go. I need to stop by the small house to pick up a few things, and then head out."

"Should I call the pilot?" she asked.

"Naw...Mississippi is close enough. I'll drive."

"Alright...and Jo...I mean Silas... Why can't you just stay here? It's been too long, you living back in that little house."

"I'm comfortable there." He tilted his head towards her. "Besides, I can exercise; run the field with the dogs and study in my old safe room. It's my foundation, my building blocks... it's who I am."

Marsha frowned, but accepted his reasoning in silence.

He nodded several times in quick succession as Silas thought further. *Her understanding wasn't required*, he told himself... yet Jon insisted on trying again.

"My basics... the basics of my fundamentals... they're all there," he added. "It's what I need right now." Pulling the car door open, he added, "we all need it."

Silas smiled at Marsha and climbed into the Mercury. He punched up the controls on the dash and quickly drove out through the tunnel.

It was nearly dark as the trusted big sedan left the old gas station. The car climbed up highway 71 and past the mansion.

At the top of the hill, where the road to town turns to the left, Silas thought he caught a glimpse of something. Was it a reflection or shadow coming from the cliff across from his house? He stopped, adjusted the mirror and looked again. But it was gone, if it ever had been there. The Mercury proceeded on and out of sight.

Something had been there. The reflection was real. A silent shadow had stepped back from the edge of the ridge as the Mercury went by below him. The man, who created that shadow, nodded to himself as he watched the car go by. Then stepped back from view as a warm glow grew inside his chest.

Slapping his leg with it first, the figure then raised his large hat to his head. With a respectful tip of its brim toward the mansion, he turned and walked the hundred yards or so back to the sleek, dark blue Sikorski, X2 jet helicopter.

Under its rear window, the white lettering read distinctly, "Lucy Too."

"When we view this country in its extent and variety, we ought to be exceedingly thankful to divine goodness in bestowing it upon our forefathers, and giving it as a heritage for their children."

Silas Downer
at the Dedication of the Tree of Liberty, 1768.

Also by *Doug Dahlgren* :

It Was Thursday   The Tale of an Event that
                       Should Never Happen

The *SON* Series

The SON Silas Rising   Book One of the Son Series

The Only Constant   Book two of the Son Series

You've just finished Book three of the SON

Book Four is coming soon !

Watch for :
The Four Samaritans
later in 2012

www.dougdahlgren.com

Doug Dahlgren

Made in the USA
Lexington, KY
13 May 2012